THE LEBENSBORN BOY

by Roy Havelland

Vanadis Texts

2014

Cover picture by Christopher McIntosh

Overall design and formatting by Judith Kraus

Copyright © Christopher McIntosh and Tim Jeal, 2014

All rights reserved. Except for brief quotations, this book or any part thereof may not be reproduced, stored in or introduced into a retrieval system, or transmitted, in any form or by any means, electronic, mechanical, photocopying, recording or otherwise, without the prior permission of the authors

ISBN-13: 978-1500104450

ISBN-10: 1500104450

*To Daniel
with much love and all
birthday good wishes
from Opi (one half of
Roy Havelland).
Bremen, May 2016*

DEDICATION

This book is dedicated to all former Lebensborn children.

CONTENTS

PART I 3

PART II 135

PART III 176

PART IV 311

Harz Mountains, Germany, November 1943

They arrived on a cold November afternoon in 1943, when the trees were already heavy with snow. There were five children escorted by a young nurse from the home. Huddled in blankets, they sat on wooden benches fitted inside the rear section of the truck. The nurse was holding one of the children on her lap – a pale, shivering little boy, not yet three years old, with a persistent, rasping cough. She wished she could say something to bring him comfort, but she knew he understood nothing but his native Danish. During her time at the home she had seen many children come and go, but somehow this one had touched her, affected her in a special way – perhaps it was his physical fragility combined with something in his face, a spark, a kind of inner strength. Touching his forehead she realised that he had a fever and wondered with dread whether he was suffering from whooping cough. If he was, then she knew, they would not let him stay in the home. They'd send him to the nearby hospital, where he would end up in the department for "special treatment" – a cold euphemism for murder by over-sedation. She hoped fervently that his cough would have subsided by the time they reached the house.

The road wound uphill between massed pine woods, and the truck laboured as it took the steep bends, its winter tyres digging into the snowy ground. Perhaps shaken loose by the vibration of the engine, a heavy clump of snow slid abruptly from a pine branch and fell to earth by the roadside with a sound like the thud of a distant field gun. As twilight turned into nightfall the headlights of the truck made the tree trunks stand out in the darkness like prison bars. They passed a milestone, and the nurse knew that they were close now. The boy had stopped coughing and seemed to have fallen asleep in her arms. With luck, no one would notice that he was ill, and perhaps by morning, after a warm supper and a good sleep, his fever would be gone.

The truck slowed, turned off the road to the left and halted, the headlights shining on a massive double door with diagonal boarding and the name "Lenzfeld" written in black Gothic letters on a white enamelled plaque. Another plaque said: "Property of the Lebensborn Foundation. Entry by unauthorised persons strictly forbidden." Someone opened the doors from within, and the truck moved forward with a jerk that woke the boy. As the doors closed behind them, the nurse stifled a scream of horror. The boy was coughing again.

PART I

1

Berlin, summer 1990

When Erdmann heard that a woman had called him on the telephone his first thought was that there had been a mistake. No one had called him at work for years – it was out of his normal routine, and routine was what held his life together. Every morning he took the underground railway from the bleak East Berlin suburb where he lived and clocked in on the dot of eight at the Jupiter restaurant for the morning shift. In the cramped staff cloakroom behind the kitchen he put on his black suit, adjusted his bow tie in the mirror and combed his receding grey hair. Then he helped to lay the tables, putting out the menus, the knives and forks and the napkins with swift, practised movements. He had plainly been doing the job for a long time but still seemed to be a man out of his element, although resigned to it.

Deeply etched lines on his face suggested some past ordeal that had marked him permanently. But there were still traces of earlier good looks, and his eyes conveyed a quick intelligence as well as world-weariness. Other signs suggested he had not always been a waiter: crisp movements and a precise manner hinted that he might once have been a soldier. Yet there was also a touch of the intellectual about him. To his colleagues he was something of a mystery. They found him reliable, even-tempered and polite, but always reserved – a loner. Between shifts he enjoyed a cup of coffee and a piece of cake – Black Forest gâteau, when available, being his favourite.

The Jupiter was in a street close to Unter den Linden. It was one of those genteel, old-fashioned restaurants that the Communists had preserved almost intact, as places where the privileged could dine out or entertain foreign visitors. But, lacking the impetus and the resources to maintain it properly, they had allowed it to go to seed. The red velvet curtains in the tall windows had become threadbare, the ornate plasterwork in the ceiling had fallen away in places, and the wood panelling was chipped and cracked. Still, throughout the Communist years it had somehow clung to some lingering semblance of elegance. Now, with the Wall gone, West Germans and foreign tourists were beginning to come to the Jupiter, finding it quaint and nostalgic, and enjoying the absence of background music, so pervasive where they came from. But things were about to change. A new, young manager, Herr Meyer had taken over and had plans to smarten it up, install loudspeakers for music, hang paintings by modern artists and introduce a whole new range of dishes with French, Spanish and Italian names. It was Meyer who had taken the call.

"Yes," he told Erdmann "a woman with an English name – Warrington."

The waiter was puzzled. "Are you sure? I know no English people."

"Quite sure. She asked for you by name. Said she'd call back. Only don't spend too much time talking to her. Time is money."

Yet again, the older man was struck by how quickly the jargon of capitalism was invading East Germany, along with the advertisements and the people hawking party insignia and GDR flags in the street. Hard to believe it was only a few months since the Wall had fallen. It was all very confusing. Often he felt that he had sacrificed half his life for nothing.

Warrington? Surely a mistake, he told himself as the restaurant started to fill up with lunchtime customers. Even so, he found that he felt disappointed when she didn't call again. He actually waited half an hour beyond his usual clocking-off time of four o'clock, then gave up and left for home.

As he came down Unter den Linden towards the bridge over the river Spree, he saw a man in the uniform of the People's Police looking on bemused as a group of teenagers jerked and twitched to a ghetto blaster thudding out a heavy, percussive rhythm. They wore torn jeans and strident tee-shirts, and the girls' hair was dyed bright, luminous colours. The road was full of cars with western number plates – Mercedes, Audis and BMWs – making the little East German Trabants look like quaint relics of another era. Now that the period of euphoria following the demolition of the Wall had simmered down, he felt rather like an unwanted guest at a party that didn't know where it was going.

Warrington, Warrington ... his footsteps beat out the name as he crossed the Alexanderplatz on his way home. The mystery nagged at him. Could the woman perhaps be an English friend of the family in Denmark? He rejected the thought immediately. They had surely done their best to forget him.

In the Alexanderplatz a couple of souvenir vendors had set up their makeshift stalls. These days everyone seemed seized by a desire to sell their GDR memorabilia – flags, Free German Youth badges, People's Army caps, framed photographs of Erich Honecker. Officially the GDR still existed, but everyone knew that it was only a matter of time before the two Germanies were reunited.

At the entrance to the Suburban Railway station Erdmann lingered by the newspaper kiosk and browsed through the western papers on display – the *Frankfurter Allgemeine*, the

Herald Tribune, the *Times* of London. He settled for a West Berlin paper and read it on the train. It was full of the debate about what should be done with the millions of Stasi files that had been assembled over the past four decades with the help of "unofficial collaborators" who had spied on colleagues, friends and even family members. These informers now feared exposure and some were being blackmailed by people who claimed inside knowledge of the files. Rumours were rife about who had collaborated. The new democratic government of the GDR had debated the possibility of destroying the files, but that would only have increased the potential for rumour. Now it looked as though the files that had survived the Stasi's orgy of shredding when the Wall fell would be preserved and made publicly available. Somewhere, if it had not been destroyed, there would be *his* file. Had someone managed to get hold of it and now meant to blackmail him? But why an Englishwoman?

He emerged from the suburban railway station at Marzahn into a landscape of bleak high-rise housing blocks, one of which he lived in. He opened his mailbox in the entrance hall and found it empty, then he took the lift up five floors to the spartan one-room flat that he called home. As he was opening the door he heard someone behind him and turned to see the bulky figure of his neighbour from across the hallway, Frau Kowsky.

"Sorry to disturb you, Herr Erdmann. But a woman's been round here, asking for you." There was a look of sly amusement on her plump, middle-aged face. "Quite a young woman." She was obviously titillated by thoughts of the mysterious female visitor.

"When was this?"

"The day before yesterday ... in the evening. I found her

hanging about the entrance to the house, and she asked if I knew you."

He remembered that evening, because he had gone to a film and not come back until nearly midnight. "Did she say who she was or anything else?"

"Only that it was a private matter. She asked for your telephone number, but I didn't know it, so I told her where you worked." She fingered her apron nervously. "I hope I didn't do wrong."

He touched her arm reassuringly. "No, not at all, Frau Kowsky. You did the right thing. Many thanks."

She wanted to linger on the landing, probing for more information about who the woman might have been, but he said goodnight and closed the door.

Next day at the restaurant he started every time the telephone rang, but the morning passed and there was no call for him. Then, when the place was filling up for lunch he heard the telephone ring again and this time saw Meyer signalling to him from the bar, holding up the receiver. "This is a bad time. So make it quick. Time is money."

He took the receiver, still not quite believing that the call was for him.

"Who is this?" He spoke loudly against the babble of conversation.

"You don't know me," said a bright woman's voice. The accent was foreign, but not an English one, more Scandinavian. "My name is Sonia Warrington. I tried to find you at your flat, and one of your neighbours told me that you work here."

"I see ..." but he didn't see at all. "What can I do for you?"

There was a pause, then the woman said hesitantly. "It's a delicate matter ... too delicate to talk about over the phone. Could we meet?"

Meyer was looking at him impatiently and tapping his wristwatch.

"I ...don't know." Should he refuse? If it was blackmail, she would find some other way to confront him. From her tone of voice she didn't sound like a blackmailer, but still he hesitated.

"Please, trust me," the woman pleaded. "It's important. It's about the past."

The past. The word set off alarm bells. There were too many traumas in his past.

Better put down the phone, he told himself. Perhaps she'll back off. He wanted to hang up, but something stopped him. "All right. But I can't get away until four o'clock."

"That's fine. I'll meet you at five on the Lion Bridge in the Tiergarten. Do you know it?"

"No, but I can find it."

"Then see you there. I'm in my early twenties, dark haired. I'll be carrying a red umbrella."

As he replaced the receiver Meyer said. "Thanks for keeping it brief. Time is money."

At the end of his shift he clocked off and changed into his everyday clothes. As he set off for the rendezvous he grew increasingly apprehensive, gripped by the old dread of being "found out". What could she have found out? And how? Desperately he searched his mind, stirring memories that had long been deliberately buried. As he approached Unter den Linden, his memories transported him back twenty-four years to that fateful journey. He was back on the bus travelling down this same street, a young man of twenty-five setting off on what promised to be a great enterprise..

2

Berlin, February 1966
He tried to merge with the other passengers on the bus, while putting them down as misguided failures. An hour earlier they had set out from the prison camp before dawn, and up to now none of them had said a word; the habit of watchful silence was so deeply engrained so that, even on their farewell journey, they were worried that the wrong word might send them back to prison. Up to the last moment the Stasi men had unsuccessfully tried to convince them to change their minds. Now they were non-persons, bacilli to be removed as quickly as possible from the body of the workers' state. He hoped that none of them suspected anything about him. In his case the prison camp had been a charade. Clever idea of his bosses, he thought, to have him masquerade as a dissident and arrange for him to be bought free along with the others. They imagined they were escaping to a freer world, but he knew better. The West was a fool's paradise. He was proud to be part of the fifth column that was going to hasten its collapse. And, what was more, somewhere over there was his mother – a mother whom he had never known about until they had told him. Now he was going to find her.

With the palm of his hand he rubbed a peep-hole in the misted-up window of the bus. A hole in time. Beyond it, already vanishing into the past, the East Berlin suburbs rolled by, overlaid by a reflection of his face with its flop of sandy hair, blue, slightly sunken eyes and sharply chiselled nose and chin. A handsome face with a hard edge to it.

Made it, he said to himself with a deep breath. *Made it*. For years he had dreamed of this moment – through all the training, the time served in the lower ranks, the menial jobs, the boot-licking, the condescending superiors. A captain at the training centre in Potsdam had called him an "egghead" and told him that he would always be a back-room boy – just because he had a brain and a scientific education. Well, screw him. He was on his way to the West. He was going to use his brain and serve the cause at the front line. He would need all the knowledge and skills that he had so painstakingly acquired. And he would need his special charisma, partly natural, partly cultivated. When he was a teenager his Uncle Rolf had told him: "You have something rare, the ability to make people see in you what you want them to see, to influence their will. But you need to develop it. I can help you." He had always been grateful to his uncle for bringing out that ability, and he intended to use it to the full. There was no way he was going to screw this one up and be sent back to the dingy basement laboratory in Leipzig where he had spent two years among the smell of formaldehyde. No way.

As they went deeper into Berlin, a middle-aged woman's voice broke the silence.

"Why are there always ten?" She was grey-haired and slightly plump. In her old-fashioned red winter coat and beige felt hat she looked like a waitress on her day off. She addressed the question to no one in particular, but just in front of her, a middle-aged man, wearing a battered brown Homburg hat, turned round and asked: "Ten of what?"

"Us," the woman said, "people being sent across. It's nearly always like that – ten altogether. I heard it from my brother-in-law, who knows a thing or two – connections, you know. I wonder why."

The man laughed. "Well, it stands to reason. There are five fingers on each hand. If there were more than ten of us the guards at the border would have trouble counting."

A youth sitting close by said: "Good thing we're leaving the country. I've known people get a prison sentence for making jokes like that." The speaker sat awkwardly in his western-style leather jacket, with his long legs stretched out into the gangway. "Actually," he added, "we're not over the border yet."

"Soon will be. It's only about another quarter of an hour to the Friedrichstrasse Station," said the woman.

At the front of the bus a man's face poked out from behind a seat and looked back at the woman. "If your connections are so good," he said in a sarcastic tone "maybe you can tell us how much the West Germans are paying to buy us our freedom." He had bulbous eyes and a bushy moustache that twitched argumentatively as he spoke – the type who likes to have the last word in a bar-room debate.

There was an awkward silence, then the man with the Homburg hat said: "We're not supposed to know that, but I do. Forty thousand marks a head - that's on average."

"They must pay even more for some of us. I don't mean for the likes of myself, but for well-known dissidents," said the woman in the red coat, trying to hold her ground as the one with inside knowledge.

"You bet they often pay more. Nice little earner for the GDR," grumbled the young man in the leather jacket. "No wonder it's done so quietly on both sides."

Erdman had listened to his fellow passengers with a

feeling of well-concealed amusement. What fools western politicians were to pay for the "privilege" of supporting these misfits. A sound from the seat behind made him turn. A young woman was holding a handkerchief to her face to stop the sobs that had just started to bubble up. A black woollen cap covered her dark hair and part of her pale face. He wondered whether she was crying out of relief, or on account of a loved one she had left behind, or perhaps because some part of her still wanted to cling on to the bronze statues of Marx and Engels in the middle of the Alexanderplatz, and to the propaganda posters with their images of smiling workers and peasants with striding feet and pointing hands.

Erdmann said: "Are you all right? Can I help you with anything?"

She shook her head and dabbed her eyes with a handkerchief. "No one can do anything. The bastards took my baby son from me. Told me I couldn't be trusted to bring him up with socialist values – just because I had applied to emigrate. Put me in prison for six weeks and then told me they were throwing me out of the country. God knows whether I'll ever see him again."

He wondered what her offence had been? Must have been pretty bad for them to take away her child. People's justice could be harsh but it was always necessary for the greater good.

The others began to talk more freely, and a buzz of long-suppressed excitement grew louder. Even in the drab streets outside, they found things to point at and laugh about, tentatively at first, then with greater confidence as the realisation sunk in that they were really leaving - going to a place where laughter didn't bring you suspicious looks, and where you could make jokes about the system and not be reported. Only Erdmann, the young man with the fair hair and athletic build, kept silent. They were passing the neo-classical pomp of Karl Marx Avenue, with its towers, colonnades and porticoes, the white tiling of the facades crumbling away between the windows of the showcase workers' flats.

"Do you know what time it is ... Herr ...?" asked the middle-aged man in the Homburg sitting across the aisle. This man was not the only one who seemed to be growing anxious about the slowness of their journey.

"My name's Erdmann ..." He had been about to say his first name "Lutz", but instead he added "Henrik". That was his "real" first name he had been told. If he managed to find his mother she would surely want to call him by the name she had given him. Even so, he still found it difficult to think of himself as a Henrik. He looked at his watch. "It's seven-thirty now and our train leaves at eight, so we still have enough time."

"Erwin Borchert," grunted the man, thrusting out a hand to introduce himself. "I hope you're right. I don't want anything to go wrong this time."

"This time?"

"I've been out of the GDR before. I escaped across the Hungarian border into Austria so I could join my son in Stuttgart, but on a visit to West Berlin I was kidnapped by the Stasi and taken back here. In my case they were only interested in a profitable ransom deal, and when my son managed to arrange one I was quickly released. That's how I know how much they paid. But what about you, Herr Erdmann? What's your story?"

Erdmann was quiet for a moment, frowning slightly as

though pondering whether to reply at all. Finally he said: "My story is complicated. I was a war child, born out of wedlock ... in Denmark. I was adopted, lost my first adoptive parents in the war and then grew up with a family in Wittenberge. I never felt I belonged. They tried to make me forget my real mother, but I always knew in my heart that she was still living. I never gave up hoping to be reunited with her. I tried to escape over the border twice and ended up with two long prison sentences. Then, like all of us, I was ransomed."

"And now you hope to find your mother?"

"More than anything."

He could imagine how shocked Borchert would be if he knew that he was talking to a spy whose mother would unwittingly provide him with the perfect cover for his mission.

Borchert said kindly: "It seems to me that you have the noblest motive of all of us for going to the West. If there is such a thing as divine justice, you will succeed."

From a side street, a garbage truck pulled out in front of the bus, blocking the way while dustmen collected metal bins from the pavement. The minutes ticked by, and the bus driver lit a cigarette, apparently unconcerned. Finally, after four bins had been loaded, the truck pulled off and the bus was able to proceed. Erdmann looked at his watch and saw that it was twenty to eight. Still enough time if there were no more traffic delays and the exit formalities were quick.

The woman who had been sobbing earlier also glanced at her watch as if she could hardly bear to check it. But the tension eased as they crossed the river by one of the smaller bridges and saw the railway, on its elevated tracks, and the grimy glass and steel vault of the Friedrichstrasse station. The bus drew up and the ten passengers dismounted and entered the station, each carrying everything they owned in old suitcases, shoulder bags and rucksacks.

The way to the steps leading up to the platforms was barred by a police border control post. The expressionless official behind the glass window examined the documents of the tall young man, then opened a door in the booth, signalled to the youth to place his suitcase on a metal table and began to rummage through it. Those waiting behind were growing apprehensive. If they missed the train there wouldn't be another for half an hour, and the lawyer from West Berlin would be waiting at the next station on the other side of the wall. They were sprats in the mouth of a shark that had opened its jaws to spew them out. There was no telling when the teeth might suddenly and capriciously clamp down on them again. At last the official thumped the young man's papers with a rubber stamp before letting him through. Now it was the turn of the woman in the red coat. She had two bags and the official insisted on searching both. It was already five to eight when he finally stamped her passport and let her through. When Borchert came up the official's pale, glassy eyes examined him indifferently.

"Destination?"

"Stuttgart."

"What is your purpose in Stuttgart?"

"I have family there." Borchert tried to keep his voice calm, even though the official had no business asking him such questions. He knew these little power games they played. One had to humour them.

The official examined the documents again, then picked up a telephone, dialled and waited. Erdmann, standing at the back of the queue with the tragic young woman in front of him, looked at his watch and saw that it was two minutes to eight. From above came the wheezing sound of brakes then the opening and shutting of carriage doors. "Dear God!" the young woman moaned. "Do they have to torment us right up to the last minute?" She was trembling with rage and distress. "Doesn't he know we have a train to catch?"

The official was speaking into the telephone, tapping his finger on the documents. Then he put down the receiver, picked it up and began to dial again.

"Please, our train ..." Bochert could not keep the desperation out of his voice, but it was already too late. As the official continued to dial they could hear a whistle blow and then the sound of the train pulling out. The official disappeared from his booth. Borchert swore under his breath. The young woman was on the verge of hysteria.

"It's all right," said Erdmann kindly, laying a comforting hand on her shoulder. "We'll get the next train. The others will be waiting for us at the Lehrter station." She looked up at his handsome, chiselled face, and her expression of gratitude and trust caused him no surprise.

The official reappeared and told Borchert that he would have to search his luggage. With only three minutes to go, it was looking as though they would miss the second train as well. Borchert went purple and looked ready to smash the window of the booth with his fist.

Erdmann thought: now is the time to use what Uncle Rolf taught me. First, do something unexpected. He pushed his way forward and slapped loudly on the window of the booth. "Everything is in order." He slid his own documents through the hole in the glass, at the same time fixing the official with his eye. "Now, if you don't mind, we have a train to catch." He spoke firmly and a shade louder than his normal voice.

The man looked up, startled. His eyes took on a glassy look. He hesitated for a moment, then he nodded. He gave Borchert and Erdmann their documents and let them pass, then quickly checked the young woman's papers and waved her through as well. They reached the platform with a minute to spare. Then they were pulling out, and a moment later they were passing over the "Great Anti-Fascist Protection Rampart" and into West Berlin.

As they approached the Lehrter station, the first stop on the western side, the young woman, sitting close to Erdmann said to him: "You certainly have a way with you. I thought we were never going to get past that stupid man."

Erdmann laughed: "Funny you should say that. Other people have remarked on it too. Well, here we are."

On the platform they were met by a slightly build, grey-haired man in an expensive looking dark blue overcoat who introduced himself as Dr. Meyer-Hoppe from the Legal Protection Centre, the body responsible for negotiating the buy-outs. Meyer-Hoppe expressed his relief that they had arrived and ushered them to a minibus. They drove through the Tiergarten, along the Street of the 17th June and then turned north, passing the sprawling Charlottenburg Palace with its delicate neo-classical facade. On the domed tower above the entrance a winged figure of the goddess Fortuna stood on one foot, poised for flight. Near the palace, the minibus drew up in a tree-lined street in front of a modern low-rise office building with an unobtrusive steel plaque bearing the name: "Legal Protection Centre".

They were shown to an airy waiting room with a picture window looking onto a small garden. Here they were given coffee and forms to fill in, before being seen individually by the staff. The young woman lawyer who saw Erdmann offered him more coffee and pushed a plate of biscuits across the desk. She seemed new to the role and was straining to combine putting him at his ease with remaining crisp and businesslike. She explained that he would be given a settling in allowance for six months and would be accommodated in a shelter for refugees and asylum seekers until a job and proper living quarters could be found for him.

Looking at his form, she said in a more feeling tone: "You've been through a lot, Mr. Erdmann – abandoned, sent to the Lebensborn home … then persecuted in the GDR. If there's anything more we can do …"

"Thank you, you're very kind,' he said firmly. The last thing he needed was to have women like this chasing after him, checking up on how he was getting on. 'If there is I'll let you know."

"Please do." Still seeming unwilling to let him go, she added: "No doubt you will try as soon as possible to make contact with your mother in Denmark. I see that you have put down Hamburg as your preferred place of residence as long as you remain in Germany, so you can stay in the shelter there for the time being. Hamburg seems a sensible choice. You'll have a better chance of finding employment there, and you'll be within easy reach of Denmark."

He nodded. "That's precisely what I've been thinking too."

*   *   *

"He is a cool one," said the young woman to Borchert as they sat in the waiting room after Erdmann had gone. "And you saw how he dealt with that border official."

"Yes, I did" Borchert said thoughtfully. "Rather odd how he did it. Positively uncanny. But it worked, so we should be grateful to him. He got us out of a tight spot."

3

To his surprise Henrik Erdmann was growing to like Hamburg. Tree-lined streets, wistful view of the skyline over the Alster lake, waterside parks, half-hidden canals, the great red-brick warehouses along the harbour, the new office towers built on bombed-out sites, the patrician houses in the smarter districts. Wealth discreetly worn in the Hanseatic style. A Russian who had been there had once said to him: "It makes you wonder who really won the war."

He was staying in a home for refugees and asylum seekers near the Autobahn to Berlin. Now he wanted something less transitory, and was working his way through the rooms advertised in the property sections of the newspapers. After another long day roaming the city, he felt tired and footsore as he emerged from the Reeperbahn station into the demi-monde of St. Pauli.

He walked through a maze of side streets, passing dingy pubs, sex shops, a florist, a laundry, and came out into the street he was looking for, the Bernhard-Nocht-Strasse, a broader thoroughfare that ran parallel with the Elbe river. He stopped in front of an old apartment building, some of its decorative plasterwork still clinging to the worn stucco façade. On the wall of the alcove enclosing the battered front door was a rusty metal panel with a column of push-buttons and labels for the names of the occupants. He pressed the button next to the topmost sign, which read: Claudia Schmidt, Psychotherapist. He was puzzled by this unfamiliar word.

The woman's voice over the crackly entryphone was barely audible. "Yes?"

"My name is Erdmann. I've come about the room."

"Oh ..." An awkward pause. "Actually, someone's been here already."

"So the room is let?"

"Well, yes ... but since you're here you may as well come up and see it. Third floor."

He climbed the worn wooden stairs, his footsteps echoing in the skylit stairwell. The last room he had looked at had sounded promising on the phone, but had overlooked a busy traffic intersection, and he wanted peace above all else. Other rooms had already been let (or so he had been told) by the time he had arrived to view them. Perhaps his East German accent had counted against him, or his clothes – he had not yet bought a West German outfit. In truth he hadn't cared for the rooms he had seen so far and had therefore made no effort to be persuasive.

She was waiting for him in the doorway of her own room on the third floor – a tall, dark-haired woman in a long, loose dress of what looked like Indian material with a swirling pattern of dark reds and browns. Through the open doorway came a pleasant aroma of fresh coffee mingling with a surprising scent of incense.

"We can go straight up to the room," she said briskly. "It's in the attic. I have the top floor of the house as well as this one." On the way up, she asked: "Do you have a job?"

Henrik shook his head. "I've just arrived from the GDR."

She looked suddenly doubtful, causing him to say reassuringly: "The resettlement people are helping me find work. I'm a trained chemist, so they're quite hopeful. In the meantime the allowance they give me will cover my rent."

The room was small, with a sloping ceiling and a dormer window with a narrow view of the river between the houses behind. It was sparsely furnished, but quiet he was glad to note.

"It's exactly what I want." He looked around appreciatively. "But you say there's already an interested party?"

"Yes." She sounded almost apologetic. "A woman came to see it earlier today and said she wanted to take it. I can let you know if she decides to cancel."

Use the technique, he told himself. Eye contact, voice, body language ...

He looked her in the eye and said in a firm, slightly deeper voice: "I'm sure you can find a way to let me have the room."

She hesitated, fingering her necklace of beads. "I ... I don't know ..." Her eyes had taken on an absent look.

"I'm sure you can find a way," he repeated, slowly and deliberately.

"Well, the woman did say she could only move in at the beginning of April."

"But I can move in at once!" He flashed her a disarming smile – optimistic and boyish. "This room is just what I need. It's so peaceful up here." His blue eyes held hers. "I think it would help me solve some personal problems I have."

A frown creased her brow and her eyes were back in focus. She would see people with problems every day and might not want someone with personal problems living so close to her. "I don't mean 'problems' exactly...I have to find my mother...that's all. I was adopted and now I want to meet my real mother in the West. No big deal except she may not want to meet me."

The woman said gently: "If you make the right approach, of course she will."

"You really think so?"

"That's what I said." She smiled. "All right, Mr Erdmann, since you can move in at once, you can have the room. Can you pay a two month deposit?"

He told her he could, and they agreed that he should move in at the weekend.

When she invited him in for coffee, he shook his head as if genuinely sorry to decline. "I'm afraid I have an errand to do before the shops close. Next time I'd love to."

He hurried back to the Reeperbahn station and caught a suburban line train to the inner city. As he emerged, he looked at his watch, swore aloud and started to run. The bookshop might already be shut by the time he got there. He crossed a canal bridge then zig-zagged down a busy shopping street, dodging the pedestrians. Coming out into a smaller square, he slowed to a walking pace and took a deep breath of relief. Ahead of him was the bookshop and outside it a table with a display of the cheaper second-hand books. There was no one else in the shop except the bookseller, who sat at a desk in a niche at the back, reading in a pool of soft light.

"Can I point you in the right direction?" he said, looking up over a pair of half-lens glasses.

"I hope so. Do you have a copy of *The Decline of the West?*"

"Ah," said the man, putting down the book he was reading. "I take it you mean Oswald Spengler's classic work."

"Precisely." He didn't care for the little jokes that so amused his colleagues.

"You're in luck. A copy just came in." He took a weighty volume from a shelf behind his desk and handed it to Henrik. A folded piece of paper was slipped in between the pages like a bookmark.

Henrik did not immediately look at the piece of paper. Instead he opened it at another page and some lines of text caught his eye: "The bushes and vines do not move of their own accord. It is the wind that plays with them. Only the tiny mosquito is free; it dances in the evening light; it goes where it will."

Out of the corner of his eye he saw that the bookseller was watching him intently, as though willing him to look at the slip of paper. Some mischievous impulse made Henrik continue reading, flipping the pages and stopping occasionally to read a passage. The expression on the bookseller's face grew more and more anxious, until finally Henrik opened the slip of paper and read: "The Bismarck Monument tomorrow evening at six. Wait there for five minutes then walk to the Dom Fairground, where you will be contacted."

He pocketed the note, and, as he handed back the book, spoke the pre-arranged words. "Thank you, but not for me I think."

"No problem." The bookseller took the volume, visibly relieved. The message had been delivered to the right man..

4

The monument was in a park near the eastern end of the Reeperbahn, where the red-light district ended and the commercial city centre began. In the middle of the park the statue of Bismarck towered grey and massive above the treetops. As Henrik walked up the hill towards the monument he heard the bells of St Michael's church chiming six.

He let five minutes pass and then walked over to the funfair, which sprawled across an open area close to the St. Pauli football stadium. A syrupy aroma came from stalls selling popcorn, doughnuts and heart-shaped pastries. Other stalls sold sausages, pickled herring, smoked eel. Their customers drank beer as they ate, while children tugged at their parents' sleeves, eager to go on rides.

At a place where avenues of stalls diverged in several directions he looked around, sensing that he was being followed. Walking on, he passed machines that spun people at crazy angles, and a shooting gallery called the "Cabinet of Horrors" where punters fired at a Frankenstein's monster, a vampire, a giant spider, a skull. Beyond an old-fashioned gypsy caravan belonging to "Madame Zabulengro, world-famous Romany fortune teller", the avenue petered out in a straggle of stall-holders' caravans. The noise of the funfair was quieter here. Following another avenue, he passed a carrousel whirling to a brassy tune. Close by was the "Bavarian Big Wheel", its enormous spokes lit by rows of coloured bulbs. The cabins swayed slightly as they moved. In one of them high up he saw a tiny figure shake a handkerchief to someone on the ground. On an impulse he went up to the ticket booth, paid and entered a cabin. Just before the door closed another customer, a man slightly older than himself slipped in and took a seat on one of the narrow benches.

"Excuse me, do you know your way around in Hamburg?" he heard the man ask. Henrik turned and met a pair of hard, unwavering grey eyes.

"Only a little," he replied.

"Then perhaps you know the Magdalenenstrasse?"

Henrik knew immediately that it was not the Magdalenenstrasse in Hamburg that he was referring to but rather the one in East Berlin, the address of the Ministry of State Security, the Stasi. "I believe it's close to the Normannenstrasse," he said, naming an adjacent street. "Then you must be ..."

"Barschke," said the other. "Kurt."

Henrik shook Barschke's extended hand. "Henrik Erdmann, at your service."

Kurt was athletically built, with a long, lean, bony face and close-cropped fair hair, receding into a widow's peak. He was dressed in jeans and a jogger's jacket, just tight enough to reveal a burly chest and powerful arm muscles. He looked a classic outdoor type.

Kurt surveyed the younger man critically. "Those clothes won't do." He pointed at the badly tailored jacket of flimsy material, the trousers growing shiny at the knees, the cheap, down-at-heel shoes. "Get some new ones. When are you going to make contact with your mother?"

"Soon. It's a question of finding the right approach."

Kurt said. "I have a mother too, you know. Widowed. Lives in an old people's home in Weimar. At the end of war she was raped by American soldiers at gunpoint, while they forced me to look on. She never got over it. I hate the Americans and everything they stand for."

The cabin completed a circle and rose slowly higher for the second time. Fairground noises and the city traffic merged into a sound like that of a distant waterfall.

"Don't just turn up on your mother," Kurt said. "You must write first."

"I've thought of that already."

"Then act on it." Kurt smelt of sweat, as though he had been running or working out in a gym. "Remember that West German intelligence may be watching you to see whether you really came to the West to contact your mother. The sooner you make contact, the sooner they'll be reassured. As you will have been told in your training, you must never risk getting into trouble with the law or do anything to draw attention to yourself. And be especially careful when it comes to women. You can screw the whores in St. Pauli, but don't get emotionally involved with anyone. Call me if you have a problem."

Call you an arrogant ape, thought Henrik. He knew the type. Met lots of them during the Stasi training. Sword-and-shield-of-the-Party men. Good at the rough stuff but no education or subtlety to speak of.

They were nearing the top of the wheel and the whole of Hamburg was spread out before them. Henrik gazed south to the other side of the river, at the docks, warehouses and cranes which stretched to the horizon. To the north the lights of the office buildings and hotels around the Alster lake were beginning to glow in the twilight.

"A beautiful city," he remarked, more to himself than to Kurt.

Kurt gave a disdainful snort. "As long as you only look at the glitzy parts." He pointed towards the city centre. "Over there you've got the rich, respectable Hamburg." Then he turned towards the heart of St. Pauli. "And over there the other Hamburg, making millions every year out of sex and prostitution. That's capitalism for you. This whole country's a rotten door waiting to be kicked in."

In his mind, Henrik added: you can do the kicking while I do the brainwork.

The wheel had stopped as new fares were being taken on below, and only started again when the passengers were on board.

"We can consider ourselves privileged," Kurt declared, while the wheel was still motionless, "to be playing a decisive role in the historic struggle. In Denmark the scales are so finely balanced that a small weight can tip them. That's why your assignment there is so important, and why everything must go as smoothly as possible with the family."

"How will I play my 'decisive role'?" asked Henrik with a sarcasm that Kurt missed.

Kurt gave him an approving smile. "There are threats that have to be neutralized – reactionary politicians who want to keep the country in the western alliance. You'll be given targets in due course. Do you have further questions?"

"Yes. When I was recruited into the service I was told I'd be able to use my knowledge of organic chemistry – doing industrial espionage, getting hold of western medical technologies to make them available to our people. How long do I have to ..."

Kurt held up a hand. "All in good time. For the moment there are other priorities."

A sudden, swelling cheer came from the St. Pauli stadium.

"Sounds like a goal" Kurt said, tilting his head. "I used to play, you know. Inside right for Dynamo Berlin, reserve team. Thought of turning pro at one time. Any more questions?"

Henrik shook his head. The cabin reached the ground and

the door opened to a blast of Bavarian music.

"Look," Kurt said, pausing in the doorway "I'm a tough team captain but a fair one. Keep your eye on the ball and do what I tell you. Then we'll smash the opposition. Well, I think I'll stick around for a while – try my luck at one of the shooting galleries. Maybe I'll win a teddy bear." He laughed mirthlessly. A moment later he was gone, merging into the bustle of the fairground, with its brassy music, its tawdry sideshows, and its crowds buying candy floss.

5

Alone in the silence and pale light of his attic room, Henrik pondered over an atlas, open at a page showing north Germany and Denmark. He ran his finger over the untidy configuration of islands and peninsulas lying scattered along Denmark's eastern seaboard where some Nordic god, in a fit of rage or playful vandalism, had apparently gone down the coast with his hammer, smashing off chunks and flinging them into the sea. One of the chunks was marked Lysholm, and a dot near the north-west side bore the name Norvik. That dot was his destination. The Stasi's careful enquiries had revealed that the Karlssen family were still living there, running a fruit and vegetable farm. Somewhere in that dot was where they lived and worked, Birthe Karlssen and her husband Sven and their two grown children, Niels and Kirsten, as well as Niels's wife and two small children. He pictured a cosy farmhouse set in blossoming orchards, the family happily living in the illusion that the past was safely buried.

Kurt had been right about one thing: Henrik certainly had to write a letter. He pushed the atlas aside and reached for a sheet of paper and a ball-point pen. The first problem was which language to use. At the Stasi Academy he had studied English and later Danish. His Danish reading comprehension was good, but his speaking and writing were still rudimentary. Perhaps his mother spoke German, but he could not be sure. English seemed the best option, but now he realised that it was one thing to take a course in English at the Stasi Academy and quite another to write a delicately phrased letter to a mother who might not even want to be reminded that he existed. The instructor on the course had been an elderly ex-schoolmaster, Dr. Schulz, who had taught for a year at a minor English public school back in the 1920s and prided himself on his command of colloquial words, idioms and phrases, of which he composed long lists that he made his students learn off by heart. Lutz Erdmann had been a diligent pupil, but the English he had learned now seemed pitifully inadequate and potentially old-fashioned. How was he to begin?

"Dear Mrs. Karlssen," he wrote at last. Formality seemed more appropriate at this stage. "I am making so brave as to write to you, knowing that this letter will come as a great surprise and may awaken sleeping hounds that should perhaps better be left to snooze. Please excuse my rusted English, but I thought it would be better to write in that language, not knowing whether your German is up to the scratch. When I wrote your name a moment ago I wondered whether to write 'Mother', because that is what I believe you to be..." In his mind he added: "...even if I can't think of you as my mother."

Henrik found it painfully ironic that he should have to write the most important letter he had ever written using a language which he had never studied in any depth. If his mother tossed it aside and refused to see him he would soon be back in the GDR and going nowhere in his profession. Oriental music floated up from Claudia's rooms on the floor below, a slow, heavily rhythmic sounding of gongs and drums, accompanied by deep male voices of what sounded like Tibetan monks. After some minutes it ceased and heavy, percussive rock music made the floor vibrate. He was growing used to Claudia's alternating moods. One minute she was meditating, the next she was in party mode. He struggled to focus his mind on the letter again, searching for the right words and expressions.

"I have no optic memory of you, and you would probably not recognise me as your son, as I was only an infant when you last saw me. I am now twenty-five and desperately nourishing the hope of seeing you once again."

He wondered about his father. He knew virtually nothing of the man except his name, Heinz Ackermann, and the fact that he was a German corporal and had been killed later in the war. He found himself speculating how they might have met. Maybe the corporal had raped her. If that was what had happened, then his mother would be doubly reluctant to see him. For the first time in his life he began to wonder seriously about the man whose genes he carried, and about his unknown German relatives. Somewhere in Germany he probably had uncles, aunts and cousins – he might even have passed one of them in the street without realising it.

He finished the letter, giving his address and phone number in Hamburg and saying that he hoped she would call or write, even if it was only to say that she would not see him. He put the letter in an envelope and attached a stamp, intending to post it at once. Today was Sunday, but it would be collected first thing in the morning, and with luck would reach her on Tuesday or Wednesday.

He left his room and walked down the narrow wooden stairway and past the hall of his landlady's quarters. The door of her living room was ajar, and he glimpsed a row of plants in blue and white china pots on a window ledge, a bookcase, an antique sofa with scrolled wooden arms, casually draped with a floral patterned fabric.

"Is that you Henrik?" she called over the rock music. She had already, within a few days of his arrival, started calling him by his first name and the familiar "Du".

"I'm going out," he replied, already on the stairs below her landing.

In East Germany any woman interested in Oriental religions would be considered decadent, a traitor to the scientific achievements of her own culture. And anyone practising meditation, and using Tibetan prayer wheels, would be compared with the deluded young people on the "Hippy Trail" to Kathmandu. As for Claudia's "psychotherapy" – *that* would have had her in serious trouble in the GDR. But though he mistrusted Claudia's gilded Buddhas and the like, Henrik had been surprised to find himself liking her from the moment she had first showed him his room. He thought she was about ten years older than himself, around thirty-five. Not exactly a stunning beauty, with her central parting and her hair pulled back severely from her face, but in her own way appealing. The thought of taking her to bed was tempting, not least because he was sure she was attracted to him, but he remembered Kurt's warning.

There was a yellow mail box on the corner of the street but as he walked up to it he began to have second thoughts about posting the letter. What if it came as such a shock to his mother that she refused to contact him at all? And what if it were opened by another member of the family? He lifted the metal flap of the mail box and thrust in the letter, but he did not drop it. Two teenage girls approached, one holding a letter. "Come on, lad," she said, "shove it in or don't shove it in, but make up your mind!" They both giggled. He let the flap down and walked down the street with the letter in his hand, hearing the laughter of the two girls behind him.

Ten minutes later, still undecided, and needing a drink, he found himself walking down the Reeperbahn in search of a bar. Walking at random, he turned into a street called "Grosse Freiheit", a side-arm of the Reeperbahn with the same sex shops and girly night clubs, but half way down it turned into a normal Hamburg street. He stopped in front of a hostelry called the Star Club. A sign proudly proclaimed that the Beatles had played there in 1962, and there was a photograph of the famous quartet in their tight-fitting jackets and page boy haircuts. He had heard of the Beatles – their fame had spread through the semi-underground pop music scene of the GDR despite the disapproval of the regime. Other names of groups which had played there were written higgledy-piggledy on a big white sign over the doorway, and were mostly unfamiliar to him: Ray Charles, the Hurricanes, Gerry and the Pacemakers, Screaming Lord Sutch, Chubby Checker, Bo Diddley, Gene Vincent. There was also an advertisement for the current attraction: the Amazing Yellow Polka Dots.

Finding the bars in Grosse Freiheit uninviting, he turned back in the direction of the river. He walked down a flight of steps to the bank of the Elbe. Pontoon jetties creaked and strained in the swell. Cargo vessels, passenger cruisers, and even a square rigger were moored nearby. It was strange to think he had grown up on this same river, upstream beyond the border. The Elbe had been the boundary of his universe then. The land on the other side and slightly downstream had been "enemy" territory, mysterious, out of bounds. And here he was, contemplating the vastness of Hamburg harbour and realising that this alien yet fascinating world could become "his oyster" – as Dr. Schulz had once taught him to say. Only for a second did it trouble him that he was living a contradiction by the way he was beginning to enjoy the west. To hell with that! Contradictions were what drove history forward. Every Marxist knew that. He took in a satisfying, deep breath of harbour air and walked on.

His mind went back to his schooldays in Wittenberge. At first his schoolmates had called him the "Lebensborn Boy" or the "Cuckoo's egg", the slang term for bastard, but soon he had won them over by a mixture of natural charm and physical bravery in fights. Early on he developed keen survival instincts, playing his part in the state-ordained rituals and not standing out too much.

At the age of fourteen he proudly took his Youth Initiation, the communist version of confirmation. His class marched with a brass band to the town hall and stood on a platform under a banner that said "With heart and mind for the high and noble cause of Socialism". The local party boss presented them with a coming-of-age certificate and then gave a speech urging them to play their full part in serving the Socialist Motherland. And he had played his part as well as he could. He had worked hard and tried to please his teachers and on the whole succeeded, although once or twice he had been reprimanded for drawing pictures in class. With his mates he had known how to be just irreverent enough to be popular and what jokes could be told without risk of repercussions.

When he was sixteen he took part in a competition at the school which involved giving a speech on the theme of "Socialism and Youth". The weekend before the event he was staying with his Uncle Rolf and Aunt Emma in the country, and his uncle told him: "I believe you can win the competition. I sense you have an unusual talent, but like all talents it needs to be worked at." His uncle had taken him for a walk in the woods and made him speak to the trees as though he were speaking to a room full of people. He had explained how to captivate an audience or a single person through the eyes, the voice, gestures, speech patterns. "It's a knack," he told his nephew. "Hitler had it too, but he misused it. You must use it well."

Two days later he stood in front of the assembled school, trying to remember his uncle's advice *Look round at the audience, wait at least half a minute to build up suspense, then begin to speak – slowly and quietly at first.* "Friends, fellow pupils, comrades ..." *Pause again.* "... at this crucial moment in the great worldwide class struggle, youth, that is you and I ..." *Point at the audience.* "... have a crucial role to play ..." Gradually his voice grew louder and more emphatic, as he spoke the stock phrases: "Imperialist enemy ... solidarity with the oppressed ... fight against capitalist exploitation." *It's working*, he thought with surprise, as he saw the audience looking up at him with shining eyes. He brought the speech to a climax: "The final victory of socialism is near, and you, and you, and you ..." *Point, make eye contact with selected members of the audience.* "... and I are going to be part of it. That is our historic destiny!"

When he finished his schoolmates applauded wildly, while the teacher looked uneasy. He was voted the winner by a large majority, but he realised he had broken one of the cardinal rules of the GDR: "Don't stand out too much". After that he was careful not to use his talent conspicuously, although he found it useful when it came to girl friends.

When he reached the age of seventeen he had every reason to think that he would be one of the few who would be allowed to take the Abitur examination in his final year and be guaranteed a place at university. At the end of the penultimate school year it was usual for the chosen ones to be called into the headmistress's room and given a solemn lecture on how privileged they were and how she expected them to be worthy of the trust that had been placed in them. So when he received a summons to the headmistress, Frau Stock, he went with happy anticipation.

As soon as he entered the room he sensed that something was wrong. Frau Stock's expression was even more severe than usual. She was a woman of fifty or so with a pale face, dyed black hair, two thin black lines where her eyebrows should have been, and a black mole on her upper lip. A face that was both cold and emphatic, like a traffic sign. And her voice was equally emphatic as she told him that he would not be allowed to take his school graduation exam and so would be barred from going to university. She gave him a whole list of offences that he had committed – telling disrespectful jokes about Walter Ulbricht, questioning the role of the Party, making drawings in class when he should have been paying attention to the teacher, and, worst of all, being heard in the lavatories singing an East Prussian song, *The Land on the Baltic Strand*. When he protested that he remembered the song from his childhood in Königsberg, she snapped at him: "East Prussia doesn't exist! And neither does Königsberg! It's now the

Russian city of Kaliningrad, as you well know."

He wanted to use his technique on her, but he couldn't catch her eye, and every time he started to speak, she shouted him down. She reached into a drawer of her desk and pulled out one of his classroom drawings – a pencil sketch of a centaur wistfully playing a Pan-pipe, which he had made in a bored moment. "And then there are these artistic efforts of yours – decadent fantasies like this one, which your teacher rightly confiscated. There are many other delinquencies that I could mention, but I think that's quite enough to justify the decision I have made."

Now his fate, she said, would be to leave the school at the end of the semester and be sent to a vocational establishment to learn a trade. He left the room shattered, his whole future in ruins. But a week later an inspector from the Ministry of Education, Dr. Petzold, came to the school and asked to see him. To his astonishment, the inspector told him that he was after all to be allowed to go to university to study chemistry. And, almost as an afterthought, Petzold had suggested that he might like to think about a career in government service, the Ministry of State Security, for example. "I have heard that you have an unusual talent for persuasiveness," he said "which could be very valuable to the Ministry." In fact, Petzold added, if he signed up right away, his future would become a lot easier. Then Petzold gave him a paper, declaring his "willingness to apply for the position of professional officer in the Ministry of State Security" and through diligent study to prove himself worthy of the Ministry's confidence in him. There was a space at the end for him to sign and date the document and another space indicating his parents' signature. Before they parted, he gave Henrik his telephone number and told him: "If you ever need advice or just a friendly chat, give me a call." Eager and grateful, Henrik took the paper home, and he and his parents signed it.

After that, life was at first a series of open doors – the studies at Halle University, graduation with a degree in organic chemistry, the job in the Stasi-run chemical firm of Lamda at Schwerin, the special training at the Stasi Academy in Potsdam – weapons drill, unarmed combat, surveillance methods. When he had completed his training he expected some interesting assignment where he could put his chemical knowledge to good use. But instead he had been sent to the grim Stasi regional headquarters in Leipzig, the so-called "Round Corner", a run-down turn-of-the-century building set on the corner of two thoroughfares. There he worked on developing synthetic material for forged rubber stamps and finding ways of preserving the body odours of suspected persons on pieces of specially prepared cloth, so that the Stasi's sniffer dogs could identify the places where they had been, the chairs they had sat on, the objects they had handled. The samples were kept in a basement room – shelf upon shelf of vacuum-sealed glass jars containing the cloth samples, each jar neatly labelled with a name and a code number. It always struck him as bizarre to think that the odours would probably live on in the jars long after those people had died.

Sometimes he thought he could not have survived the tedium of it without Petzold. He travelled to Berlin several times to meet him, first at Petzold's office and then at his cosy old-world house in the suburb of Weissensee. It was Petzold, with his kind, avuncular manner and charismatic way of talking, who kept him going. "The great beauty of the laws that Marx discovered," he could hear the elderly man saying between puffs at his pipe "is that they are both true and just. It is both inevitable and right that the working class will triumph. And the world will soon see that. You mark my words. Once the great capitalist lie is exposed for what it is, people all over the world will embrace our truth as flowers open to the light and warmth of the rising sun." He always came away from these meetings cheered and inspired.

Even so, he was close to resigning out of frustration until one day he was summoned to the office of Major Mallitsch, head of the archive and documentation unit, and told the news that had turned his life upside down. They had been gathering information about the former Lebensborn homes trying to fill in the gaps in the records of certain former inmates. Some of the records had ended up in Russia, and recently the KGB had sent a load of them back. They included some records from the Lenzfeld home in the Harz Mountains, including documentation about one Henrik Karlssen, illegitimate son of a Danish woman and a Wehrmacht corporal. The child had been re-named Lutz and adopted by a couple in Königsberg, Pastor Praetorius and his wife. And now, Mallitsch told him, there was no shadow of doubt that Henrik Karlssen and Lutz Erdmann were one and the same person. Then the major told him that, because of his Danish background, he had been chosen for a privileged assignment that would take him to the West. Once again, he had been cast down and then lifted up again as though by a powerful wave.

He came away from that meeting exhilarated. A golden future lay ahead of him. He remembered Petzold saying that inevitably the West would soon fall to Communism. He was going to help to bring that about. How could he fail, with his brains, his charisma and the laws of history behind him? After he had carried out his assignment he would go back to organic chemistry, set up his own laboratory and make discoveries that would bring him world renown.

He fingered the letter in his inside pocket, as he moved past warehouses, shipping offices, and, at last, on a corner by the Fish Market, spotted an inviting pub. From the open doorway, he heard a woman singing to an accordion. The tune had a lilting, bitter-sweet quality, and the voice had a rough edge, conjuring up schnapps, the smell of cigarette smoke, and passionate nights. The woman stood holding a microphone, just inside the doorway, beneath a sign: "Hildegard's Corner".

Drawn into the brown and amber interior, Henrik saw portholes in the wood-panelled walls *with trompe l'oeil* ocean liners and spouting whales painted in them. He caught his reflection in a mirror framed by a life-belt, pleased with how western he looked in the dove-grey tweed jacket and pink shirt that he had bought the day before. From the ceiling hung brass lanterns, a bell and a diver's helmet, lit from inside by a bulb. The place was like some overdone film set. At the far end was a bar with shelves above it crowded with ships in bottles, a fish in a glass case, a mug in the shape of a head with a sailor's cap and beard. Passing the singer, he realised her voice had misled him. She was no *femme fatale*, but a woman of about fifty, with butterfly-wing glasses and a mop of grey hair over an apple-cheeked face. Beside her sat a young blind man playing the accordion. The song was about the sea and faraway places:

>...*über Rio und Schanghai,*
>*über Bali und Hawaii ...*

The audience sang along - burly dockers, sailor types with cheesecutter hats, elderly couples, younger ones exchanging amused glances, aware that the place was an anachronism. He found a seat at a table already occupied by a middle-aged German couple and a pair of American tourists, standing out because of their clothes and the self-conscious way they looked around.

He ordered a beer from a passing waitress, and said half jokingly: "I don't suppose you'd have a piece of Black Forest gâteau?"

"What do you think this is? The Four Seasons Hotel?" She made a face of mock indignation.

"Okay, an apple strudel." Why the hell shouldn't he indulge his sweet tooth while drinking beer? She went off, giving him a sidelong smile, and came back with the strudel and a bottle of Astra.

Suddenly Hildegard stopped singing, as she struggled with a sallow-faced, grubby-looking man, his hair tied back in a pony-tail. "I told you, we don't want your type in here!" she cried, blocking the door. As the man pushed her roughly aside, Henrik leapt up, angry at the intruder for spoiling the atmosphere, just when he was beginning to enjoy it. With a dance-like movement born of his Stasi martial arts training, he spun the man back into the street, where he staggered and fell. A second later he was on his feet, lunging forward, and crashing a fist into Henrik's face. Henrik grabbed the man's collar, crouched and threw him over his shoulder. The man scrambled uneasily to his feet and ran off.

"Thank you young man," shouted Hildegard as he made his way back into the bar.

Hildegard bustled up to him. "Looks like you've got a black eye for your pains. Uschi," she called out, "give the young man anything he wants."

There was a ripple of applause as Henrik returned to his seat and accepted a free schnapps. Everyone was talking loudly and clinking glasses.

Henrik downed his schnapps and the waitress brought him another. Hildegard sang *Lili Marleen*, and everyone joined in. Henrik's head began to swim, and the apple strudel sat heavily in his stomach. He decided it was time to leave.

He walked uphill and away from the river to avoid the crowd. A drunken tramp was leaning in a doorway. An instant later, Henrik was grabbed from behind by the drunk, who held him firmly in a half nelson. The man was clearly not a drunk and Henrik cursed himself for not having been more vigilant. Another man stepped in front of him and he recognised the sallow complexion and ponytail of the man he had fought with at the bar.

The man spat at him and landed a fist in his face. His other fist slammed into Henrik's stomach. He doubled up in pain - then, with all the strength he could summon, thrust his right elbow backwards into the stomach of the accomplice behind him. He heard a gasp, and the grip loosened long enough for him to land a blow with the side of his left hand into the man's neck, simultaneously kicking the man with the pony tail in the stomach. The man dropped to the floor, clutching his stomach and groaning. From the end of the street people were turning and pointing. Someone shouted: "Call the police!"

Stay cool, he told himself. *Walk, don't run.* He turned the next corner and walked quickly up a back street. Had he been set up? Were those two goons from West German intelligence? There were spots of blood on his jacket from the bleeding nose they had given him. He would have to get it cleaned.

Well, at least he had got the better of them. The Stasi combat training had paid off. He walked on, guessing that the street led back in the direction of his lodgings, but it ended in a junction with another side street. He could hear shouts and a police siren behind him. If he was picked up by the ordinary police, looking the way he did, they would probably have him up on an assault charge. Time to vanish. He walked away down the side street as quickly as he could.

6

At the junction of the two streets he turned right and found himself back among market stalls selling flowers, fruit and vegetables. They filled a large, open plaza running slightly uphill away from the river. It was nearly closing time, and people were crowding around the stalls, hoping for bargains. The stall-holders were bawling out prices. One was even flinging unsold bananas into the crowd.

He felt safer in the crowd and allowed himself to be swept on past a group of stalls with live poultry in cages. Beyond them the crowd began to thin out, and ahead he could see a pedestrian subway leading off under a road. He followed it and emerged in a small park, where he slumped on to a bench. He rested until he had got his breath back, then slowly made his way through side streets avoiding the crowded river esplanade. Ahead was the spire of the St. Pauli church, rising above the trees in the graveyard. A few minutes later he was comforted by the sight of the familiar decaying stucco façade and battered front door of his apartment building.

Henrik started up the stairs, hoping to reach his room at the top without attracting Claudia's attention, but she had heard him. Looking up, he saw her waiting in the doorway of her apartment. His head was hurting badly and he felt shaky. There was no use pretending that he did not need help.

"My God!" she gasped, as he stepped into the light of her sitting room. "What happened to you?"

"Some thugs attacked me. Only cuts and bruises."

She frowned at him in a way that told him she suspected there was more to it than that. He tried to smile but his cut lip stopped him. "Some schnapps went to my head."

"Sit down while I get my first-aid stuff."

He sank back into a deep chair. As the shock wore off he began to ache in the places where he had taken the blows. In her living room he always felt as if he was invading a kind of sanctum. The room was lined with shelves stacked with books on various -isms and -ologies: psychology, mythology, mysticism, occultism, astrology, alchemy. There were little ornaments and curios on some of the shelves: a pyramid in black marble, a bronze figure of a dancing Indian god with many arms, a Tibetan singing bowl. In the country he had come from religion meant the embattled churches and not much more. Psychology meant homes for the mentally ill or institutions where political dissidents were treated with mind-altering drugs. Claudia had told him she was a "Jungian", as if that might help him. Then she had tried to explain the collective unconscious before abandoning the attempt when she realized he wasn't taking in a single word. That had been when she had asked him about himself and he had given her the censored version of his story - his "hero's quest", she had called it after hearing about the Lebensborn home, his Danish family and his wish to establish contact with them.

She returned with a bowl of warm water, a face cloth,

cotton wool, and several medicine bottles. He leaned back and let her long, deft fingers wash his face and dab his lip with disinfectant.

"Do you often fight, Henrik?"

Her face was intent on his and he noted the characteristic furrow between her brows that was always there whenever she was aggrieved or puzzled.

"Hardly ever." This was not quite true, but he was glad he'd said it, because her face gradually relaxed into the steady, friendly smile he liked.

"I'll put arnica on your bruises," she said, taking up a little bottle containing a brown liquid, which she poured on to a pad of cotton wool and then dabbed the places where he had been hit. Soothed by her calm, confident movements, he sank back even further into the soft armchair and closed his eyes. A moment later he was asleep.

*   *   *

He awoke with a jerk, unsure how long he had been asleep, to find Claudia looking at him with a worried expression.

"Henrik ..." she said softly. "Henrik ... it's all right. It was only a nightmare. Relax. I've just made some coffee." She sighed, lifting the pot and pouring him a cup. "I shouldn't have been listening, but I couldn't help it. Some of the time you were shouting ... something about a train and how you wanted to get off."

"Really?" he said, trying to hide his alarm. The nightmare from which he had awoken so abruptly was still in his mind – the one he had dreamt a thousand times. Once again he had been on the train, terrified by the strange faces that surrounded him and by the sound of explosions that came from somewhere in the distance, so many that they merged into an endless roar, like some vast dragon in terrible pain.

She gave him a searching look as she handed him his cup. Was this the way she looked at her clients? She would want him to explain the dream to her, and he had an urge to oblige her. That part of his life was no secret, but an instinct warned him to back off and be careful in case he gave away more than he intended. The disquieting thought came to him that maybe he had talked about other things while asleep. "Tell me what else I said."

"It was all a bit muddled. Oh dear, I wish I'd written it down. Earlier on ... before the nightmare that woke you up, there was something you kept repeating. About your mother...Your quest, I suppose. Then a lot I couldn't hear properly."

So that was all stuff she knew already. He felt relieved and made a joke of it. "Next time I'll try to be more coherent."

She smiled at him. "Please do. I'd love to help you find the real Henrik."

"The real me? Can anyone ever find that?"

"You can find it, Henrik, if it's what you really want." Her intense, unsmiling expression disturbed him. Honesty could be frightening as well as admirable. Outside in the street the afternoon was growing dimmer, but Claudia didn't move to switch on a light. She said, "There's something closed-in about you. Cut off. Underneath your charm you're sad, Henrik." Her pale face stood out against the soft, sombre colours of the room. He felt an impulse to lean towards her and take one of her hands in his. Careful, he told himself. Keep a safe distance.

She stood up and went to the window. "There's still a bit

of the afternoon left. We could drive over to Blankenese and walk down to the river then maybe have dinner there – if you want."

Better refuse, he told himself; but the thought of returning to his empty room was suddenly uninviting. He liked being the subject of her concern and it wasn't difficult to fend off her questions and perhaps he might turn the tables and ask her a few searching questions about her past – see how much she liked searing honesty. Maybe he would ask her about the men in her life. Then they would see who liked honesty most.

"All right," he said. "I've heard Blankenese is nice."

Outside, they climbed into Claudia's battered red Audi. He was startled by the speed with which she accelerated past the St. Pauli church and down a cobbled street of quaintly dilapidated, turn-of-the century houses, making the car shake alarmingly. She was a thoroughly reckless driver, zooming over traffic lights just as they were turning from amber to red and braking at the last minute as a car emerged from a side road and nearly hit her.

"For God's sake, Claudia!" he snapped.

"What?"

"He had the right of way."

"Did he?" Clearly her mind was already elsewhere. "So what do you plan to do, Henrik? About your mother, I mean."

They were in the quieter streets of Altona, driving parallel to the Elbe. Out on the river a ship's hooter gave a long and mournful blast, like the sound of a cow calling for a lost calf, or maybe driving it away, he thought bleakly.

"I wrote a letter to her today but didn't post it. I'm not sure it's the right thing to do."

She thought for a moment. "Perhaps a direct approach

isn't best at this stage."

"What do you think should I do?"

"There might be another option"

At that moment they reached the end of the Elbchaussee, and she parked the car at a point high above the Elbe. The cosy little houses of Blankenese set in miniature gardens spilled down the slope towards the river, their windows glowing in the twilight.

He smiled at her. "What's the other possibility?"

"An intermediary; someone she trusts; someone who could soften the shock."

"An intermediary," he repeated. "How do I know who to trust?"

"By choosing well."

"I plan to go there in the next few days – to reconnoitre before making contact, take a look at the house, get an idea of what sort of neighbours they have."

"Maybe an idea will come to you then. You need to let things happen as well as make plans."

Just when their talk was starting to become useful to him, she opened the door and got out. "I'm hungry. Let's find somewhere to eat."

They descended towards the river through steep alleyways. One of the old sea captains' houses had been converted into a restaurant. There they sat by a window overlooking the river and ate a fish dinner with white wine, while Claudia probed him about his life. Once, when he crossed the room to go to the men's lavatory he caught sight of her in a mirror, looking at him in a different way, as though she were trying to work out a puzzle.

When she asked him why he had decided to become an

organic chemist, he was relieved. That was a subject that he could talk about without holding back.

"When I was a growing up in Wittenberge," he told her "I used to go for weekends and holidays to the uncle and aunt of my adoptive father – I called them Uncle Rolf and Aunt Hilda. They lived in a village called Dobzin, about an hour by bicycle from Wittenberge. I always felt more at home with them that with my adoptive parents. The village was in a beautiful area full of birds – storks, herons, geese, red eagles. I became fond of watching and drawing them.

"Uncle Rolf was a blacksmith, but he was also a kind of folk healer with an amazing knowledge of traditional plant remedies. He was a rather fierce looking character with a great handlebar moustache and penetrating eyes, but underneath he was very gentle. He had enormous hands, rough and calloused from his work in the forge, but when he handled a plant they took on a great fineness and precision. He used to take me for walks through the woods and meadows, pointing out plants and telling me their properties – how valerian was good for insomnia, and artemisia for menstrual pains, and periwinkle for eczema – and the different ways you prepared them. He also told me which plants were poisonous, and how even some of the poisons could be used to heal when given in minute quantities. When I asked him how plants made these remedies he said they took substances from water, air and earth and mixed them in different ways. It thrilled me to think of each plant being a kind of mini-laboratory, and I wanted to know more about what actually happened inside them."

As he talked, Claudia reached out and touched his hand. "I love to hear you talking like this, Henrik. And I love your uncle already."

"Because of him chemistry became my favourite subject and I went on to do organic chemistry at university. I was fascinated by the alkaloids, the reactive substances that plants produce, some of which are therapeutic, others highly toxic. I became obsessed by the complexity of their chemical formulae. There are thousands of alkaloids that can be used for healing, but only a small number have been synthesized in a laboratory. And that's where there is really valuable work to be done. My dream is to have my own research laboratory, where I can work at creating synthesized alkaloids for therapeutic purposes."

Claudia touched his hand again. "I feel sure you'll get that laboratory."

Afterwards they walked down to the beach and stood looking across the river, the black water streaked with silver in the fading light. The air had grown chilly, and Claudia shivered, turning up the collar of her jacket.

"How long will it take you to drive to the island?" she asked.

"Maybe three hours including the ferry journey."

He half expected her to say that she was ready to come with him to Denmark, and he had his answer ready. He had to face the task on his own. But she did not offer to accompany him. He sensed that she wanted him to move closer to her, take her hand or put his arm around her, but he remained motionless, hands thrust into his pockets.

On the drive back the car radio was playing American jazz music, and Claudia had switched to her bouncy mood. There was a note of forced light-heartedness in her voice.

"What kind of music do you like, Henrik?" she said, moving her head in time to the rhythm. "What's your favourite band?"

He sensed that she was teasing him. Well, two could play at that game.

"The Amazing Yellow Polka Dots."

For the first time since he had met her she threw her head back and shrieked with laughter. "You're kidding! Is there such a band? I suppose they must have taken the name from that stupid song about the Yellow Polka Dot Bikini."

"Bikini ...?" he repeated, puzzled.

"When we get home I'll play you some decent stuff. You've heard of the Beatles?"

"Of course. They played here in Hamburg, at the Star Club."

"You're very well informed for someone just arrived from the GDR."

With the curtains drawn, the living room became even more of a rarified sanctum – green shaded lamp on the mantlepiece, candlelight flickering over her books and oriental ornaments, catching a trail of smoke from a joss stick burner.

She opened the lid of a record player, put a record on the turntable, and a moment later the voices of the Beatles singing *A Hard Day's Night* filled the air. She moved towards him, swaying to the music, moving with surprising grace and agility.

"Come on, Henrik!" She took his hands, drawing him into the dance. Awkwardly, he tried to follow her movements, moving stiffly, not knowing where to put his feet. At school he had learned the waltz and other ballroom steps, but never the freer, uninhibited stomping and arm-waving that he associated with westerners moving to the sound of their pop music.

When the song came to an end she said: "You're full of blockages. We've got to loosen you up." Now she was talking that strange language again. Like the Beatles' music it made him feel uneasy. He hated being made to feel inept, not least because it so rarely happened to him.

"How about some coffee?" he said, eager to change the subject.

"All right, I'll make some."

They drank in silence, and then she asked what he was thinking about.

"My mother. What else?"

"I see." She stood up to clear away the coffee things. "Well, I'd better turn in. I have a long day ahead of me tomorrow."

At the door she turned and said: "The sooner you go to Denmark the better."

7

In a second-hand Volkswagen beetle, bought from a dealer in a back street of Altona, he drove up from Hamburg through the province of Schleswig-Holstein. He looked out at the countryside, flat and reassuring with its herds of sheep and black-and-white cattle, rape fields poised to turn into blankets of yellow, woods and hedges brushed with a green mist of early foliage. The letter lay in the glove compartment of the car, just in case he got the chance to use it. Maybe he would somehow find the right intermediary as Claudia had suggested he might, or maybe he would, after all, simply put it through the Karlssens' letterbox. But first he would take a look at the house, if he could find a suitable vantage point. He planned to pose as an ornithologist in case anyone challenged him. After all, ever since his childhood he had loved to draw birds, even though he was no expert on the different species and subspecies.

The road led on to a peninsula that jutted out into the Baltic and came to an end at the small harbour of Puttgarden where he drove the car on to a ferry. An hour later, just after midday, he drove on to Danish soil at the port of Rødby on the island of Lolland. He bought a ham sandwich at a filling station and ate it in the car while he studied his map. The village lay about forty kilometres away via four islands connected by bridges. A cheap hotel or guest house would serve as a base. It might be several days before he could make direct contact with the Karlssens, and to stay in Norvik itself would be highly risky. In no time the news of a strange young German staying in the village would have reached the family through the local grapevine, and the whole delicate operation would be jeopardised. There were no hotels or bed and breakfast signs in the tiny port where he had disembarked, so he drove on, across countryside that was flat like Schleswig-Holstein, but barer, and more exposed to the Baltic winds. On the next island, in a larger port, he found what he was looking for: a modest hotel-cum-café near the harbour, where he checked in for the night and said he would return later.

He drove over another bridge to another island. The land became barer, the trees more stunted, braced against the wind that swept over the wide, flat beaches, tossing the gulls higher against a sky that was now overcast. Just when he was beginning to feel that he had reached the end of the known world he saw ahead of him another bridge and another, smaller island, Lysholm. As he drove towards it his first thought was: why on earth would the German army have bothered to occupy such a God-forsaken place? He could only see a bare shoreline, the rusting carcass of a wrecked ship on the endless mudflats and, inland, bleak-looking fields and more trees bent over by the wind, but further along, after a sharp turn in the road the island suddenly became greener, more welcoming. There were woods of fully-grown trees, cultivated fields, cows and sheep grazing, and in the distance a village, Norvik. He could see some houses and, beyond them, rising above a line of trees, a church steeple. The sight of the steeple gave him the germ of an idea. There would be a pastor. If he was a sympathetic man, and if Henrik could approach him discreetly, possibly, just possibly he could be the intermediary. It was worth considering, but first he had to scout out the land a bit more.

He slowed down and, at a safe distance from the village, parked the car on a broad shoulder of the road overlooking the shore. He rummaged in the boot and a few minutes later had donned an anorak, a rucksack and sturdy walking boots. In the rucksack were a pair of binoculars, a sketch book and some pencils. As though to test his disguise, he pointed the binoculars briefly at a V-shaped flock of geese setting off for their summer quarters in the north. He hoped he knew enough about birds to pass as an ornithologist.

He walked up the road, every so often pausing to lift the binoculars to his eyes as if sweeping the horizon for more birds. After half a kilometre the road turned inland and went slightly downhill towards the village. As he focused the binoculars on it, he was reminded of villages he had seen in old children's books - all red-tiled roofs, pastel-coloured stucco, and window boxes filled with geraniums.

He stepped off the road into a field and, skirting the village, walked towards a wood that looked as though it would provide good cover. The hardwood trees were still bare, but there were enough evergreens to provide concealment. Sweeping again with his binoculars, he saw a road sign: Strandvej. That was where the family lived, at number five, but which was the house? It was difficult to tell where the street began. Few of the houses seemed to have numbers, and in one place a dirt track with no road sign led off at a right angle to more houses and small farms. As the wood ran along the edge of the dirt track, he decided to follow it, keeping in the cover of the trees. He passed a brash new bungalow with a double garage and a front garden filled with kitschy statuary – probably a weekend home for a rich Copenhagen family. Then came a derelict red-brick house with boarded-up windows. For a moment he wondered whether that might be their house, abandoned, but now he could see another likely property about a hundred yards ahead on the other side of the track. This one looked more promising. To continue through the wood and reach a vantage point opposite the house, he found he would have to climb over a barbed wire fence, probably making himself a trespasser, if he was not one already. What if the owner of the land found him there and reported him to the police? He might be prosecuted, and deported, and what would his mother and her family think of him then – if he had even managed to meet them?

He hesitated, but then, after looking around to check that no one was watching, he stooped down and wriggled through the fence between two strands of barbed wire, holding the lower one down. Making his way stealthily through the undergrowth, he soon found himself opposite the house, which he could see clearly between the trees. A wrought-iron figure 5 was riveted to one of the brick gateposts flanking the driveway. He aimed his binoculars at the house, which looked about a century old and was larger than most of the others he had passed. It had stuccoed walls painted a pale ochre colour, generous overhanging eaves and windows with blue-grey wooden shutters. A beam over the front door bore an inscription in old-fashioned white lettering, perhaps an edifying motto or biblical quotation. On the upper floor a window was open and a lace curtain stirred gently in the breeze. In front and to the right was an L-shaped garden and, beyond it, a fenced chicken run. Moving to a different angle, he could see part of a courtyard with some barns and outbuildings. To the left of the driveway, one of the barns had been converted into a shop with a sign above the door that said "KARLSSEN – HOME-GROWN AND LOCAL PRODUCE". Through the open doorway he caught a glimpse of baskets of fruit and vegetables, shelves stacked with jars of preserves, a counter and a young, dark-haired woman moving about behind it – perhaps Birthe's daughter (he found it helpful to think of Birthe by her name, rather than as "mother"). Beyond the house, he presumed, lay fields and orchards. There must, he guessed, be one or two other personnel besides the family to keep such a business going. There was no one in sight, but he could faintly hear voices somewhere in the house or the courtyard. Their dog, a large, shaggy, black creature, was tethered by log lead to the shaft of an old iron pump in the courtyard.

The front door of the house swung open and he raised his binoculars to see another young woman emerge, holding a spade. She was stocky, with untidy reddish hair, and wore a brown sweater, jeans and rubber boots. There were two small children with her, a boy and a girl, clearly her own from the colour of their hair and her tone of voice when she spoke to them. So this must be Birthe's daughter-in-law. The children played with a ball while the woman began to dig at an asparagus bed, banking the earth up around the new shoots.

After about twenty minutes the red-haired woman stopped her digging and went back into the house with the two children. A few moments later he heard raised voices from within the house, then the door burst open and a young man emerged, fair-haired with a moustache and a lean, taut face. The woman came running after him and tried to stop him, clutching at his arm and saying something in a tearful, pleading tone. Henrik tried to catch a word or two, but at that moment a car went past, drowning their voices. Henrik felt sure the young man must be Birthe's son and the woman must be his wife. Henrik saw the man shake her off with a curse and climb into a Land Rover standing in the drive. The woman stood helplessly as her husband started the engine and drove away. Henrik watched the woman go back slowly into the house.

A middle-aged woman on a bicycle approached the house from the direction of the village. She was wearing a pale beige raincoat and a red headscarf. She was crouching forward on the bicycle, the headscarf pulled low over her forehead, so that Henrik could not see her full face, but he had the impression of a woman of middle age. Surely she must be Birthe. The sight of her brought a disturbing mixture of confusion, resentment and sympathy. For the first time he wondered what it must have been like for her to give away her child. Steady, he told himself. She was his cover. He must win her and the family over but stay inwardly detached.

She halted for a moment and put one foot on the ground while she said something to the younger woman. Then she pedalled off into the courtyard behind the house. A light rain had begun to fall. Henrik decided that he had seen enough for the time being. He would go back to his hotel and return in the morning.

At least he now had some idea of what Birthe looked like. Sooner or later he was going to have to approach her, but first he would have to gather more information about her – such as how she spent her days and what her movements were, so that he might find an opportunity to speak to her alone. Perhaps she had a particular friend in the village, who might become an intermediary? Clearly he would have to do a lot more reconnoitring, but not today.

As he walked back down the road the rain began to fall more heavily. Coming into sight of the car, he saw that three teenage boys had gathered around it, evidently intent on doing some sort of damage. Annoyed at himself for not hiding the car, he ran towards it. The boys were scooping up mud from the ground and smearing it over the white paintwork. Maybe they had punctured the tyres as well. He yelled angrily as he approached. They looked startled for a moment, then laughed and made obscene gestures. He heard them shout the word, "Tysk", and then "Nazi". A moment later they ran away, disappearing across a field. When he came up to the car he saw that they had smeared muddy swastikas on the sides and bonnet, but the tyres and windows seemed undamaged. He wiped off the swastikas as best he could, then he sat in the driver's seat trying to compose himself. With anti-German feeling like this in the village, he was going to have a hard job winning over Birthe, let alone her husband.

He started the engine and swung the car round. As he did so a vehicle swept past from the village - a Land Rover, possibly the one in which he had seen Birthe's son drive off earlier, although he did not see the driver clearly. He drove off and was soon crossing the bridge to the next island. He came to a main road and, seeing that he was approaching a transport café, decided to eat. In the parking lot he saw the Land Rover parked among the heavy lorries.

The café was a plain red brick building, brightly lit, with coloured photographs in the windows showing hamburgers and plates of spaghetti and fish and chips. Inside, the place smelt of cooking fat and tobacco smoke. Conversation, kitchen noises and American big-band music filled the air. Fetching a plate of cod, peas and chips from the counter, he sat down near a window. Across the room, at a table in the opposite corner was a young man munching a hamburger and reading a tabloid newspaper. When he raised his head Henrik realised it was the bad-tempered man he had seen at the house, whom he had assumed to be Birthe's son and his own half-brother. Not at all the kind of relative he would have chosen. Henrik watched as the man finished his hamburger then ate an ice cream, still reading his newspaper. Suddenly he looked at Henrik with an expression of intense hostility then stood up to leave.

Henrik watched him walk out into the car park, turning up his jacket collar against the rain. Instead of making for his Land Rover he stalked up and down the car park, smoking and every so often looking grimly towards the café entrance. He finished one cigarette, lit another and tossed away an empty book of matches. He was still there when Henrik emerged from the café.

As Henrik approached, the young man took a pull at his cigarette, then threw it to the ground and stamped it out, unleashing a volley of unintelligible words, none of them flattering to judge by his tone. Henrik dreaded being dragged into another fight. For a split second the man seemed to be about to grab him by the collar, but then thought better of it. He glared for a moment longer, then turned on his heel and walked across the car park to his Land Rover. As he drove off, he gunned the engine furiously.

Walking to his car, Henrik noticed the discarded book of matches on the ground and picked it up. There were a couple of matches still in it. On the shiny black flap he read the name "Severin's" in white Gothic letters, with an address in Hamburg and a telephone number. Instinct told him that it might be useful and he slid it into a pocket.

8

Two days later Henrik climbed the short flight of steps that ran sideways up to the front porch of the Pastor's house, a long barn of a building in red brick, more imposing and severe than the other houses in the village, and set in its own grounds behind the church. It was Monday morning. The previous day he had returned to the village, parking the car a kilometre or two away, among some trees, down a deserted farm track. At first he had heard and seen no one from the house. Then, as the church bell began to ring, Birthe had emerged, evidently dressed for the service in a long, dark green overcoat, a beige bonnet over carefully pinned-up hair, and old-fashioned high-heeled boots, laced to the ankle. He had followed her into the village, keeping a couple of hundred yards behind and had seen her enter the little white-stuccoed church with its slate-covered spire, pausing at the door to greet and shake hands with members of the congregation. Evidently she was a regular church-goer and probably on friendly terms with the Pastor. So Henrik's mind had been made up. The Rev. Hans Arup, whose name was on a board in front of his church, was to be his chosen means of meeting Birthe.

Standing at the door, he wondered whether he would be able to find the right words, never having known a pastor, except for the man who had been his adoptive father up to the age of four, Pastor Praetorius, whom he barely remembered. A typed notice on the door told him that he had come outside the Pastor's regular consulting hours, but this was after all a special situation. He grasped the iron bell pull attached to the wall and gave it a tug. It was stiff and in need of oil, and he had to pull it three times before a cold, dull clang sounded somewhere in the house like a mocking reminder of mortality, of things that were better left safely buried and forgotten. A couple of minutes passed before he pulled the bell again. He heard a movement, then someone irritably rattling at the lock of the inner door. It opened and the Pastor appeared in the porch, a slightly built man in late middle age, with dark hair turning grey, a small, bushy moustache and a high, balding head. He was wearing a brown cardigan over an open-necked shirt and looked slightly dishevelled, as though he had just woken from an afternoon nap. He opened the outer door wide enough to poke his head out and look at Henrik with a vexed expression. He said something in Danish and pointed at the timetable.

"I'm sorry," Henrik said in German. "Perhaps I came at an awkward time."

"Ah, you are German" Arup said, as though being German explained the unwelcome intrusion. "This is outside my consulting hours. You can come back tomorrow." He began to close the door again.

Henrik stopped the door with his hand. "It can't wait till tomorrow." For a second he thought of thrusting the letter into the Pastor's hands, but instead he said: "I have something urgent to discuss with you. It concerns Birthe Karlssen."

The door opened a little and the pastor gave him a searching look.

"You know Mrs. Karlssen?"

"Yes ... well, not exactly ..."

Arup hesitated, puzzled. "Well, perhaps if it's an important matter ... He held the door open for Henrik to enter. "But I can only spare a few minutes."

He showed Henrik into the drawing room and said: "Please take a seat. I'll be back in a moment."

The room was cold like the sound of the doorbell. Lace curtains at the window let in a washed out light, and the air had the dull smell of rooms that are routinely cleaned but little used. There were chairs and a sofa, stiffly upholstered in green brocade, a glass-fronted cabinet filled with bone china, a few old prints of farming and fishing scenes, set a little too high on the wall as though to keep a respectable distance from the viewer. It reminded Henrik of the reconstructed rooms that he had seen in the museums of provincial towns in East Germany. This one would have a sign that said "Pastor's drawing room, mid-20th century" and then something about how religion was part of the apparatus of class oppression and how the furniture reflected the Pastor's status as a member of the bourgeoisie. Henrik broadly agreed with this: Christianity was an elaborate pretence.

When Arup reappeared wearing his clerical collar and a

black jacket, Henrik was reminded of an actor making his entrance. The pastor seated himself opposite Henrik and carefully folded his hands in his lap, as he probably folded them on the edge of the pulpit before beginning a sermon.

"So," he began, "you are from Germany." He spoke correct German but with a strong Danish accent. "Not a country I know well, although of course I have read much German theology. Melanchthon has always been a special inspiration for me, and I've found a lot to admire in some of your more recent theologians, Otto, Bonnhöfer, Tillich. Yes, there is much of great value that has come out of your country." But in his tone Henrik fancied he could hear the unspoken thought: ... *and much that is appalling as well: Hitler, the war, and now people like you and hordes of German tourists coming here and behaving as though you still occupied the place* ... This was going to be a difficult meeting.

Arup unfolded his hands and pressed the fingertips together. "So what can I do for you, Herr ...?"

"Erdmann, Henrik Erdmann."

As Arup took in the name, his eyes registered a startled look. *He knows*, thought Henrik. *He knows the whole story. She must have told him everything.*

"What can I do for you, Herr Erdmann?"

Since Birthe was probably a long-standing member of this man's congregation, it was almost inevitable that she would have told him her story. How had Arup reacted? With sympathy, shock or stern disapproval? Henrik's hand reached into his inside pocket and touched the envelope.

"Herr Arup, I have a favour to ask of you."

A look of suspicion crossed Arup's face.

"I have brought with me a letter for Mrs. Karlssen."

"A letter?" The Pastor appeared to be taken aback, as though he were thinking: *Does he take me for a postman?*

"Yes, it concerns a delicate matter. The letter will come as a surprise, perhaps a shock. That's why ..."

Arup raised a hand to interrupt him. "Herr Erdmann, I believe I know what you are going to tell me. Mrs. Karlssen has already spoken to me of this matter. You were wise to come to me and not approach her directly. You see, Mrs. Karlssen has decided to close that particular chapter of her life. There would be no point in trying to re-open it. She would refuse to see you, or ask you to leave and not return." Arup sat quite motionless, hands folded calmly and resolutely, like a judge who has delivered a harsh verdict but will not be moved.

"I see. So you know all about me."

"Yes, I guessed who you were as soon as I heard your first name." Arup made an apologetic movement with his hands. "I realise this must be very disappointing for you, but there is nothing I can do. Mrs. Karlssen's mind is made up. Now, if you don't mind ..."

"Did she say why she wants to close the chapter, why she won't see me?"

Again Arup's hands gestured apology. "I really can't say anything more about the matter. I would advise you to go back home to Germany right away."

Henrik looked the Pastor in the eye, holding his gaze. "That's for me to decide," he said in a deeper voice. "You tell me my mother doesn't want to see me. But how do I know that's true? I can hardly believe she wouldn't even look at a letter."

Arup sighed and sat hunched forward, while a clock on the cabinet ticked away the seconds. "All right," he sat upright again and looked at Henrik, "there are things that perhaps you should know." Suddenly he had dropped the stiff, clerical manner. "I was just about to make a cup of tea when you arrived. Come into my office and I'll make one for you."

He led the way down a corridor and into a smaller room, half-filled by a big mahogany desk, which was cluttered with papers. The walls of the study were lined with bookshelves, containing imposing volumes in sombre bindings. The Pastor offered Henrik a chair, while he plugged in a kettle and rummaged for tea things in a corner cupboard.

"I'd offer you a biscuit as well," he said apologetically, "but I seem to have run out. My wife died a year ago, and I'm still learning to look after the house myself."

Henrik noticed a picture on the wall between the bookshelves, a sepia photograph in a black oval frame, showing an old man with a gaunt, bony face, his white hair, beard and mutton-chop whiskers merging into an enormous white aureole. The picture was captioned "Nikolaij Frederik Severin Grundtvig, 1783-1872, theologian, poet, philosopher, educational reformer and founder of the Danish Folk High Schools".

"Ah," said Arup, seeing the direction of his gaze. "You are looking at one of my great heroes, N.F.S. Grundtvig, founder of the Danish Folk High Schools. My dream is to start a Grundtvig School here on Lysholm, but I can't do it alone. I'm trying to persuade Mrs Karlssen ... your mother ... to help me, but she's reluctant. She's afraid that if she stepped into such a public role there might be problems." He handed Henrik a cup of tea and then stirred his own thoughtfully. "That brings me to the subject of the past. How much do you know already...about your father, for instance?"

"Only that he was a German corporal named Heinz Ackermann and that I was conceived soon after the German invasion."

"That's correct." Arup went on slowly stirring his tea. "And your mother genuinely loved him. He came from Flensburg just over the border and spoke some Danish. That was one of things that made him different from the other German soldiers. Anyway, at the time they met she was married but living apart from her husband, Sven. She had really only married him because she had become pregnant. Then when she had a miscarriage he went to pieces, started drinking and being violent with her, so she moved out and went to live with her uncle and aunt. Then she met your father." He paused, sipped at his tea and said: "I'm not sure whether I should really be telling you this. Your mother told me the story in confidence, but I suppose as her son you have a right to know."

"I'm grateful to you for telling me."

"They planned to marry as soon as she could get a divorce from Sven, but your father was transferred to France for mine-clearing duty and just after that your mother discovered that she was pregnant. He wrote for a while, but then his letters stopped and eventually your mother heard that he had been killed by a mine." Arup paused again and said quietly: "This must be upsetting for you. I'm so sorry."

"It's all right, go on."

"Well, Sven went to see your mother and begged her to return – said he would forgive her and accept the child and give up drinking."

"And she agreed?"

"Yes, what else could she do? She gave birth to you in the

spring of 1941. At first Sven tried to keep to his promise, but he could never really accept you as his own, especially after the birth of her second child, your half-brother Niels. Then, you see, the war began to go against the Germans. Your mother was afraid of what would happen if they were driven out of Denmark. She would be branded as a German soldier's whore, and vengeful people might try to hurt you. At best you would suffer a stigma for many years, possibly for the rest of your life. It was then that the SS offered her a way out. They would take you and look after you in one of their special homes in Germany, until you could be adopted. You would be well cared for and free of the dangers and prejudice that faced you here. It seemed for the best ... above all for you. But still she hesitated. Who wouldn't? You were her son after all. Then she became pregnant again - that was in the spring of 1943 - and that's what finally made her make the decision. After the war it was clearly going to be difficult for the other two children, almost as much as for you. She delayed throughout that summer, then decided she needed to act before the new baby was born. So one day a woman from the SS came to take you away, by ship."

Arup stood up and put a hand on Henrik's shoulder. "All this is terribly painful for you, I know, but you must also realise how it is for your mother. It's only two decades since the war ended. There is still a great deal of resentment against the Germans and especially against those who, shall we say ... fraternised with them. Mrs. Karlssen has had a long struggle to live down her past and become accepted by the community. It's not been easy for her or her family. Now at last things have simmered down a bit and she can live here more or less peacefully. But if she were suddenly to acknowledge you as her son it would reopen old wounds. Things could become very unpleasant, even dangerous for her and the family."

"Dangerous?" Henrik repeated.

"Yes. There could be anonymous phone calls, bricks thrown through windows at night, death threats. Such things have happened in other parts of the country, deplorable though they are. Think how terrible that would be for Mrs. Karlssen and her family, especially for her grandchildren. It could be dangerous for you as well. Every time you came here, your presence would be a provocation."

Henrik looked silently at the Pastor, thinking of the youths' attack on his car and recognizing that the man had a point, but also knowing that it would take a lot more than a dozen such attacks to make him abort his mission.

"Do you see now," Arup said "why it would be so unwise for you to contact your mother? It will be very hard for you to accept my advice. But if you think of your mother and her family and put them first, I believe you will want to avoid causing unnecessary suffering."

At the front door Arup said gently: "I wish it could have been otherwise." He shook Henrik's hand, turned back into the porch, and a moment later came the rattling sound of the lock turning.

Henrik walked away from the house. He wanted to sit down with a drink and think things over, but it wouldn't do to go into a local pub and make himself conspicuous. Across the village square from the churchyard was a little grocery shop, which probably stocked schnapps and brandy, but there was a cardboard sign hung in the glass door that said "closed". He made his way back to the secluded track where he had parked his car.

Driving away from the village, he passed the spot where he had interrupted the youths vandalising his car. Then he turned a bend in the road and saw a woman approaching on a bicycle from the opposite direction as if making her way to the church. His pulse quickened as he made out the beige raincoat and red headscarf that she had been wearing the first time he had seen her. The next few moments might determine the success or failure of his entire mission. He took a deep breath and slowed down as she came towards him. For a moment his eyes met hers as she passed. A hundred yards past her, he braked hard, stopped, then wrenched the steering wheel around and drove slowly back down the road towards the figure on the bicycle.

9

In the quiet of the reading room at the Hamburg Public Library Claudia sat at a table with a pile of books, thinking about Henrik. When she had first begun to fall in love with him she had tried to keep a cool head by analysing him as objectively as if he were one of her clients. On the table in front of her lay a notebook open at a page on which she had written in a neat, upright hand:

"Henrik Erdmann. 25 years old. Refugee from the GDR. Childhood marked by traumas – rejection by Danish mother, period in Lebensborn home, adoption, stigma of birth. Personality type: something of the "eternal boy" – charming, with a strange sort of charisma, but self-centred and a bit ruthless. Strongly driven to prove himself to himself and the world. Prominence of Hero archetype. Determined, intelligent, idealistic, but masking feeling side. Out of touch with Anima.

Impaired capacity for bonding due to uprooted childhood. Evidence that he is holding something back when talking about the GDR. Speech patterns and body language change subtly when the subject comes up. Something he is ashamed of in his past? Altogether a bit of a dark horse."

She closed the notebook and turned to the pile of books. With Henrik away in Denmark on his "hero's quest", as she called it, she had decided to find out more about "the real Henrik" starting with the place where he had been born and that other place where he had been sent as a small child. "Lebensborn" – "wellspring of life" – the name had an old-fashioned, poetic quality that belied the cruel reality. She opened a magazine containing an article about Lebensborn. The scheme, she learned, had been launched in 1935 on the orders of Heinrich Himmler, Reichsführer of the SS, in order to end the loss of "good German blood" through abortions. Lebensborn had started as a chain of maternity homes for unmarried mothers of sound German stock as well as for the wives of SS men. But when the war came Himmler urged people - whether married or not - to produce children for the good of the Reich. This included military men, who were encouraged to mate with women of the occupied countries. Children resulting from such unions could be looked after in Lebensborn homes until adoptive parents could be found for them. At the time Henrik had been given away, it seemed there had been no Lebensborn homes in Denmark, which was evidently why he had been sent to one in Germany.

The article was illustrated with photographs of several homes – all of them fine houses set in spacious grounds. One picture showed some of the staff and inmates on a sunlit terrace overlooking a garden. There were small boys in leather shorts with shoulder straps, girls in loose white dresses, buxom young women in nurses' aprons, holding babies. It looked idyllic, but the article told of the grim human consequences. The orphanage children had all been separated from their mothers. Many had been kidnapped in the occupied countries and brought to a Lebensborn home where they were given new names and forced to speak only German. Small wonder many of them had that blank, withdrawn look. Then there were the cases of chronically sick children who were simply eliminated through over-doses of morphine. But the worst traumas had come after the war, when the children had been regarded as pariahs and often brutally treated. As Claudia read on she found herself close to tears just thinking that one of those little blond boys in the picture might have been Henrik. She felt that she was beginning to understand him better.

When she went back to her table after a coffee break, she had the distinct impression that someone had looked through what she had been reading. The books and her notes lay on the table where she had left them but she could have sworn that they had been shifted a fraction. Probably just the idle curiosity of another reader, she told herself, but it gave her an uneasy feeling. She couldn't help wondering if it had something to do with the other odd things that she had noticed lately, like the grey Volvo that she had noticed following her car from time to time. She would have been even more uneasy if she had realised that someone was watching her through a gap in one of the bookshelves – a tall, athletically built man with a bony face and close-cropped fair hair. When Claudia left the library the man followed at a discreet distance.

10

The woman on the bicycle did not at first notice that Henrik had turned and was slowly following her. Now he could see her face properly: friendly blue eyes, high cheekbones, a generous mouth and a slightly snub nose, only a few strands of grey in the blond hair falling out from under the scarf. Use the gift, he told himself.

"Mrs. Karlssen?"

"*Ja.*" Her face took on a look of surprise, as though she were wondering how a strange German would know her name?

"Excuse me ... you don't know me," he began in German, unsure whether she would understand him. "Let me explain. Just one moment." He leapt out of the car and went around to where she was standing. She was beginning to look alarmed, one foot on a pedal, ready to push off.

"Mrs. Karlssen, I'm very sorry to surprise you like this, but ..."

She was shaking her head. *"Undskyld! Jeg forstår ikke."*

So she didn't understand German. He tried English: "You may find this hard to believe, but my name is Erdmann ... Henrik Erdmann."

Her face froze and went a shade paler as he said the name. He reached into his jacket pocket and brought out the letter. "I wrote you a letter. I didn't want to take you by surprise." Now her face registered alarm. *"Jeg forstår ikke,"* she repeated.

"Can't understand", she was saying. Or did she really mean she didn't want to? He tried to hold her eyes with his, but she kept looking away. Just when he needed it most, his charisma wasn't working. "I wanted to avoid shocking you… that's why I didn't come to your house or telephone you or send you the letter directly in the mail. I thought you would need time to adjust ... I thought with time to think it over ..." He gave up trying to explain and held the letter out to her. "I wasn't sure whether you understood German, so I wrote in English."

She stared at the letter, not moving. He sensed that she wanted to take it but was afraid to do so. He held it out a little closer to her, willing her to accept it. With a shake of her head she pushed off again on her bicycle and pedalled away.

Henrik wondered whether to go after her, but decided there was no point. Trying to force her to take the letter would only alienate her more. Despondently, he watched her figure grow smaller as she cycled away. So what had happened? Judging by the pale, shocked look on her face when he had spoken it, she had recognised his name. That would mean she had known who he was and had rejected him. So the Pastor had been right. She really did want to "close the chapter." Why hadn't his charisma worked? In a flash he realised the answer – it was because the moment he saw her face he was no longer detached, like an actor playing a part, and she was no longer just his "cover". He was beginning to want her to accept him as her son.

Feeling the need to calm himself, he left the car by the roadside, walked onto the beach and sat down on a piece of driftwood. It was high tide, and the waves were being whipped up by a cold wind. Along the tide line he saw the usual depressing detritus amongst the seaweed - a dead seagull, an old plastic bag, the severed head of a child's doll, a detergent bottle.

He took the letter from a pocket and stared at the envelope, bearing Birthe's name and address in case he should decide to post it. But there wasn't much point in doing that now. He thrust it carelessly back into a side pocket of his waterproof jacket. If he couldn't have a drink, at least he could have a smoke. Fumbling for his cigarettes and matches, he didn't notice that he had dislodged the letter and didn't see it fall to the sand. A fierce wind was blowing, and he had to crouch forward and make a shield with his jacket before he could light up. As he inhaled, he saw, from the corner of his eye, something caught by the wind, and tossed into the air. Something white. He patted his pockets and started running. But the envelope was blown so high and at such speed that he lost sight of it almost at once. All he could do was hope it would come down in the sea.

To his surprise he found himself wanting Claudia's calming presence. He could tell her about what had happened with the Pastor and his abortive encounter with his mother on the road, and she would respond in her soothing, level-headed way. In a few days he would return and try again, perhaps with another intermediary. In the car he rested his forehead on the steering wheel for a few seconds, and then drove away.

11

When he arrived back in his attic room in Hamburg in the mid-afternoon he had the feeling that someone had been there uninvited. The shape of his pillow seemed different and the bedclothes were tucked in far more carefully than he would ever do. Whoever had been searching between his blankets and under the mattress would have been disappointed since he had hidden nothing there. Nor would they have found anything in the wardrobe and the chest of drawers apart from his clothes and his drawings. He wondered if it could it have been Claudia and whether she suspected that he was not what he seemed. Perhaps she was even reporting on him to the police or to the West German intelligence service. Or the intruder might have been Kurt. Either way, the incident was troubling.

He was sitting on the edge of the bed wondering whether to have it out with Claudia directly, when he heard the sound of the street door opening and shutting. He went down to the first-floor landing, in time to see her coming up the stairs. She climbed towards him with slow, heavy steps, carrying a shopping bag. When he called down to her he expected her to shout up a greeting or at least to hurry up the stairs. But she plodded on at the same pace, and when she looked up at him, he saw that her face was wan and drawn, with dark shadows around the eyes.

"Hello, Henrik," she said listlessly.

"You don't sound very pleased to see me."

"Give me a chance," she muttered, as she reached the door of the flat.

"What's the matter, Claudia?"

She made no reply as she dropped her bag in the hall with a thud. Feeling seriously worried, Henrik followed her into the living room. At last, she said in a flat, almost aggressive tone: "Let's have a drink."

She went to a sideboard, took out glasses and a bottle of brandy and poured two generous measures. She took a gulp and slumped down into the sofa. In the awkward silence that followed, Henrik sat beside her.

"I went to the island," he told her "and found my

mother's house."

"Oh yes?" she said absently, staring into her glass. Her listless tone felt like an accusation. What had she found out about him to make her behave like this? When... if she had searched his room, had she found some clue that he had overlooked?

There was another tense silence. Claudia emptied her glass with one gulp and stared blankly into the distance. Then she gave a slight shake of her head: "Something strange is going on. Someone is spying on me."

"Spying!" he repeated, alarm bells going off in his mind.

"Yes. Several times over the past few days I've had the feeling that I was being followed. I don't know who it was because I didn't see them, but I knew they were there – trailing me around, watching where I went, what I bought, who I spoke to."

"Are you sure you weren't imagining it?"

"Yes, quite sure. I was reading some books in the city library and when I went for lunch I left the books on a table along with some notes I had been making. When I got back to the table I was sure that everything had been moved slightly. Someone had looked at the books and the notes. And there's a car, a grey Volvo, that I'm sure has followed me several times. But what shocked me most was when I came home one evening and found that the flat had been searched."

He knew Kurt drove a grey Volvo.

"I knew it," she went on, "as soon as I walked in. Of course they'd done it very professionally, leaving nothing disturbed. But everything had been replaced a little too carefully – things were still lying about higgledy piggledy, the way I tend to leave them, but they were a little bit too deliberately higgledy piggledy, if you know what I mean. And the strange thing is that nothing was stolen. That made it more worrying than if it had been a straightforward burglary. Now I'm too scared to go out, and I wake in the middle of the night at the slightest noise. It's like being violated. If it goes on like this I'm going to go to pieces."

She covered her face with her hands and began to cry. He put his left arm around her shoulders and said gently: "Claudia ... look, if someone was really spying on you we must get to the bottom of it. I'll do what I can to help." Now he was sure it was Kurt who had broken in and searched both Claudia's apartment and his own.

She leaned her head against him and clasped his right hand in hers. "I'm thankful you're here, Henrik." She dabbed at her eyes with a handkerchief. "I'm sorry, I didn't mean to put a damper on your return. You must tell me what happened on the island. Did you meet your mother?"

Henrik emptied his own glass before replying. "I met her in a country lane, on her bicycle. It wasn't planned. Just fate. She didn't want to see me."

"What did she say?"

"I spoke to her in German and then in English. She pretended not to understand."

"Maybe she really didn't. Perhaps you scared her."

"I think I did. I spoke to the local pastor earlier, hoping he would be an intermediary, like you suggested. But he told me she would be persecuted if people got to know that I was her son. He said I ought to go away and forget her. There's a lot of anti-German feeling in Denmark. I don't really blame her for not wanting to know me."

Claudia was looking at him with astonishment. "You can't

give up like this, Henrik. Go to the house if you have to. Choose a moment when she's alone there."

"First I have to learn to speak Danish properly."

"Then do that."

"It'll take me several months." He did not tell her that he could already read Danish well and had a basic speaking competence thanks to the crash course at the Stasi language school. Over the next few weeks he hoped to progress rapidly, with the help of tapes and his good ear for languages.

She squeezed his hand and smiled. "Anyone can learn a language with a bit of work." She leaned forward slowly until their faces were almost touching.

Through one of the two doorways leading off the living room he could see into her bedroom – all soft lights, velvet fabrics and a tapestry on the wall showing a flower-strewn meadow, fruit trees and in the distance a fairy-tale castle. She tilted her face, and a moment later their lips met – lightly at first, then lingering. When they drew apart she reached up and pulled out a hairpin, so that her dark hair spilled down over her shoulders and neck, lying in thick strands against her pale skin.

"Claudia," he said, pulling back. You don't really know me ..."

She turned her dark, serious eyes on him. Her face, framed in the dark hair, was no longer severe. She looked soft, almost vulnerable. "But I think I'm beginning to know you, Henrik ... the real Henrik."

Beyond the doorway her velvety inner sanctum beckoned. For a moment he was tempted but remembered Kurt's warning. He was wondering how to extricate himself when the telephone rang. She let it ring several times, then walked to the table where it stood and lifted the receiver. All at once she was her everyday self again, speaking in her therapist's voice, dependable and reassuring with just the right degree of professional distance. It was evidently a client who wanted to change an appointment. "Yes," he heard her say. "Wednesday at five will be fine. I'll see you then."

Henrik stood up as she put the phone down. "Claudia, I'm really sorry, but I have to go." The sound of the phone ringing had reminded him that he was supposed to report to Kurt immediately after returning to Hamburg and that he was late already. He also wanted to confront Kurt about the break-in and about Claudia being followed.

"I'd like to stay, but …" He could feel her disappointed eyes following him as he left the room.

12

The afternoon sunlight broke in flashes through the scudding clouds. A family of three made their way down the beach with their dog. The boy and the dog, a black poodle, ran excitedly ahead, while the man and woman followed a hundred yards or so behind. The six-year-old boy had picked up a stick from the driftwood and was scampering along the tideline, poking at the flotsam and jetsam, while the dog darted to and fro, sniffing at the rich smells that rose from the tangle of seaweed and detritus. The woman, wearing street shoes unsuitable for the pebbly beach, took small, cautious steps and clutched at her skirt to stop it blowing up in the wind. She had pale, freckly skin and her face, under a mop of frizzy fair hair, was sharp-featured, the mouth habitually pursed with disapproval.

"I don't think it was such a good idea to come down here today, Holger," she piped. "I'm getting frozen. And look at

Rasmus and Skippy! They shouldn't be poking around in that rubbish. Heaven knows what might be in it."

"Oh, let them be," said the man wearily. "They're having fun. Let's just enjoy the walk." He was tall and lanky, with a reddish moustache and a face that was rugged but kind. He walked with long strides, not minding that his feet in their big boots were sinking deep into the sand with each step. It was his afternoon off-duty, although he knew that of course a policeman is never really off duty, especially a country policeman. Like the pastor and the doctor he had to be on call for the emergencies, real and imagined, that even a little village can produce when least expected. Even on a beach like this you never knew what you might find - like the corpse that had washed up seven years earlier and turned out to be an East German seaman who had jumped ship and failed to make it to the shore.

Instinctively scanning the beach for anything unusual, he saw his son pick up something from the sand and then come running towards him, the dog leading the way, barking and wagging its tail.

"What have you found, Rasmus?" he called, as the boy came up out of breath.

"I didn't find it, Skippy did. It was nearly covered by the sand. "

"You should have left it there," his mother said. "You never know what you're touching when you pick things up on beaches. What is it?"

The boy ran towards her, waving his new-found treasure over his head triumphantly: "It's a letter!"

13

"A woman called you," Claudia told him when he returned to the flat. "Said she would call back at seven o' clock. Didn't give her name, but she had a foreign accent."

"Did she sound Danish?" Henrik asked, startled. Could it have been one of the Karlssen family? "You should have asked for her number," he said a little testily.

"I did ask, but she refused. She may only be able to phone when she's alone."

"Point taken. I'm very glad you answered my phone."

He pressed her hands between his warm palms, but before she had time to savour the moment, he had pulled away, saying that he things to do in his room. In fact he wanted to be alone to think about what he would say if, by some miracle, it was one of the Karlssons who called.

The phone beside his bed rang promptly at seven.

"Hello, Henrik Erdmann speaking."

There was a slight pause, then he heard the bright, eager voice of a young woman say in English: "It's Kirsten Karlssen."

Speechless for a moment, he heard her say: "Hello? Can you hear me?"

"Yes ... yes. I'm so glad you called."

"Henrik, it's so wonderful to hear you. I hope I may call you Henrik."

He tried to keep his voice calm. "Yes, of course. It's wonderful to hear you too, Kirsten."

"We got your letter. A boy – Police Officer Andersen's son – found it on the beach."

For a second anxiety pricked him at the mention of the

policeman. Then it struck him that chance had made Anderson his intermediary instead of the Pastor.

"My mother couldn't call you herself," Kirsten went on "as she doesn't speak much German or English. To tell you the truth, at first she didn't want me to contact you either. She still feels terribly guilty about giving you away and she can't quite bring herself to believe that you would ever forgive her. I hope you have forgiven her, Henrik."

"Of course. Please reassure her that I have."

"I'll try, but there's also the problem of the rest of the family. Mother is afraid there is going to be a great row when they hear about you. They don't know about your visit or your letter - not yet anyway. I was there when the letter came, and Mother showed it to me. It's funny, but part of me wasn't really surprised. I had thought about you a lot over the years, and when I saw the letter my reaction was: yes, of course, Henrik has come back to us, as I knew he would."

"Thank you, Kirsten. I hope the rest of the family will come to see it that way as well."

"I hope so too, but for the moment my mother and I would prefer to meet you alone."

"Of course. Where would you like me to meet you?"

"We are going to Copenhagen on Saturday. Can you meet us there?"

"Yes."

"Fantastic. Now listen. On the harbour there's a quay called the Langelinie. Everyone in Copenhagen knows it. We'll meet you there at noon opposite the statue of the Little Mermaid."

"I'll see you there."

"You certainly will. I can't wait."

14

"So give me your report," Kurt said, flicking a cigarette butt into the river, "and make it quick. I don't have much time. Have you made contact with the family?"

They were standing side by side on the front deck of a ferryboat travelling down the Elbe. In the mid-afternoon there were few passengers, and they had the deck to themselves. The smell of engine fumes and the rolling of the boat were beginning to make Henrik feel faintly nauseous.

"Yes, I've spoken to my half-sister on the phone. I'm going to meet her and her mother in Copenhagen on Saturday."

Kurt's face registered surprise. "Good," he said pleasantly, before his brow furrowed again. "But why only the mother and sister? And why in Copenhagen?"

The boat's hooter gave a blast, making Henrik pause for a moment. "They have to be cautious. My mother's had a hard time living down the past and building a new life for herself. If her German soldier's bastard suddenly turns up out of the blue it could make things very difficult for her. And then there's the rest of the family. I'd be surprised if they were happy about my arrival – especially the husband."

"How many family members are there?"

"Apart from Birthe and her husband, there's a son, a daughter-in-law and two grandchildren, and a daughter, Kirsten, the one I spoke to on the phone. The daughter-in-law is having trouble with the son. I suspect he's got something going on the side, so I plan to look into it."

Kurt lit another cigarette with a deft flick of his lighter. "Okay, but first you've got to win over the mother, and from what you tell me that's going to be tricky. You've got to pull out all the stops, be prepared to weep and make her heart bleed. She's sure to feel guilty about what she did to you. She needs reminding. Nothing brutal of course, but get your hands on her emotions."

"Anything else?" Henrik asked with a touch of sarcasm.

Unexpectedly, Kurt clapped Henrik on the back. "I know how hard this mission is for you, Erdmann. Meeting your mother and her family and getting to know them, and then having to keep part of yourself hidden from them. I want you to know I understand all that." He released Henrik's arm. "I'm not a monster, you know." He chuckled at the very idea that Henrik might have had such a preposterous thought. "But in our business we have to be one hundred per cent committed. We can't take risks."

"What does that mean?" demanded Henrik.

"It means you've told that landlady of yours far too much."

"Only that I'm looking for my mother. It's good she knows that."

"She's become inquisitive about you. She's been at the City Library reading books about Denmark and about the Lebensborn homes."

"What's wrong with that?"

Kurt studied Henrik coldly, snakelets of smoke coiling from his nostrils. "Maybe she suspects there's more to you than meets the eye."

"She knows nothing she shouldn't." Henrik felt anger rising in him. "But if you go on following her, break into her flat again or do any other pointless thing to upset her, she's going to start thinking there is something odd about her new lodger to explain this level of attention."

"You're not telling me she's noticed anything?"

"I'm telling you exactly that. You've scared her senseless."

"Then she must have something to hide. One of us has to make sure she isn't a risk."

Henrik struggled to control his anger.

Kurt lit another cigarette with a flick of his lighter and drew in a deep breath, before exhaling slowly. "Are you sleeping with her?"

"No. But what's that got to do with anything?"

"I don't want you getting too fond of her. Focus on your family, all right?" A sudden happy thought made him pause. "Though come to think of it, if you could get her into bed perhaps she could be recruited."

"I don't think so."

Henrik was feeling increasingly sick from the fumes and the swell. With relief he saw that the boat was approaching a landing stage.

"Another thing," said Kurt grimly. "A policeman has been visiting her flat."

Henrik shrugged: "Hundreds of people have dealings with the police – reporting a mugging, a burglary, a stolen car …"

"And maybe reporting a spy. We have to be careful."

"Okay, she's fond of me, but nothing serious. Just enough to make her curious about my past. That would account for why she was reading those books. And, as for the policeman, she's a psychotherapist. He's probably a client."

"Let's hope so," Kurt grunted, as the boat drew up at the landing stage. "Now listen – while you're in Copenhagen you can start work on your mission. These are your next set of instructions." He drew a manila envelope from an inside pocket and handed it to Henrik. "Study the contents carefully and then destroy them. Report back as soon as you can. The bosses don't like to be kept waiting." As the boat was made fast and the gangplank went down, he gave Henrik a look of mock sympathy. "Best stay on board till the next stop. You look a bit green around the gills. The river breeze will do you good." And with a couple of long, bounding steps he was down the gangplank and away.

Henrik looked around to make sure that no one was observing watching, then took a greyish sheet of paper with a short, typewritten message on it out of the envelope. It was anonymous, but he knew that it came from Section Z, the unit responsible for "Agitation":

"As part of the effort to combat western politicians and other public figures hostile to détente with the countries of the Warsaw Pact, active measures are to be undertaken against the Danish politician Arnold Borup, leader of the reactionary Integrity Party. In view of Integrity's probable increased success in the coming Danish general election and the prospect of Borup obtaining a key post in the next government, it is of the utmost importance to secure his neutralisation before the election, planned for the autumn of this year. Measures to that end, including intimidation, disinformation and, if necessary, force, must be undertaken and a progress report submitted without delay …"

It included brief biographical details about Borup – his background, his career as a businessman, his family, place of residence, friends and private interests. Section Z had done its homework thoroughly.

He read the message again carefully. This was his first assignment, a tough one, but he was determined to carry it out well. Borup appeared to be a man with an impeccable record – suspiciously impeccable. A man like that always had a shadow side, as Claudia would say, and he would find it. He tore the sheet of paper into tiny pieces and threw them overboard.

He alighted from the boat at the next landing stage and decided to walk the four or five kilometers back to St. Pauli along the minor road that ran parallel to the river alongside a narrow strip of pebble beach. The daylight was already beginning to fade, the early March air still had a wintry edge, and the wind was making white flecks on the water. The landward side of the road was lined by fine, turn-of-the century houses, set back behind well-tended gardens. The windows of warmly lit rooms glowed in the thinning light. In one of them a teenage girl with long, fair hair sat playing a piano, the notes faintly audible between gusts of wind. The sound followed him as he walked down to the beach, where he stood and smoked a cigarette, watching the flow of the great river and thinking that Petzold would have compared it to the inexorable force of history. At that moment a large cargo ship slid past, and he saw that it was flying the flag of the Soviet Merchant Marine: a star and a hammer and sickle in red against a white background with a blue stripe along the bottom. He could make out the ship's name Krim, Crimea, in cyrillic letters on the side of the prow, and a couple of sailors standing on the deck, hands on the railing, taking a farewell look at Hamburg. He resisted an impulse to wave at them. Probably they would have been kept on board in quarantine during the time the ship was moored. Only a few trusted officers would have been allowed to go ashore, and always accompanied by a KGB man. Such restrictions were regrettable but necessary, he told himself. It would only take one sailor to be corrupted by the temptations of a city like Hamburg, and the infection could spread to the other members of the crew and be carried back to Russia.

He watched the ship disappear downstream, then tossed his cigarette into the water. As he did so his eyes caught a movement in the waves, somewhere close to where the ship had been. For a moment he took it for some aquatic or amphibious creature – a seal perhaps. Did seals come this far up the river? Then he saw that it was no seal but a man swimming. Who would be mad enough to be swimming the Elbe in this weather and risk being mown down by a ship? The figure came closer, and now Henrik realised that the man was struggling, waving an arm and shouting something. In seconds Henrik had discarded his jacket and shoes and run down to the water's edge. He was about to plunge in when he heard what the man was shouting: "Pomogitye! Pomogitye!" That cry for help in Russian told him everything. The man was clearly a sailor who had jumped from the Russian ship.

A deserter, he thought. Let him drown. It's my duty. Walk away.

The beach was deserted save for a man and his dog a hundred yards off, walking in the opposite direction. No one else could have seen the swimmer. He turned to walk away, but hearing the man's distress cries again he halted. He hesitated for a moment then hurried down to the water's edge. He discarded his jacket and shoes and plunged in, stiffening as the icy water penetrated his clothing, and struck out towards the drowning man.

As he came close to the sailor he saw a smaller cargo vessel bearing down on them from upstream. Unless it changed course it was going to plough into them, but there was still time to save himself if he turned back and swam towards the bank. Instead he kept going until he reached the sailor, who was now struggling to keep his head above water. Supporting the man with one arm, he struck out for the shore, and a moment later the vessel surged past them. Its wake swept over them and then tossed them towards the beach like flotsam. Reaching the shallows, Henrik dragged the man up on to the pebbles, where he lay shivering and gasping for breath. Henrik now saw that the man was very young, possibly in his early twenties, with fair hair and a square snub-nosed face, like a stereotype peasant hero in a propaganda poster. When he could speak he kept repeating the word "spasibo", thank-you.

Henrik was thinking: the bosses won't thank me for this if they find out. Get away before the police arrive.

He yelled to the man with the dog to come and help him, then rapidly put on his shoes and jacket as the man approached.

"My God, what happened?" the stranger gasped, while his dog yelped and sniffed at the sailor.

"He fell from a ship. Please stay with him while I call an ambulance."

"Of course." The man removed his overcoat and laid it over the sailor, while Henrik hurried to the house where he had seen the girl at the piano. When he rang the bell she came to the door and looked startled to see him standing there dripping wet. Behind her he could see a softly lit hallway with a bookshelf and some prints and paintings in gilt frames.

"There's a man on the beach who nearly drowned. He needs an ambulance."

The girl turned towards a tall, elegant woman with carefully streaked grey hair, who had just appeared in the hallway. "What is it Eurydice?" the woman asked.

"Mama, the gentleman wants to call for an ambulance." The girl spoke in a calm, grown-up voice. "Apparently someone nearly drowned ..."

"Certainly," the woman said without hesitation. "Come in. I'll show you where the telephone is."

"Kind of you," Henrik said "but could you make the call? I'd better go back and see what I can do to help while we're waiting for the ambulance."

"Yes, I understand. I'll see to it."

Henrik thanked her and turned away. In the twilight he could see the dog owner kneeling beside the sailor. There was no one else in sight. Instead of returning to the beach he walked quickly away down the road in the direction of St. Pauli. Although he suppressed the thought at the time, in later years he would look back on the incident as his first act of disobedience against the system he served.

15

Sitting on a bench with a view over Copenhagen harbour, he lit his third cigarette since arriving, then looked at his watch. It was twenty past twelve, and he began to wonder how long he should wait for them. Henrik refused to let himself think that they might not be coming. Too much rested on this meeting. There could certainly have been no misunderstanding about the rendezvous point. There was the bronze figure of the Little Mermaid, sad and wistful on her rock in shallow water near the shore.

A group of British sailors came towards him, loud-voiced and merry, swaggering in their tight jackets and bell-bottom trousers. "Hey, look at Ted and Barry!" one of them shouted, pointing to where Ted and Barry, arm in arm, were dancing an impromptu can-can, while some Japanese tourists looked on with puzzled smiles and took photographs.

"Hello, Guvnor," one of them said, as they came up to him. "Is that the Mermaid?" He spoke with some broad regional accent that Henrik found it hard to understand.

"I beg your pardon?"

"The Mermaid. Is that 'er?"

"Oh, the Mermaid ... Yes, that's right."

They were standing around him, five of them, but he had no interest in them. He looked again down the shore and at last, yes, there were the two women approaching – Birthe and a younger woman who must be Kirsten. They were walking quickly, almost running, obviously anxious that he might already have left. They had not seen him yet.

"Nice tits," said one of the sailors, gawping at the mermaid.

"Yeh, but I wouldn't fancy getting into bed with that, would you? Like fucking a salmon!"

Now the women caught sight of Henrik and Birthe pointed and then waved. He stood up and waved back. Birthe was dressed up as though for a church fête – pink jacket with a lace collar, matching skirt, and green cloche hat with a big artificial yellow rose – and her eyes were looking at him eagerly. She was hurrying towards him, and Kirsten keeping up beside her. Suddenly he realised how unprepared he was for this meeting which would probably change his life and theirs too. The noisy sailors still surrounded him.

"What do you say, Guv? You look like a man as got good taste in women. Would you go to bed with 'er?"

Henrik forced a smile. "I might, but the trouble is I don't

speak Mermaid."

The sailors laughed loudly, and one clapped him on the back. "Nice one, Skipper!" They moved off, leaving him alone as Birthe and Kirsten came up.

It was Kirsten who spoke first. "Henrik?" It was half a question, half a greeting, as though she was uncertain how to address him. "I'm sorry we are late." She spoke in English, as she had done on the telephone. "Our train was delayed." She held out her hand. "I am Kirsten." She had her mother's high cheekbones and slightly turned up nose, but had dark hair and eyes that were greenish, like a cat's, rather than blue.

They shook hands and, as he turned to shake hands with Birthe, Kirsten said: "This is my mother. I think you have already …" She was about to say "met each other", but stopped herself with a nervous laugh. "Mother doesn't speak English and only a little German, so I'll translate."

Birthe clasped his hand in both of hers and looked at him, smiling but hesitant, as though repressing an impulse to take him in her arms. She held his hand for what seemed like ages then said something in Danish, and Kirsten translated. "Mother says thank you for your letter. She says she's very glad to see you."

The three of them stood there, uncertain what to do or say next. There was no protocol, no convention for a situation like this. A few paces away the sailors were still laughing and joking.

"Can we go somewhere?" Henrik said. "A place where we can talk – a café or restaurant."

Kirsten said: "We could walk down towards the New Harbour and the Royal Market Square. There are some places there."

They started to walk down the shore and Kirsten said: "You don't mind if we call you Henrik? We don't need to be formal, do we?"

"No, first names are fine." He wondered whether he could ever get used to saying "Mother" to Birthe. In the meantime, her first name would do.

As they walked down towards the city, Kirsten said: "We must show you a bit of Copenhagen, Henrik." Kirsten had entered eagerly into the role of guide, perhaps because it prevented any tense silences. As they walked on she kept up a commentary, stopping every so often to point out a building or a monument – the 17th century fort, embassies, the royal palace, a department store that looked like a French 18th-century château, a theatre that reminded Henrik of the Dresden Opera House, and finally a great wedding cake of a hotel with a façade of frothy white stucco. Henrik pointed to the hotel. "Let's go there," he said. "I invite you to lunch."

The two women looked at each other, taken aback, and then at Henrik. "Oh no!" Kirsten protested. "That's one of the most expensive hotels in Denmark. We couldn't allow you ..."

But Henrik had stepped between them and was already steering them by the elbows towards the door. "Please, I insist! This is an important occasion, perhaps the most important ever."

The restaurant of the hotel was a long, light room, festive with big vases of flowers and a row of tables along the windows, with little yellow-shaded table-lamps casting pools of warm light on the white table-cloths. The room was half empty. As soon as they were seated a waiter in a dinner jacket came hurrying up and handed them menus in heavy folders made of imitation red leather with the hotel coat of arms embossed in gold.

"Shall we have starters?" Henrik said, glancing at the list: caviar with blinis and sour cream, terrine of lobster, crab with avocado, confit de canard...

"I'm not very hungry," said Kirsten, obviously shocked by the prices of the dishes. "One dish will be enough." Her embarrassment made him feel genuinely sorry for her. She was so unpretentious and natural that suddenly the hotel looked gaudy and overblown, the other guests pompous and self-conscious in their expensive clothes.

"All right, let's look at the main dishes. There's chicken cooked in red wine, roast beef, duck with an orange sauce ... or how about fish? A salmon casserole ... halibut ... fried plaice?"

The women held a consultation in subdued voices, then Kirsten said: "We would both like the salmon."

"Good, then I will have the halibut." The waiter returned, and Henrik placed the order, adding that they would like a bottle of white Burgundy.

At first their conversation was halting and subdued, with long, awkward pauses, accentuated by the sounds of the restaurant – dishes and cutlery being cleared away, a waiter clearing his throat.

When the wine had been poured. Henrik raised a glass. "What shall we drink to?"

"To your return, Henrik," murmured Kirsten. He was struck by how eagerly she had slipped into the role of the half-sister, and he felt unsettled by his almost instantaneous reciprocal tug of affection.

They drank and Birthe and Kirsten gazed at him. Wanting to stop Birthe looking at him with such anguished intensity,

Henrik laughed to ease the emotional atmosphere: "I really mustn't leave it another twenty-three years until my next visit!"

It was meant as a joke, but when Kirsten translated his words Birthe's eyes welled with tears. She reached over the table and touched Henrik's hand, then spoke in Danish. She spoke so quietly, her voice choking with emotion that Henrik didn't catch what she was saying.

"Mother says she knows how you must have felt all these years," Kirsten explained. "It's been hard for her too, but harder for you. You must have felt terribly betrayed. Some time she will explain everything to you – and about your father of course. Some time she will tell you the whole story."

Birthe nodded and spoke again in Danish. Kirsten said: "Mother says she is sorry about the way she behaved when you spoke to her on the road. You see, she thought you were someone else – a reporter."

"A reporter!" Henrik gave an incredulous laugh.

"Yes, my sister-in-law Gertrud saw you in the wood opposite the house, looking through your binoculars. And my brother Niels was convinced that you were following him."

Henrik now realised why Niels had been so aggressive in the car park by the restaurant.

Birthe withdrew to the ladies' room, and he was grateful for a moment alone with Kirsten. "Now it's my turn to apologise. I wanted to prepare myself before I met you – to see what kind of people you were."

"I see. Well unfortunately ..." There was an embarrassed tone in Kirsten's voice. "Unfortunately the rest of the family were upset about being spied on. They were all convinced you were a reporter. Stories about war-time Lebensborn children still appeal to muck-raking newspapers. We haven't yet told the rest of the family about your letter or this meeting. We said we were coming to Copenhagen to go shopping."

Henrik looked anxious at the thought of what lay ahead, and all the consequences of possible failure. "And how do you think they are going to react when you let the cat out of the bag?"

"When we what?" Kirsten sounded perplexed.

"When you tell them I am Birthe's son."

"Ah, yes … well it will be difficult, and they will take time to accept you, especially Niels and my father. To tell you the truth we're all a bit worried about Niels. He and Gertrud, my sister-in-law, have been quarrelling rather a lot lately and he is always going off on mysterious trips for two or three days at a time to Copenhagen, Hamburg or Lübeck. Business trips, he calls them, but he never gives us any details."

"And what about your father?"

Kirsten sighed. "I think it's going to be especially difficult for him. He's still very hurt by what happened in the war."

"It's so long ago now."

"But it still hurts a lot. I'm sure in the end he will accept you. I'm sure they all will. Give us time to prepare them. Then you can come up and meet the whole family." She gave him a bright smile. "That'll be nice," she added, as though arranging a picnic.

Birthe, returning to the table, said something to Henrik in a questioning tone and then looked at him expectantly. He turned to Kirsten, who translated: "Mother says that your birthday is coming up in three weeks. She wants you to meet the family before that, so you can celebrate your birthday with us."

For an instant he thought they must be confused about

the date. The third of May was more than a month away, the birthday that had been arbitrarily chosen by his second set of adoptive parents. Then he remembered that they were talking about his real birthday, the nineteenth of April, which had come to light with the discovery of the Lenzfeld records. "Well of course I'd love to," he said "as long as everyone else is happy about it."

"Don't worry, they will be," Kirsten reassured him.

They agreed he would arrive a week before and stay in a hotel initially. If the other family members reacted well, he would stay at the house for his birthday.

When they had finished their main course Henrik insisted, despite their protests, on ordering a dessert, and the waiter came up with a trolley loaded with cakes, trifle, tiramisu, chocolate mousse.

Henrik spotted a Black Forest gâteau. "My favourite cake. I can never resist it."

Kirsten timidly asked for a tiramisu and Birthe a chocolate mousse. They were starting to loosen up a little, and Kirsten's cheeks were flushed from the wine. With her hair down, instead of wound into a knot at the back of her head, she looked much prettier, losing her air of primness as she relaxed.

They finished the meal with coffee. While the waiter fetched the bill Kirsten said: "You're very generous, Henrik. You have a good heart. It's wonderful to have you back." As she laid a slender hand on his, he felt a deep ache in his chest as if a stitch had pulled at his heart.

They didn't prepare me for this.

Detachment was the first rule of his profession and he felt ashamed of his moment of weakness. Winning their trust and love was one thing; reciprocating was quite another.

16

As they left the hotel Henrik told them that he would be staying on in Copenhagen for a day or two "looking for a job". But he would walk them to the station. Together they strolled through the tangle of old streets in the city centre, now more at ease with one another, Kirsten periodically taking Henrik by the arm to point out more of the sights – the Town Hall, the entrance to Tivoli Gardens, the statue of Hans Christian Andersen. "You must get to know the things that make Denmark what it is," she told him "now that you know it's your real home".

On some hoardings outside the station, Henrik spotted a political poster that made him halt in mid-stride. "Integrity stands for Danish values," was the slogan printed in huge letters beneath an imposing picture of the man whom he had been ordered to bring down. Borup's clear, penetrating blue eyes were set in a strong, sun-tanned face. An aquiline nose and thick, grey hair, combed back carefully from a generous forehead, made Borup the embodiment of the virtues his party proclaimed. As he gazed up at this confident face, Henrik's mission seemed slightly absurd.

Seeing the direction of his gaze, Kirsten smiled. "Arnold Borup is our big hope in Denmark right now."

"Why?" asked Henrik, moving on reluctantly as people kept pushing past him into the station.

"He's promised to look after country people," replied Kirsten eagerly. "Small farmers, fishermen, market gardeners."

"But isn't he a bit of an opportunist?" inquired Henrik.

"Opportunist?" Kirsten's voice was shrill and indignant. "Oh, Henrik, what do you know of Danish politics? You shouldn't believe everything the papers say about Borup."

Before seeing them onto their train, Henrik managed to smooth their ruffled feathers by agreeing that he knew very little about politics outside East Germany and had a lot to learn. He kissed them both as they boarded, sensing that they expected it, and waited on the platform till their train pulled out - the two women standing at the carriage window, Kirsten bright-eyed, smiling and waving briskly, Birthe waving more slowly and pausing to wipe away a tear.

He walked out of the station into the sunlight, feeling satisfied with what he had achieved so far. There was still the rest of the family to deal with, but his mother and half-sister had clearly accepted him. It was a good beginning.

In front of the station a beggar thrust a paper cup at him, rattling the coins in it and asking if he could spare some change. The man stood there, thin and pale in his grubby jacket and tattered jeans – a living reproach to this rich capitalist country. Henrik took a one hundred Krone note from his wallet – probably a day's earnings for the beggar. "Have a few drinks on me," he said, putting it into the cup. "I've got something to celebrate today." The man looked incredulously at the note, then smiled and thanked Henrik profusely.

Henrik walked back towards the town centre, past Tivoli, across the Town Hall Square and into the narrow streets of the inner city. On the way, he saw more posters put up by the numerous political parties that were already gearing up for the autumn election – the Social Democrats, the Conservative People's Party, the Christian People's Party, the Left, the Radical Left, the Communists – and of course Arnold Borup's Integrity Party. Borup's resolute face stared at him – the man that his mother and half-sister had placed their hopes in. What would they think if they knew that "their" Henrik was going to destroy Borup's career, while they provided him with cover? He pushed aside the thought and walked on.

He was staying at the Marco Polo hotel, close to the station. It was a decidedly ordinary place with a cramped reception area, fake palms in white plastic pots, and a stack of brochures on the counter advertising night spots and escort agencies. Its tiny bar smelt of old carpets and cigarette smoke. It was the antithesis of the place where he had taken the two women to lunch, but it suited him. He could pass comfortably for a travelling salesman.

Next morning he read a local newspaper over breakfast. It appeared that Danish politics were a motley affair. No single party had held an absolute majority in the Parliament for over half a century, so even very small parties could have a decisive influence in the legislature when the vote was close. This was why the Integrity Party was a force to be reckoned with – the joker in the pack that could decide the game. Henrik was already beginning to see why Borup would have to be rendered hors de combat. His first step, he had already decided, was to read some older newspaper reports on Borup and see if he could detect an Achilles heel, some hint of a scandal buried somewhere in his past.

At the hotel reception they gave him the address of the Central Library in the Krystalgad. It was a solid red brick building covering half a block, with a phalanx of bicycles along the pavement in front of the entrance. The various floors of the building opened on to a skylit atrium. In the department of press archives was a series of long tables at which readers sat studying back numbers of newspapers in large cloth binders, each containing several months' issues. He asked a mousy, pale-faced girl at the information desk for an index of subjects, but she said there wasn't one. He would have to work his way through the back numbers until he found what he was looking for. She explained how the shelving system worked and he found a place to sit at one of the tables, next to a dishevelled man, with a look of the elderly Einstein about him, dozing in his chair with some scribbled notes on the desk in front of him.

Henrik decided to start from the beginning of 1959, the year when the Integrity Party had been founded, an event which he soon realised had been greeted with general scepticism in the press. Initially the articles were condescending, describing Borup as a store magnate and property speculator with his eyes on a political career. But the tone changed over the next few years as the party's support grew. In the previous general election Integrity had been a real contender and now had six members of Parliament including Borup himself – a remarkable achievement for a new party. Suddenly Borup was the rising star on the political scene. In a long interview in one of the quality papers he showed how he could skilfully steer a middle course between left and right. He played to the left by declaring his support for welfare and social justice, and to the right by taking a strongly pro-Western stance on the Cold War. He also used his war record as a Resistance fighter very effectively, cleverly linking it with his position on NATO and the Western alliance. As he repeatedly stated: "I didn't fight the Germans only to hand Denmark over to the Soviet bloc".

Now Borup's party was poised for the next election. With a few more seats they would hold the balance of power, and then Borup would be in line for the post of Foreign Minister, which he was known to covet. If that happened the anti-NATO faction in Denmark would be drastically weakened. Henrik could see why the Stasi and the KGB were so anxious to eliminate the political threat that Borup represented.

He read on, searching for skeletons in the cupboard, dark secrets, anything that would give him an entry point, but there seemed to be nothing. He may have been controversial, but Borup was apparently clean. Many of the articles had pictures of him – Borup playing golf, Borup on his yacht, Borup with his family at their country home. Nothing remotely incriminating. A bell rang somewhere in the depths of the library and the mousy girl announced that the building would be closing in ten minutes. He turned a few more hurried pages. As another bell rang, he noticed that the Einstein look-alike was leaning over, staring intently at the page that lay open in front of Henrik.

"Reading about him are you?" The elderly man leaned forward closer to Henrik and pointed a grubby finger at a picture of Borup.

"Yes, that's right." Henrik recoiled at the pungent smell of sweat, nicotine and unwashed clothes that suddenly enveloped him.

Hearing Henrik's accent, the man went on in German. "It's a scandal that people like him are being elected to Parliament … running political parties. The rats are taking over the ship. Mr. Integrity! Ha! The Resistance Hero. What a joke!" The man lowered his voice dramatically. "If they knew what he really did in the occupation …"

"What do you mean? Isn't he the Resistance hero everyone thinks he is, then?" Henrik looked at him sharply.

"What do you know about him?"

The man sniffed. "I don't exactly know anything. And you won't find anyone writing about it in the newspapers." He ran a hand through his greasy hair and looked directly at Henrik. "Except for that one reporter ... Published an article a year or two ago. But of course after that he stopped writing – Borup saw to that."

"Who was this reporter?"

At that moment the bell rang again, and a voice said through a loudspeaker: "The Library is now closing. Would all readers please leave the building."

"Maybe I can find it quickly," the old man said, making for the shelves, but the mousy librarian stopped him. "I must ask you to leave the building. We are closing." From the impatient tone in her voice it was obvious that he had caused her problems before. The man snarled and made for the exit stairway.

She cast an apologetic glance at Henrik and said: "We'll be open again tomorrow at nine. Is there anything we can put aside for you until then?"

"No, thank you," muttered Henrik. He raced across the room and flung open the door on to the stairwell. The man had vanished. On reaching the ground floor, he pushed his way through the knot of people around the front door. Out in the street he looked right and left but there was no sign of him. Turning left at random, he walked for some minutes through the streets, scanning the crowd, then returned to his hotel.

At the bar he downed a Carlsberg then, to delay returning to his dreary room, headed out again to think things through. On the face of it he had done well so far. His mother and stepsister had accepted him, and he had picked up something on Borup that sounded like a promising lead. He was worried about Claudia too, wondering if Kurt still had her under close observation and whether she might be beginning to suspect it was linked to him and his arrival at her flat.

A nervous feeling had him hurrying to a phone booth and dialling her number. As the ringing went on, he had a mental picture of Claudia coming out of the kitchen and going into the living room, then hesitating before picking up the phone.

"Schmidt," he heard her say.

"Claudia, it's me, Henrik."

"Hello, Henrik." He had expected her to be overjoyed by his call, but her voice sounded flat and distant and at the same time tense.

"I'm in Copenhagen, Claudia."

"Yes, I know."

"Claudia, is something wrong? You sound so …"

"No, nothing's wrong."

But he knew from her tone that she was holding something back, and her denial worried him more than if she had burst into tears and told him that Kurt had broken into the flat again.

"Listen Claudia, I could come back to Hamburg tomorrow if you like …"

There was a click and the connection was lost. Perhaps she'd just cut him off. That seemed most likely. When he dialled again he heard the engaged signal. He hurried back to the hotel and called again from his room, but this time the phone just went on ringing. He called reception and told them he would be leaving early next morning.

17

He drew up in Bernhard-Nocht-Strasse and found a parking space a hundred yards down the street from the house. As he walked back towards the house he saw Claudia's red Audi by the front door, a newspaper and a beige woollen scarf dropped casually on to the passenger seat. The sight of these everyday things suggested that everything must be all right and she would probably be surprised and hopefully pleased to see him. Climbing the stairs past her landing he saw a "Do not disturb" notice on the door, which meant she had a client. He thought he would take a walk and check out the club advertised on Niels' book of matches.

The early evening air was heavy as he emerged into the street, and the western sky was thinly veiled by cloud, turning the light of the setting sun into a sickly orange miasma. He heard the clock of the St. Pauli church strike eight and as he walked down the Davidstrasse he saw the prostitutes taking up their positions along the western side of the street, but not on the eastern side where the red-brick police station stood, solid and austere, keeping watch over the frenzied sexual bazaar that surrounded it.

He took the book of matches from his wallet and checked the address printed on it. He had suspected that he had seen the street name on an earlier walk through the red-light district. Now he knew he had: Kastanienallee, a side street off the Davidstrasse. The building looked quite ordinary, with lace curtains and potted plants on the window sills, except that the basement was entered through a door fitted with large, black, wrought-iron hinges and mountings, to make it resemble the entrance to a dungeon. Above was a neon-lit panel with the name Severin's, the "s" forming a curling whip, and on the wall was a painted sign describing in various languages, including German, English and Danish, what was on offer. English customers were promised an "exclusive live SM floor act".

He descended the steps and stood in front of the door. So this was his guilty secret. Birthe was not going to be happy if she found out where – and how - her dear Niels got his kicks. Henrik hesitated for a second or two but before he had decided between walking away or raising a finger to the bell, the door swung open, and a large, heavily built woman filled the doorway. She had bare arms and shoulders and an enormous white bosom cupped in a glistening leather corset which looked as though it might burst at any moment. Her stocky legs were encased in leather trousers and crammed into knee-length boots with high heels. Her face, which looked as though it had been carved out of a block of grey-white soap, might have belonged to a female wrestler or perhaps a prison wardress, the jet black hair drawn tightly and severely back over her head. Her large, dark eyes, ringed by mascara, surveyed him with a deadpan, faintly disdainful expression.

"Well, don't just stand there!" she said in a deep, hoarse voice. "Come in if you're coming."

In the entrance hall was a cloakroom and a small cash desk where a middle-aged, well dressed couple were buying tickets. Through an open doorway he glimpsed a room with black-painted walls on which hung a row of whips, leather straps and cat-o'-nine-tails. Suspended from the ceiling was a trapeze with leather manacles hanging from chains.

"There's a twenty-mark entrance fee," the leather-clad woman explained. "That entitles you to the floor show and a table with waitress service. Then if you want a private session in one of the dungeons that costs a minimum of thirty marks per half hour. There's an extra charge if you want special effects or costumes." An evening here would be expensive, certainly quite a lot for someone like Niels Karlssen.

Henrik had seen enough. "Thank you, but not tonight I think. If I may I'll take a few of these." He reached for some books of matches lying on the cloakroom counter.

Walking back through the sex bazaar of St. Pauli he began to feel turned on. Would there be any harm in sleeping with Claudia? She had given him clear enough signs that she would like that. When he returned to the flat he was relieved to find no trace of the frightened woman Claudia had been a few days earlier and he thought it wiser not to mention his phone call to her from Copenhagen that had ended so abruptly. But there was something strained in her manner, a sort of brittle brightness that made him uneasy. Her client, she said, had just left – "her policeman", she called him - and he realised that this must have been the man Kurt had seen entering the house. Henrik allowed himself to be led to an armchair, and then told her what had happened in Copenhagen, adding that Birthe and Kirsten were going to tell the rest of the family who he was and that he would be going back there again to meet them very soon.

"How hard it must have been for your mother," she said, without as much enthusiasm as he had expected, "and how wonderful for her to have found you again after all these years."

"It was wonderful." He was about to ask her why she had sounded so tense when he had called her from Copenhagen, but at that moment the telephone rang again and she was kept for several minutes talking to another client. He would try to find the right moment later in the evening.

They had a supper of lasagne and Chianti in her little kitchen, lit by a candle on the table. Afterwards, while they were still sitting facing one another, she surprised him with a sudden change of subject. Studying his face closely, she said: "I never found out what you really thought when I told you I had been followed that time."

"Concern for you of course."

She stared into her glass, frowning slightly. "Is that all, Henrik, for something so unusual and alarming?"

"Actually I reckoned that in your business that sort of thing probably happened from time to time…clients becoming too dependent…wanting to be close to you all the time…maybe even hanging about outside."

"But never entering my apartment and searching my things. We're not in the GDR, Henrik. In West Germany ordinary people are not spied on. Isn't it natural for me to wonder why my room was searched only a short time after you came to live here?"

So that was what had been troubling her. Henrik did his best to smile. "Sure, I can understand your thought; but with husbands and wives telling you so many private things, I can think of lots of reasons why someone might want to break in."

She leaned closer, her eyes challenging him. "But would they do it so professionally that most people wouldn't have noticed anything?"

He said blandly: "Maybe one of them hired a private detective."

"Maybe," she replied in a quiet, pensive voice, almost as if relieved that at last he had said something that might be true. Then suddenly she was bright and brisk again, standing up and saying that she would make some coffee.

He felt the pressure of desire grow stronger. Why not do it? To hell with Kurt's warning. He had to find a way to stop her questioning, and there was one obvious way to do so.

As she stood at the kitchen counter filling the coffee maker he came up behind her and put his arms around her waist. Turning, she said: "I'm not sure about this, Henrik. I thought I was, but things have changed somehow."

"You lie," he said quietly, looking into her eyes and pressing forward against her. "You want me as much as I want you."

"I ... I don't know."

"Of course you do."

He pressed his lips against hers, feeling her body, tense under the loose dress, then suddenly relaxing as she gave a little stifled cry.

She let him hold her for a moment, then took his hand and led him out of the room, along the corridor and into her bedroom.

When he awoke in early morning light it took him a few seconds to adjust to the unfamiliar room, the pale light falling on the flower tapestry, the clutter of little jars of make-up and herbal oils on the dressing table, his clothes and hers tossed on to a chair. He felt the warmth of Claudia's body beside him and remembered their love-making with pleasure, but when he turned his head towards her he saw that she was gazing at him, and her searching expression did not please him.

He realised from her face that she meant to subject him to more questions. The main point of sleeping with her had been to make her compliant. Yet here she was trying harder to get under his skin. The uneasy thought came to him that, perhaps the fact that they had slept together made her feel she had the right to know more. He slid out of the bed and began to dress.

"Henrik," she said intently, piercing him with her dark eyes. "You've not been telling me the truth."

He stared back at her, speechless for a moment. "What are you talking about, Claudia?"

"Don't pretend you don't understand, Henrik. You remember how I told you that I wanted to know who the real Henrik is. I wanted to share in your quest. I even started to read books about Denmark and the Lebensborn and the island that you talked about. But even then I must have sensed something about you that wasn't quite real."

His heart had started to thump. Don't sound panicky. Call her bluff. Tough it out again.

"I don't know the whole truth, but there's a pattern. Your arrival, my being followed, the flat being searched, all sorts of things about you that don't add up. Last night when we talked you replied evasively, as though you had something to hide. You're not a spy are you?"

She had put the question in a mock-serious tone, but immediately she saw from his face that it had shocked him.

"Oh my God, Henrik, don't tell me it's true!

"Claudia ..." he said, looking away "you don't understand".

"Henrik, I'm desperately in love with you. You must know that, but ..."

"But what?"

"You remember when you got into the fight, and you slept in my room later and talked in your sleep?"

"Did I talk again in my sleep last night...Is that why you

think…?" He let his voice fade away.

"Yes, you did, and this time it was clearer."

He began to pace the room, avoiding her gaze, playing for time to think. He had no way of knowing what he had said in his sleep and therefore could not deny it. Instead he forced a small laugh. "It's just pure rubbish."

"Most of it didn't make any sense but there were a few things that were very clear. You used the word 'mission' repeatedly and at one point you said very distinctly: 'They don't know about my mission.' And I also heard you say something about 'State Security'. Well, even I know what the Ministry of State Security is. So tell me the truth, Henrik. Who are you? And what is your mission?"

"Don't go jumping to wild conclusions, Claudia! My mission has been to find my mother, that's all. And as for State Security – everyone in the GDR is scared of them. I was in one of their prisons, for God's sake! No wonder I talk about them sometimes in my sleep."

She reached for a paper handkerchief and dabbed her eyes. "I want to believe you, Henrik, I really do, but I don't know what to believe anymore. Do you really expect me to think that the break-in and the person shadowing me have nothing to do with your coming here?" Her words came in a tearful, croaking voice. "What if it was your mother who had heard you talk in your sleep? Would you lie to her?"

"Don't bring my mother into this!" he shouted, and a moment later he realised that he had confirmed all her suspicions. There was a long, tense silence, then he said in a quiet voice: "No more questions, Claudia. And say nothing about this conversation to anyone. I have to go now."

He left the room and the flat and began to walk through

the streets, wondering how long it would take Kurt to work out what had happened with Claudia and dreading the conversation that would take place.

18

Stepping out of his car and approaching the Karlssens' house, Henrik began to feel an apprehensive tightening in his stomach. Time to pull out all the stops – use his charisma to the full. But would it work against the hostility that he expected from the male members of the family?

They must have been watching for him, because the front door opened as if by magic, and there were Kirsten and Birthe, coming out with radiant, loving faces to greet him with their kisses, and lead him into the house. The dog ran up to join the reception party, barking, wagging its tail and leaping up at him until Kirsten told it to calm down.

He was ushered into the living room where the family members were waiting like a committee. There was an atmosphere of subdued, awkward solemnity, accentuated by the formal room, the bulky sofas and chairs, the stiffly hanging dark green curtains, the skull and antlers of a stag looking down mournfully from the wall over the unlit stove.

"Well," said Kirsten in English, as they entered "let me introduce you to everyone. This is my sister-in-law Gertrud, that's my father and that's my brother Niels." Though she said this very brightly, Henrik sensed her nervousness. Now he saw that there was also a cat, black with white boots and waistcoat, that came padding cautiously towards him, sniffed briefly at his leg and then walked off. "She takes a while to get used to people," Kirsten explained.

Gertrud seemed tense as she shook Henrik's hand. Sven and Niels stayed where they were and merely nodded stiffly. Niels said: "Yes, we've already met – under not very pleasant circumstances."

"Really, Niels!" exploded Kirsten. "That was all a misunderstanding. There's no need to bring it up now." Turning to Henrik, she said: "I apologise for my brother. Please sit down, Henrik. I'm sure you would like some coffee. And look what mother has made for you – Black Forest gâteau! We remembered it's your favourite."

Henrik felt touched. Sitting on the sofa, feeling the hostile eyes of Sven and Niels on him, he took the plate and the cup and smiled across the room at Birthe, who was cutting more slices of cake. "Thank you. How kind of you to remember."

Sven, who had still said nothing, took a slice of cake and began to wolf it down greedily, but Niels took only the coffee. Between sips he drew moodily on his cigarette, tipping the ash into his saucer.

For a while the women made polite small talk with Henrik, asking about his journey from Hamburg, how he liked Denmark and how he was getting on with learning Danish. Thinking it prudent to appear more of a beginner than he really was, he said a few things that he had learnt from his books and tapes, and they clapped with delight. When he heard them talking to each other he was pleased to find how well his ear was attuning to the language, although he was glad Kirsten was there to interpret. When Birthe asked him if he liked the cake, he understood and replied directly that it was excellent.

"We'll make another one for your birthday next week," Kirsten said. "You are going to be here for your birthday aren't you? After all, it will be a very important one – the first since our reunion."

At that moment Sven spoke for the first time: "Now wait a minute, Kirsten. Before we take any decisions like that we need to talk the whole thing over. That's why we're here isn't it?" He turned towards Henrik and said in a gruff tone: "You have to understand, this is damn difficult for us. We need to find a solution the whole family is happy with."

Getting the drift of what he had said, Henrik said quietly: "Of course I understand. And I'm sure you will understand that it's not easy for me either." He tried to catch Sven's eye, but Sven merely grunted and looked away. It's not going to work with him, Henrik thought, and probably not with Niels either. If their view prevailed, that would be the end of his cover. His mission hung in the balance.

Birthe spoke up. "I don't think there's much to discuss," she said firmly. "It's Henrik who's the aggrieved one here. We threw him out all those years ago, and he went through hell in that children's home and that awful, grim country where he grew up, longing all the time for his real home. Now by a miracle he's come back. And he has forgiven us for what happened, which we had no right to expect. Well, of course he can stay for his birthday – forever, as far as I'm concerned."

Niels stubbed out his cigarette roughly. "It's not as simple as that. How do you think Dad feels? Henrik is not his son. Does he want to be reminded of it every day? And don't forget that news of this will spread very quickly. People around here have long memories. Our business could suffer. We could be ostracised, maybe even attacked. It would be very wrong to expose us all to that kind of danger."

Blushing fiercely, Kirsten cried: "For God's sake, no wrong can compare with the wrong that was done to Henrik.

We've all felt guilty about it ever since – you too, Father, even though you won't admit it. It's been like a poisonous blister in the -family. Now we have the chance to cure it, to make up for what we did, to make amends to Henrik and to start to be honest with each other." Seeing her glaring defiantly at her father and brother, Henrik did not need to understand every word that had been spoken to understand the argument. He felt another burst of admiration for her courage, and another twinge of guilt.

"You're getting carried away," said Niels. Then he jerked his head in Henrik's direction. "He's not the only one who has rights here. He must know what a hornets' nest he's stirring up by coming here. I think he's being downright selfish." He turned and looked directly at Henrik: "Well? You've just been sitting there like a dummy. Can't you speak for yourself?"

Pulling out a packet of cigarettes, he stuffed one into his mouth with an angry movement, then reached into his pocket, fumbling impatiently for matches or a lighter. While Niels was still searching, Henrik, acting on impulse, reached forward, holding out a book of matches from Severin's club. Niels hesitated before taking the matches from Henrik's palm. Henrik saw a startled, questioning look in Niels' eyes. Slowly Niels took the matches, tore one out and lit the cigarette, then handed the matches back without a word.

Henrik said quietly in English: "The last thing I want to do is impose myself on any of you. You have your own lives to lead..." He looked around the room. "I know I don't have the right just to arrive out of the blue and demand to be taken in..."

"Oh, but you do, Henrik," Kirsten interrupted. "You have every right. I must translate what you said for mother and father."

"Let's give everyone a chance to speak," Birthe said, after Kirsten had translated for the men. Turning to her daughter-in-law, Birthe asked her what she thought.

The others turned and looked at Gertrud, sitting a little apart at the side of the room, as though it was not the first time they had sought her mediation. There was something sturdy and reassuring about her solid figure and plump, common-sense face framed by thick, coppery hair. "Well, we've only just met Henrik ..." She spoke in a quiet, sensible tone. "We hardly know him yet. And he hardly knows us. Why don't we at least get to know each other better. Celebrating his birthday with him would be a good way of doing that." Her speech and her calm, down-to-earth manner defused some of the tension in the room, but Sven was not quite ready to give in. "That's all very well, Gertrud, but no amount of getting to know each other can alter the basic problem."

Niels, who had been sitting pale and stonily silent for several minutes, now broke in again: "Gertrud's got a point. Getting to know each other wouldn't be a bad idea."

The other members of the family looked at him, astonished at his sudden change of position, especially Sven, who now looked confused and angry. "Well," he grunted "it seems I can't talk sense into anyone."

"Then it's settled," Birthe said with a satisfied clap of her hands. "We'll celebrate Henrik's birthday here. In fact, Henrik, why don't you stay here until then?"

Henrik sensed that he was on probation with Gertrud, and that Sven was still hostile. Niels had performed an about-face, but he might revert to his previous position. After Kirsten had explained to him that his mother hoped he would celebrate his birthday with her and stay the night, Henrik replied hesitantly: "That's very kind of you, but I have a room booked in Vordingborg. I was planning to drive back to Hamburg tomorrow." He had promised Claudia that they would go out for dinner on his birthday.

Kirsten gave a delighted laugh. "You still have time to cancel the room. I'll call them for you. Where were you going to stay?"

"The Ferry Hotel."

"Oh yes, I know the people there. I'll explain things to them in a moment, don't worry. And you will stay over until your birthday, won't you? We insist."

Henrik was about to protest again, but Birthe said something which Kirsten translated: "Mother says we'll put you in the spare room. Do you have a bag with you?"

"Yes, in the car." He realised he would have to call Claudia and postpone their dinner.

"Niels will show you where you can park," insisted Kirsten. "You can't leave it there blocking the drive." Niels had evidently understood and led the way out of the house. Pointing to a covered car port in the yard, he amazed Henrik by saying in English as good as his sister's: "Park there, next to my Land-Rover."

As Henrik eased the car into the yard, he saw that Niels was hovering around the car port. When Henrik stepped out of the car Niels said abruptly: "Where the devil did you get that book of matches?"

Henrik closed the door of the car and said quietly: "That one you dropped in the car park at that restaurant. These ones," he added, taking several more from his pocket, "I found at Severin's. Do you go there often?"

"Don't start getting the idea that you can blackmail me. What if I did go there once as a guest?" Niels' voice was surly and defensive.

Henrik shrugged. "Live and let live."

"So you're not shocked?"

Henrik laughed. "It takes much more than that to shock me." He wondered what Niels would think of some of the things he had seen behind the two-way mirrors in the brothels that the Stasi used to entrap western visitors.

"And you won't tell Gertrud?"

"If I were you I'd tell her myself."

"You're not serious?"

"Women are more sensible about these things than men are. It's not like having an affair."

Niels seemed to be considering the idea seriously when they both heard Kirsten calling merrily from inside: "What on earth are you two talking about? Come in and have something to drink before supper."

19

In the early hours of the morning Henrik woke up with a shout, his heart racing, still half in the nightmare – the same one that had tormented him repeatedly. Once again he had been in the pandemonium of the Dresden station, gripping Mutti's hand as they hurried down the platform, the train gathering speed, and then the terrible moment when he was thrust on board and the woman he called mother was left behind. The dream had ended with him crying out desperately to her and waking himself up with his cry. Where was he? And how long had he been here? He had to make a conscious effort to remember that this was the third night he had spent in the Karlssen home and that today was his birthday.

As the dawn light seeped into the room, he lay in the deep, soft bed with its down quilt, conscious of smells that were becoming familiar: the polish on old wooden furniture, the scent of pine logs and the wood-burning stove, the faint mustiness of the carpets, and the early morning whiff of damp earth wafting through the half-open dormer window. Soothed by this homely room, he dozed off again, and the next thing he was aware of was a knock at the door and Kirsten entering, dressed in a nightgown and carrying a tray.

"Good morning, Henrik. Happy birthday!"

"Thank you, Kirsten." Seeing her radiantly pretty face, he had to remind himself that she was his half-sister.

"Look, I brought you some tea. There'll be a big breakfast downstairs in the kitchen later on." She placed the tray on a side table, gave him a kiss on the cheek and then perched on the edge of the bed. Looking at him with a concerned expression, she said: "I don't think you slept very well, Henrik. You made such a lot of noise in the night."

"Noise ..." he repeated in a thin voice. What might she have heard through the wall that divided their rooms? Had he talked about the mission, as he had in Claudia's bed?

"Poor Henrik. You must have been having terrible nightmares. What on earth were you dreaming about?"

He felt a flood of relief. "Oh, just a memory from my childhood. It comes back to me sometimes in dreams."

"Tell me about it," she said gently, handing him a cup of tea. "That's, if you want to."

For a moment he was worried that if he told her the story she might press him to tell her more about his past, and then he might accidentally tell her too much. On the other hand, sooner or later he was going to have to tell the family more about what had happened to him soon after he left the Lebensborn home. So far he had only told them the bogus later part of his story – his "escape attempts", his "imprisonment" and his transfer to the West.

"All right." He took a sip of tea and then leaned back in the chair, feeling a sudden desire to surrender to his memories.

"Strange," he murmured "an old melody just came back to me." He hummed a few notes and then sang softly:

"Do you know the land on the Baltic strand,
The amber gold, the gleaming sand?"

"That's lovely," Kirsten murmured. "What is it?"

He took another sip and went on: "It's an old song from East Prussia. That's where I was taken after the Lebensborn home – Königsberg on the Baltic. I was adopted by a pastor, Jan Praetorius and his wife Martha ... good, kind people. They had no children of their own, and they must have been overjoyed when they were able to arrange the adoption through the Lebensborn organisation. Of course I knew that they weren't my real parents, but I soon learned to call them Mutti and Vati all the same."

Kirsten was listening intently. "So that would have been ..."

"The spring of 1944. I was only three years old, so I don't remember anything about my arrival, but I do have a few later memories of that time – services in the pastor's church, the old house full of books, the bears in the Königsberg zoo, my adoptive mother taking me down to the shore to fly a kite, watching it climb higher and higher then plunge suddenly into the sea. By then the writing was on the wall for Germany, but everyone refused to believe it – so the mass exodus didn't begin until early 1945 when the Russians were actually on the doorstep. The pastor delayed his departure – I expect he wanted to make sure that all his congregation got away safely. At any rate, he sent his wife and me on ahead. I was not quite four, but I can still remember bits of that journey. At first it seemed like a great adventure, setting off one winter morning while it was still dark, boarding a crowded train and waving to Vati, who stood on the platform waving back until we could see him no longer. Our destination was Berlin, where Mutti had a sister who was willing to put us up. We changed trains a lot. I had no idea why. I suppose bombing alerts caused cancellations and diversions. There was pandemonium at every station, with people literally fighting to board the carriages."

Henrik closed his eyes, frowning, as though forcing himself to see the scene in his mind's eye. "Somehow we reached Dresden late that evening and Mutti said we had to change trains again. I remember clinging to her hand, terrified that I would get separated from her in the chaos. The platform was teeming with people – soldiers with bandaged faces and arms in slings, mothers with countless children, everyone clutching suitcases and makeshift bundles. The noise was deafening, with people shouting, steam hissing and the whistle blowing as we ran for the train. Mutti yelled at me to hurry, and I ran until my lungs were bursting. As the train began to move, a woman standing by an open carriage door saw us and held out her arms to take me, so that Mutti could climb aboard with the luggage. She heaved a heavy bag on to the train and was about to board herself when she slipped and fell back on the platform. I saw her pick herself up again and run after the train, but it was too late. We were travelling too fast. I still have an image of her in my mind, running along, her face distorted with anguish, screaming at the woman holding me to wait at the next station. It was the last time I ever saw her. Dresden was bombed a few hours later."

Kirsten touched his arm. "Henrik … I had no idea …" Her eyes were welling with tears. "It must be hard to talk about it." The emotion in her voice was intense, and he felt his own voice cracking as he went on.

"Yes, but somehow it's a relief. I've never told the full story to anyone before."

"What happened after you lost her?"

He closed his eyes again, seeing the strange faces peering at him in the crowded carriage, hearing the sound of the train rushing through the night.

"At first I was too terrified to cry, let alone answer when they asked my name and where I came from. By chance, an old man in the carriage had lived in our street. Suddenly, he announced to everyone: 'I know this child. I've seen him in Königsberg. He's the Lebensborn boy that Pastor Praetorius and his wife adopted.' Everyone turned and stared at me when they heard the word Lebensborn.

"Then the woman who had lifted me on to the train said something like: 'Poor lad, he must have been through a lot. And now this!' Funny how I seem to hear her saying that quite clearly, while other things about that journey are just a blur. Hanna Weber was the woman's name, and she was already a war widow, as I later discovered – her husband was killed at Stalingrad. She was travelling with her elderly parents, heading for Wittenberge where she had a sister.

Eventually we arrived at Leipzig and had to change trains again. That must have been when we heard the news about

Dresden. I remember Hanna saying that there was no point in waiting there for Mutti. She would take me on to Wittenberge and look after me until she found out where Mutti was. Her parents were worried at first about having another mouth to feed. But after a while Hanna's mother patted me on the head and said I would be all right with them. I could tell she liked me."

Kirsten smiled a little. "So even as a child you were charming, Henrik. What happened after you reached Wittenberge?"

"They never did trace Mutti. It was pretty certain she must have died in the bombing. And Vati was probably killed when the Russians bombarded Königsberg. So Hanna ended up adopting me. Not long after that she found a second husband, Dietrich Erdmann, and I was given the name Erdmann."

"No wonder you became confused about who you really were. What sort of parents were the Erdmanns?"

Henrik sighed. "They did their best for me, but then they produced two children of their own and I got pushed aside. I was always somehow the Lebensborn boy. But I survived. I did well at school, got on with the teachers, had friends, girl friends …"

"And when did you find out … about us?"

"Only much later. When I was sixteen I began to make enquiries through the Central Registry Office, but could find out very little about myself. If there ever were documents – a birth certificate and so on – Mutti was probably carrying them with her when Dresden went up in smoke. I knew that I had been in a Lebensborn home, but had no idea which one. Apart from that, there was very little to go on except my first name, my age and the fact that my mother had been Danish. For years I heard nothing from the Registry Office, and I had almost given up hope. Then one day a cache of Lebensborn documents turned up, proving who I really was." He hoped that she wouldn't ask him how they turned up, but she was silent, listening intently. "Suddenly I knew everything – my mother's name, my father's name and the Lebensborn home to which I was taken – Lenzfeld in the Harz mountains. There was only one child in the records of the home who fitted my description – Henrik Karlssen, born of a Danish mother on 19 April 1941. Well from then on I became obsessed with the idea of finding my mother. And you know the rest – my escape attempts, the prison sentence, my being ransomed and sent to the West." The final part of his account was not a direct lie, he told himself, only stretching the truth a little.

She patted him silently on the arm, a suspicion of tears in her eyes. He saw how deeply he had touched her.

As she bent down to take away the tray, the neck of her nightdress slipped down, half-revealing her breasts. With a conscious effort he looked away, trying not to think about the slim body under the white fabric. He touched her hand and felt an answering squeeze of her fingers – a sisterly squeeze, he told himself.

"It is wonderful that you are here, Henrik," she said softly "like a dream come true. I can hardly believe you've only been here since Saturday. It seems so natural to have you in the house."

"Does it? I'm not sure everyone feels that way."

Kirsten dismissed this with a sweep of the hand. "Don't worry about Father and Niels. They'll come round. I thought it was marvellous how you kept your temper when they were so hostile the other day." She gave him a sidelong, playful look. "Do you ever lose your temper, Henrik? No, I don't believe you do. How will I ever live up to my perfect brother?"

He found himself laughing out loud: "Don't be ridiculous, Kirsten!"

He realised that he had never before been treated in this light-hearted, affectionate way. It made him wish that they had grown up together, had common memories, and that he had no secrets that would have to be kept from her.

Kirsten moved towards the door and said: "I'll tell mother everything you've told me. Now I have to get dressed and go shopping. We're all looking forward to your birthday dinner." She turned in the doorway, smiled and was gone.

*   *   *

Coming down twenty minutes later to the kitchen, he found a place laid at the table and Birthe busy at the stove, filling the room with the aroma of ham and eggs. The family cat, still wary of him, darted across the room and jumped on to the window sill. Birthe gave him a shy smile as he came in, as though she could not quite believe that he – her firstborn son – was really here, and had spent his first few nights in her house.

"Glædelig fødseldag! Happy Birthday, Henrik." She came up and kissed him. "Please ... sit. I hope you like big breakfasts." She spoke Danish, but slowly and clearly, so that he had no difficulty in understanding her, especially as she threw in a few German and English words.

"The others have gone out," she said. And he realised with alarm that this was the first time he had been alone with her. After she had offered him a choice of tea or coffee and he had chosen the latter, she opened the lid of an archaic looking metal coffee-grinder, poured in beans, then turned a handle. "We are a little gammeldags – how do you say? – old-fashioned. It would be nice to have one of those electric machines. So much quicker. But expensive." The coffee fell into a glass holder, which she detached, then tipped the contents into an enamel coffee pot.

When the coffee was ready she sat down at the table and drank with him as he finished his breakfast. Every so often she would look at him with that shy smile, as though happiness were an unfamiliar guest in whose presence she was not yet quite at ease. He could not remember ever having sat like this with his adoptive mother, just quietly drinking coffee together and enjoying each other's company. She had always been harassed and in a rush. This kind of intimacy was new to him.

"Twenty-three years is a long time, Henrik, ikke sandt? Is it not so?" Close up, he saw that Birthe's face still had a soft beauty, the lips full, the eyes clear and fresh despite the lines and touches of shadow around them. She put her hand on his and went on speaking, slowly and hesitantly. "Of course I know how much you must have suffered, Henrik. I know that you cannot forget the past, and I don't expect you to forgive me immediately for the wrong I did you. I expect that it will take time, perhaps many years." Her eyes were looking at him with a sad, almost tearful expression. "In the meantime anything I can do for you will give me joy and make me feel better – even small things like cooking meals and making life pleasant and comfortable for you when you stay here. Don't feel obliged to me in any way. In my eyes it's generous of you to allow me to do these things for you."

He realised that she had already become more to him than just his cover. He reached out and put a comforting hand on her shoulder. "Please ... I have already forgiven you." He was speaking Danish, reaching for words in a way that accentuated the feeling in his voice. "I understand why you had to act as you did – I mean when you gave me to the Lebensborn home."

As he spoke he saw her eyes fill with tears and felt an unfamiliar swell of emotion. She leaned towards him, breaking into sobs as she embraced him, kissing his cheek. "Henrik, my dear, dear boy ... That you would find it in your heart to forgive me ..."

He returned her embrace. At that moment he realised with terrible clarity that if his mother ever found out the full truth about why he was there, it would probably destroy her. Certainly it would finish any relationship she might have built up with him. He also knew how desperately he wanted to stop this happening, and not just for the sake of his mission.

Birthe leaned back, pulling out a handkerchief and dabbing her eyes. "How wonderful that this should happen on your birthday. Since you left it's always been the saddest day of the year for me. But this time it's the happiest of my whole life."

She gazed at him in silence while an old pendulum clock on the wall ticked away the seconds. Then she said with a sudden apologetic frown: "Henrik, I'm sorry that I was so unfriendly that time ... on the road, when you tried to speak to me and give me your letter, but I was so surprised and confused. We really did think you were a reporter after Niels saw you in the wood, pretending to be a bird-watcher."

Henrik laughed. Thinking he had better steer the

conversation away from the subject of his reconnoitring, he added: "As it happens, I am very fond of birds. I like to draw them."

Birthe's eyes lit up. "You don't know how happy it makes me to hear that! You're father loved birds as well. This island, with all its different species, was a paradise for him."

She began to speak more rapidly, so that now he had difficultly in following. She seemed to be trying to ask him something about the Lebensborn home, but he did not understand her question. At that moment Kirsten reappeared with a basket of shopping, which she placed on the sideboard. Birthe said something to her, and she turned to Henrik.

"Mother says there is a lot she wants to ask you. She realises that it must have been awful for you in the Lebensborn home, but at least there was that nurse who took special care of you. What was her name, Mother? Neumeyer, that was it, Astrid Neumeyer."

Henrik tried to conceal his surprise. He had thought of the Lebensborn episode as a blank page in his life, except for the terse records that the Stasi had retrieved from the KGB. As he had left the home to be adopted at the age of three, he had no memory of the place or any of the staff. Now, hearing the name of someone who had apparently worked there and known him, he was taken aback. If there were such people around, how was it that the Stasi, with their formidable thoroughness, had not sought them out? The memories of someone who had looked after him in the home would have given him a much more complete picture of that key part of his childhood.

"Yes," Kirsten went on, "Fräulein Neumeyer somehow found out our address and wrote to us after the war – to say that you were safe and well. Apparently, after a long search, she finally found out where you were and went to see you."

"I'm sorry," he said "I don't remember her visiting us. But I was only four when the war ended. When exactly did she say she saw me?"

Kirsten conferred with Birthe for a moment, then said: "Mother thinks it was around 1946. Fräulein Neumeyer said how happy she was that you had been adopted by a good family and that you were living in such a pleasant town in a beautiful area on the edge of the Harz mountains …But wait a minute …" She was about to sit down at the table and paused, her hand on the chair. "Didn't you say …?"

Henrik frowned. "Yes, that's strange. I didn't grow up in the Harz. I grew up in Wittenberge on the Elbe." He felt suddenly unsettled, seeing Kirsten's puzzled look.

She laughed a little nervously. "Well, I expect she made a mistake. She was probably thinking about the surroundings of the Lebensborn place."

"That must be it," replied Henrik, eagerly. Yet he thought it unlikely that anyone could confuse Wittenberge with the Harz. Something was clearly wrong, but he felt a passionate desire not to admit this even to himself. He had to steel himself to ask one all-important question: "Did she tell you the name of my adoptive parents?"

Birthe said something rapid and incomprehensible. Henrik was more nervous than at any stage since his arrival. Why was Kirsten taking so long to translate? At last she said: "Mother doesn't remember whether Fräulein Neumeyer mentioned any name. Mother thinks she probably took a risk in writing to us and did not want to say too much. Mainly she was anxious to tell Mother that you were safe."

"I see," he murmured, relieved but still uneasy at the thought that the adoptive parents mentioned in Fräulein Neumeyer's letter might not be the Webers in Wittenberge. Maybe the nurse had made a mistake. She could have been talking about a different Lebensborn child. Perhaps there were several children she had taken an interest in and followed up after the end of the war. So she could have got names and adoptive parents mixed up. Yes, that must be it – when writing to Birthe about Henrik she had mistakenly assigned him to a place in the Harz, which actually was the home of another of her charges. But a moment later this seemed far-fetched. Clutching at straws, he wondered whether there might be two ex-Lebensborn boys called Henrik Karlssen. He was only half listening as Kirsten went on talking.

"Mother can't remember the other details that Fräulein Neumeyer talked about, and the trouble is that we can't find her only letter. It's gone from the box in the attic where Mother keeps old family stuff. Maybe it will turn up some day."

Henrik was relieved that the letter had been lost. He wanted more than anything to belong to this family, and not just because he would be sent back to the GDR and probably demoted if his relationship to the Karlssens was undermined. He had started to feel happy with Birthe and Kirsten, and yes, at home. Perhaps for the first time ever. And now there was this chafing doubt because of what he had been told about the nurse. Suddenly he needed to be alone, to try to work it all out in his mind.

He heard the front door bell ring. Birthe went to answer it and there came the sound of a familiar male voice. "Come into the kitchen," he heard Birthe saying, and a moment later she came in with Pastor Arup. "Hans was just passing, so I invited him in for a cup of coffee," she said. "Do sit down, Hans."

The Pastor stopped when he saw Henrik sitting there. He looked back at Birthe and then at Henrik again, and it was clear from his surprised expression that he had understood the whole situation immediately and strongly disapproved.

"I believe you've met my son, Henrik," Birthe said.

The Pastor shook Henrik's hand stiffly. "That is quite correct." He looked at his watch and said, making little effort to sound convincing: "Actually, I'm afraid I don't have time to stop for a coffee, although it's most kind of you to offer me one. I just remembered that I have to see someone at the pastorate at eleven."

When he had gone Henrik said: "I'm afraid you will have to excuse me as well." He desperately needed to be alone, to think things over. "I have to drive over to Vordingborg. There are some things I need to buy."

"Don't be offended by him, Henrik," murmured Birthe. "I'm sure he will come to like you."

Henrik smiled bravely. "I hope so." He moved to the door.

Kirsten said brightly: "Now don't go buying things for us. It's your birthday and you mustn't be late for your big supper. We'll start at six o'clock so the children can be there as well."

"Yes, of course, I'm looking forward to it. A delicious breakfast...Thank you." He retreated from the room.

As he drove off he began to consider questions and possibilities, which only an hour earlier he would have found laughable. Could there have been some absurd mix-up in the records? Could the Stasi have confused him with some other Lebensborn child? It seemed highly unlikely, since it would have been so glaringly obvious to them that any mix-up might cause an embarrassing international incident. But there was still the possibility that the lost letter from Frau Neumeyer might turn up. While this would probably confirm that he was the Lebensborn boy, it just might contain facts the Stasi never knew about. Should he phone Kurt about the problem? Probably he ought to, but he hated the thought of having to ask Kurt for advice.

Distracted, he ignored a red traffic light, nearly colliding with a car emerging from a side road and causing the other driver to give an angry blast of his horn. Steady, he told himself. Getting arrested for careless driving was the last thing he wanted right now. He pulled to the side of the road, leaned back and took some deep, slow breaths, telling himself that there must be a perfectly reasonable explanation for everything. He forced himself to think it out logically. Suppose Fräulein Neumeyer had got two boys mixed up – himself, brought up in Wittenberge, and another boy, brought up in the Harz. And suppose she had visited Wittenberge when he was too young to remember it later. That was surely the only scenario that fitted the facts. But how had she tracked him down after the war? The Lebensborn adoption record would have led her to Königsberg, but from there the trail would have gone dead because his adoption by the Webers had been a purely chance affair. It was a million to one that she could have traced him to Wittenberge. So it looked as though she had correctly reported that Birthe's son was living with a family in the Harz. Therefore he himself could not be Birthe's son. The logic of it seemed inescapable, although he still resisted it. He would have to call Kurt after all.

He drove on and stopped at the diner where he had

nearly fought with Niels, found a telephone and dialled Kurt's number, but there was no answer. He sat for a couple of hours, drinking beer and trying the number intermittently without success. Then he looked at his watch and saw that it was already five-thirty. The family was expecting him back for his birthday party at six. He would have to hurry back and postpone the talk with Kurt until he returned to Hamburg the next day.

As he drove up to the house, Kirsten was standing by the gate, waving at him agitatedly. She was wearing a turquoise party dress and white high-heeled shoes. As he drew into the drive and opened the car door she said: "Henrik, where on earth have you been? We've been waiting for you to start the birthday party."

He looked at his watch and saw that it was already quarter past six. "So sorry," he mumbled, feeling genuinely contrite. To see her standing there in her party clothes, with an anxious expression on her face, touched him almost painfully. "I lost my way coming back." It was a hopeless excuse, but would have to do. "I'll just get changed and then I'll be with you."

She took his arm as he stepped out of the car. "Nonsense, Henrik. You look fine. We'll go straight in." Her evident joy at seeing him made him want to take her in his arms.

She led him through the front door and down the corridor towards the living room.

"Here he is at last, the birthday boy!" she shouted as she opened the door.

The sight overwhelmed him: the family in their party clothes standing around the table – all white linen, best china and silver, and in the middle a vast white cake with candles already lit and a message written in chocolate saying: "Happy

Birthday Henrik and welcome home!" Kirsten led him to his seat at the head of the table, and the family sang Long may he live! as champagne glasses were raised and even Sven managed a cheer. Kirsten's eyes were shining as she lifted her glass towards him, and it struck him how intensely adorable this young woman was who now seemed most unlikely to be his sister. Surrounded by so much good will and love, all he could think of was the Lebensborn nurse and the dark cloud cast by her letter..

PART II

20

When Colonel Fuchs arrived at his office in the East Berlin district of Lichtenberg at 8.30 in the morning he found a heap of files lying on his desk. Clipped to the drab manila cover on the top one was a typed memo that said:

To: Col. Ernst Fuchs, Director, Overseas Intelligence, Ministry of State Security.

From: Major Paul Kobitz, Officer in Charge, Section Z.

Date: 15 April 1966.

Herewith, as requested, files relating to Danish operations, the Doppelgaenger Project and the agent "Renatus".

At the bottom was Kobitz's signature in his small, obsessively neat handwriting.

Fuchs was pleased that Kobitz was dealing with this operation. Despite his rather over-intense manner, he was utterly reliable. So Fuchs was thankful that it would be Kobitz briefing him before his crucial appointment with General Nikolai Chernikov, head of the KGB's liaison office for the GDR. Unusually, the General was coming over in person from the KGB enclave in the suburb of Karlshorst. The Russian had been his mentor and protector since the old days in Moscow during the war when Fuchs had been one of the youngest members of the group of German communist exiles being groomed for service in the new German state that would arise under Russian tutelage. Fuchs knew from long experience that Chernikov, for all his avuncular manner, was rigorous and exacting, so he tried hard to keep him happy.

Fuchs began to go through the files, periodically making notes as he read. The essential information was already familiar to him, but he wanted to make sure he had the important facts at his fingertips when Chernikov arrived. There was a file on the so-called Trade Delegation of the GDR to Denmark, opened six years earlier as an attempt to create a de facto embassy and hasten Denmark's official recognition of the GDR. Other files contained information on efforts to infiltrate various sections of Danish society; and of course there was the main object of his attention: the Danish project involving Henrik Erdmann, alias Renatus. He had asked Kobitz to give him an up-date report on the project.

The door to the adjacent office opened and a plump young woman came in holding a tray with a coffee pot, a cup and saucer and a jug of milk. "Ilse," he said, as she put the tray on the desk, "When General Chernikov arrives, can you have some more coffee ready?"

"Certainly, Colonel."

"Major Kobitz will be at the meeting too. In the meantime, please try to ward off anyone else for the next hour. I need to concentrate on this report from Kobitz."

"Of course, Colonel." She withdrew, softly closing the door behind her.

Fuchs poured himself a cup of coffee, took a sip, then opened the report, headed "Doppelgaenger Programme". In case the quaintly named programme failed in the end, Fuchs intended, if asked, to say he couldn't remember precisely who had dreamed up the original idea. But whoever it had been, Kobitz had taken it up enthusiastically, despite Fuchs's initial reservations, and when Chernikov had given it his blessing there had been no going back, whatever the risks.

Fuchs read the opening section headed "Background to the Programme":

"The general context in which the idea for the Doppelgaenger programme arose was the new geo-political situation that came about as a result of the building of the Great Anti-Fascist Protection Rampart in 1961 in order to secure the border between the German Democratic Republic and the imperialist lackey state of the so-called Federal Republic of Germany, and thereby thwart the latter's efforts to undermine our socialist achievements. Whereas before 1961 our agents had been able to come and go more or less freely, we now had to find both new ways of channelling operatives into enemy territory and credible forms of cover under which they could work ..."

Fuchs could hear Kobitz's tense, monotonous voice in his head, trotting out the stock Party phrases: "Anti-Fascist Protection Rampart ... imperialist lackey state ... socialist achievements" – all ideologically correct but hardly necessary in an internal report. He read on:

"Our attention was then drawn to a possible source for recruitment, namely people who had spent their early childhoods in the SS Lebensborn homes as illegitimate offspring of Danish or Norwegian women who had mated with men from the occupying German forces. These people had great advantages as potential agents. For one thing they had a credible reason for wanting to go to the West, namely to be re-united with their mothers. Furthermore, if they could prove the mother's identity they had an automatic right to a passport of her country. Alternatively they could opt for a West German passport if they wished. This meant that each one could be planted in at least two countries with a very convincing cover. Consequently we began seeking recruits from among selected former Lebensborn children.

Unfortunately most of the individuals we approached were unsuitable. As a result of the Lebensborn experience they tended to be depressive, anxious, apathetic and un-motivated. In other words they were distinctly unqualified for this kind of work.

"However there was another idea that occurred to us. Instead of employing someone who had been a Lebensborn child, we could 'borrow' his identity and 'graft' it on to one of our regular agents. The agent could then masquerade as the real Lebensborn child, unbeknownst to the latter, taking on his name and biography. Hence the name of the programme: Doppelgaenger. The masquerader or doppelgaenger would be supplied with papers, forged if necessary, proving his identity. He could then seek an exit visa and, when he reached the West, apply for a passport of his "mother's" country and, hopefully, make contact with her and other "relatives". Alternatively, to make him even more convincing, we could organise a fake escape or have him imprisoned and then ransomed in one of the secret deals with the West German government."

Fuchs finished the cup of coffee and poured himself another. You really had to hand it to Kobitz. The scheme had a crazy, eccentric brilliance that was distinctly appealing, and probably workable – so long as these young agents could cope with being slobbered over by middle-aged women who'd been fooled into thinking they had found their long-lost offspring. The report went on to describe how two agents had already been supplied with Lebensborn identities and successfully transferred to the West. One had infiltrated the high-power American radio listening base in West Berlin; the second – a woman – had managed to become the personal assistant to a senior member of the Christian Democratic Union. The report continued:

"While we had good reason to be satisfied with the success of the Doppelgaenger programme in its initial phase and the performance of the first two agents placed, we were aware of the unusual strain that was being put on them. Even for those with long experience in undercover intelligence work it is difficult to keep up the pretence of being person X in front of that person's family. Therefore the ideal Doppelgaenger would be one who really believed that he was person X, in other words an unwitting Doppelgaenger, but one who was also willing to work as an agent for us. He would be able to play the part with complete conviction, without the attendant strains, except for the lesser strain of having to conceal his role as an agent."

"Obviously it was going to be extremely difficult to find a suitable candidate, someone who could be convinced that he had the biography of the particular Lebensborn boy that we wanted him to impersonate. But let us first consider the person we deemed ideal to be impersonated – a Lebensborn boy in his late twenties, son of a Danish woman named Birthe Karlssen and a German soldier named Heinz Ackermann. He was brought to the Lebensborn home Lenzfeld in the Harz mountains at the age of nearly three in the autumn of 1943 and remained there until the end of the war, when he was adopted by Otto and Waltraud Siebert in the nearby town of Sangerhausen, taking the surname of his adoptive parents, but keeping his first name of Henrik. Naturally it was a matter of concern to us how much he knew of his background and whether he felt any urge to seek out his natural mother. If he did so, it could of course endanger our operation. Fortunately our investigations revealed that the adoptive parents have told him little beyond the fact that he had a Danish mother and a German father. They themselves possessed no documentation about him and did not know the names of his real parents. Such documentation as we possess was found in the house when the area was liberated by the Russian Army in 1945 and later passed on to us. It included an entry in the registry of the home giving the name of his natural mother and his place of birth in Denmark. Our investigations have also revealed that Henrik Siebert has little curiosity about his Danish origins and appears to be devoted to his adoptive parents. He is a docile, somewhat timid character, married but without children. He worked as a plumber in Sangerhausen before moving to Berlin with his wife and taking a job with the firm of BOKA Plumbing, Heating and Sanitation. His wife Uta is an accountant with the Ministry of Economic Planning, a Party member and a strong personality. He appears to be easily dominated by her. We believe it is most unlikely that he will ever initiate any search for his real mother.

"Our next task, an awesome one, was to find the perfect man to impersonate him. He had to be someone who had almost no knowledge of his early childhood, but just enough to make our story credible to him. By an extraordinary piece of luck we found an ideal candidate in the person of a young man named Lutz Erdmann, who, while a schoolboy, had signed a pledge to work for us. All he knew about his early years was that his mother had been Danish and that he had been in a Lebensborn home – he did not know which one. From there he had been adopted in 1944 at the age of three by a couple named Praetorius in Königsberg (now Kaliningrad). In the last year of the war his adoptive mother was taking him westwards by train, and while they were changing in Dresden he was put on to a train that was moving out, and somehow his mother failed to board. Shortly afterwards came the British bombing raid on Dresden and Mrs Praetorius was killed. She apparently had all his documents with her, so they were irretrievably lost. On the train the boy was looked after by a war widow called Hanna Weber, who took him with her to Wittenberge. There she married a man called Dietrich Erdmann, and they adopted the boy and gave him their surname. Dietrich Erdmann worked in a copra-processing plant and his wife in a textile factory, so he grew up in a working class home.

"The boy got into trouble at school for anti-socialist attitudes and behaviour and was under threat of expulsion, which was when he was persuaded to sign our pledge. After taking his Abitur examination with good marks, he studied chemical engineering at Halle University, joining the Socialist Unity Party in his final year. After graduation he was sent to the Ministry-owned chemical firm of Lamda at Schwerin, then to our Academy at Potsdam for training, and then to the Leipzig branch of the Ministry. Early on our attention was drawn to his unusual record and his suitability as an unwitting Doppelgaenger. Another thing in his favour was that he appeared to be free of the personality defects that we had found in other former Lebensborn inmates. Having decided that he would be an ideal candidate for the Danish operation, we kept him for a time in a tedious job in the Technical Department in Leipzig, then presented him with some 're-discovered' documents, supposedly from the KGB archives, proving who he 'really' was. Then we offered him the chance to go to Denmark and contact his 'mother' provided that he continued to work for the Ministry, which he accepted. We arranged for him to have a crash course in Danish and gave him the code name Renatus, 'reborn'."

Fuchs paused and lit a Marlborough cigarette. He had initially been sceptical about this extra Machiavellian twist to the scheme. It was outrageously daring, and elaborate precautions would be needed to keep Erdmann in the dark. On the other hand Kobitz had a point. If the deception meant that Renatus could play his role better, then perhaps the thing had merit, although he was not sure that Chernikov would see it that way. He continued:

"Renatus was successfully transferred to West Berlin under the ransom programme. To give him added credibility he was placed for several weeks in a prison camp near Frankfurt an der Oder. From there he was transported by bus with nine other ransomed detainees to Berlin and then sent by train via the Friedrichstrasse station to West Berlin, where he was taken under the care of the Legal Protection Centre. He told them that he wished for the time being to live and work in Hamburg, from where he could make excursions to Denmark and attempt to establish contact with the Karlssen family. The Legal Protection Centre gave him a settling-in allowance and offered to help him find a job (up to now he has not actively sought full employment, wishing to concentrate on his mission). In Hamburg he was placed under the control of an experienced handler, Kurt Barschke, who has kept us informed of Renatus's progress (see Barschke's own report, attached). Barschke is fully informed about Erdmann's real identity. Renatus has, after some initial difficulties, established friendly relations with Mrs. Karlssen and her daughter and is hopeful that he will be accepted by the rest of family. Meanwhile he has already started work on his first important assignment – to neutralise the politician Borup …"

Fuchs put down the report, picked up his telephone and dialled Kobitz's extension. "Ah Kobitz, would you mind stepping in?" Kobitz always made him a bit uneasy – a dark horse, rather intense and humourless – not the kind of colleague with whom you could enjoy a drink and joke in the officers' canteen at lunchtime, but you had to admit he had a remarkably inventive mind.

The door opened and Kobitz came in. With his serious, pale face and hair very short at the sides but longer on top, he looked a little like a monk. A few centuries earlier he would probably have been an inquisitor, fighting the enemies of the Christian faith instead of the Communist one.

"You wanted to see me?" He spoke out of the left side of his mouth, as though he were used to making surreptitious asides to someone sitting next to him in a meeting.

Fuchs invited him to take a chair on the opposite side of the desk, then opened the folder and flicked through it. "Well, Kobitz, I've read your up-date on the Doppelgaenger project. The only part that still worries me a bit is this 'unwitting Doppelgaenger' as you call him. Are you sure that nothing could turn up from his past and give the game away?"

"Absolutely, Colonel. Even we don't know which Lebensborn home he was in, much less who his real parents were. Any evidence that existed was destroyed when his adoptive mother was trapped in Dresden during the bombing."

"I see, but can we be absolutely sure that the West German Intelligence Service or the Danish equivalent haven't unearthed any new information since then?"

"Our sources inside those services would tell us if there were any undue suspicions."

Fuchs was stroking his chin while looking at the document. "What about this man Siebert, the real Lebensborn boy? Are you sure he has no thoughts of tracing his Danish family?"

"As sure as we can be, Colonel. He appears to be devoted to his adoptive parents in Sangerhausen, and to our knowledge has never shown any curiosity about his birth and early childhood. In any case, his wife is a Party member, so we can probably persuade her to assist us."

"Alert you to any signs of disquieting behaviour?" asked Fuchs.

"Exactly."

Fuchs' telephone rang and he said: "Thank you, Ilse. Please show him in." A moment later Ilse appeared with a tall man of late middle age. Today he was wearing a grey suit instead of his KGB uniform, making him look more than ever like a university professor, or a champion chess player, or perhaps a poet, with his long, thoughtful face and wistful grey-blue eyes.

"Come in, Nikolai Nikolayevich!" Fuchs rose to shake his hand, then introduced him to Kobitz. They moved to a corner of the room where there were comfortable armchairs and a low, round table in pale wood.

"Major Kobitz has just been bringing me up to date on the Doppelgaenger operation," Fuchs explained. "Major, would you mind giving General Chernikov a brief summary of your report."

Chernikov listened, pensively puffing at a pipe, while Kobitz talked. When Kobitz reached the part about the Danish operation Chernikov frowned. After Kobitz had finished, the Russian remained silent for several seconds. Kobitz began to look as though he were in the dock awaiting sentence. Then Chernikov threw back his head and gave a loud laugh. "Trust you Germans to think up a scheme like this."

Kobitz attempted a wan smile, and Chernikov went on: "Actually, I'm impressed. An impersonator who doesn't know he's impersonating is something I've never come across before in our business. But if it works, that's what counts. From what you tell me Renatus has begun his task well."

"I believe he has, General," Kobitz affirmed.

"But belief is not enough, Major. We need certainty." Chernikov removed his pipe and poked it at Kobitz. "This Danish operation is vital – more vital than even some of our own colleagues realise. Do you play chess, Major?"

"A little."

"Good, then imagine Europe as a chess board." His hand gestured at the imaginary pieces. "White to the west, red to the east. The end of the war marked the beginning of a new game, and the opening phase is already over."

Kobitz nodded eagerly. Fuchs had heard all this before, but he knew how Chernikov loved to talk in chess metaphors, so he listened patiently as the Russian went on.

"We fought a strong opening game, and we have some red pieces strategically placed inside white's territory. However, white's defences are good, and their main pieces are well protected. So we have to focus on the pawns – Denmark, for instance. If we can take Denmark we'll easily go on to take other pawns – Norway, Sweden, Holland, Belgium. Then we'll be well poised for the final game when the big pieces fall one by one, red closes in on the white king, check mate and the game is ours." Chernikov sat back triumphantly and refilled his pipe before continuing his monologue. "Denmark is such an intriguing member of NATO - officially part of the western bloc, but the politicians and the public as a whole are deeply divided about that. And these small countries resent the dominance within the alliance of larger ones. The peace movement is still growing and who knows whether it will one day wield the political clout to cause the Danes to disarm and pull out of NATO altogether? Many people there would like to see Denmark become a fully neutral country, which would be ideal for our purposes. It would open up a crack in the western alliance, and in time, as I said, the country could be steered over to our side. So that's why it's vital to boost the peace and neutrality movement, and create alarm about NATO."

While he was talking, Ilse reappeared with a fresh supply of coffee. The Russian looked up and rubbed his hands. "Ah, I've been looking forward to a cup of your excellent coffee, Ernst. It's quite unrivalled from here to Vladivostok. Where was I?"

"Creating alarm about NATO," Fuchs prompted,

"Ah, yes. This is where your Renatus comes in, by helping us undermine the anti-Soviet, pro-NATO faction and its leaders. So I'm very glad to hear that Renatus has started work to discredit this man Borup with his Integrity Party. Keep me informed about his progress. But remember, this is only the beginning. We plan to launch our major propaganda campaign five months from now, and that's when he will really have to prove his mettle."

21

Clutching her third mug of coffee since breakfast, Claudia walked over to the window and again peered cautiously into the street, almost hoping she would see something that would at last confirm her fears. She had slept badly, as she almost always did these days, and needed more coffee than was good for her. The worst of it was the uncertainty. Not knowing whether the dishevelled figure slouched on the doorstep of the house opposite was the down-and-out that he appeared to be, or was someone masquerading as one; wondering why, when she was driving, she kept seeing a grey Volvo with the same number plate behind her. Normally on a Tuesday morning she would go shopping, browse in a bookshop, drop in for a coffee at one of her favourite cafés, where she would be almost certain to meet a friend or two. But since the break-in she had become more and more reluctant to leave the flat.

In the afternoon she saw two clients – a middle aged wife who had been abused by her father and could not bear her husband to touch her, and a young homosexual man in denial. As though from a distance, she watched herself playing her calm, understanding therapist's role, while they poured out their secrets to her – but all the time thinking: how trivial, this talk of complexes, emotional crises and the search for one's true self, when she had a spy living in her home – a spy she was in love with.

By the time the second client had gone it was late afternoon. She had given up waiting for Henrik to call, and she couldn't face another evening alone in the flat. She decided she would just go out anyway. If she was followed, who cared? They wouldn't try anything stupid on the busy streets of the city. Better leave one light on, she thought as she put on her coat, and she switched on a heavy brass lamp with a pale green glass shade, which stood on top of the bookshelf behind the sofa. Glancing around the familiar room, peaceful in the soft twilight with the lamp over the bookshelf casting a circle of warmth and intimacy, she thought with sadness of the many contented evenings she had spent curled on the sofa with a book, meditative music playing in the background. Her life used to move in a serene cycle of work, books, music, friends … But since Henrik's arrival everything had been turned upside down. Her room offered no comfort any more. She needed noise and people, anything to stop her thinking.

She filed away the notes she had made on the last client, putting them into a neat binder which she kept in a bookshelf by her desk. As she closed the door of the flat behind her she thought how easily she could remain detached from the things her clients told her – disturbing though they sometimes were – and how different it was with Henrik. She had not helped him directly, but knew that he was a spy and had done nothing about it because she had fallen in love. That made her feel like an accomplice. She carried the thought like a burden out into the twilit street. To know a guilty secret was to share the responsibility for the damage it might do, unless one revealed it – and she knew she could never do that.

She came to a tree-lined, cobbled square, surrounded by old houses, where a corner café beckoned – its windows glowing with amber light. Inside, ranks of bottles gleamed behind a mahogany bar, and the babble of voices mingled with the brassy sound of jazz coming from loudspeakers. It was a place she had visited quite often in the past, but not at all in recent months. It drew a young, faintly Bohemian clientele from the neighbourhood – social workers, political activists, struggling artists and would-be writers. As she entered, she recognised a group sitting at a table near the door and scanned the faces, putting names to them: Harry and Elke … Dirk,

Uschi and Sabine. They were acquaintances, not really friends, and most were several years her junior. For as long as she stayed here she would be safe.

"Claudia!" one of the men called as she approached. "Claudia! Long time no see. Come and sit with us. What'll you drink?" And she found herself swept up into their easy intimacy and laughter. For a moment she had an impulse to confide in them, but when one of them asked her what she had been "up to lately" she just said with a laugh: "Oh, still the usual things – trying to sort out screwed up people." The secret she carried was a wall that separated her from their innocence and gaiety. So she kept the secret to herself, laughing loudly at every feeble joke, and chaffing the teller in return. And in time the glow of alcohol and the insistent rhythm of the jazz made her forget her cares. In wars people managed to live for the moment, and so could she.

It was late in the evening when the group broke up and Claudia walked home alone through the echoing streets. Sober, she would never have risked being out at a time when every dark alley and pool of shadow could be hiding the man who had been following her. But in her befuddled state, her fears about being shadowed seemed absurd and cowardly. At the corner of the Antonistrasse she stopped, swaying slightly, to peer at the goods displayed in the window of a junk shop. Turning her face up to the light rain that was now falling, she walked on with half-closed eyes, nearly colliding with a lamp post. Tomorrow she would wake up with a hangover, but never mind, the evening had been worth it.

As she approached her front door she saw her car parked close by and decided to put it into the underground car park around the corner in the Hamburger Hochstrasse, where she usually kept it overnight for fear of thieves and vandals. She reached into a pocket for her car key, telling herself that she was not so tipsy that she couldn't manage the drive of a few hundred yards to the garage. The route went through a one-way system, so there would be no oncoming traffic. As she drove towards the intersection with the Davidstrasse she looked in her rear mirror and noticed a car pull out and drive in the same direction. It was about a hundred yards behind her, and in the dark she couldn't see the make, but the shape looked like the grey Volvo.

At the corner of the Davidstrasse she made a split second decision to turn right to see if the car would follow her. The turning took her downhill towards the Landing Stage and the harbour. Sweat started to trickle down her back, and a surge of adrenalin made her suddenly feel more sober. A main road ran east, parallel to the river, and she followed it. Glancing in the rear mirror, she thought she could see the Volvo still following her, two cars back. She drove past the massive brick warehouses along the harbour then, on impulse, turned south, making for the bridge across the Elbe and the motorway leading south into the Lüneburg Heath, the quickest route out of Hamburg and into the country. A plan was forming in her mind. She would drive to Lüneburg where her friend from student days, Brigitte, lived with her doctor husband. She would be safe with them for the night.

The rain was becoming heavier, mingling on the windscreen with the spray from the heavy lorries trundling in an endless line down the right-hand lane. In the wet and dark, the oncoming headlights were dazzling. She turned up the speed of the windscreen wipers, but the glass was greasy and the rubber smeared the section at the centre of her vision. A sign with the name Lüneburg flashed past, and she wondered whether she had missed the exit.

Realising that she was driving too fast, she eased back the accelerator and moved over to right-hand lane. In her rear mirror she saw the Volvo do the same. It was now immediately behind her, and she recognised the letters "JD" on the number plate. Yes, it was the same car that had trailed her in Hamburg.

Beyond the curtain of rain she saw another sign. Wasn't that the turn-off? She swerved towards it, then realised it was the wrong one and swerved back again, causing a lorry driver to hoot angrily at her. In the rear mirror she saw the Volvo continuing down the turning that she had been going to take, the driver evidently confused by her manoeuvre. With a sigh of relief she accelerated away down the middle lane, watching in her mirror for a chance to turn into the fast left-hand lane. Abruptly the curtain of rain parted to reveal a lorry that had pulled into the middle lane right in front of her to overtake another lorry. She wrenched the steering wheel to the left and missed the lorry by a hair's breadth, but the front wheels were no longer obeying the steering column. The car slid uncontrollably over the sheet of water on the road surface. There was a deafening scraping, grinding sound as it smashed against the metal fence between the north- and south-bound tracks of the motorway, bouncing back into the thick of the traffic. She heard the screech of brakes, the sound of cars behind her colliding. She tried to bring the car under control, but she was sliding across towards the embankment on the other side of the motorway, through a narrow gap in the line of lorries. In a flash of clarity she read the name on the side of one of them: "Hoffmann Frozen Foods, Bremerhaven". She wrenched the steering wheel again and the car went into a spin, making her think of the dodgem cars at the Dom fairground. From some distant point of consciousness she saw herself and the car spinning round and round in an insane dervish dance that seemed to have no end.

22

Henrik woke shortly after dawn, with a tight ache in his stomach and doubt still nagging at him. At his birthday party he had carefully drunk just enough to appear that he was enjoying himself while still remaining alert. Birthe would have thought the evening one of the happiest in his life, as it would have been if it weren't for the uncertainty that now hung over him. He knew he had to find out the truth. At the same time the truth was what he was most afraid of.

In the cool morning light, he looked down from the open dormer window at the rows of daffodils lining the path leading down to the orchard and saw the cat setting off with a lordly air on its early morning round. The idyllic peace of the scene only added to his worries.

When he had called Claudia and said he would be postponing his return, she seemed accepting although he knew she was holding back her disappointment. He realised he didn't want to go back to Hamburg at all. Claudia would sit there looking at him with her dark, serious eyes, expecting him to talk profoundly about "how it had felt for him". Then she would want him to sleep with her again, and he knew how dangerous it would be to encourage her to hope that they might one day have a real relationship. But now she knew the truth about him, he couldn't just abandon her. At some point he would have no option but to recruit her.

He shaved with cold water from the china ewer on the chest near the fireplace, dressed and then stepped cautiously on to the creaking landing, pausing as he heard the loud voices of Sven and Niels rising from the kitchen below. They were probably grumbling about him. Perhaps he should wait until they had eaten and left the room, but then that would leave him alone with the two women, who would want to discuss the events of the previous day. Maybe it would be better to risk being with the men and hope that he could parry any dangerous questions. The clock was ticking on the floor below, a deep, solid sound far slower than the beating of his heart. Stepping carefully, he tried to pass Kirsten's room without being heard, but as he came level with her door she came out as if she had been listening for his steps.

"Come in," she commanded. "We have to discuss what happens next."

"Next?" He tried to keep the alarm out of his voice. What did she mean? He followed her into her bedroom, noticing the still unmade bed and how the room smelt of her presence. It was disturbing to be so close, standing right beside her in the small space between her dressing table and the bed, aware of her faster breathing and her nervousness. At least she was dressed.

"Yes – about you and us ..." She looked around uneasily, almost as if expecting the door to burst open. "Mother and I want you to come and live with us here as one of the family right away. I needed to be able to say this to you on your own, without my father or Niels butting in."

"I want to come... of course I do, but I have to go back to Hamburg tomorrow. There are things I have to do there."

Kirsten nodded agreement. "Of course there are. But

couldn't you move here in a week or two?"

Henrik edged closer to the dressing table. He wanted to tell her that he would do anything to be close to her, that he worshipped and adored her. His voice faltered as he said: "I don't think we should rush your father and your brother."

"He's your brother too, Henrik."

"I know, I know. Half-brother anyway – a very bitter half-brother."

"They'll both come round far sooner than you think," she whispered encouragingly.

"You're so sweet," he told her truthfully. "I'd love to stay here right away, but I need to earn money. I can't let Birthe pay for me. Imagine what Niels and Sven would feel if I just moved in and did nothing. I need to find a job. I'll be looking on both sides of the border – Hamburg, Copenhagen, Flensburg … I wouldn't be far away and I can visit all the time."

"You promise?" she asked, urgently. "It matters so much to mother. It would really hurt her if you stayed away for weeks at a time. She wants to right the wrong she feels she did you."

He placed his hands on her shoulders and looked into her green eyes. "Trust me." He had intended to end the conversation there but he watched dismayed as tears welled in her eyes and spilled over her dark lashes.

"Of course I trust you, Henrik. I'm so sorry. You came back to us after all you had been through. We have no right to expect any more than whatever you are prepared to give us."

He held her for a few moments and then suggested that they go down to breakfast. The two men were still at the table. They gave Henrik a perfunctory greeting, then a few moments later left the room. A pleasant aroma of coffee filled the air. On the table were fresh rolls, boiled eggs, cheese, ham and a bowl of fruit.

Birthe placed a mug of coffee in front of him: "I hope you slept well, Henrik," she said, putting a hand on his shoulder.

He gave her a warm smile. "Perfectly, thank you, Mother."

Hearing him call her that for the first time, she squeezed his shoulder and her eyes lit up. When Henrik explained that he would be leaving for Hamburg the following day in order to look for work, Birthe dabbed her eyes with the corner of her apron, then said quietly that she understood and made him promise that he would come back soon.

* * *

The next morning, Birthe and Kirsten walked with Henrik to his car. He tossed his case onto the back seat and turned to kiss the two women, but Birthe said: "Wait a minute! I just remembered there's something I want to show you."

She dashed back into the house and came back holding a small photograph. She handed it to Henrik, and he saw a little boy in a bathing suit on a beach, holding a spade.

"You at two and a half," Birthe announced. "I've been looking for it ever since you arrived, and I found it last night in a drawer. It's easy to see that it's Henrik, isn't it Kirsten?"

Kirsten leaned over and gazed at the picture. "Oh yes, I can see it in the eyes, the chin ..."

"So can I," Birthe chimed in happily "and you can even see his birthmark. Strange, I had forgotten all about that mark until now." She pointed at a diamond-shaped mark on the left thigh of the boy in the picture.

Henrik felt his heart pounding hard as he looked at the photograph. The birthmark was as plain as could be. He forced himself to say: "How marvellous that you found it. May I borrow it? I can have copies made."

"Of course, Henrik dear. I'm so glad that it turned up."

In a daze, he kissed the two women on the cheek, climbed into the car and drove off. In the driver's mirror he caught sight of Kirsten waving. Alone with his thoughts as he drove away along the bleak coastline, four things kept hammering at his mind. He had no birthmark. Kirsten was not his half-sister. He was desperately in love with her. He could never tell her the truth.

23

When he arrived back in his room in the Bernhard-Nocht-Strasse Henrik tried several times to phone Kurt without success. He was studying the picture of the child with the birthmark, when the phone rang.

"Did you call while I was out?" he heard Kurt say.

"Yes, listen. I'm not the son of Birthe Karlssen. Our people must have mixed up the records. I could be exposed at any moment, so we'll have to ditch the mission. The family ..."

"Just a minute." Henrik had expected an astonished reaction, but Kurt's voice was calm and iron-hard. "So what if the records did get mixed up and you're not Mrs. Karlssen's son? What's important is that she thinks you are, and the rest of them do too."

Henrik, thrown off balance, said slowly: "You mean ...

you expect me to stay on and pretend I'm someone that I'm not?"

"In our business we do it all the time."

"Not twenty-four hours a day, living side by side under the same roof."

"Yes, it is twenty-four hours a day," Kurt said "seven days a week. A full-time job."

Henrik told Kurt about his talking at night, the letter from Fräulein Neumeyer, the birthmark, but his words came out in an angry rush, verging on incoherence.

"Listen," Kurt cut in "there is no way – repeat no way this mission is going to be aborted. Too much depends on it. Fuchs is demanding success. If it fails, we're both in the shit, and I can't let that happen. Calm down. I'll look into this question of the records. Maybe there's a perfectly good explanation. In the meantime you're just going to carry on as before."

"But what if they catch me out on something?"

"They're not going to catch you out. If the letter from the nurse turns up and doesn't match your story, you can tell them that all the staff in the Lebensborn home were Nazis and nothing they say can be believed. And as for the birthmark, we can arrange for one to be tattooed on to your leg. I'll look into it. There are plenty of good tattooists here in Hamburg, and I know of one who is sympathetic to us."

"Tattooists!" Henrik laughed scornfully. "Are you serious?"

Kurt's voice took on a harder edge. "Just do as you're told. The Ministry attaches great importance to this mission."

"It's all very well for them, sitting safely on their arses in Berlin," Henrik shouted. "They don't care what it's going to be like for me trying to keep up this act day after day, having to lie to decent people and pretend to love them as though they were my family. This was not part of the deal when I agreed to the assignment."

"Anything we ask you to do is part of the deal," Kurt snapped. "If your cover's blown, we'll get you out before any harm is done. It'll be easier to deceive people you're not related to. So stop complaining and get the hell back to the Karlssens' place, otherwise they're going to get an invitation to your funeral. Do you understand me?" Kurt hung up without waiting for an answer.

Henrik knew that he should have talked to Kurt about Claudia. Should he admit to Kurt that he had slept with her and that she had found out the truth about him? If he did then Kurt would want him to recruit her. Kurt would probably be happier if she had already been recruited by the time he told him about the affair. Maybe he should bite the bullet and talk to her about it.

He went down to Claudia's room and knocked. "Claudia!" he called, "Claudia, are you there?" No answer. He would try again later. As he turned away from the door he saw that Blok, the caretaker, with his pale, bleary-eyed face, had come out of his ground-floor flat and climbed half way up to the landing.

"Ah, Herr Erdmann," he wheezed, giving off a miasma of beer fumes and cigarette smoke. "You're looking for Frau Schmidt?"

"Yes. Where is she?"

"Frau Schmidt's dead," Blok coughed: "Road accident. There was a report on Radio Hamburg. Apparently she was driving like a maniac down the Autobahn to Lueneburg and skidded off the road. Tragic business. If you want to stay on in the flat you'll have to deal with the lawyers for her estate. No doubt they'll be in touch with you. Otherwise if you're paid up you can leave at any time. Tragic, tragic." He disappeared back into his flat, shaking his head.

For several minutes Henrik sat crouched on the stairs in a state of shock. Suddenly he felt sick. He stared at the door of Claudia's flat, picturing the cosy living room with its books and exotic ornaments, and her tapestry-lined bedroom where they had made love. Claudia dead? Surely there must be some mistake. He felt the blood drain from his head as he thought about Kurt and his surveillance of Claudia. Could that have anything to do with her death?

He went back to his room and feverishly dialled Kurt's number.

"Claudia's dead." He felt the bile rising in his throat. "Did you have anything to do with it?"

"What do you mean? Tell me what happened."

"All I know is that she was killed last night in a road accident on the motorway to Lueneburg. Was that your doing?"

"Of course not! Why do you think I had anything to do with it?"

"I don't believe you. I know she was a bad driver, but not that bad."

Kurt was silent for several seconds, then he said evenly. "We need to talk. Meet me at the jetty by the Fish Market. If you're not there at seven, I'll be back at eight."

A click and their conversation was over.

24

As he left the house, Henrik passed a weeping woman in the hallway. From her features and colouring, he guessed she was Claudia's mother. He wondered how many other people were grief-stricken at her death, and he couldn't help thinking that if he hadn't taken the room in her house she would still be alive.

Outside, the air was cold from a recent rainfall, but the evening sun had come out, glinting sadly from the wet pavements. He turned up the collar of his raincoat as he crossed the empty expanse of the Fish Market, hearing the clock of the St. Pauli church tolling seven o'clock. It was low tide and the ramp leading to the pontoon jetty sloped steeply downwards. The railings on either side of the ramp were hung with spiders' webs that caught shafts of evening sunlight. One of them quivered as a fly landed and was trapped, and he saw the spider eagerly dart towards it. He felt as desperate as the fly, struggling vainly to free itself.

The pontoon jetty ran parallel to the riverbank, forming a T-junction with the ramp. He could make out Kurt's figure standing alone at the extreme left-hand end of the jetty, smoking a cigarette, a hundred yards or so beyond where a ferry was disgorging its passengers and taking on new ones. Henrik waited on the ramp until the ferry cast off again before walking down to where Kurt stood.

"So tell me the truth. Were you chasing her when she went off the road?"

Kurt's face darkened and he grasped Henrik's arm. "I ask the questions here. I was tailing her, but I turned off the Autobahn by mistake before she crashed. It was an accident."

"Why were you following her?"

"She knew too much. She had become a liability, especially after you slept with her. Kurt smirked as he saw Henrik's face whiten. "I wanted to keep her under observation."

"And now she's conveniently out of the way."

"In a war there are bound to be unintended casualties. In our profession we have to accept that." Kurt tossed the stub of his cigarette into the water, then turned and faced Henrik, a hard, fierce look in his eyes. "Let me tell you something. A couple of years ago I was assigned to take care of a dissident who had escaped to the west and was causing problems for us. I found out that he and his wife and daughter were going on a caravan holiday in Normandy, so I followed them, parked my caravan next to theirs on a camping site and made friends with them. One evening they invited me round for hamburgers. I told them I was a vegetarian, but I volunteered to do the grilling. When they weren't looking I laced the meat with a toxin that simulates food poisoning. The wife vomited hers up immediately, and the daughter refused to eat, but the man kept his down and that was the end of it. The wife and daughter were lucky to escape, but even if they hadn't I would have accepted it as collateral damage. And that's what you must do now."

Henrik's anger was succeeded by a feeling of resignation. In their business "collateral damage" happened and innocent people like Claudia died. He would have to live with the fact that he, more than anyone, had been responsible for her death.

"Now," Kurt said, punching his right fist into the palm of this left hand as though to indicate that there were more important matters to talk about, "it's time you started concentrating on the job." He moved closer. "The people in the Normannenstrasse are getting impatient for results."

"Then they shouldn't have made such a monumental error with the Lebensborn records."

A gull landed momentarily on the railing a few feet away, then was chased off by another gull and they flew away over the river, screeching and swooping at each other furiously. Kurt looked at Henrik with a mixture of distaste and anger.

"Be careful what you wish for. If you get yourself sent home, you're finished. And don't forget that our bosses didn't like the news about the birthmark."

"I'm not thrilled either."

Kurt gave a sigh of exasperation. "Get it into your head that this may be the one chance you and I ever get to distinguish ourselves in Fuchs's eyes. Look ..." He handed Henrik a scrap of paper. "This tattooist is the best around. Don't go anywhere else – he's expecting you."

Kurt ran a hand through his hair. "You said you were on the trail of something with Borup?"

"Something in his war record. I found a newspaper article and got a lead to a journalist. I'm researching it."

"Let's hope it's good. The people in the Normannenstrasse are keen to see results quickly. I'll report back and ask them to be patient."

*   *   *

The following morning, Henrik went to Kurt's recommended tattoo parlour, which was in a dingy side street parallel to the one in which Severin's was located. The shop had a display window showing coloured pictures of the designs available – a Viking's head, an Indian chief, a Chinese dragon, a heart with a

163

dagger thrust through it. As he entered the shop the owner emerged from behind a bead curtain – an elderly man with neatly combed grey hair, mild eyes behind rimless glasses, and the quiet, patient manner of a watchmaker. He raised his eyebrows a little when Henrik explained his request.

"Often people want a tattoo to mask a birthmark. The other way round is less usual; but no problem either way. The colour can be brown or purple. I will show you shades to choose from. You must draw the shape for me. Ah, you have a photograph … better still."

Half an hour later Henrik emerged with a mid-brown, diamond-shaped blotch on his left thigh. Not altogether convincing, he thought – especially if it had really been purple – but it would have to do. Perhaps these marks could change over time.

From the tattoo parlour he returned to the desolate house in the Bernard-Nocht-Strasse to collect his belongings. He found that Blok had left a note for him in the hall, saying that a cremation would take place at the Ohlsdorf Crematorium in four days time. Too late for him to attend. His last act, before driving out of Hamburg, was to visit a florist's shop. After choosing a small spray for Claudia's coffin, he struggled to write a message on the accompanying card. He wrote a few predictable words addressed to Claudia. Not sure how to sign off, he decided on "your friend". In a gloomy mood, with an image of Claudia's smiling face stubbornly refusing to leave his mind, he left the shop.

25

Fuchs knew how seriously Chernikov was taking the situation by the fact that the Russian had summoned him and Major Kobitz to the KGB liaison office in Karlshorst at 7:30 in the morning. Fuchs expected the Russian to keep them waiting as a further sign of his displeasure, and he did – on a bench in the corridor outside his office. After nearly an hour a secretary admitted them to an anteroom where they waited a further ten minutes before being shown into a large room where Chernikov sat at the far end behind a large wooden desk on which stood three telephones and a plaster bust of Lenin. The room was decorated in the heavy, bombastic style typical of the upper echelons of the Soviet Union. The three windows on one side were hung with dark red velvet curtains. On the opposite wall was a large map of Europe with a thick black line marking the boundary between the Soviet and the western blocs. There were also bronze reliefs of Marx and Engels and the inevitable photograph of Felix Dherzhinski.

The Russian was dressed in full uniform. At a wave of his hand they sat down on plain office chairs before his desk.

"Well," he said, clasping his hands together, "you know why I called you here. This business of the Doppelgaenger Renatus. So he's found out that he's not who you told him he was. Is that correct?"

Fuchs spoke up first. "Yes, Comrade General." He thought it better on this occasion not to call him Nikolai Nikolayevich. "According to Agent Barschke, Mrs Karlssen showed Erdmann a photograph of the real Lebensborn boy in which the lad he is impersonating appears to have a birthmark on his leg, where he himself has none. It was something we couldn't have foreseen."

The General gave an impatient grunt and said: "But you might have guessed that something of the kind was likely to happen. Are you sure there's nothing else I ought to know?"

Fuchs felt a heavy flush spread across his face. Out of the corner of his eye he saw that Kobitz was looking equally embarrassed. "Apparently, Comrade General, a letter may exist – Mrs Karlssen can't find it at present. It was sent to Mrs Karlssen by a nurse who looked after the real son in the home, and visited him after the war when he had been adopted."

Chernikov banged his fist on the table and glared angrily at the two Stasi men. One of the telephones rang. Chernikov picked it up and spoke some words in Russian while Kobitz, pale and tight-lipped, crossed and uncrossed his legs nervously. The General replaced the receiver and continued to look at them in silence for a moment.

"The question is," he went on "what do we do now? Major Kobitz, this was your idea. What is your assessment of the situation? And what options are open?"

Kobitz coughed and shifted uncomfortably in his chair. "Well, General, I am convinced that this development will not endanger the mission. Agent Barschke reports that, despite knowing that Mrs Karlssen is not his mother, Renatus is eager to continue with it and is confident that he can still carry off the impersonation. The family have accepted him completely and have no suspicions of any sort. Barschke has arranged for Erdmann to have a false birthmark tattooed on to his leg to protect him in the unlikely event of any member of the family seeing his upper leg…"

Chernikov looked at them with an expression of extreme scepticism, prompting Fuchs to intervene: "Barschke is the man on the spot who can best judge how resilient Renatus is. He wouldn't recommend continuing if he thought Erdmann didn't have it in him. Barschke will potentially be in danger too if Erdmann's cover is blown."

Chernikov drummed with his fingers on his leather-topped table. "You realise that if Renatus breaks down under the strain and gives the game away it would endanger our entire Danish operation. In fact it would blow apart your whole Doppelgaenger project. The Karlssens may have found that missing letter by now. The Danish secret service might already be watching him."

"Then, what would you recommend, General?" Fuchs asked in a mild, compliant tone.

Chernikov gazed for a moment through the windows at the chestnut trees in the grounds while continuing to drum on the desk with the fingers of one hand. "In such a case," he said, still gazing into the garden "it might be best to sacrifice a pawn."

Fuchs and Kobitz stared at Chernikov in silence. Each knew that their plan was discredited. It was all over.

Chernikov stared back at them unflinching. "Arrange an accident – no body must be found. We lose an active agent but the position is still covered and no one is any the wiser as to his true identity. We find another way to complete the mission with another agent." He turned to Kobitz. "Can Barksche be relied on to carry this out?"

"Yes, but can't we just recall Renatus?"

The Russian shook his head. "I think it's a little late for that now. The thing has to be cut short here. We sacrifice one to protect the many."

"Very well, General," Fuchs replied calmly. "If that's what

you think best we can do it. Only … I wonder if we should wait just a little. Barschke reports that Renatus is on to something important with Borup – some scandal from the war. It could be just what we need. Borup is a hard nut to crack, and this is the first promising lead that we have had. Another agent might not be able to pick it up again. And we're under time pressure with the elections coming up."

Chernikov looked out through the window again, stroking his chin. "You're asking me to gamble on the nerves of an inexperienced agent who could be exposed at any moment?"

"I believe it's worth taking the chance, Comrade General," said Fuchs. "He's performed well in the past and he has every motivation to succeed. He knows he's expendable."

Chernikov nodded several times. "That's very well put, Fuchs. All right, we'll give Renatus two weeks to come up with something on Borup and hope that he keeps his nerve." He consulted a calendar on his desk. "That takes us to 10 May. If he hasn't come up with anything by then Barschke eliminates him. Is that clear?" Chernikov stood up to indicate that the audience was over.

Fuchs nodded. "Quite clear, General."

They were making for the door when Chernikov said: "By the way, the real Lebensborn boy – what's his name?"

"Henrik Siebert," Kobitz replied.

"I assume you are keeping a close eye on him"

"I already have him under surveillance."

"Good. We wouldn't like to have any other unexpected problems cropping up."

26

Henrik drove straight to Copenhagen and checked into the Marco Polo again. On Monday morning he walked to the library, praying that the Einstein look-alike might be there again, but the man was nowhere to be seen. Confronted with the unending ranks of bound volumes of newspapers, he felt a sense of utter hopelessness. The article had appeared "a year or two ago" according to the man. So Henrik decided to go back three years and work his way through all the main newspapers, hoping to spot the piece. At first he conscientiously looked up unfamiliar words in his pocket dictionary, but soon realised that he was going far too slowly. He decided to trust to luck and instinct. By the end of that day he had only finished one year of the mainstream daily Berlingske Tidende and was beginning to feel that the task was beyond him. When he returned despondently to his hotel he found a slip of paper waiting in the pigeonhole next to his room key. The receptionist had scribbled a telephone message: "Delivery for Norman expected by 10 May, otherwise penalty clauses in contract will be invoked." He swore under his breath as he carried the message up to his room. Only fourteen days, and all he had to go on was a vague mention of an article that might prove to be a dead end.

For the next four days, until the library closed on Saturday, he worked feverishly through two more years of the Berlingske Tidende, then spent Sunday drifting uneasily around the city, along the canals and through the Tivoli Gardens, unable to enjoy the fine weather and the bright mood of the city awakening to spring. All the time the deadline hung over him.

On Monday, as soon as the library opened, he returned to the task, now skimming through the papers without reading every headline. Every so often he found an article about Borup and the Integrity Party, but nothing remotely like what the Einstein look-alike had described.

Next day, leaving the hotel, he caught sight of an electric clock over the reception desk, which showed the date, 3 May, the birthday that had been arbitrarily given to him by his adopted parents, the Erdmanns. Not that they had ever made much of the event – it had always seemed to get submerged in the aftermath of the Mayday workers' holiday. He spent his notional birthday at the library and worked grimly on through the newspapers in their heavy, cumbersome bindings, but once again he finished the day empty-handed. Seven days to the deadline, and one of them a Sunday. It seemed unlikely that he would make it.

The following day, Wednesday, he began with a different newspaper, Kroniken, a low-brow tabloid with the usual mixture of sex, crime and scandal. Again, he came across several articles about Borup, but by midday he had still not found what he was looking for. He was unable to shake off the sense that it was a futile task. He might as well resign himself to his fate if he hadn't found anything by the end of the day. Half way through the afternoon he found another article about Borup with a picture of him addressing an Integrity Party rally, but it was the usual routine report. He turned over mechanically then turned back again to look at another article on the same page that had fleetingly caught his eye. He felt a flutter of excitement when he saw the headline: "SORDID SECRETS OF THE DANISH RESISTANCE". Under it was the name of the reporter, Christian Jenssen.

"Something is rotten in the state of Denmark," the article began. "Shocking new evidence has come to light about the way in which the Danish wartime resistance movement was used as a cover for criminal activities, including robbery, extortion and murder." The article went on to describe how criminals, calling themselves resistance fighters, had carried out robberies, run protection rackets and killed people who got in their way, avoiding justice by claiming that their activities were all part of the armed struggle against the Germans. Some of the perpetrators of these crimes were later fêted as resistance heroes and went on after the war to build successful business empires. The reporter described a conversation with the widow of one of the victims, but did not name her. Her husband had been in the retail business in Copenhagen and Aarhus and had got in the way of a competitor who was an influential figure in the resistance. This competitor had fabricated evidence "proving" that her husband was a collaborator, and had then had him shot while he was taking his usual Sunday morning walk in a local park. After the war, when she tried to bring the murderers to justice, she encountered a wall of silence. No one in the judiciary or the political establishment wanted the resistance to be shown in a bad light, and all crimes committed in its name were now de facto amnestied. And, of course, she had no hard and fast proof of the crime. Still, to her dying day, according to Christian Jenssen, she had gone on hoping that her husband's murderers would be punished. Henrik's apathetic mood vanished instantly. It was perfect, perfect beyond his wildest dreams.

The "competitor" was not named directly, but the article was insinuatingly placed on the same page and right beside the photograph of Borup addressing the rally. It was a blatant hint.

If Borup could be linked to this crime, his political career would be finished, and Henrik's skin would be saved. But without more details it would be difficult even for the Stasi to manufacture convincing evidence. He leafed through all subsequent issues of Kroniken up to the present but found no further mention of the story. So "Einstein" had been right. Jenssen had somehow been silenced. If Jenssen was still alive, Henrik had to find him quickly and the newspaper would be a good place to start. He hurried to the desk where the girl obligingly looked up the address for him.

Half an hour later Henrik was at Kroniken's reception desk, talking to a uniformed janitor, who proved uncommunicative until he was given three hundred Krone. The man, who wore thick-lensed glasses, looked around furtively, before leaning across the desk and saying in a confidential tone: "Jenssen, yes I remember him. Sharp one, maybe too sharp for his own good. Left the paper and bought a small hotel in Roskilde. Always said he wanted to run a hotel. Old dream of his. Well one day, somehow, suddenly he could afford to make his dream come true. Good luck to him."

Leaving the newspaper building, Henrik imagined how Jenssen just might have been able to afford it. That afternoon Henrik made the half-hour train journey to Roskilde, and found the hotel with ease. He hailed a taxi and said he was looking for a hotel run by Mr. Jenssen, a former Kroniken journalist. The driver knew immediately which hotel he meant, and ten minutes later he was stepping out in front of a wooden chalet with a weatherworn sign over the porch: "Hotel Nordlys". When he asked at the reception desk for the proprietor he was told that Jenssen was away until Saturday, but perhaps the gentleman would like to leave a message or speak to Mr. Jenssen's wife. Henrik declined, but said he would return. On the way back to Copenhagen he though about telling Kurt straight away about the article, but decided to wait until he had seen Jenssen.

He returned Roskilde on Saturday morning and found Jenssen working at a desk in a poky, smoke-filled room behind the reception area – a burly, round-faced man with receding red hair and a beard. Beside him was an ashtray full of cigarette stubs. Henrik introduced himself as Manfred Korff, a journalist from the Spiegel, who had come across Jenssen's piece while researching an article on the Danish resistance. At first Jenssen insisted that he had nothing more to say on the subject, but at the mention of the name "Borup" and a hint that Henrik knew about the bribe, Jenssen became agitated and demanded shrilly: "What do you want?"

Henrik said in a calm and reasonable tone: "All I want is a couple of names – the man killed on Borup's orders and the person who killed him – plus the basic details about when and where it happened. I'll keep your name out of it."

Jenssen pulled at his cigarette. "So that's all you want, is it? Well, sod off. If I were you I'd be careful. Borup doesn't like people asking awkward questions."

"Maybe," Henrik said quietly, "but he can't stop the story coming out. I've taken precautions in case anything happens to me – a letter with my employer listing the people I've been talking to and why. So the choice is yours: either we publish with your help but without your name, or vice versa."

Seeing an anguished look pass across Jensen's face, he decided the time had come to show him the money – he'd had the stick, so now the carrot.

"Now, of course I realise information of this kind doesn't

come free, and I can be very generous." He reached into his pocket and pulled out a thick manila envelope. "I imagine it's hard to make a profit out of a hotel like this. There's ten thousand Krone in here. That'll pay a few of your outstanding bills. It's all yours if you tell me what I want to know, and I swear your name won't be mentioned."

Jenssen was now staring fixedly at him, his eyes narrowed. "You're not from the Spiegel at all! Who the hell are you?" Henrik could sense fear oozing out of him.

"Let's just say I don't like Borup any more than you do. There's a price to pay for everything and now it's Borup's time to pay."

He held out the envelope and Jenssen slowly reached out and took it.

"All right, I'll tell you what I know."

*   *   *

"Kraal was the name of the victim, Henning Kraal," Henrik told Kurt the following morning. "Kraal was a rival store owner who got in Borup's way. Borup had him shot by a resistance death squad led by a man called Gunnar Jakobsen. Shortly afterwards Jakobsen and three of his men were arrested by the German security forces and shot. You'll find the details in my report."

He handed Kurt a single sheet of paper. They were standing in a small, dank men's lavatory in a car park beside the motorway near the north German coast. Their voices were muffled by the heavy lorries roaring past. It was Monday, the day before Henrik's deadline expired.

Kurt glanced over the report. "You've done surprisingly

well." As though unwilling to give unqualified praise, he added: "The details are a bit skimpy, but look adequate. Our forgery experts at HQ can concoct a report of Jakobsen's interrogation by the Gestapo in which he confesses to the contract murder of Kraal on Borup's orders. It will be ready for you within a week. You can pick it up from Petersen's photo shop in Copenhagen. He's one of our people. Say you have something to collect for Mr Norman and hand him a slip of paper with Renatus written on it."

"And what then?" Henrik asked. "Release the report to the press?"

Kurt shook his head. "Not immediately. Send him an anonymous letter enclosing a photcopy of the forged report and demanding his resignation. He'll try to tough it out. Follow it up with an anonymous phone call. Give him a deadline, and if he doesn't keep to it, give the report to the press. Petersen will handle that."

Kurt picked up a canvas hold-all from the floor and handed it to Henrik. "There's a gun in here," he said. "You may need it." Henrik took the bag, feeling a little light-headed. "Fuchs and the other big boys won't forget it if you pull this off. Most agents work a lifetime and never get a chance like this. You'll have played a major role in making Denmark tip our way." He stepped towards the doorway and glanced up and down the car park to make sure that there was still nobody within earshot." And by the way, the bosses are posting me to Copenhagen. They need an experienced man on the spot. I'll be keeping an eye on things – discreetly of course."

The thought of Kurt coming to the island filled him with dread. With a sinking heart, Henrik watched him stride away to his car..

PART III

27

Hinnerk Siebert lived with the awareness that his world was full of boundaries – thresholds between what was safe and approved and what was forbidden, out of bounds, dangerous. Sometimes the boundaries were marked out with signs and barbed wire. At other times they were discernible only thanks to the survival instinct that he had developed since childhood. Now, on his way home from work in the late afternoon, he found himself at the corner of a street in the south-western part of the city and knew that he was in one of those danger zones. He would never have dreamed of approaching it unless he had been working nearby, but now some overwhelming impulse made him turn into the street, then stop and look ahead. Behind a row of derelict houses lay the Wall – the supreme boundary, the one that legitimised all the others and kept them in place. He found it enticing and terrifying at the same time. He was too close to it. He should not be there, he knew that, but still he took a step forward and, having crossed the invisible threshold, he walked on.

Most of the streets along the East German side of the wall had been sealed off. Either the windows of the houses had been bricked up on the side facing West Berlin or the houses had been evacuated and pulled down and the land fenced off. But here stood a row of houses that had been abandoned but not yet demolished. Most of the ground-floor windows that remained had been bricked or boarded up, but in one house the mortar had crumbled and bricks had fallen out, leaving large gaps. He peered through, and on the other side, he could just see a row of grey concrete slabs, reinforced by steel girders that projected above the concrete, with barbed wire strung between them. His heart beat faster. On the other side, he knew, lay a death strip as wide as a sizeable road, overlooked by watchtowers at intervals, constantly under observation by the border police, heavily mined and patrolled by ferocious Alsatian guard dogs. On the far side of it was an outer wall, almost as formidable as the inner one. Even if you managed to tackle the inner wall and the barbed wire, and then succeeded in crossing the strip without being shot, mauled by a dog, or blown up by a mine, you were quite likely to set off one of the automatic firing devices – inconspicuous little grey funnels that could be mistaken for loudspeakers until you activated one of them and it sprayed you with tiny, sharp-edged metal cubes that ripped your body open in a hundred places. And if, by some miracle, none of that happened, you still had the outer wall to get over. By then the alarm sirens would be going full blast and the place would be swarming with border police. Long before you reached the outer wall you would be riddled with bullets. So if he ever tried to escape, supposing he could conquer his fears, it would definitely not be that way.

When the Wall had gone up back in August 1961 he had still been living in Sangerhausen at the edge of the Harz Mountains and thoughts of escape had been far from his mind. He had just qualified as a plumber – a menial job for someone who had wanted to study at university, but a safe and respectable one. And then had come his marriage to Uta and the move to Berlin. Uta seemed to have a knack of obtaining privileges – a Trabant car, a decent apartment not far from the centre, foods that were normally hard to find. Life could be worse – that's what he had tried to tell himself despite another quiet voice inside him insisting that "could be worse" was not good enough. Gradually that voice had become louder. He had begun a process of "inner emigration", as they called it in his country, taking refuge in literature and in his own secret writing. He might have remained in this bubble of his own making had it not been for the evening when he saw the Danes.

His thoughts were abruptly interrupted by the sound of footsteps. A voice barked: "You! What are you doing here?"

He turned and saw a thickset man in the grey uniform of the Border Police, helmeted and black-booted, a machine-gun with a round magazine slung over one shoulder and a walkie-talkie over the other. A pair of small, dark eyes, set in a pig-like face, stared coldly at him.

Hinnerk struggled to control the slight stammer that came over him when he was nervous or frightened. He was frightened, caught out of bounds. "Going h-home." He held up his leather bag containing his plumber's tools. "Been doing a p-plumbing job in Leipziger Strasse."

"What's your name?"

"Hinnerk ... that is, Henrik Siebert." He had never felt that the name Hinnerk - one of the familiar forms of Henrik or Heinrich - really suited him. But his adoptive parents had called him that from the start, and now it was the name that everyone called him by.

"Show me your personal identity card." The policeman thrust out a hand, and Hinnerk gave him the document. The man looked carefully at it then reached into a pocket and pulled out a small black notebook, evidently a check list of names, because he ran a stubby finger down the pages before putting the book away.

"Who do you work for?"

"BOKA Plumbing, Heating and Sanitation."

"Don't move, I'll have to check your credentials."

He spoke into the walkie-talkie, a clumsy grey box with an aerial attached to it. As Henrik watched him, he felt sick with apprehension, cursing himself for having strayed so near the Wall.

"Becker here, Border Police," the man was saying. "I've just apprehended someone loitering in the Zimmerstrasse. Name of Henrik Siebert. Address Metzer Strasse twelve, Prenzlauer Berg. Says he's a plumber working for a firm called BOKA. Can you check him out ... That's right, Siebert, Metzer Strasse twelve."

Several minutes passed while the policeman waited for an answer. Overhead, a helicopter swept along a length of the Wall, then hovered so low that Hinnerk could see a man in the cockpit peering out through binoculars. A moment later the aircraft tilted, picked up speed again and flew off.

"I see," the policeman said into the walkie-talkie. Hinnerk felt his legs go weak. From the way the man said "I see" it sounded as though the name Hinnerk Siebert had bad connotations to the person at the other end.

The policeman handed back the identity pass. "All right, the records have confirmed who you are. But that doesn't mean you won't hear more about this. You may do or you may not. For now you can go home."

Hinnerk took the pass and walked rapidly away, relieved that he hadn't been arrested immediately. Did they already have a file on him? Up to now, as far as he knew, he had given them no reason to open one. But you could never be sure. He might have been heard making a joke of the wrong kind, seen speaking to a suspect person, or observed failing to cheer loudly enough at some official parade. Or perhaps his

Lebensborn childhood and Danish mother had been enough to make them start a file. If they hadn't done so already, this incident would probably ensure that they did so now. Perhaps one of his colleagues in the plumbing firm was already sending regular reports on him to the Stasi. He could imagine the kind of comments they would contain: "The subject stands out by virtue of his non-working-class attitudes. He appears to live in a world of his own, socializes little with his fellow workers and takes no interest in political issues."

And it was true, he did live in a world of his own. In his spare time he liked to read good literature, when he could get hold of it: Goethe, Fontane, Rilke – although of course he never talked to his colleagues about it, let alone about his own writing. It had started with a sort of diary, an old exercise book into which he had begun to write sporadically about his inner life – his thoughts, dreams, hopes and fears. Then he had progressed to writing poems and short stories in between the diary entries.

Recently he had begun to write a story called *One Hour of Freedom*. It was about a society in which everyone's life was programmed down to the last minute and lived according to a rigid set of rules and prohibitions. No deviation was possible, because everyone was under observation the whole time. There were not only spies and surveillance cameras everywhere but also devices that could measure and interpret brain activity, so that not even thoughts were free. There was only one tiny chink in the prison wall. At some point in your life you were granted a single hour of freedom – one hour during which you could do, think or say whatever you wished. The trouble was that you never knew when the hour was going to come until the morning of the day in question. Then the telephone would ring and a recorded voice would say: "Congratulations, Fellow Citizen, you have been assigned your hour of freedom today from …." Of course the hour of freedom was really the cruellest device of all in the regime's system of control, for what could you do with a single hour, with hardly any time to prepare for it, and knowing that it would never come again in your entire life? You would search frantically for a meaningful way to spend the time, and as the minutes ticked away you would grow increasingly frenzied. In the last few moments many people committed suicide in a final, desperate attempt to perform a free act.

He knew of course that the contents of the notebook, and especially this story, would be enough to get him a long prison sentence, which was why he kept it hidden under the floorboards of their storeroom in the attic. Although he was sure that no one knew about it, whenever he put the notebook away he left a small trace. Last time he had placed a dead fly on the book before replacing the floorboards.

A terrible thought came to him. After the incident by the Wall perhaps Stasi agents had already been ordered to search the flat and the storeroom, and were on their way there, while he was travelling home. Maybe they were already sifting through his things, waiting to arrest him the minute he got home. He told himself not to be ridiculous, but he had a desperate urge to return home as quickly as possible and find out whether he was doomed or not.

28

He almost ran the few blocks east to the Spittelmarkt underground station. The platform was crowded with people going home from work. There must have been some technical problem further up the line, as there so often was, because he waited twenty minutes until a train arrived and he squeezed into the already crowded carriage. Catching a glimpse of himself, reflected in a window of the carriage, he thought ruefully that the security police would have no difficulty in tailing him if they wished. He stood out from the crowd around him – above average height, stocky build, a large pale face, dreamy and innocent blue eyes and a shock of dull brown hair that flopped over his forehead. Anyone who looked closely at him saw a certain cumbersome slowness in his body movements, as though he were constantly anxious that he might be out-manoeuvred by people who were smaller and nimbler than himself.

Until a month ago it would never have occurred to him to go and look at the Wall or even consider the possibility of escaping. It had been Uta's birthday and he had taken her to dinner at the Kosmos café on the Alexanderplatz. The place had been more crowded than usual that evening, and they had sat at a table in the middle of the room under a crude, star-shaped glass chandelier that gave out a pale, greenish light. Loudspeakers played soft, anodyne dance music while they waited for their order.

A group of eight sat at the next table, six foreigners with two Germans, the foreigners marked out by their clothes which were top quality. One of the men, a large "Viking" of a man with reddish hair and a thick beard, raised a glass and said "*Skål*" as the others followed suit. The grey, middle-aged German was probably Stasi. The woman he was with was younger with a thin severe face that occasionally broke in a tight-lipped smile when she spoke to the foreigners. It became clear to Hinnerk from the conversation that they were Danish and he strained to listen in. The sound and the cadence of their voices sounded oddly familiar. He had the frustrating sense that he should be able to understand them if he could just press the right button in his mind. The voices felt like a song that he remembered deep in his mind, something he could not quite remember but that would come back to him if he listened long enough. He was dazed, thrilled and troubled all at the same time.

He felt Uta's hand on his arm: "What is it, Hinnerk?" she said in her grating voice. "Is something the matter?" She was looking at him with an expression that combined concern and annoyance in equal measure.

He shook his head. "No, it's nothing, just a bit light-headed. Probably the beer on an empty stomach. Ah, good, here comes our food!"

When Hinnerk asked the waiter who the Danes were, the man lowered his voice and said: "Delegation from the Danish Communist Party. Fraternal visit." Hinnerk had a desperate urge to go and talk to them, but he held back. It would be a stupid thing to do and what would he say?

The Viking type was saying something in German to the escorts, and Hinnerk strained to hear the words, but they were drowned by Uta's chatter as she went on about how nice it was to have a visit from a "progressive" group within the enemy bloc. Her voice grated on his nerves until he could stand it no longer. Something snapped inside of him and he sprang to his feet.

"Hinnerk! Hinnerk … what on earth …?" Horrified, Uta watched him stride towards the Danes and hold out a hand towards their leader. The Viking turned, startled, then extended his hand to Hinnerk, but the two escorts were now on their feet, and grabbing him by the arms, steered him back to his table.

The grey, middle-aged German said sternly. "It's forbidden to speak to these people without our permission. Show me your identity card." Hinnerk gave him the document and he examined it for several seconds, as though memorising the name and address, before handing it back.

Uta's face was a picture of fear and agonized embarrassment. "So sorry, Comrade. He meant well, you see. We had just been talking about how nice it is to have a fraternal visit from …" But the man wasn't listening. He and the woman went quickly back to their charges.

Uta hissed: "You've wrecked our evening. We're leaving now."

Afterwards he tried to put the episode out of his mind, but it kept coming back to him in the days and nights that followed – especially the nights when he dreamed about Denmark, about an island and a farm and about a terrible black ship that came out of the darkness and carried him away over a raging sea, embroideries of his imagination fed by the few scraps of information he had been given about the brief period of his infancy before he had been brought to the Lebensborn home.

As he stood in the crowded underground train, his mind went back to his earliest tangible memories – the house in the Harz mountains, the smell of institutional food that always seemed to hang about the place, the games of hide and seek in the grounds with the other children, the big, blond nurses in their white uniforms – especially Fräulein Neumeyer, the one who had always taken special care of him, told him stories and held him in her arms when he cried. Then the day came when he had to say goodbye to her, tears rolling down his face as he was taken away by his "new father and mother", Otto and Waltraud Siebert, to their plain, red-brick house in the nearby town of Sangerhausen. Once, a year or two after the war, Fräulein Neumeyer visited the house to see if he was happy there and had gone away reassured. He never saw her again. Otto worked in the big copper mine that dominated the town, and his mother was a seamstress in a clothing factory. They were kind people who had never had children of their own and doted on their adopted son. As he grew up in his new home and came to love his adoptive parents, he pushed the knowledge of his early self into a dim corner of his mind and rarely even thought about it. As Hinnerk Siebert, for better or for worse his life was here in the country that had adopted him.

After the episode in the restaurant something had changed for him. If pressed to explain it he could not have done so, except to say that these confident Danes had awoken a sense of new possibilities within him. Whereas previously he had gone his modest way uncomplainingly, trying to make the most of his job and his marriage, thankful for the things he had – the flat, the mild excitement of living in the capital and the solace of his books and his secret writing – now he was increasingly struck by the anonymity of life in the city, a sense of rootlessness, of being no-one from nowhere. The child in him that was Henrik had re-awoken along with an insatiable desire to rediscover his lost origins. He was warmed by a new sense that there was somewhere he might actually belong.

He stepped off the train at the Senefelder Platz and set off at a run down the street towards his home. He prayed the

Stasi wouldn't be tearing the place apart when he reached home. With any luck Uta would not be home yet either. They lived in a small flat in an old building in one of the streets that had managed to survive the war. They had a living-room, bedroom, bathroom and tiny kitchen. Very basic, but they were lucky to have their own place. Somehow Uta had managed it through her Party connections.

He looked up at the windows of their flat and saw with relief that there were no lights on. He let himself into the dimly lit entrance hallway of the building and walked up the stone stairway. So far, so good. As he passed a door on the first landing, it opened a crack and for an instant he saw Frau Fischer's thin, pallid face and watery eyes peering out, before the door closed again silently. Frau Fischer and her husband looked after the building and she could recognise every passing footstep. Did she know something that he didn't? Had she seen agents climbing the stairs?

He passed the second floor where he lived and raced breathlessly up five more flights to the attic. Pushing open a bare wooden door, he came to a corridor lined by storerooms partitioned with walls of flimsy wooden lattice. Unlocking a padlock, he entered his storeroom, pushed aside a cardboard storage box and, using a penknife, prised up a floorboard with trembling fingers. He sighed with relief. In the gap lay a small exercise book in a brown cover. He was about to reach down for it when his heart started pounding loudly in his chest and he felt a sudden wave of giddiness wash over him. The fly was gone. Could a spider have taken it or eaten it? Did they do that kind of thing? Or would it only eat a fly that it had caught in its web? Had somebody discovered the notebook, read it and then replaced it, without noticing the fly. Could it have been Uta? If it was her, he couldn't imagine her missing an opportunity to tell him what she thought of him. It must have been somebody else. But that would definitely mean that he was under active observation. In a state of controlled panic he replaced the book and the floorboard and left the attic.

When he walked through the front door Uta was in the small kitchen putting a kettle on the gas. He wondered whether to tell her about the incident by the Wall, then decided not to. If anything came of it she would find out soon enough. She gave him a light kiss and turned towards the kitchen cupboard. "Let's have a cup of coffee, shall we?" She took out cups and saucers, a tin of condensed milk, sugar and one of the small blue and white paper sachets of instant coffee, which normally cost a couple of hours' wages, but which she somehow got hold of at cut price.

He stood awkwardly in the tiny kitchen, feeling large and clumsy, squeezed between the door and the kitchen counter, watching her, deft and petite, as she spooned a careful measure into each cup and then poured out the hot water. Since they had married three years earlier she had become more brisk and businesslike, her blond hair cut short, page-boy-like, her face devoid of make-up. But her movements still had the tightly coiled eroticism that he had always found so enticing.

Sometimes he wondered what it was that had attracted her to him. Maybe something in her restless, brittle nature had needed the solid reassurance of his slow and dreamy gentleness. They had met in Halle at the college where he was training to be a plumber and she was studying bookkeeping. At her initiative they had become lovers, then after graduation they had married. By that time she had joined the Party, and maybe she had thought it politically appropriate to be married to someone with a good working-class profession. She only found out later that he had really wanted to go to university to study literature, but had been unable to do so for want of a school graduation certificate. Mysteriously, he had been refused permission to take the graduation exam. He had assumed that the circumstances of his birth and early childhood were to blame. A "Lebensborn boy" with a Danish mother would always have a black mark against him in a system that clung to the puritanical morals of a bourgeoisie which it claimed to have eradicated. And so, he had spent two years learning how to lay pipes, weld joints and repair gas leaks. In a country which supposedly glorified the working class, it was strange that his training was still considered inferior to a university education.

She handed him a cup and he took a sip, searching in his mind for some way to find out if it was she who had found the notebook.

"How long have you been home?" he asked.

"Oh, about an hour. I got off work early."

"So you've had *'one hour of freedom'*." He said it to test her reaction, mouthing the title of his story with slow emphasis, as if placing it within quotation marks. He watched her closely, but her face betrayed nothing. Perhaps he was being paranoid. There had to be another explanation for the missing fly? He felt guilty about his suspicions. Uta was a good wife, he told himself. He was grateful for the extra comforts that she had obtained for them both. Tonight he would make a special effort to be nice to her. He took another sip of the coffee and said:

"I'm thinking of going to Sangerhausen at the weekend. Would you like to come? I'm sure Mother and Father would love to see you." But even as he said it he hoped that she would say no. He wanted to go alone for a quite specific reason.

She shook her head. "I can't. There's a district Party meeting I have to go to." She raised her cup, about to drink, then put it down again. "Why do you want to go? You saw them two weeks ago."

"I know, but there are th-things …" Growing nervous, he found his stammer returning. "There are th-things that I would like to discuss with them that we didn't manage to talk about last time."

She shrugged. "Well, you'll have to go by train. I need the car, I'm afraid."

"That's all right," he said, relieved that she hadn't asked him more questions.

They carried their coffee cups into the living room, which had once been twice the size before the flat was divided up. All that remained of the 19th century period details were a few fragments of plaster frieze. The room was furnished in the safe, nondescript style typical of the GDR – beige wallpaper with a semi-abstract pattern of stars and criss-crossing lines, bright red curtains, armchairs, a sofa upholstered in imitation black leather and a coffee table. "I was thinking about our summer holiday," said Uta as they sat down. "We can afford to go abroad this time – say to Lake Balaton in Hungary or maybe to the Black Sea coast. Look, here's an article in *Neues Deutschland* about Bulgaria."

Hinnerk took the paper that she pushed across the table, but he wasn't really listening. He was thinking of another sea and another coast.

"Sometimes," he said, "I wish we weren't so cut off here

in the GDR." Then, as soon as he had said it, he wished he hadn't.

Uta put her cup down and stared at him with a shocked expression. "Cut off? What do you mean when we've all the socialist brother-countries to go to? Where would you want to go, for heaven's sake?"

Suddenly he wanted to stop being evasive with her, to put everything out on the table. "Well, Denmark, for instance."

She stared at him for a moment then spat out the word "Denmark!" with furious indignation. "Are you stark, raving mad? I'm amazed you've got the gall to mention Demark after you disgraced me at the Kosmos by running up to those Danes. I never want to hear another word about your damned Danish origins. Do you hear?"

He raised conciliatory hands. Her fits of anger soon passed, unless he fed the fire by arguing. But this time her mood did not improve as quickly as he had hoped. Instead she covered her face with her hands, and, when she took them away, said in a tone of exasperation: "When will you realise you'll never get back those years? You may as well forget them – and your mother. She abandoned you didn't she? What could you possibly gain by finding her? It would just drag up all the old suffering for both of you."

He sighed and answered her anyway even though he risked making her really angry. "You d-don't understand. You had a normal childhood. You have a place where you belong …"

"And so do you," she snapped. "You belong here in the present, with me. You love me, don't you?"

"Yes," he said quietly "of course I do, but …"

"Well then, what do you think it's going to mean for me if

you pursue this fool's errand? It would seriously compromise me with the Party. They might even throw me out. And then I would probably lose my job as well. It would screw up everything for both of us."

"Uta," he said, trying to sound calm, "aren't you exaggerating a bit? I just want to find out who I am, where I come from, who my real mother is."

She stood up, face flushed, and stamped her foot. "Yes, and probably the next thing I'll hear is that you've buggered off to Denmark, leaving me to face the music!" She turned and disappeared into the bedroom, slamming the door behind her. A moment later he heard the sound of her sobs.

Leave her alone, he told himself. But as always a deep anxiety about her anger drove him to make up as soon as possible. As he entered the bedroom, she was gazing out of the window, staring fixedly at the drab flats opposite. "Uta," he said "don't be upset ..." He wanted to reassure her, but couldn't find the words. He was on the point of saying he would forget about Denmark and his mother when she turned towards him, tears rolling down her anguished face.

"Who *wouldn't* be upset when you're about to risk everything we've worked for – this home, our jobs, our whole life together." Her voice became quieter and more plaintive, as it often did when he opposed her. "Oh, Hinnerk ... how could you even think of doing such a thing?"

The sight of her flushed and tearful face always aroused him. Today was no different, though he doubted that she was as upset as she wanted him to believe. She knew she could get round him and was prepared to let him make love to her to remind him what he would soon be missing if he continued to cross her. Hinnerk stroked her hair gently and then bent down and kissed her, reaching to unbutton her blouse, feeling her arms encircling him. Yes, he thought – suddenly angered by her dishonesty – two can play at deceit.

"I promise I'll forget about Denmark," he told her haltingly, between kisses, and felt her body pressing closer to his.

29

Arnold Borup and three other men played off the 18th tee of the Grevelund Golf Club and set off down the fairway, Borup walking ahead of the others, a big, solid man, dressed in a yellow sweater, pale grey trousers and flashy golf shoes with white uppers. The golf course was laid out along the coast, protected on one side by a stretch of rocky shore and on the other by a row of expensive houses set in large grounds with high fences around them. The immaculate greens and fairways were set in a serene landscape of lakes and woods, with intermittent picture-postcard views of the sea. This was one of the most exclusive golf clubs in the country, with a long waiting list and a commensurately high membership fee. It was the perfect club for a man like Arnold Borup.

His drive had landed perfectly in the middle of the fairway with a clear line to the hole. Taking out an iron, he swung powerfully at the ball, landing it crisply on the green and punched the air with satisfaction. On the green he sank a long putt and held up his club in a victorious gesture. One of the other players said: "Home and dry, Arnie!"

Borup laughed. "Who said anything about dry? I'm buying drinks at the 19th hole."

Half an hour later they were sitting in the spacious bar of

the club in comfortable leather armchairs by a picture window overlooking the course. They had just finished the first round of beer when a waiter came up to the table and said: "Excuse me, Mr Borup. Urgent message for you."

Borup sighed. "Even at the golf club! When will they ever learn to leave me alone?" He opened the envelope and his face blanched. Calling back the waiter, he said in a hard voice: "Who left this message?"

The waiter went off to enquire and moments later came back and said: "We don't know, Mr. Borup. It was left at reception. Nobody remembers who brought it."

"Is there a problem, Arnie?" one of the men asked.

Borup slipped the message into an inside pocket and managed a forced laugh. "No, nothing that I can't deal with when I get back to the office."

The following afternoon Borup was sitting at his desk in the Integrity Party's new premises in Copenhagen. The décor in his office was expensively minimalist: tubular steel furniture with black leather upholstery, parquet floor, one wall almost filled by a painting consisting of a white canvas with a red splash in the middle. A glass wall opposite looked out over the harbour. Borup liked to be interviewed seated at his vast leather-topped desk with the imposing view behind him. Today he was priming himself for a filmed interview for television, so when the phone rang he assumed that the interviewer had arrived. It wasn't a voice he recognised and it issued a threat.

"You have until the day after tomorrow, Wednesday, to announce your resignation from the leadership of the Integrity Party. Otherwise we will release the Gestapo report proving that you ordered the killing of Henning Kraal."

Borup had turned pale, but he tried to keep his voice

even. "Blackmail won't work with me."

"Wednesday, Mr Borup," said the voice, and the line went dead.

Borup buzzed his secretary in the outer office. "Greta, please get me the press officer." A moment later he said: "Ah, Bernd, that old libel's cropped up again. We've got to stifle it. I need to discuss it with you when I've finished the TV interview."

30

Coming down the stairs on his way to work, Hinnerk saw Frau Fischer's door open just wide enough and long enough for him to catch a glimpse of a pale eye peering through the crack. Up to now he had thought of Frau Fischer as a sad old busybody, but now he wondered whether she was the Stasi's eyes and ears in the building. The door closed again quietly, and he went on, the sound of his feet echoing on the bare stone steps, past the first-floor landing where the rickety banisters had fallen out and been replaced by crude wooden boards, hurriedly nailed into place in one of those temporary repairs that had a habit of becoming permanent.

At the bottom of the stairs he nearly stumbled on one of the loose floor tiles as he pushed open the front door with its dirty, cracked pane of glass. Outside in the street it was raining lightly. If it had been a fine morning he might have walked to work, but instead he turned up his jacket collar and set off for the metro. After a few paces he sensed that he was being observed. He turned and saw that there was no-one behind him except for two children on their way to school. A hundred yards ahead of him, two Trabant cars were drawn up at the kerb, and beyond them was a grey van with the name "Star Bakery Combine, People's Own Enterprise" painted on the back.

He walked on towards the intersection where a viaduct of iron girders carried an overhead stretch of the metro. A train rattled along the tracks, heading south, and he felt depressed at the thought that, if it weren't for the wall, he could have taken the line to Kreuzberg, Schoeneberg and other places in West Berlin, places that were so close and yet might just as well be on another planet. Railways always made him think of places far away. And "far away" was where he came from. When he saw his adoptive parents in Sangerhausen at the weekend he would ask them to tell him more about his childhood. He might even visit the Lebensborn home and find out whether anyone remembered Astrid Neumeyer, his nurse. It was a wildly dangerous thought, but it cheered him as he walked on through the rain.

As he came alongside the baker's van he wondered idly what it was doing. There were no bakeries in the street. He was stunned when three stocky men got out of the vehicle and stopped him. Before he realised what was happening, his arms were forced roughly behind his back. He heard the click of handcuffs and felt the steel bite into his wrists. They shoved him into a small, cramped cage in the back of the van and padlocked it, then slammed the van doors shut, leaving him in darkness.

He couldn't move in the tight space. The handcuffs hurt his wrists and he was kneeling on the floor of the cage. The space was too tight for him to shift his position to a more balanced one. As the van moved off he lost his balance and banged his head against the side of the cage. He could feel panic rising along with the bile in his throat. He hated dark, confined spaces and this replicated his worst recurring nightmare – fed by his deep fear. His adoptive parents had believed it stemmed from his early childhood. The only difference was that in his nightmare he was stationary. He wasn't sure if that was really better or worse. What did the Stasi want with him that would warrant them picking him up off the street? It had to be the Stasi. He had heard stories of people being picked up and simply disappearing, with a bullet in the neck and a nameless grave in a remote wood. Was this about his visit to the Wall or the situation in the restaurant? Or was it because Uta had found his story?

He had felt the van do a U-turn as it moved off, so he knew it must be travelling east. That could mean that they were heading for the Stasi headquarters in Lichtenberg. On the other hand they might be taking him directly to Hohenschoenhausen, the infamous Stasi prison with its rubber-lined cells where you could be locked up in total darkness until you went mad.

He could feel his arms growing numb from the cramped position and the tight handcuffs. How long had they been travelling? Surely longer than it would take to get to Lichtenberg or – God forbid – Hohenschoenhausen. Maybe they were taking a long detour to confuse and disorient him. They were still in Berlin, to judge by the sound of the street traffic.

Abruptly the van slowed down and swung to the left and the street sounds became muted. The engine was turned off, and a moment later the van door was flung open. One of the men unlocked the cage, dragged him out of the van and removed his handcuffs. He was in a garage.

"Come this way!" one of the men barked at him, opening a heavy steel door in the garage wall, while the other two propelled him forward by the elbows. He had to duck slightly as he went through the doorway into a dimly lit corridor. The air felt stale and heavy, as though compressed by the rough grey concrete walls and ceiling. They hurried him to an elevator, which rose several stories and opened on to a brightly lit corridor, with brown linoleum on the floor. The man leading the way turned for a moment, and Hinnerk saw a heavy-featured face with the grave, impassive expression of an undertaker at a funeral. The man stopped in front of one of the doors, opened it and waved Hinnerk in, telling him to wait there.

The room was small and windowless, with just a pine table and two metal chairs gracing it. Hinnerk sat down on one of the chairs and waited. On the wall opposite him were three photographs: one of Leonid Brezhnev, one of Walter Ulbricht and one of Felix Dzerzhinsky, founder of the Soviet secret police, the Checka, and role model for security forces throughout the eastern bloc. With his thin, bony face, sharp nose and pointed goatee, he could have played the part of Don Quixote. His eyes were cold and ruthless.

Half an hour must have passed before the door opened again and a thin, pale-faced man entered the room and sat down at the table opposite Hinnerk. The "undertaker" slipped in behind him and stood by the door.

"I am Major Kobitz of the Ministry of State Security" said the pale man, speaking in twitchy jerks out of the corner of his mouth. "You are probably wondering why you have been brought here. Let me reassure you that we merely wanted to ask you some simple questions."

He opened a manila folder and began to leaf through it. They have a file on me, whispered a terrified voice in Hinnerk's head.

"Tell me," Kobitz began, "why an apparently able person like yourself is only working as a plumber."

Fighting his terror, Hinnerk said: "Well, I've never s-seen it that way." He tried to keep his voice calm, but his stammer had returned. "You see, I was b-brought up to believe that there's nothing better than a good working class profession."

The Major frowned slightly and drummed his fingers on the table. Careful, Hinnerk told himself. Don't be too clever. Men like this one did not care to have the paradoxes in the system pointed out to them.

Kobitz pursed his thin lips: "But there are different ways of serving the working class. The intellectuals have their place in the struggle as well, and I have the impression that you are an intellectual at heart. Am I right in thinking that you are fond of literature ... poetry?"

Hinnerk nodded, badly shaken. How could this Major Kobitz have known that, unless Uta had informed on him?

"And perhaps you yourself have ambitions to be a writer. Am I right?"

Hinnerk understood it all completely. It was Uta. Uta had found the hidden notebook and told Kobitz. And of course she had said nothing to him about it, because Kobitz had told her not to. What Kobitz said next took him completely by surprise

"Well," the Major went on, "maybe we can help you. But I need to know more about you. Do you trust the Party?"

Henrik wondered whether a trap was being laid for him. "W-well, I would certainly h-hope that I could trust it."

An expression of irritation returned to Kobitz's face. "I didn't ask if you hope. I said *do* you trust it – for example in political matters?"

Hinnerk decided to play naïve and innocent. "I'm sure I do, Major, though I d-don't understand much about politics."

The Major seemed satisfied. He leafed through the folder again and said: "I see from your records that you never took a high school graduation." His tone became friendlier. "We could arrange for you to take it and then go on to university. How would you like to study literature – at the Humboldt for example?"

So that was their game, Hinnerk thought – the stick and the carrot. First they terrorise me with the handcuffs and the prison van, then they offer me a place at the most prestigious university in the country. But what was it all for? Why were they going to so much trouble for a small fish like him? There had to be something behind it, something important that he didn't understand.

He said as if dazed with pleasure: "Well, Major, I d-don't know what to say. A place at the Humboldt ... it would be a dream come true. But how have I deserved such an honour?"

"Sometimes even the most efficient social systems can hold back deserving people." For the first time Kobitz smiled – a thin, fleeting smile. "Perhaps you underestimate yourself," he suggested. "The country needs people like you – good reliable men who have proved their working class values and can go on to serve as intellectuals, teachers, writers. I take it, then, that you would like to accept our offer?"

"Well ... yes ...most gratefully."

"Good," Kobitz said, "but there's just one little formality that we have to get out of the way ..." He searched in the folder again and found the place he was looking for. "My apologies for raising the delicate matter of your parenthood. I am only doing so for bureaucratic reasons. I understand that you were born during the war to a Danish mother and a German father – a soldier, that you were later sent to a Lebensborn home and that you were adopted at the end of the war by Mr. and Mrs. Siebert."

"Yes, that is correct."

"At this point in your life, do you harbour any thoughts of finding your natural mother, perhaps even returning to Denmark?"

Again the question came as a shock. Kobitz plainly suspected that he did think about going to Denmark and finding his real mother.

He gave a sad shrug. "Anyone in my position would wonder sometimes about his natural mother. But it was a long time ago. My mother abandoned me, and I have no memory of her. So, no…my life is here. The past is buried. I've no wish to dig it up again…in Denmark or anywhere."

Kobitz nodded and drew a document out of the folder. "That's what I hoped you would say. In that case I'm sure you will not object to signing this declaration. A formality, you understand, but the Humboldt will want to be sure that you intend to stay in the GDR. By signing this you will be declaring formally what you have in effect just told me: that you wish to sever all possible connections with your natural mother and renounce any intention of returning to the country of your birth."

Again Hinnerk urgently tried to fathom why they were doing this. There had to be something behind it. Surely they would not do the same with every Lebensborn child? They were desperate to keep him in the GDR for some reason. He had no option but to play along. Not doing so would bring unwanted consequences. Kobitz pushed the document across the table and handed him a ballpoint pen. He glanced quickly over the text and signed – thinking, as he did so, that if he were ever caught escaping, this document would be Exhibit A at his trial… if they bothered to give him one.

31

On Thursday Henrik looked in the morning paper that came to the house and scanned the other dailies on sale at the village shop. There was still nothing about Borup's resignation. From a telephone box in the village he called Petersen's photographic shop, as Kurt had instructed him to do, and said: "The order hasn't been delivered. It's time to make alternative arrangements." Petersen, he knew, had contacts in the press and would do his best to make sure that the Kraal story was all over the headlines the following day.

It wasn't in the newspapers on Friday or on Saturday, although they advertised the fact that Borup would be speaking at the party conference on Saturday morning. Apparently Borup had the press well in hand. Henrik began to think that it would take other measures to dislodge him.

Later in the day he joined the family when they gathered around the small television set in the kitchen to watch the early evening news, hoping for a report of the rally. The set was old and the reception bad, so Sven had to fiddle with the aerial to get a picture. A woman newsreader flickered into view, and behind her was a blown-up photograph of Borup in orator's pose. "We now go over to the Ringstedt Congress Hall in

Copenhagen," the woman announced "for a report on the dramatic events at today's the Integrity Party rally."

Everyone leaned forward eagerly as part of the conference was re-played. The camera swept over the packed auditorium and focused on Borup standing at the podium, flanked by members of the Party executive. On the wall behind him hung a huge banner that said "It's time for Integrity!"

"We are gathered here today," Borup was saying "at a crucial moment for our party. Integrity has heard the call of the Danish people. And the Danish people have heard the message of Integrity."

As the audience cheered, an elderly woman was seen making her way slowly up the central aisle towards the podium. She was white-haired, small and rather frail-looking, but she moved as though she were sure of her purpose. In one hand she was carrying a piece of printed matter. Those who noticed her must have assumed that she was a member of the conference staff taking some document to one of the people on the podium. She stopped directly in front of Borup, who was saying:

"Friends, on the eve of this election – possibly the most important in Denmark's history – we stand ready …" Seeing the woman looking up at him, he faltered then carried on "…ready to carry our commitments, ready to fulfil the mandate that you have given us."

"Murderer!" the woman shouted.

Borup stopped speaking and stared at her, his face suddenly pale.

"Murderer!" she shouted again. Then she held up a newspaper. "You murdered my husband, Henning Kraal! I always knew it, and now I've seen it in black and white." As a pair of stewards hurried towards her she waved the newspaper at Borup. "You gagged the Danish press, but you couldn't gag the German papers. It's all here in the *Hamburger Allgemeine Zeitung*. You *will* pay for what you did."

Two stewards, men in dark suits with the build of nightclub bouncers, grabbed hold of her and started to hustle her away down the aisle, as a murmur began to flow through the audience.

Borup raised a calming hand. "As I was saying ..." he went on, hoping to raise a laugh.

But now a middle-aged man near the front of the audience stood up, waving a copy of the same newspaper. "I've seen the article as well," he shouted. "We want an answer!"

Borup supporters tried to shout him down, but other voices joined in support. As the uproar increased, the film ended and the broadcast switched back to the woman newsreader, who asked a pundit for his opinion on what had happened. The pundit, an earnest-looking young man with black-rimmed glasses, reported that Borup had eventually resumed his speech. Applause at the end had been distinctly subdued, and it was clear that the incident had dampened the atmosphere. Of course, the pundit said, he couldn't comment on the accusations that the woman had made, but the party's supporters would obviously be asking for full clarification.

"Well, what was all that about?" Birthe said after Sven had switched off the television.

"Probably a storm in a teacup," Sven grunted. "The woman was obviously a lunatic."

But an article in the Sunday newspaper next morning took the incident seriously. So did several others papers that Henrik bought at the village shop. After the report in the German paper and Mrs. Kraal's accusation at the rally, the Danish press could no longer submit to pressure from Borup.

Over the next few days Borup made no public pronouncements. Henrik guessed that he must be agonizing over what to do. If he carried on as leader the party's chances in the election would be damaged. If he resigned it would look like an admission of guilt. If he sued for libel he might lose. Meanwhile the Deputy Leader, Leif Korsgaard, an ambitious man, was acting as spokesman for the party.

A week after the incident Henrik was talking to Kirsten in the yard when they heard the boy, Per, calling from the kitchen door. "Grandma says to come quickly. There's something on the television ... about Mr. Borup."

32

After Hinnerk had signed the paper, Kobitz became very cordial, shaking him warmly by the hand, congratulating him on his decision, phoning his firm to explain the situation and ordering a car – a black Volga limousine – to take him back to his place of work in a courtyard near the Alexanderplatz. Later, crouched in a manhole repairing a leaking gas pipe, he hardly noticed the discomfort and the sickly smell of the gas. His mind kept going back to the conversation with Kobitz and the suspicions that nagged at him about Uta. There had to be another explanation for how Kobitz had come to know about his interest in Denmark and his fondness for literature. Uta, for all her self-centredness and ambition, would surely not have gone so far as to spy on her own husband. And yet, once the suspicion had entered his mind, he found it hard to shake it off.

Later, while waiting for Uta to come home from work, he became ever more nervous. His earlier faith in her suddenly seemed proof of how easily she manipulated him. He realised that how she reacted to the news of Kobitz's offer would tell him whether she had been talking to the Stasi about him. When, at last, he heard her key in the door, he put away a book of Rilke's poems that he had been reading, eager to forestall one of her withering remarks about "bourgeois individualist rubbish", or "the poetic plumber". Then he hurriedly switched on the television, which was showing a programme about coal mining targets – a subject more to her taste.

"Well," she said, after giving him a quick kiss, "did you have a good day, today?"

Alert as he was to any sign of her deceit, at once it seemed strange that she should ask him in those words precisely. Usually she only described her own day and asked him nothing about his.

He followed her into the kitchen where she began to fill the kettle for coffee. "Since you asked, I did have a good day, actually." Watching her closely, he went on: "I've been offered a chance to go to the Humboldt University, to study literature."

"Really? That's marvellous," she said before switching on the kettle. Despite the enthusiasm of "marvellous", she didn't seem nearly surprised enough. He'd known that anything less than outright amazement would be suspicious, and had dreaded being faced with the truth. Now, there was no escaping the truth. Uta was his enemy.

"Tell me more?" she said, fiddling with her little sachets of coffee.

When he had finished telling her about his interview with Kobitz, she gushed about how privileged he was to be living in a country where such a thing was possible. "I don't imagine that any plumber in any imperialist country could ever be given such a glorious opportunity. When will you start?"

"October." He smiled as if delighted, knowing that he would either leave East Germany or die in the attempt.

"Well, I suppose that means you'll have a university post one of these days. 'Professor Doctor Siebert' ... And I'll be 'Frau Professor'." There was an undertone jealousy and resentment in her voice.

Looking at her, busy with the cups and the instant coffee, it hit him forcefully that she had no idea he had worked it all out. The thought gave him a thrilling feeling of power, but at the same time he knew he would have to be very careful. She would be watching his every move, reporting on the slightest sign of backsliding. He would also have to keep her happy – in bed and out – since resentment would sharpen her vigilance.

"We should celebrate," he said. "We could go to the Kosmos or maybe the Moskau."

"It's a strange thing," she said, gazing at him with more interest than he could remember in years, "but I'd have thought you'd be scared to go to an élite institution like the Humboldt."

He held her gaze without giving in to his usual tendency to lower his eyes. "I'm not so stupid that I don't know a good chance when I see it."

The next moment she put her arms around him and kissed him on the lips – another rare event. "I think we should celebrate your good fortune right now!"

"What about the coffee?" he asked

"Leave it. I don't really want any."

While she led the way towards the bedroom, Hinnerk tried to seem excited by this most untypical display of desire for him.

As they passed through the living room, the television screen was filled with the image of a miner, face blackened under his helmet, wielding a shuddering drill that sounded like several machine guns, while a histrionic commentator's voice proclaimed: "The Bottkus Mining Combine in Saxony are setting the pace with their amazing achievements." There was a burst of martial music and the voice went on: "In a single day they harvested the unbelievable total of 2,720 tons of coal – an unprecedented triumph thanks to the tireless dedication of these heroes of socialist production."

Hinnerk reached down and fiercely twisted the knob to silence the voice, but the same programme became faintly audible from the flat above. The sound even followed them into the bedroom. He could no longer hear the words, only the triumphant tone of voice, and the martial music. It made him want to scream with rage, tear the room apart, knock Uta down and tell her how much he despised everything she and her Party stood for. The moment he felt angry, confidence surged through him. Something else helped too – the fact that *he* was in the driving seat now, instead of her. He was the stronger one. He felt his penis stir and throb. As she tugged at his hand to get him to lie down on the bed beside her he knew it was going to be all right. He slid a hand up her skirt at once and tugged at her underwear in a way that he had felt too inhibited to attempt in the past. Ridiculous that he had often treated her like fine china.

"This isn't like you, Hinnerk," Uta giggled, wriggling out

of her clothes and helping him out of his. Her hand touched his erection and she gasped at the size of it.

From above came the voice again and a crescendo of brass and percussion. Fuck them too, he thought, as Uta's legs curled around him and he pushed into her. Hearing her cries he thrust faster and faster, eager for release, and yet feeling more detached than he could remember. There she was acting out the passive role while thinking that she had him in her power; when, in reality, he was one step ahead of her and drawing a powerful charge from that knowledge. With his hands under her buttocks, he drove into her with an ardour that brought them both to an overwhelming climax.

After they had dozed for a while, Uta turned over and smiled at him. "My God, Hinnerk, what happened then? You're not usually so forceful."

"I suppose it's down to getting a bit of appreciation for once."

"From me?"

"From the Humbolt. I can't believe I'm so lucky!" and he began to stroke her breasts absently. "Think of what I'll be able to do for us both when I graduate."

"Darling," she murmured, squeezing his hand. "Such a pity I have to go to that Party meeting. Otherwise we could stay at home and do this all weekend. Are you still going to Sangerhausen?"

"Yes, and that reminds me of something else I wanted to tell you. I'm going to join a cycling club."

She sat up and looked at him, genuinely surprised. "A cycling club! What gave you that idea?"

Still lying on his back, Hinnerk said casually: "Some of the lads at work are members of a local club, and I decided to join.

One of them has found me a second-hand racing bike that I'm going to buy. It'll help me keep fit while I'm studying." He almost laughed at the thought of himself in shorts, pedalling along in the midst of a throng of other cyclists, while crowds lining the roadside cheered them on, but he would have to be careful to give Uta the impression that he was deadly serious about it. "I plan to start getting in some long-distance practice on country roads while I am in Sangerhausen. I'll take the bike with me on the train."

Uta was looking at him with a teasing expression. "You're going to be pretty fit." She reached down and stroked his thighs. "These are going to get almost as hard as something else."

He could imagine her telling Major Kobitz the news, and him writing it up approvingly in a report for the file: "The subject has taken up cycling and joined a club, providing a further indication that he has a sound collective mentality and is committed to building his future in the GDR." Probably the news would be relayed to the Stasi's contacts in Sangerhausen, so that if some "unofficial collaborator" saw him setting off into the country on his bicycle they would confirm that the subject had been training for his club. In fact, he would be on the first leg of his journey to freedom.

33

Borup had been found drowned in the Isefjord near his country house on the north side of Zeeland. The body had been discovered late the previous evening. That was all the first television announcements had to say.

Birthe was shaking her head in disbelief. "I can't

understand it. Why would he do a thing like this? Just when everything was going so brilliantly for him and his party."

"How can you think it was suicide?" demanded Sven. "A man like Borup doesn't kill himself. I reckon it was murder. The communists must be behind it."

"Give me a break, Dad!" Kirsten said. "You seem to think the communists are behind everything."

By noon there was speculation about suicide and a sex scandal, which Borup's good looks made almost inevitable. But by lunch, fear of exposure for corruption was the front-runner. At last, by mid-afternoon certain hard facts had emerged. Borup had walked into the lake, fully dressed, and had not been dumped there. So the police were treating the death as suicide. The deputy leader of the Integrity Party, Leif Korsgaard, looked set to succeed Borup as leader, but Korsgaard was an unknown quantity, and the party's prospects in the elections were now very uncertain.

The late edition of the Copenhagen evening papers reached Lysholm at about six – a little later than usual – and Sven had to queue at the village shop and post office to make sure he got one. The mood around the supper table was sombre as the evening paper was passed round. "ARNOLD BORUP COMMITS SUICIDE," the front-page headline said "INTEGRITY PARTY IN DISARRAY". When the paper was passed to Henrik he saw a recent photograph of Borup addressing a party rally, and beside it a picture of his wife and two teenage daughters standing outside the family home looking tearful and bewildered.

"I don't believe that story about the assassination," Birthe said. "Borup was a man of integrity, just like his party."

The dog, sensing that something was wrong, was creeping

around the table, whining and looking for comfort. To ingratiate himself with the creature, Henrik slipped him a piece of cold meat. It pleased and disgusted Henrik, in almost equal measure, to imagine how Kobitz and his colleagues in the Normannenstrasse would be celebrating the news. Kurt, at their next meeting, would praise him patronisingly and probably tell him he would be getting a bonus for the job.

He realised Kirsten was speaking to him. "What do you make of it, Henrik?"

He continued to hold the paper, looking at the picture of Borup's family and hoping that he wouldn't have to be responsible for any more "collateral damage". He had carried out his assignment perfectly. Now hopefully he could be assigned to industrial espionage.

"Well," he said thoughtfully "there's obviously more to this than meets the eye. Borup must have had a lot of enemies. And he didn't seem the type to commit suicide." Then some reckless impulse made him add: "Maybe Sven is right about the communists being behind it." As he did so, he could hear Kurt's voice shouting: "Are you mad? What the hell are you saying?" As though to defy Kurt, he went on: "I know only too well what those people are capable of."

"Maybe you should tell that to the press, Henrik," Niels said. "If the voters thought that Borup was the victim of a communist conspiracy they might vote for Integrity out of solidarity. The party could end up doing better than ever in the coming election. We don't know much about Korsgaard, but he might turn out to be a very good leader."

"That's right," Kirsten agreed excitedly, "start a wave of sympathy for Integrity."

Henrik suddenly realised that, if he wanted, he could

make the whole Borup mission backfire and effectively sign his own death warrant.

He shook his head. "That wouldn't be a good move for me."

"Would there be any need for your name to be mentioned?" asked Kirsten softly. "You could just be quoted as 'a refugee from East Germany'. Does anyone here know any journalists?"

Alarmed by the direction the conversation was taking, Henrik said: "Anonymity wouldn't work. The police would want to interview me. Every journalist in western Europe would be after me. Money would be paid to the immigration people. The Stasi would find out who I was, and that would be the end of me." He emptied his coffee cup and stood up. "Excuse me, but I have to post a letter to catch the last collection." It was the only excuse he could think of on the spur of the moment for getting away from further questions.

The Borup family's grief kept nagging at him. All his conditioning told him that such casualties were inevitable in the just war that he was fighting, but did a noble end justify foul means? A dam burst inside of him, releasing a flood of doubt. Things that he had long suppressed came swirling to the surface: the people shot or blown up while trying to cross the death strip, those who had died under unexplained circumstances in the Stasi prisons, the young woman on the bus leaving East Berlin whose baby son had been taken away from her, and the countless other people crushed in the wheels of the system he served – the system that he was working to export to the whole world. He had begun to reject it. And the worst of it was that it was too late for him to turn back.

Another chilling thought struck him. Although he had

completed his mission successfully, it had made him more vulnerable. Would they keep him under strict surveillance? Would they be worried that he might make a mistake and betray himself? Now that he knew he wasn't Birthe's son he was watching for the unguarded moment when he might say something that would set off an inevitable chain reaction – like his comment about the communists. Kurt was already in Denmark. His Hamburg phone number was disconnected. Once or twice Henrik had thought he had caught a glimpse of Kurt in the trees by the house, but he was gone before Henrik could get a fix on him with his binoculars.

At the post box, he felt an idiot with nothing to post; and, after waiting a moment, turned back towards the house. Retracing his steps and approaching the white gateposts on either side of the Karlssens' driveway, he paused in the dappled shadows cast by overhanging trees. For a short time he had believed this house among the trees was his real home. Being here had given him back a part of what he had felt while staying with his adoptive uncle and aunt in Dobzin – a sense of something wholesome and enduring that had to do with the presence of intact nature and a life lived in harmony with the seasonal rhythms. Marx had spoken of the idiocy of rural life, but had he ever watched the flight of an eagle or the wild, dervish dance of the starlings at twilight? Had he ever even looked at a single tree and sensed the wonder of it? What was Marxism, with its weight of dry theory, in comparison with these vital realities?

By rights another person should be walking towards the house, feeling a glow of homecoming on seeing the red-tiled roof and the loving inscription over the doorway. Where was he now Henrik wondered, the man whom the boy in the photograph had grown up to be? In all probability, even if he were alive, he would never discover his true identity. Henrik had never expected to discover *his*, before the Stasi had deceived him into believing he was Birthe's son.

As he passed a thicket of bushes to the right of the road, he heard a faint a rustling sound. An image flashed through his mind of Kurt crouching in wait in the undergrowth with a high-powered rifle. But surely Kurt would not take the risk of shooting him down in broad daylight? That wouldn't be his style, would it? Yet something or somebody was moving there. His right hand slid instinctively inside his jacket towards where the gun holster would have been if he had been wearing it. But the gun, he remembered, was concealed in the car. With a thudding heart, he kept walking.

34

Watching Waltraud, the woman he called "mother", busy with the breakfast things in the parlour of the house in Sangerhausen, Hinnerk felt a pang of sadness. This house was the only place he had ever really been able to call home. At the breakfast table, surrounded by old, familiar things – the heavy, dark wood sideboard, the green porcelain stove, the pot plants on the window sill, the framed family photographs on the bookshelf – he felt a sense of inner comfort that he knew he would miss when he was "on the other side" – if he managed to get out alive.

Otto, his adoptive father, came into the room, a stocky man in his sixties with soft, kindly eyes and skin made grey from twenty years' work in the local copper refinery. Taking a seat at the table, he said: "Well Hinnerk, as I was up early I cleaned and oiled your bike for you and pumped up the tyres. Nice machine. Where are you going to head for?"

Hinnerk knew that, even if he succeeded in escaping, it was going to be very difficult to find his real mother. No one had even told him her name, and without it, the prospect of finding her was remote. But it was just possible the nurse from the Lebensborn home might remember not only his mother's name but also which part of Denmark she was from. He had no idea where the nurse was now living, but there was a chance that she might still be in living near the Lebensborn home.

"Thanks, Papa," he said, then added as casually as he could: "I've always wanted to take a look at that place where I lived before you and Mutti adopted me. Wasn't it called Lenzfeld?"

Otto sighed and looked down at the table. "Oh, Hinnerk, do you really want to go there? Isn't it better to let sleeping dogs lie?"

Waltraud, coming in with the coffee, interrupted him: "Now, Otto, Hinnerk's old enough to make up his own mind. Maybe it will do him good to visit Lenzfeld – help him come to terms with that part of his past."

"Exactly," agreed Hinnerk gratefully. "Of course I've always thought of you as my real parents, and nothing can alter that. It's just that, as Mutti says, I need to come to terms with my birth mother's decision to give me up. It might help if I could find and talk to that nurse – if she's still in the neighbourhood. You told me her name years ago, but I never wrote it down."

Otto was silent, looking even more uncomfortable, but Waltraud said: "Oh, what *was* she called? Niemeyer or Neumann ... no, Neumeyer, that was it. I'm afraid I can't remember her first name. Heaven knows where she's living now."

"Well, I can ask around. What was the nearest village called?"

"Selz-Krombach. The house was just outside the village – about two kilometres away. How could I forget the day we went there to collect you? The house was like a lovely old hunting lodge, surrounded by woods."

Otto nodded resignedly. "All right, Hinnerk, if you're set on going, I won't hold you back. It must be about thirty kilometres from here. You should be there by midday. I'll give you a map."

Waltraud stood up and patted Hinnerk on the shoulder. "Good, that's settled then. I'll make you a packed lunch."

*   *   *

Two hours later he was cycling through Selz-Krombach, a once pretty but now run-down place, huddled against a wooded hillside. There was a street of red-roofed, half-timbered houses with crumbling plasterwork, a little red-brick church that was boarded up, and a pub with the drab look of a people's own enterprise. He pedalled through the village and continued uphill for about three kilometres. Intent on looking out for Lenzfeld's gates, Hinnerk didn't notice the cyclist shadowing him.

Finally he found the remains of a double gate. The rotting wooden doors were propped against the gateposts, having fallen from their hinges. Weaving his way between pot-holes in a decaying driveway, heavily overhung by trees, he emerged after a couple of hundred paces in an open glade, and saw, ahead of him, the vestiges of a large house – foundations, part of a cellar, a terrace with a crumbling balustrade. Everything was overgrown, and a few birch trees had seeded themselves in the spaces that had once been rooms.

Resting his bicycle against a pile of bricks, he picked his way over the rubble, the remnants of the house touching off disconnected fragments of memory. Here was where the main door must have been, here the hallway and there, beyond the terrace, the garden where he would have played with the other children.

Behind him, the sound of footsteps on the rubble jerked him abruptly out of his reverie. He turned to see a tall man with a thick, black beard, wearing leather breeches, a green jacket and a green chasseur's felt hat. He was carrying a shot gun, which was levelled at Hinnerk.

"What are you doing here?" the man barked at him. "This is Forestry Department property."

Hinnerk began to panic at the thought of being arrested for trespassing. He would be questioned by the Stasi, and Major Kobitz would hear that he had been seen cycling near the border. Instead of being sent to the Humboldt he would probably be sent to a labour camp. He decided to stay as close to the truth as he could.

"I'm s-s-sorry," he said, his stammer returning. "I didn't realise it was private. I was looking for a place called Lenzfeld, a former children's home."

"This is Lenzfeld ... or was," the man said, still suspicious. "What did you want here?"

"I once lived here ... long ago, during the war. I was a Lebensborn child."

Now the forester relaxed a little and lowered his gun.

"Well, as you see, there isn't much of it left. After the war nobody wanted to look after it; eventually it was pulled down and the land was given to the Forestry Department. Why have you bothered coming back? You can't have happy memories of the place."

He took out some cigarettes, gave one to Hinnerk and took one for himself.

"Thanks," Hinnerk said, leaning forward towards the man's lighted match. "Actually I have very few memories of it. I was only four when I left. But I do remember there was a nurse who worked here, who took a liking to me and looked after me. I suppose it's crazy, but I was hoping she might still live somewhere in the vicinity."

"And what was this woman's name?" The man was looking at him with a puzzled frown.

"Neumeyer," replied Henrik. "I'm afraid I don't know her first name. You don't know anyone of that surname, do you?"

"My God!" the man gasped, as he squeezed Hinnerk's hand. "Are you in luck today! Not only do I know the woman you mean, but I can take you to her." He pressed his hand again. "I am Andreas Vogler. My elder brother Jürgen's wife is called Astrid, born Neumeyer. She used to work at Lenzfeld, and I think you are one of the children she talked about. You must be …?"

"Hinnerk, but she would have known me as Henrik."

"Henrik … yes, of course." Vogler clapped him on the shoulder and said. "She'll be overjoyed. We'll go there right away. Jürgen is also a forest warden, and their house is only a few minutes' walk from here." He pointed to a track leading into the woods. "You can push your bike."

They followed the winding track through the woods and

ten minutes later came to a solid, single-storey house with white stucco walls, generous, overhanging eaves, the front door opening on to a wooden verandah, where a big Alsatian dog was sitting. The dog stood up and came towards them, its tail wagging.

"Astrid!" the forester called out as they approached. "Astrid!"

The door opened and a tall, strongly built woman, with fair hair turning grey, stepped out on to the verandah, an expression of astonishment coming over her face as instinctive recognition dawned.

35

Another sound of movement in the bushes made Henrik stop again, and in that instant a stone flew through the air and struck his forehead. "Nazi swine!" a voice shouted, and from the bushes came one of the louts who had earlier tried to vandalise his car, a thick-set youth with small, pig-like eyes set in a pimply face. Hearing more footsteps behind him, he swung round and saw the other two – one of them a gangling giant with a face that was half jaw, the other one, small and ferrety, his thin-lipped mouth twisted into a malicious grin. Even as they approached he felt grateful that they looked like locals rather than Borup's friends or associates.

Henrik's martial arts training came to his aid. He ducked a blow from the tall one, seized his arm and tripped him to the ground. Then, in one continuous movement, he landed a kick in the crotch of the pimply youth and a punch in the stomach of the thin one. Both of them reeled back, moaning with pain, but then the tall one was on him again from behind, one arm round his neck in a choking grip. Henrik bent forward and butted his opponent in the stomach, winding him just long enough to break free, but as he ran towards the house he tripped and fell. All three were on him at once, kicking at his body with their heavy boots. Lying doubled up with pain, trying to shield his head with his arms, he heard Kirsten's voice as he had never heard it before – a long scream of outrage and loathing. From the corner of his eye, he saw that she had picked up a fallen branch from the side of the road. Now she swung it at the tall one, catching him on the side of the head. He staggered back moaning and clutching his skull.

The other two stood their ground for an instant, and the thin one sneered: "Whore! Nazi fucker! Get out of the village – you and your whole family! Get back to the Vaterland. And take him with you!"

Kirsten rushed at him, swinging the branch furiously. "Scum!" she screamed. "Get out of here before I call the police!" She kept thrusting the branch at him until finally he ran off down the road and a moment later the other two followed him, the tall one holding a hand to his head as he ran unsteadily away.

When they were gone Kirsten knelt down and cradled Henrik's head in one arm, while her other hand stroked his face. One eye was turning black, and there was a gash in his forehead where the stone had hit him. "Poor Henrik. Those bastards! Are you badly hurt?"

He propped himself up on an elbow, wincing. "I'll be all right."

She bent over and kissed his wounded forehead and his cheek, then for an instant her lips met his. He sat up and for several seconds held her encircled in his arms. Her warmth and softness and closeness enveloped him, so that for a moment he could hardly breathe. This was the absolute limit of the permissible (perhaps beyond it) and he was in anguish. Never again must he let himself be this close to her physically or he would lose all control. He started to speak, but his throat was dry and the words came out in a hoarse croak. "Kirsten ... Kirsten ... remind me never to get on the wrong side of you!"

She looked uneasy for a moment, then quickly recovered herself. "We must get you back to the house. Can you stand?"

He picked himself up, feeling the bruises in his legs and back. "Yes, I'll be fine."

She took his arm - how reluctantly he had no idea - and very slowly they made their way to the house.

36

Astrid reached across the table and put her hand on Hinnerk's. They were sitting in the homely wood-panelled living room of her house, warmed by a wood-burning stove.

"I recognised you straight away, even though it's twenty years since I saw you as a little boy – your eyes were unhappy then, and still are, poor man; but you stood so firmly, the way you do today. It broke my heart."

Sitting there with Astrid and her husband and brother-in-law, Jürgen and Andreas, in the wood-scented room with the stags' antlers on the walls and the cupboards and furniture painted with rustic floral patterns, Hinnerk felt himself relaxing, warming to these kindly country people. Jürgen, the husband, was a big man like his brother, but clean-shaven with sharp, rugged features and very light blue eyes, probably in his mid-forties like Astrid. Somehow Hinnerk had the impression that they had no children.

Astrid had served venison stew and dumplings for lunch, and now they sat at the corner table, sipping a home-made quince brandy. Astrid talked of her memories of Hinnerk as a child and how ill he had been with bronchitis when he arrived at the Lebensborn home and how she had nursed him through it. And she spoke of the letter she had written to his mother after the war to tell her about the kind couple who had adopted him. When she told him his mother's and his father's names it felt to him like a re-birth – joyful but full of pain as well – pain at the thought of how his mother had rejected him and of how he had been denied this knowledge for so long. Part of him felt cheated of his whole childhood and youth. And yet he still longed desperately to find his mother.

"Can you remember where my mother lived?" he asked Astrid.

"Oh dear, it was such a long time ago. But it was on an island off the east coast of Denmark. Let's see if I can find it on the map." She went to a bookshelf and came back with an old atlas, then flipped over the pages until she found Denmark. "It was somewhere here." She pointed to the straggle of islands facing the Baltic coast of the country. "I think it began with 'L'. Let's see. Yes, this must be it – Lysholm. And this was the town, Norvik. Sorry, I can't remember the exact address."

Looking at the spot she was pointing at, Hinnerk felt a deep throb of excitement. He now had a precise goal if he should ever make it to the West. And how could he allow himself to fail after the years of disappointment, of incompleteness? Eyes still fixed on the atlas, he knew that only death would stop him reaching this place and this person who could unlock his past and make his future possible. Seeing the look of concern on Astrid's face, he wondered how frank he should be about his plans to escape.

Astrid put the atlas away, then returning to the table put her hand on Hinnerk's shoulder. "Well Hinnerk, now that we've made contact again after all these years, I hope we'll see more of you."

"I hope so too," he said, "but that rather depends on where I'm going to be living."

The sudden silence in the room made him realise that he had nearly said too much. Instinctively he knew he could trust Asrid, but Andreas and Jürgen, as foresters, were officials of the state. If they knew about his plans they would either have to betray him or make themselves guilty of treason.

"Y-you see," he went on quickly, his stammer returning. "I have b-been offered a place at the Humboldt University ... to study literature. Eventually I hope to become a professor, and that means I could be posted to any university in the country."

He realised he had not sounded very convincing. The GDR was a tiny country. Wherever he was going to be living, it wouldn't be more than a few hours' journey from the Harz.

"Well that's exciting, Hinnerk," Astrid said a little hesitantly. "I'm sure you'll be an inspiring professor one day."

Jürgen refilled the glasses with the home-made brandy, and they talked of other things – of wild life, of game hunting, of the air pollution that was killing many of the trees, of how it was become increasingly hard to meet the government-imposed timber quotas.

In the early afternoon Jürgen stood up and clapped his brother on the shoulder. "Come, Andreas, let's fetch our guns and see if we can get a rabbit or two for the evening meal. I'm sure Astrid and Hinnerk have a lot to talk about ."

When they were alone, Astrid laid a hand on Hinnerk's arm and said quietly: "There's something on your mind. What is it?"

Then he told her everything. Suddenly having someone to confide in made him blurt it all out in a gush – his dreary job, his miserable marriage to Uta, her treachery, the episode with the Danes, Kobitz's stick-and-carrot treatment, and his resolve to leave the GDR.

When he had finished he said: "I'm sorry, Astrid. I shouldn't have told you all this. I'm already a criminal in the eyes of the state for merely wanting to leave the country. Now I've made you a party to my crime."

She kept her hand on his arm and gave it a squeeze. "I'm glad you told me. Do you have a plan?"

He shook his head. "Nothing definite, but I know the border runs through the Harz. I thought there might be some weak spot, perhaps where a stream crosses it, where I could slip through."

The sound of footsteps on the threshold made them turn. Andreas and Jürgen had re-entered the house, guns tucked under their arms, angry expressions on their faces. "There's a rainstorm brewing up," Jürgen said. "Now what the hell's going on? We heard what you just said, Hinnerk."

"Fool!" Andreas shouted. "Do you want to get us all arrested? Is this the way you repay our hospitality?"

"Calm down, Andreas," Astrid pleaded.

"No, I won't calm down. This is insane. The best thing we can do is forget what Hinnerk said and never mention it again."

"It's hopeless, Hinnerk," Jürgen grunted. "You'll never

succeed, and you'll endanger us all."

"Please, Jürgen ..." Astrid began, but Hinnerk interrupted her.

"They're right. It was irresponsible of me to talk about my plans. I'll leave right away. I should be getting back to Sangerhausen anyway."

"Oh, Hinnerk ..." Astrid was almost in tears. "Do come back, won't you?"

"I will, if I am allowed to." He kissed her on both cheeks, then turned to the two men. "Sorry, it was foolish of me." They shook hands and a moment later he had slung on his rucksack and was gone, mounting his bicycle and setting off into the rain.

He cycled back up the road with an acute sense of guilt and fear – guilt at having compromised Astrid and her husband and brother-in-law with his escape plans, and fear that the two men might already have decided to report him. The mere intention to flee the GDR could get him several years hard labour, especially with the other black marks against him, like the incident with the Danes, his straying too near the Wall, and above all his story *One Hour of Freedom*, which he was sure they had discovered.

There came the sound of a vehicle behind him. Had Andreas and Jürgen already alerted the local police or did they plan to make a citizens' arrest? Desperately he looked for a possible hiding-place, but there were no trees or bushes for several metres on either side of the road. He would be spotted immediately. But a stone's throw ahead, he saw a narrow dirt track leading off into the forest. He glanced back. The vehicle was hidden by a bend in the road. With any luck the driver had not yet seen him. He turned into the track, zigzagging between potholes and fallen branches. Abruptly the heavy silence of the wood was broken by something moving in the trees to his right. The undergrowth burst open and a large stag leapt across his path, causing him to brake violently, lose balance and fall. The stag paused, tossed its antlers at him and disappeared into the forest on the other side.

As he picked himself up and started to climb back on to the bicycle he heard a shout from the direction of the road. Someone was calling his name. The vehicle, an open truck, had pulled up and the driver had climbed out and was walking towards him, waving. It was Jürgen.

"Glad I caught up with you, Hinnerk," he said in a friendly tone as he came up. "Why in heaven's name did you take this path? Never mind, come back to the house. You can sling your bike in the rear of the truck." Relieved and puzzled, Hinnerk obeyed.

"We've been talking," Jürgen said as they drove back. "Maybe we can tell you a few things that will help you."

"God knows why we're doing this," Andreas said when they were all seated around the table again. "It would have been our duty to turn you in, but Astrid has told us a bit more about your circumstances and we've taken pity on you, so we'll do what we can. We hate the regime as well. No true forester could ever be a communist."

Jürgen nodded gravely. "We foresters live among trees, the noblest creations in the plant kingdom. But to the Party men they are just lifeless things to be cut down and made into hideous furniture in some people's own enterprise. They wouldn't know a noble thing from a pile of shit."

"First of all," Andreas said "You won't find any place in the Harz where you could break through the border. It's absolutely impenetrable – watchtowers, mines, dogs, automatic shooting devices, patrols everywhere … you name it. And don't forget there's a no-go zone five kilometres wide all along this side of the frontier, so you probably wouldn't even get near the border itself."

"It's that bad?" Hinnerk felt crushed. "I suppose I'll have to find some other way."

"The ways are becoming fewer, Hinnerk," Jürgen said. "Unless you have someone on the other side to help you it's going to be very difficult … and dangerous."

His brother stroked his dark beard silently for a moment, then said: "There's one way that he might just stand an outside chance of making it – if he's a good swimmer."

"Ah, you mean across the Elbe," Jürgen put in. "Well, are you a good swimmer, Hinnerk?"

Hinnerk shrugged. "Not bad, I suppose. I used to compete in swimming races at school."

Andreas said doubtfully: "The Elbe isn't a swimming pool. There are strong currents. But if you're willing to take the risk … then the question would be where to make the attempt."

Astrid said nothing and merely looked at Hinnerk, tears welling, while her husband fetched a map of the GDR, which he spread out on the table.

"There's only one place." He ran his finger along the line of the Elbe. "Along this stretch the river forms the border. Anyone swimming across here would land in the West German state of Lower Saxony. Normally it would be impossible even to reach the river because of the no-go zone. But … you see this road?" He pointed to a red line on the map. "Here it runs through the no-go zone within about three hundred metres of the river. If you could get to this point on the road you might just make the river without being caught. But even over such a short stretch there are going to be many hazards – patrols, mines, trip-wires, Alsatian dogs. The dogs are perhaps the greatest danger, because they'll be able to sniff you from a distance, and they're ferocious beasts. I've seen them being trained on dummies. Some of them go around with the guards on their rounds. Others are tethered on leads of up to a hundred metres long and trained to patrol up and down just in front of the death strip. You'll just have to hope that if one of them sniffs you, you'll be able to make it to the river before he gets his teeth into you."

Astrid raised her hands to her face.

Hinnerk leaned over the table, studying the map. "So if I could cycle to that point ..."

Jürgen shook his head. "Not a good idea. Even if they let you into the no-gone zone you would be suspect and they would be likely to keep you under surveillance the whole way. You would have to leave your bicycle at the edge of the zone and walk from there, but then you would have much further to go to reach the river – more like two or three kilometres – and that would increase the risk of your being spotted or running into a trap. No, the best thing would be for someone to drive you into the zone."

"Someone with a good reason for driving along that bit of road," explained Andreas, "such as a forester with a permit to inspect forested areas inside the zone."

There was a moment's silence in the room, broken only by the ticking of an old cuckoo clock on the wall. Jürgen was looking at his brother with a fearful expression. "What are you saying?"

"That I'll do it." Andreas held up a hand to ward off any

protest. "I'm not married like you, Jürgen. I have very little to lose. And if I can strike a blow by helping Hinnerk, I'll do it."

Astrid stood up sobbing, and left the room. Jürgen went after her, and a few moments later she returned. "I'm sorry," she said. "I just hate the thought of Hinnerk and Andreas taking such a risk. And even if he survives and gets across we may never see Hinnerk again." She wiped away a tear. "But I mustn't be selfish. I know you want to find your mother, Hinnerk, and that's only right. Tell him what you suggest, Andreas."

Andreas looked searchingly at Hinnerk and asked: "Does anyone know you want to escape except the people in this room?"

"Before I left Sangerhausen I t-t-told my parents I wanted to visit Lenzfeld b-but nothing about escaping to the West." Under pressure, Hinnerk' stammer had returned. He feared that Andreas would think it was because he was hiding something.

Jürgen said gently: "Might anyone else know you're cycling in the Harz?"

"My wife, Uta. B-b-ut she has no idea why. I said I was joining a club so I could improve my f-f-fitness. She believes I'm thrilled about the Humboldt, so it'll never occur to her that I may be planning an escape."

Andreas shook his head sadly." If she's told her party friends you're in the Harz, they'll be sure to think you're trying to trace your blood family. I expect you were followed here."

As Hinnerk hung his head, Jürgen patted him on the back. "We'll just have to act fast. Are we all agreed?"

Looking at their solemn faces as each one assented, Hinnerk realised what he was asking of them.

"You d-d-don't have to help me. P-p-please don't feel you must."

"Relax, Hinnerk. We know that."

For the next two hours they discussed the plan, which was set for the following Saturday. To explain his absence, he would have to tell Uta that he was paying another visit to Sangerhausen. Inevitably, she would be furious with him for returning there so soon after his last visit, but he would only tell her at the last moment to avoid three or four days of mounting anger. In fact he would not be going back to his parents, whose house might be watched, but instead would board a west-bound train, taking his bicycle with him, and alight at Ludwigslust, located on the main road that passed through the no-go zone some sixty kilometres further on. From there he was to cycle westwards as far as the village of Pritzheim.

"As you go through the village," Andreas told him "you'll pass a red brick church, then a crossroads. Half a kilometre beyond the crossroads on the right you'll see a sign marked "Forestry Precinct" and a track leading off into the woods. Go a hundred metres along it until you come to a large boulder to the side of the track. Wait for me there."

The rendezvous was arranged for eight o'clock in the evening. They would wait until darkness fell and drive to the no-go zone. Andreas would be driving the open truck, loaded with saws, ladders and other equipment, covered by a tarpaulin. Hinnerk would leave his bicycle in the wood and board the truck, concealing himself under the tarpaulin. Just before they reached the edge of the no-go zone he would leave the truck, skirt around the sentry post at the entrance to the zone, and board the truck again further down the road. Half way through the zone Andreas would stop and tap on the rear window as the signal for Hinnerk to jump out and run like hell for the river. It all sounded marvellously simple, but a stumble, a vigilant dog or a single bullet would be enough to end it all.

Before leaving, Henrik wrote a letter to his adoptive parents, Otto and Waltraud. Wishing to protect them when they were inevitably questioned, he begged them to forgive him for keeping his escape plans secret from them. When they received the letter he would either be on the other side of the border or dead. Not wishing to entrust this letter to the mail, which he knew was monitored by the Stasi, he gave it to the Voglers to deliver secretly. Astrid slipped the letter under a sideboard and pushed it out of sight. "Don't worry, we'll find a way of getting it to them – after you're safely out of the country."

37

The message arrived at Stasi headquarters on Monday morning. Seeing that it was marked "urgent", the woman in the cramped telex room in the basement carried it up two flights and hurried down the dimly lit corridor towards Major Kobitz's office, the heels of her clumpy shoes clattering on the drab green linoleum floor. Kobitz was talking on the phone as she entered the room, and he signalled to her to place it on his desk. When he had finished he picked up the telex and read the message:

"From: Lt J.K. Schwarz
Ministry of State Security

S-E Harz Territorial Office, Sangerhausen

To: Major P. Kobitz
Ministry of State Security, Head Office, Berlin
Overseas Intelligence, Section Z

8 May 1966

In conformity with your instructions, the object, Henrik Siebert, was kept under observation during a visit last weekend to his adoptive parents, Mr and Mrs Siebert, at Benderstrasse 19, Sangerhausen. He was observed cycling to the village of Selz-Krombach in the Harz, where he visited the site of his former Lebensborn Home "Lenzfeld", now demolished. He was seen there in conversation with the forestry official Andreas Vogler and subsequently went with him to the house of Vogler's brother Jürgen and the latter's wife Astrid. At 14:21 he left the house and took to the road on his bicycle, but one of the Vogler brothers went after him in a truck and brought him back to the house. At 17:37 he finally left the house and cycled back to Sangerhausen. It was not possible to overhear the conversation that took place. I await your further instructions and in the meantime will keep the Voglers under observation."

When he had finished reading Kobitz went to a book case, pulled out an atlas and turned to a page showing the Harz Mountains and environs. He studied it for several minutes, then reached for the telephone and started to dial.

38

A week had passed since the attack on Henrik. In the shop, Kirsten closed and locked the till at the end of the day's work, but instead of leaving the shop she reached under the counter for a piece of notepaper. She picked up a ballpoint pen and sat for several minutes staring at the blank sheet, uncertain how to begin. Then she began to write in the same neat, upright hand that she used for keeping the account books.

> Dear Henrik,
>
> It seems strange to be writing you a letter, but I have to. There are unspoken things between us that <u>must be</u> spoken, but when I am with you I can't bring myself to be blunt. Where to begin? I've always known that I had a half-brother. I knew that mum still thought of him every day and was agonized by what she did all those years ago. So of course I longed for a miracle that would bring him back to us. Then the miracle actually happened, and there you were – out of the blue.
>
> What an impression you made on me that day that mum and I met you for the first time in Copenhagen – so handsome and charming and fascinating with your talk of plants and birds, your stories of life in the GDR and how you found out about us and tracked us down after you were 'bought out'. Of course mum and I were determined to believe that you were who you said you were. Why would you wish to lie to us and give us so many convincing reasons to think you were genuine unless you truly were? It seemed impossible you could be an imposter. And of course we wanted to believe in you and

so very badly. But just when we were so happy to have found you, Mum mentioned Fraulein Neumeyer's visit to your family in the Harz, and you said you could not remember her at all, though we knew she'd been the nurse who protected you in that awful home. You'd been very young of course and some people remember nothing before the age of five. But your adopted family lived in Wittenberge. So how could Frau Neumeyer have confused Wittenberge with the Harz where her little Henrik had gone to live? Mum didn't press you to explain. I think it was because she loved you so much and couldn't face having to change her mind about you. I was scared too, although I kept expecting that you would reassure us all. But you didn't.

I told myself you needed more time and made all sorts of excuses but at the very same time – and I am so horribly embarrassed to admit this – I was starting to fall in love with you, Henrik, just when I was doubting you more. You were so different from any of the young men I had met up till then – so much deeper and cleverer and more experienced. You were mysterious too, so I had no idea what you were thinking. Somehow this distance made me want you all the more. I even began to wonder what it would be like to have you as my lover. Then I realized why I was feeling this way. It was <u>because</u> you might <u>not</u> be my half-brother. Suddenly I could love you without breaking any taboo. Your lies became less important – though I'm ashamed to say so.

Just at this time you were attacked on the road. After I had chased the attackers away and was kneeling beside you on the ground, you gave me a fleeting kiss on the lips and then held me in a way that no brother would. Though it might have been an accident, and you moved away and acted normally afterwards, I sensed that you'd enjoyed this moment too. In that instant, I thought: <u>yes</u>, that was how it would feel to be held by the man you love, and <u>no</u>, I must never risk losing him. I didn't mention this to you, or my other suspicions, because I was terrified that if I did you would leave us without a word before Mum had had a chance to ask for your explanation. Nobody would claim another man's identity unless they were escaping from something or were using their new name and life to commit some crime.

Even now though I'm scared, I still love you. You see I've no idea whether I'll have the courage to give you this letter. Whatever you say will be terrible for me. If you're not my brother you are a cruel liar and have stolen what is not yours. But if you really are my brother and have told us the truth, I must stop loving you. Even though there can be no happy outcome, this dreadful uncertainty still has to end.

The other day to discover the truth without having to ask you, I went up to the attic with a torch to search for the letter mum remembered receiving from Fräulein Neumeyer. I hadn't been up there for years. It was all dim and musty and piled high with all kinds of family junk. I looked through some suitcases filled with old mementos – photo albums, post cards, letters – but there was no sign of the letter. I was disappointed and overjoyed at the same time. Oh Henrik, I have to know one way or the other, but dread the truth and not just for myself. If you love any of us, please find a way to be truthful without destroying my poor mother and tearing yourself away from me.

Your loving and unhappy,
Kirsten

She sat at the counter and re-read the letter several times, reached for an envelope to put it in then changed her mind. She walked over to a small wood-burning stove, unlit as it was summer, and opened the metal door to the grate. Screwing up the letter, she put it into the grate and set it alight with a match.

39

Astrid and Jürgen had just sat down to an afternoon cup of coffee when from outside came the sound of the dog barking and growling furiously. They got up from the table, startled, and heard a shot, then a yelp of pain from the dog, then silence. Opening the front door, they were aghast to see the dog's body lying near the front garden gate and four men coming up the path towards the house. The men were wearing the grey uniform of the Stasi troops. One of them, with the epaulettes and collar tabs of a captain, held the pistol with which he had just shot the dog. The other men had rifles with bayonets slung over their shoulders. One was younger than the rest, with fair hair and an almost schoolboyish face. The other two were dark, thick-set and coarse-looking.

"Jürgen Vogler?" the captain rasped. "We are from the Ministry of State Security. We need to ask you some questions."

Jürgen was still staring, shocked, at the fate of the dog. "Why the hell did you shoot him?" he said in a strangled voice.

"He sprang at us." He gestured with his gun, indicating

that they were to go back into the house. When they were inside the captain said: "I'll come straight to the point. A man called Henrik Siebert was seen coming to this house a week ago. Now he's gone missing. We have reason to believe that he intends to leave the country illegally. I'm sure you'll want to help us stop him. Now what do you know of Siebert's escape plans?"

Astrid now spoke up. "We know nothing about any plans. Hinnerk Siebert came to see us because over twenty years ago he was one of my charges when I was a nurse at the Lenzfeld Lebensborn home near here. He wanted to see me again, that's all."

"I see. And where is your brother-in-law, Andreas? We checked his house, but he's not there. Rather a coincidence, don't you think?"

"Andreas is away on forestry business."

"You're lying!" the captain shouted. "Your brother-in-law is aiding Siebert to commit the crime of flight from the GDR, isn't he?"

Jürgen and Astrid remained silent.

"Search the house!" the captain barked to the young soldier, then turned and faced Jürgen. "Perhaps *you* will be more cooperative. Now, where are your brother and Siebert, and what are they up to?"

"I've nothing to add to what my wife said."

The captain's smashed the barrel of his pistol into the side of Jürgen's face, cutting the cheek and loosening teeth. Astrid screamed. From the bedroom came the sound of the young Stasi man rifling through drawers and cupboards, smashing vases and hollow ornaments, slicing open the mattress and pillows with his bayonet. Jürgen's head was sagging, blood streaming from his mouth and from the open wound.

The captain now held the pistol up to Jürgen's temple, while the remaining two soldiers held his arms pinioned behind his back. "This is no fucking game," the captain shouted at Astrid. "We mean business. Unless you tell me what I want to know I'm going to shoot your husband in precisely one minute's time – "he looked at his watch, "starting from now."

Astrid's eyes registered terror, but she was weighing up the risk of telling them something, anything that would save Jürgen but also put them off the scent.

"You now have forty-five seconds!"

The soldier doing the search had now moved into the living room where they were standing. He looked under rugs, pulled open draws, stood on a chair to look above the sideboard.

"Thirty seconds!"

Out of the corner of her eye, Astrid saw the young Stasi man crouching down on the floor in front of the sideboard.

"Twenty seconds!"

"All right, I'll tell you what I can," Astrid said, hoping to stop the search.

But the young man was already pulling out the envelope, a gleeful look on his schoolboy's face.

"Captain, look at this!" He handed the envelope to the officer, who opened it and read the letter.

"Well, well!" He waved the sheet of paper in Astrid's face. "This is enough to get you and your husband a long prison term with hard labour, or maybe even a death sentence. So … what was it you were about to tell me?"

* * *

Hinnerk looked again at his watch and saw that it was already an hour past the rendezvous time of eight pm. He was waiting in the twilight at the appointed place by the boulder in the forestry precinct. His bicycle stood propped against a pine tree, and because he could not take it with him and could not safely make a present of it to his friends, he intended to leave it here after Andreas arrived. He ate a snack that he had brought with him, and in the fading light he took another glance up the road, but still there was no sign of Andreas's truck. They had agreed that he would wait until nine, but he decided to give it until nine thirty and then cycle back to the station. If there was no train that night he would have to sleep out in the open and then catch the first one in the morning, or perhaps hang about all Sunday and travel back to Berlin in the evening. That way he wouldn't have to explain to Uta why he had come back early.

Then a terrifying thought came to him. His adoptive parents, Otto and Waltraud did not know he had told Uta that he was going to Sangerhausen that weekend. With so much else to think of, the basic precaution of alerting them had slipped his mind. What if Uta were to telephone him there and they told her they had not been expecting him that weekend? She would inform the Stasi immediately, and every police patrol in the country would be on the lookout for him.

*   *   *

As Andreas approached Magdeburg he looked again at his watch. Estimating three to three and a half hours drive to his rendezvous with Henrik, he had left home at four o'clock, which should have allowed plenty of time to spare, but he hadn't anticipated having to stop and change a flat tyre, nor getting stuck behind a heavy lorry on one of the narrow roads through the Harz. Now it was well after five, and at best he would only just make it. A good thing they had arranged that Henrik would if necessary wait for an extra hour past the appointed time. In Magdeburg there was a badly signposted diversion because of road works, and he made several false turnings before he found himself back on the motorway. Another twenty minutes lost, and now he was eating into the fail-safe hour.

Just past Magdeburg he noticed a vehicle a couple of hundred yards behind him. It was a Russian Volga GAZ-21, a high-grade saloon car normally reserved for police, taxi drivers and officials, but it had neither police markings nor a yellow "Taxi" lamp on the roof, so Andreas guessed that it belonged to some local party official and told himself that there was no cause for alarm. Worrying thoughts began to nag at him. What if Hinnerk had been apprehended by the police and made to confess everything? Or what if Hinnerk's wife suspected something and had tipped off the authorities? Perhaps the men in the car behind were from the Stasi and were tailing him so that he would lead them to the rendezvous. He could of course simply turn around and drive back home, but that would look suspicious. It would show that he had spotted the car and was changing his plans.

As he approached the industrial city of Stendal he glanced at a map on the passenger seat and made a decision. Instead of continuing due north he would turn eastwards at Stendal. If the men in the Volga did not follow him, then he would turn back and continue as planned. If they did follow him then he would drive towards Berlin then, after about fifty kilometres, turn to the north-west, back in the direction of the rendezvous. That would take him through an area of forest plantations where he knew the foresters well, and he could easily invent a reason for being there if he were stopped and questioned. Of course, if things became too dangerous, he would have to abandon the meeting with Henrik.

After he cleared Stendal the Volga was still there, so he decided to take the alternative route. He drove on for another fifty kilometres to the town of Briesen, where the road came to a T-junction with the Autobahn from Berlin to the Baltic coast. Here he turned left, and when he dared to look in his rear mirror the Volga was nowhere to be seen. Since he was shaking from the release of tension, he pulled over into a lay-by and lit a cigarette.

A moment later he heard the sound of a siren, and a regular police car drew up beside him. He wound down the driver's window as two men dressed in the dull green uniform of the People's Police came up to him. One of them, wearing the epaulettes of a lieutenant, peered through the window and growled: "Andreas Vogler?"

*   *   *

Hinnerk took one more look at his watch and saw that it was nine thirty. Then he pushed his bicycle out of the trees, down the track and on to the main road. Off to the left he could see the spire of the church in Pritzheim. To the right the road pointed west towards the Elbe and the border. He mounted the bike and then, almost as though drawn by a powerful magnet, pedalled towards the west. He would either make it to the river alone or be shot.

Now there could be no turning back, he felt a surge of exhilaration. Speeding along in top gear, he began to roll back the twenty or so kilometres that divided him from the point where the road entered the no-go zone just past the town of Boizenburg. That meant over an hour's cycling. It would be well past nightfall by the time he reached the zone. The moon was in its dark phase, which would be good for cover, but on the other hand he would now have a long way to walk through the no-go zone and might lose his way, despite having his compass and pocket torch.

Several times over the next hour he took cover off the road while a car or a lorry passed. Once, rounding a corner he was surprised by a car coming towards him and catching him in its headlights. But the Trabant spluttered by with its tinny rattle and was gone. Another time he had to slow down when a heavy tractor appeared ahead, pulling a cartload of manure. He followed at a safe distance until it turned off into a farm drive.

The road rose steeply and he dismounted and pushed. He was not as fit as he had imagined. So how would he fare against the currents of Elbe – if he ever reached it? At last the road flattened out and he pedalled along a ridge. He stopped to shine his torch at a road sign, and saw the town of Boizenburg indicated to the left. The place lay below a ridge close to the river – and was the last town before the no-go zone. He coasted down the curving road which by-passed the town.

As the road levelled and straightened, he saw, sooner than he had expected, the control post at the entrance to the no-go zone about three hundred metres ahead. It was lit, as though part of a stage set, by lamps hanging from a cable strung across the road. He dismounted and pushed the bike forward cautiously, keeping in the shadows at the edge of the tree-lined road. What he now saw sent a shiver of alarm through him. In the yellow light he could make out a wooden hut and a pole-barrier. A military truck had just parked inside the barrier, and a dozen or so green-uniformed border guards carrying rifles were dismounting from it. Four of them had Alsatian dogs on leads. The officer in charge of the troop was already talking animatedly to a sentry standing in front of the hut. Hinnerk could not make out the words, but he heard the urgent tone of the officer's voice. The sentry nodded and saluted, then the officer turned and gave some instructions to his men. Three of them joined the sentry at the barrier, the others hurried off into the woods of the no-go zone, the four dogs barking excitedly.

Hinnerk tried to think quickly. Clearly the Stasi were now aware of his escape plans, but did they know that he was heading for the Elbe, or were they increasing security all along the border? If the latter, then he might still have a faint chance of slipping through. But now he saw something that made his heart sink again. A high fence extended from the road into the woods on either side. The no-go zone was fenced off.

For a moment he thought of turning back, and waiting until he could plan a fresh attempt in a different place. But it was too late to turn back, even if he wanted to. Instead of a place at the Humboldt he could now expect a long term of hard labour or possibly a death sentence.

He concealed his bicycle in some bushes, and then began to make his way cautiously through the trees, tracing a wide quarter circle around the control post. This soon brought him, as he had calculated, to the boundary fence. He moved down it to the left, following it through the wood. By the light of his torch he could see that it was about three metres high and made of wire mesh stretched between concrete posts, with barbed wire strung along the top. There was nowhere to get a foothold and, even if there had been, the barbed wire would have stopped him going over the top.

Were there any weak spots in the fence? Perhaps somewhere the mesh had split open or a post had loosened; but the more he looked, the more impregnable the fence appeared to be. Then his heart leapt. Where the fence ran across a small gulley made by a newly-formed stream, there was a gap. Here, the shallow water flowed muddily under the fence with a clearance of perhaps ten centimetres. A small cat could have managed it, but to get his large frame through he would have to make the hole a lot bigger.

He set to work with his bare hands, scooping out the earth as best he could, bruising his fingers on roots and deeply embedded stones. Every few minutes he peered through the mesh to make sure that none of the guards were in sight. After half an hour his hands were raw and bleeding, and the hole was only slightly larger than before. Picking up a fallen branch he shoved it under the fence and managed to lever up the mesh another few centimetres. He lay down in the stream and, gasping as the cold water soaked through his clothes, he half swam, half scrambled through the gap. When he was half way through, he heard the sound of voices – two guards, by the sound of them, were approaching the fence. He risked raising his head a little and saw their silhouettes, perhaps fifty metres away, moving in his direction. They had Alsatian dogs who were straining at their leads. Another few paces and the dogs would pick up his scent. He lay as low down in the stream as he could, face beneath the surface. He had read of people avoiding dogs or wild animals by hiding in water, but not in a pitiful muddy trickle like this. Desperate to breathe, he raised his head and gulped in air, hardly caring any more whether they heard him. To his relief he heard the voices of the men were receding. He pulled the rest of his body through the gap, crawled out of the stream and lay on the ground, wet through and shivering.

Eventually he pulled himself up into a crouching position and looked around cautiously. Light from the control post off to the right caught the trunks of the pines and silver birches, giving the scene an eerie beauty. This wood had been here long before the border had existed and would still be here when the GDR and all it stood for had vanished into dust. This thought soothed him a little as he groped for his torch and consulted his compass. If he went south-west, he would come to the Elbe, but it would be a longer walk than if Andreas had let him off in the middle of the zone – perhaps two kilometres – and every step of the way would be full of danger from patrols, dogs and man-traps. But all he could do was press on.

He set off, moving from tree to tree, pausing to look and listen every few seconds before moving on. Thorns and sharp branches tore at him and made his progress noisy.

He risked switching on the torch, hoping that he might see the river ahead, but still he saw only the endless ranks of pine trees and birches and the tangled undergrowth in between them. The beam of the torch caught the delicate patterns of spiders' webs. He shone the light along one strand that ran in a straight, gleaming line across his path about twenty centimetres from the ground, then realised with a shock that it was not part of a spider's web. He had almost walked into one of the tripwires that Jürgen had warned him about. He stepped carefully over it and went on, at intervals switching on the torch to check for more trip-wires.

Still there was no sign of the river. Perhaps he had underestimated the distance. Then, as he emerged from a thicket, he felt a hard surface under his feet. He shone his torch down and saw that he was standing on a narrow road made of concrete blocks, which ran to his right and left – obviously a thoroughfare built for the border guards. Hearing a vehicle, he flung himself into the bushes, crouching there until an armoured car had swept past. For a second, in the light of its headlamps, he had seen, on the other side of the road, willow trees. He must be very close to the river.

Hinnerk glanced up and down the road, and dashed across to where the willows and some smaller bushes formed a tangled barrier. Pushing through it, he found himself struggling down a steep bank, criss-crossed by roots. Now he could just make out the wide belt of the river and hear the gurgling, rushing sound of the great mass of water moving west, down to Hamburg and the North Sea. On the far bank the lights of a village were visible, its houses reflected in the water. His spirits soared.

Then he heard a sound that made him freeze: the barking of a dog. It was coming from the road and getting closer. He ran on down the bank, tearing aside branches in his frenzy to escape. He could hear the creature snuffling in the undergrowth close behind him. In the distance, other dogs began barking as they found his scent. Sprinting ahead, he tripped on a root, feeling a searing pain in his ankle as he hit the ground. In seconds the dog would be on him. He could hear it barking and growling only metres away. As he dragged himself to his feet, he saw it leaping and straining furiously at something holding it back. It must have reached the limit of its tether.

Half hopping, half limping, he stumbled down the shore towards the water. A siren started to wail above the shouts of the guards, and the roving beam of a searchlight swept over him. As he hit the water he heard the stammer of a machine gun and bullets spattering the surface inches away.

With all his remaining strength he struck out towards the opposite bank. The river was moving much faster than he had imagined and the lights on the far shore were sliding away to the left with alarming speed. Beneath him, the irresistible power of the current was carrying him away. The firing stopped, the lights across the river vanished. He had no idea how far he still had to go, and his strength was failing. He was struggling for breath, trying not to gulp down water, when he heard the rumble of an engine, and a moment later was dazzled by a searchlight, mounted on the front deck of the approaching patrol boat.

40

Henrik had taken to leaving the breakfast table early, hoping that Kirsten would take the hint and leave early too, so that they could talk together. One day when he had almost given up hope that she would ever oblige - so cool had she become towards him - she did follow him out into the corridor.

"Try trusting me," he said, calmly taking her arm, detaining her in the ill-lit corridor.

"Let go of me, please."

He was shocked by her tone of sharp insistence, but leaned towards her and whispered: "If I've offended you..."

She turned away with a stifled cry that could have been

anger or exasperation. He murmured: "I don't deserve to be..." But he got no further than this before she was walking away. Ever since the aftermath of the attack on him, when their lips had met and he had held her too closely, she had scarcely glanced his way. All he could think was that she knew what he felt for her and was deeply repelled - the very thing he had been determined to avoid. Every day now, he had to work hard to appear to be his normal self when encountering other members of the family. It was essential that he showed no dismay.

Later that morning, passing the children's playroom near the back door, Henrik saw Ulla kneeling on the floor, occupied with a jigsaw puzzle. She had assembled about half the pieces and was turning one piece around in her hand, trying to fit it into a gap. The rest of the pieces lay scattered on the floor. Hearing him come into the room, she looked up at him and then looked down again at the jigsaw. Her brother Per was more relaxed with Henrik, calling him "Uncle", but his twin sister Ulla remained reserved. He gave her his brightest most open smile. Usually Henrik could win over children, but Ulla seemed impervious. She was an unusually grown-up five-year-old with a pale, serious face and very fair curly hair. Sometimes, when the family ate together, Henrik would turn and catch Ulla looking at him with her intense, pale blue eyes, and he would wonder whether she had sensed intuitively that he was a sham.

"That's a tricky puzzle," he said, trying to sound friendly, "but it looks like you'll soon have it finished."

"Yes," she said coolly, keeping her eyes on the puzzle, "I've done it before." She picked up another piece and fitted it in. The picture emerging was of an old barn with a horse looking out over a stable door. On top of the red-tiled roof was an enormous bird's nest with some heads of chicks poking out over the edge and the legs of the parent birds just discernible. More pieces would be fitted in to make up wings, heads and beaks. The picture consisted of bright, crude patches of colour like a painting-by-numbers canvas.

"Those are storks, aren't they?" he said, watching her fit more pieces in. "Have you ever seen one?"

She merely shook her head.

"I'll show you a drawing of some storks I once saw. Let me get it and show it to you."

He went to his room and fetched his portfolio of drawings. Sitting on the floor beside her, he took out one that he had made during a summer holiday spent with his adoptive grandparents in the village of Dobzin when he was fourteen. It showed a similar nest on top of a roof, with one of the parent storks taking flight, the wings outstretched against a sky of windblown clouds. The drawing was vivid and full of movement. Ulla put down a jigsaw piece, took the drawing and looked at it closely.

"Is it true," she asked, "that storks bring babies?"

Dismissing the idea that the question might be a trick, he felt that he was actually beginning to break the ice with her.

"I don't know if it's really true," he began cautiously, "but it's a lovely thought isn't it? Imagine being brought into the world by such a beautiful creature. Would you like to keep the picture?"

She looked at him and nodded, her eyes shining. Then, hearing her mother come in through the front door with Per, she went to meet them, still holding the picture.

"Look," he heard her shout excitedly, "look at this picture that Uncle Henrik gave me."

A moment later Birthe and Per came into the room, Birthe now holding the drawing.

"Henrik," she gasped, "did you really draw this?"

"Yes, when I was fourteen."

"Well that makes it all the more amazing. My goodness, your father would have been proud of you. To think that you've inherited his love of birds and his gift for drawing them."

"Can I have a picture too?" Per asked.

"Of course you can," Henrik laughed.

At that moment the doorbell rang, and Birthe looked around, surprised. "Goodness, who can that be? Can you see who it is, Per?"

The boy was gone for a few seconds. They heard the door open and a man's voice saying something to him. Then he reappeared.

"It's a policeman," he announced importantly. "He wants to see Uncle Henrik."

"To see me?" Henrik repeated, managing to conceal how shocked he was. "Are you sure?"

"Yes, he said, 'I want to speak to your Uncle Henrik.'"

Henrik pulled a face. "Well, I suppose I'd better go and see what he wants."

He felt sick and breathless. So this was the end. They had found him out. Probably Claudia had, after all, told her policeman friend in Hamburg. The police must therefore have known the truth and been playing him along, keeping him under surveillance in an effort to catch his contacts too. They would have tailed him to the Fish Market and observed his meeting with Kurt. So by now they probably would have arrested Kurt as well. For a moment he thought of making a run for it, but there would be more police covering the house. He wouldn't stand a chance. Now that he knew he was going to be arrested he wished there was some way it could be done without Birthe being there, but it was too late – he heard her and the children following him to the front door where the tall policeman was waiting, cap in hand.

"Ah, Officer Andersen," Birthe said in a surprised tone. "Good afternoon. What brings you here?"

"Good afternoon, Mrs. Karlssen. I would just like to speak to your son for a few minutes ... alone if I may."

"Well whatever it's about, I think I should be part of the conversation," Birthe said with a touch of indignation. "As you say, he's my son." She squeezed Henrik's hand reassuringly.

"Please," Henrik murmured. "I think the officer is right." He was determined to spare her the painful scene that must be coming.

Birthe looked from one man to the other, her expression both angry and anxious. "All right ... if you say so, Henrik."

She withdrew with the children into the back of the house, while Henrik followed Andersen a few steps into the front yard.

"Sorry to bother you like this," the policeman said in a friendly tone, "but I understand you had a spot of trouble the other day with three lads from the village. They attacked you, is that correct?"

"Yes, it is." Henrik had to fight back tears, so acute was his relief.

Andersen shook his head. "Disgraceful! They're a plague on the community, that lot. Well, I wanted to let you know that they've been arrested in connection with another crime – a car theft. They'll be in jail for quite some time. Of course you're free to bring charges, but as they're in prison anyway you might want to save yourself the trouble."

Seeing Andersen's kindly face, for a split second Henrik felt a confusing urge to confess everything, but instead he muttered, "Absolutely right, Officer... I don't want to bring charges."

"Right, then I'll be getting along." Andersen replaced his cap, but lingered in the yard, stroking his moustache. "By the way ... although it's not really my business ... I know it's a difficult situation for you and your mother ... what with all the old resentments from the war. But here's some advice: give 'em time and they'll simmer down. Meanwhile let us know if you have any more trouble."

Andersen shook Henrik's hand and walked towards his car, parked in the drive. As he re-entered the house Birthe was already waiting in the corridor, white-faced and concerned.

"What did he say, Henrik dear?"

He had an impulse to laugh hysterically. "Oh, don't worry, it was nothing. Really."

"Nothing! How can you say that? I saw how worried you looked just now."

He knew she would give him no peace until she knew the reason for Anderson's visit, so he told her about the attack. He tried to make light of it, but the time he had finished she was in tears.

"Oh, my poor boy!" she sobbed. "That's terrible."

More than anything, he wanted to be alone, away from the house and everything that reminded him of the false life he was living. When he told Birthe that he needed to rest in his room, she planted a tearful kiss on his cheek and let him go. After a few moments he stole down the stairs, and slipped out on to the road.

Over the next two hours he walked without stopping, but in no particular direction – over fields and through woods and along the shore – feeling like a condemned man who had been reprieved but still feared the final outcome. He had heard stories of people who had almost died under surgery and then miraculously revived, and how they spoke of life taking on a new vividness and intensity. But he experienced no such feelings, only anger that fate was playing cat and mouse with him. Then there was the stand-off with Kirsten – enough on its own to lower his spirits. It was not merely painful either, since he sensed that it was dangerous too. Might she, perhaps, suspect something and not merely be offended by his feelings for her?

Eventually he came to the small harbour of Lysholm and walked out along the wall that shielded it from the Baltic storms. The air smelt of oil, dead fish and seaweed, stirring memories of the wanderlust that he had felt as a teenager visiting the little harbour at Wittenberge. In between the workaday fishing boats, piled with nets, there were sailing dinghies, motor launches and a few expensive looking yachts with neatly coiled ropes, smartly painted woodwork and gleaming brass fittings. For a moment he fantasized about sailing away with Kirsten, and escaping his mission, and all the lies. But really the way things were going he might need to escape the island on his own and quite soon at that. His suspicion that he was being watched and followed had recently approached near certainty. Today, for once, he had seen nothing to alarm him.

A curious lightheadedness, born of desperation, came over him as he walked on down the quay and whistled a tune

that he remembered from the sailors' pub in Hamburg:
über Rio und Schanghai,
über Bali und Hawaii ...

He had almost reached the last of the moorings when his eye was caught by a sturdy motor launch that looked as though it had once been a small fishing vessel. On the side of the prow was the name *Jasmin* in red copperplate letters and beside it a delicately painted jasmin flower. But what most attracted his attention was the sign fixed to the stern: "FOR SALE". He stepped closer to the vessel. It was broad-beamed and built of overlapping wooden planks. There was a small, half-open wheelhouse, with the wheel and instrument panel to the right and a few steps leading down into a small cabin under the foredeck. At the rear there was an open deck.

"Hello!" he called out. "Is anyone at home?"

Hearing no reply, he stepped on to the wooden gangplank slung between the boat and the harbour wall. He called again without getting any response, then climbed aboard and entered the cabin. Its cosy interior thrilled him immediately. When his eyes had adjusted to the dim light from the portholes and the open doorway, he made out comfortably upholstered benches down the sides, a fixed table in the middle, and a tiny galley in a corner near the doorway, with a small sink, a primus stove and a cupboard for provisions. On the surface beside the stove stood a metal coffee pot and a mug, evidently recently used, since a faint whiff of coffee still hung in the air. Ahead was another door, leading to a smaller cabin containing two bunks, tucked in under the bows, one on each side of the vessel. Looking around, he began to imagine what it would be like to have this boat as a refuge, to sit here in the cabin drinking coffee and not having to wonder who might knock on his door and ask him impossible questions. What a dream – to be alone here with his thoughts and drawings, to know that he could cast off from the quay at any time and motor away. It would be a blessed refuge – not only from the strain of being with the family but also from the feeling that Kurt might be near at hand.

Abruptly his reverie was interrupted by the figure of a man dressed in overalls and a nautical cap, blocking the open doorway. His weather-beaten, bearded face was scowling.

"You!" he said. "What are you doing on this boat?"

Henrik instinctively flashed a boyish smile. "Well, I saw the 'for sale' sign and came looking for the owner." Henrik was now determined to have the boat, come what may. With funds unused from the Borup mission, he was confident he could buy her. He would explain to the family that he was going to use the vessel for bird-watching and drawing, and as for the Stasi ... he would make up some convincing reason, perhaps that he was planning to use it for "Romeo work" with potential female collaborators in Denmark.

"Well, *I'm* the owner," said the man, somewhat less gruffly.

"So how much do you want for her?"

*   *   *

Coming down the drive towards the house, whistling *über Rio und Schanghai*, he met Kirsten coming out of the shop. When she saw him she hesitated and looked around as though seeking a way of avoiding him, but it was too late. She stood facing him on the drive, a slight frown on her face and said: "Where have you been?"

With no time to think, he said brightly: "I've been getting to know Jasmin."

"Jasmin?" Kirsten repeated, puzzled. "Who is Jasmin?"

"The new love of my life." She looked so bemused and wretched that he almost shouted: "She's a boat! I've bought her."

Kirsten's face brightened but only for a moment. "A boat?" she said, puzzled. "Why have you bought a boat?"

"I took a walk down to the harbour and saw her for sale. And that was that – love at first sight!"

"But I didn't know you were a sailor."

"I'm not. She's a motor boat. I'm going to use her for watching seabirds – and drawing them. I've been longing to get back to my ornithological drawing." He put out a hand and touched her arm. "Tell you what, why don't we go on a trip on her together? Tomorrow, if you like."

She stiffened at the touch of his hand and drew back.

"That'd be nice some time," she said in a sad, tense voice, "but I have a lot to do at the moment ... I'm stocktaking." Before he could protest she had disappeared back into the shop.

41

When they got him on to the deck of the patrol boat his legs were wobbly and his head swimming. He had to be half carried into the cabin by the two members of the crew, who helped him out of his wet clothes and gave him a heavy wool blanket to wrap himself in. For a few moments he was left alone, and as his dizziness gradually left him he realised that he still did not know whether the boat belonged to the East or the West.

Then a man in a dark blue uniform came in and pressed a small metal flask into his right hand. "Schnapps," he said. "Take a swig. It'll do you good." He wore a smart officer's cap – white headpiece, blue peak, gold braiding … and a badge. Hinnerk stared at the emblem on the badge, then opened his eyes wide. He was not looking at the hammer and compasses symbol of the GDR, but at the image of a black eagle with red beak and claws against a yellow background. Merciful God! It was the coat of arms of the West German Federal Republic. He drank from the flask and the liquid fire of the schnapps roused and warmed him.

The officer was smiling at him. "May I welcome you on behalf of the West German Customs Service? You are safely across the border. Many congratulations. We heard shots on the other side and thought someone was trying to swim across. Close thing. I don't think you'd have made if we hadn't spotted you."

Hinnerk was on the verge of weeping with joy. "Th-th-thank you," he stammered. "Thank you. I can hardly believe this is real. Where are we?"

"Some more schnapps," suggested the customs officer. "We're nearly at Lauenburg, the first town on the river on the western side of the border. We'll be putting you ashore there and you'll be taken to a hospital. You'll need checking out and a few days in bed by the look of you."

Later, when he recalled the events that had followed, everything was blurred and patchy like an old reel of film: the feel of crisp white sheets in the cheerful hospital ward in Lauenburg, where they treated his cuts and bruises and sprained ankle and kept him for three days until he was thoroughly rested; the three-hour journey south with several other asylum-seekers in a minibus of the immigration authorities; the big reception camp on the outskirts of Giessen, where several hundred refugees lived in a converted army barracks.

Within a couple of hours of his arrival at the camp he was told that he would be interviewed by an officer of the Allied forces in Germany. "Standard procedure" he was informed. The officer turned out to be an Englishman, Major Kemble, a smallish, dapper man of about fifty, with greying hair and a neatly trimmed moustache. In his nondescript khaki uniform, he appeared slightly dwarfed by his large desk, which was bare save for a notepad, a ballpoint pen, some manila folders, several rubber stamps, an ink pad and a tobacco tin. There was something of the schoolmaster or the university don about him, a quick intelligence in his dark, beady eyes.

"Do have a seat, Mr. Siebert," the major said in flawless German. He opened one of the folders. "You've certainly pulled off a very daring escape. Well done."

"Thank you, Major."

"Do you have any form of identification?"

Henrik took out his GDR personal identity document, a passport-sized booklet with pale green pages, printed all over with the hated GDR emblem. It was discoloured and coming apart after its drenching in the Elbe, but the photograph inside was still recognisable. He handed it to Kemble, glad that he no longer needed it.

Through the window behind where Kemble sat, Hinnerk could see the front courtyard of the barracks, where a bus had just disgorged a group of new arrivals – a couple with three young children, two elderly women, several middle aged and younger men – still dressed in their drab, old-fashioned GDR clothes and carrying small bags and suitcases.

Kemble filled and lit his pipe and said with a smile: "Well, Mr Siebert, we'd better see what we can do for you."

He took a document out of the folder and looked at it. "Curious coincidence," he remarked. "You have a near namesake in the camp, Heinrich Siebler. And on the subject of your name, I suggest we give you a new one for the time being."

Seeing Hinnerk's look of surprise he added: "We have to be on the alert for spies in the camp. We do our best to flush them out, of course, but sometimes they manage to slip through. From what you've told me they may be on the lookout for Hinnerk Siebert. How do you like the name Werner?"

"I could live with it for a while."

"Very well, until further notice you are Werner Beck."

He wrote the name on the document, stamped it firmly with one of the rubber stamps, signed at the bottom with a fountain pen and then handed the paper to Hinnerk. "There you go, that gives you clearance to stay in the camp. You can give it to the people at reception and they'll take care of you. You'll get a change of clothing, bed and board and 30 marks a week while the people at the Department of German-German Affairs sort out your residence papers. Then they'll help you find a job and more permanent accommodation. While you're here you can come and go freely from the camp, but don't go more than five kilometres out of the town."

Hinnerk took the document, noticing Kemble's small, neat signature in blue ink at the bottom. "I much appreciate all of this, Major, but my aim is to go to Denmark and apply for Danish citizenship."

Kemble drew slowly at his pipe, then examined the bowl as though he was trying to save the tobacco. "The trouble is you have no proof that your mother was Danish, and the Danes are not going to be eager to believe your story – that aspect of the Nazi occupation is very embarrassing to them – whereas in West Germany you have an automatic right to citizenship. I would suggest you take it. You can always move to Denmark and apply for naturalisation later if you still want to."

Hinnerk fingered the document, dismayed by what the Major had just told him.

"I see ... so how long must I stay here?"

"A couple of weeks, I should say ... three at the most. From now on it's up to the German authorities to help you. All right?" He stood up to signal that the interview was over and reached out to shake Henrik's hand. "Good luck. Come and see me if you suspect that anyone's getting nosey about you. And be suspicious of any person who tries to get too friendly."

Later that day he called directory enquiries from a pay telephone in the camp and gave the name of Karlssen and the location on the island of Norvik. In a few seconds he had the number, and his heart beat faster as he wrote it down then stood in the phone booth staring at it. Now that he was only a phone call away from his mother he realised that he had no idea how she would react when he called. If the Danes were embarrassed about that part of their history, as Major Kemble had told him, maybe she would not even want to talk to him. And could she even speak any German? Questions that he had never asked himself before, now crowded in on him. At last he lifted the telephone receiver, inserted some coins and began to dial the number. Then, as he heard the ringing tone, another thought occurred to him. What if the Stasi had the line tapped? He hung up before anyone answered. No, it would be better if he could reach the house unobserved by the Stasi and hope that his arrival would not be too much of a shock for his mother. But first he would have to wait until his residence papers came through.

That night, as he lay in the bunk bed in the dormitory that he shared with a dozen other men, he pondered what the Major had said about spies. The depressing thought came to him that he was probably in more danger now than before his escape. Back in East Berlin he had been the "harmless imbecile", safe as long as he toed the line. Now he was probably on the Stasi hit list. Kobitz had, for some reason, been desperate to keep him from going to Denmark. That probably meant that they would be watching the Danish border and possibly the house if they knew who his mother was. Even if he stayed in West Germany and tried to make himself inconspicuous there was no guarantee that they wouldn't track him down. And what depressed him more than anything was the thought that he might die before seeing his mother.

42

After another week had gone by and no more had been said about a boat trip. In fact Kirsten's reluctance to speak to him at all had become even more blatant. To leave things as they were would clearly be risky, so Henrik felt he would have to confront her about it, even at the risk of antagonizing her still more. There seemed no point waiting for a chance to occur naturally, so one morning he followed her into the shop and said quietly:

"Kirsten, things cannot go on like this."

Looking up at him from behind the counter, she said: "I quite agree with you, Henrik."

He had anticipated every possible reaction from her, but not this one. For a moment he was speechless.

"Yes," she went on "we must talk, but not here; not now."

"Then where and when?"

"On your boat. I could make time this afternoon."

Again he could hardly believe what he was hearing. Until the coolness had come between them he would have given anything for a chance like this, but now it was she who was suggesting it, he felt confused. She had given him no indication of what he might expect. So while he looked forward to the afternoon, he also dreaded it.

*   *   *

The *Jasmin*, with Henrik at the wheel, chugged along at a leisurely pace, hugging the coast of the island, past windswept dunes, broad beaches and then a stretch of steep chalk cliffs. Henrik found it hard to credit what he was seeing. Kirsten was sitting on the bench that ran around the open deck, her arms resting on the side of the boat, her head flung back, eyes closed against the bright afternoon sun, hair stirring in the light breeze. They had not yet talked about why she had been avoiding him, because whenever he had attempted to raise the subject, she had waved his words aside and promised that they would talk later. The day was too beautiful to spoil with an argument, she seemed to be telling him. So he gave in. The sea was ruffled only by small waves, and the clouds were small and high. When it was time to eat their lunch of ham and rye bread, he opened a bottle of hock, and poured two glasses, leaving it to her to take one, which she did after a momentary hesitation. He turned on his portable radio and tuned to a station playing jazz requests. And still the issue between them remained undiscussed. The music mingled pleasantly with the puttering of the engine and the gentle slapping of the waves against the hull.

Henrik sat at the wheel and drew at the same time, with his sketch pad open on his knees, occasionally reaching out with one hand to correct the course of the boat. Already he had filled three pages with lightning sketches of Kirsten, trying to capture the easy grace of her body in a few deft lines. His nervousness about what she might eventually say enabled him, like some knight in a courtly love epic, to think only Platonic thoughts.

This afternoon, under the high summer sun, caressed by the soft breeze, his longing for Kirsten had transformed itself into a renunciation that held its own kind of pleasure, like the feel of a hair shirt against the skin of a penitent. He had forced himself to give up any thoughts that he could ever be anything more to her than the half-brother that she thought he was. Starting a love affair would compound the deceit that he was already practising, unless he told her the truth, and if he did *that*, he would not only blow his cover but also put her in terrible danger. So on this warm and beautiful afternoon with the tiny waves sparkling like a million stars and the boat swaying ever so slightly, he dared hope that, by their reticence, they were achieving something of great value. Then Kirsten rummaged in her bag and produced a one piece bathing suit.

"Shall we swim?"

"Good idea." He'd realized, as Kirsten spoke, that she would now see his false birthmark for the first time - the brown, diamond-shaped blotch on his left thigh, created for him during the painful half-hour in the Hamburg tattoo parlour. No help for it. If he tried to hide the thing or kept away from her, he would simply draw attention to it.

In a secluded cove they dropped anchor and put on bathing suits, Kirsten changing out of sight in the cabin and Henrik on the deck. While he waited for her, he focused his binoculars on what looked like an Arctic tern perched on a rock near the shore, so when she came out of the cabin, he did not see her stare fixedly at his false birthmark, nor hear her little gasp.

"Henrik ..." she began.

He lowered the binoculars and saw that she was looking at him with a frown.

"Yes?"

She shook her head. "Nothing. Let's swim."

Down the short ladder slung over the stern, they slipped into the water. Henrik stayed close to the boat. Kirsten, streaking along with a graceful crawl, made wide circles around it. After twenty minutes they were ready to climb back on board, which proved tricky with the boat tipping and the ladder difficult to get a foothold on. Henrik clambered aboard first, then reached down to haul Kirsten up, catching her as she half slithered, half stumbled over the side on to the deck. Then he had her in his arms, holding her wet body, mesmerised by the beads of water glistening on her pale skin, feeling the contours of her breasts, hips and thighs under the tight bathing suit. In that moment all his renunciation was swept away and he held her no longer as a half-brother. She allowed him to hold her until his lips brushed hers, then she stiffened, pulled away, and sat huddled at the side of the deck. He handed her a towel and sat down beside her. In silence she dried herself with the towel then tossed it aside.

"Kirsten," he said "what's wrong?"

She turned and gave him a challenging look. "I think you know, Henrik ... but your name isn't Henrik, is it?"

"What the hell are you talking about?"

"I'm talking about *that*!" She pointed at his leg. "That's no birthmark. It's a fake. And you're a fake."

Her words hit him like a kick in the stomach. He felt ready to faint and at the same time everything went into sharp focus. Out of the corner of his eye he saw the Arctic tern take off from its rock and fly away down the coast. The radio was still softly playing jazz, and the bottle of hock was still in its ice bucket. A slight wind had blown up, making the boat swing round.

"I began to suspect it," she went on "when we talked about the nurse from the Lebensborn home, and how her story didn't fit with yours, but I kept telling myself that there must be an explanation. Now I know what it is - you're not my half-brother. So who are you? And what are you?"

He sat for a moment with closed eyes, hearing the maddening slap, slap of the water against the side of the boat. "All right," he sighed. "I'm not your half-brother. The name I grew up with is Lutz Erdmann, but that's not my real name either. The fact is I don't know who I am."

"How very convenient for you."

He looked at her directly, meeting her gaze without flinching. "All I know is that I am the war child of a German soldier and a Danish woman, not Birthe but someone else – I have no idea who. I was given as a small child to one of the Lebensborn homes – I don't know which one. I've told you what happened after that – Königsberg, Dresden, Wittenberge. All of that is true. What I didn't tell you is that at the age of seventeen I was persuaded to sign up for a career in the Stasi."

"No!" cried Kirsten, covering her face with her hands. "That means ..."

"Yes, I'm a spy. I could pretend that I never believed in the communist cause, but at first I did. I really thought the world would be a better place when our system conquered. The Stasi told me I would be using my knowledge of chemistry, and they promised that when I'd served a couple of years I would be given my own laboratory. At first they gave me boring work in a lab in Leipzig, then one day they told me they had found some stuff from the Lebensborn records proving that I was Henrik Karlsson, son of Birthe, and your half-brother."

Kirsten was looking at him with a frown. "Is this a lie too? Or did you really think you were my half-brother?"

"I swear that's *exactly* what I thought. When I met you and Birthe I began to feel things that I'd never felt before – especially for you. I was struck by you at our very first meeting, and the more I got to know you the stronger my feelings grew."

Kirsten was shaking her head sadly. "Oh Henrik, Henrik ..."

"At first I told myself that I could only ever love you as a brother, but then the mystery with the nurse set me wondering, and then came the shattering discovery. When I saw the photograph with the birthmark I knew for sure. The Stasi pretended at first that it had been a mix-up, but I found out that they had deliberately set me up so that I would think I was Henrik Karlsson."

"But when you knew the truth how could you go on pretending? How could you be so cruel and deceitful?"

"Because I was in love with you. It's the truth, Kirsten. But I couldn't tell you, because you thought you were my half-sister."

She was shivering in her wet costume, so he wrapped a towel around her.

"If you'd truly loved me, Henrik, you would have left us all… gone away."

"I couldn't bear not to be near you. That's why I stayed… though it was a torment being in your presence, all the time wanting to reach out and hold you but knowing that I couldn't." She was gazing at him fixedly, giving him no clue about what she was thinking. "Another thing … the Stasi were breathing down my neck. If I'd backed out they would have arranged a fatal accident for me. The mission was too important to them. I thought I'd be doing industrial espionage, but instead I was ordered to destroy a Danish politician – yes, Borup."

Seeing Kirsten begin to sob, he said: "Don't waste your sympathy on him. It was all true about the rival that he had killed during the war. He was a cold-blooded murderer."

"Are the Stasi any better?"

"No, I realise that now. And I realise that the system I've been serving is rotten to the core."

"Oh Henrik," Kirsten sighed. "Lutz … no Henrik. I can never call you anything but Henrik."

"Well now there's only one thing I can do, and that's to

give myself up to the Danish police."

Kirsten drew breath sharply. "Dear God, Henrik. Do you really have to do that?"

"I'm afraid so... I'll write a letter to Birthe explaining everything. It'll be a terrible shock for her and the family, but they would have found out sooner or later anyway. Now let's get back to the harbour. I'll go and see Officer Andersen this evening."

She went below to dress and he did the same on deck. While steering the boat back along the coast, Henrik noticed a white motor launch about half a kilometre out to sea. It was travelling in the same direction and appeared to be deliberately keeping pace with the *Jasmin*, although it was clearly a much faster vessel. When it was still there half an hour later he focused his binoculars on it and was relieved to make out a slim, blond-haired woman at the tiller rather than, as he had half feared, the muscular Kurt. As they came into the harbour the white launch continued down the coast.

*   *   *

When the *Jasmin* was moored at the quay, Henrik held out his hand to help Kirsten ashore, then stood still.

"Wait," he said. "This is probably the last time we shall ever be alone together, so let's say goodbye."

Kirsten nodded, still holding his hand, her eyes moist. "Did you really mean those things you said ... about me?"

"Every word." He drew her towards him. "We've never kissed properly. Let's kiss now. Just this once."

She raised her face towards his and their lips met. A moment later they were embracing feverishly, their bodies clinging together, all the pent-up force of passion between them suddenly released. When at last they drew apart she moved towards the cabin, making it clear that she meant him to follow. After a moment's hesitation he did.

*   *   *

In the semi-darkness of the cabin she at first avoided his eyes, clinging silently to him as they sat on the edge of the narrow bunk. For several minutes he held her motionless, feeling the beat of her heart against his chest and the rise and fall of her breath. Then he lowered his head and kissed her again. She allowed him to peel off her clothes, and in seconds he had taken off his own. Afterwards and for the rest of his life he would remember every detail of those moments – the sweet, fresh aroma of her skin, the pleasantly dank interior of the cabin, the sounds of the harbour, the distant cry of seagulls, the feel of her body awakening in response to his arousal, the way they moved gently at first then more fiercely, their mingled cries of passion coming faster and louder.

After they had slept for a while she opened her eyes and looked up at him with an earnest expression.

"Henrik, don't go to the police. I won't tell anyone. I couldn't bear it if they imprisoned you or sent you back to the East. I'd tell any lie to avoid that." She reached out and stroked his cheek. "Wouldn't it be lovely if we could just stay here forever on this boat? If we could sail away to exotic places ... and forget about the world?" Then in a faraway voice: "We love each other. That's all that matters."

He leaned forward and took her in his arms. "Yes, that's *all* that matters," he repeated very softly, feeling in his heart a flame of joy that seemed to enfold them both and justify everything.

43

In the days that followed his arrival at the reception camp, Hinnerk often asked himself which of his fellow camp inmates might be a spy. Was it perhaps one of the dozen men with whom he shared a room – the schoolteacher who had become tired of having to devote part of every lesson to party propaganda, the border guard who had not wanted to shoot at "traitors" fleeing the country and had one day walked through a checkpoint that he had been guarding, or perhaps the young Protestant pastor who had been harassed in a hundred different ways by the zealously atheist mayor of his town?

Then of course there was the man with the similar name, Heinrich Siebler, who lived in another dormitory down the corridor. When introduced to him one day over lunch in the canteen, Hinnerk nearly said, "So you are my near namesake", but stopped himself just in time. Siebler even bore a certain resemblance to Hinnerk, with his dark brown hair and round, pale face, even though he was shorter and slighter in build, and wore steel-rimmed glasses through which he peered out at the world with a quizzical expression. He might have been a librarian or perhaps a minor civil servant – Hinnerk never did find out what he had done back in the GDR because only a few days after they had met, Siebler disappeared one drowsy Sunday afternoon. The police had been alerted, and the story was in the local newspapers along with a photograph of Siebler and an appeal for anyone who had seen him on that afternoon to come forward. The next day there was a report that he had been seen in the Old Cemetery, a well-known beauty spot in the south-eastern part of the city.

When the subject came up in the canteen, while Hinnerk was having lunch with the pastor and the schoolteacher, Hinnerk said: "This man Sie... Siebler ..." and he realised that he had nearly said his own name, Siebert. "This man Siebler – why do you suppose he went to the cemetery?"

"Oh, he went there a lot," the schoolteacher said, cutting into a Vienna sausage. "He said the presence of so many graves made him feel alive. A little morbid, don't you think?"

"I wouldn't say that," the pastor objected. "Graveyards remind us that, after all, there is an eternal life beyond this one."

But Hinnerk was not listening to them. His near slip with the name had made him see it all – Stasi agents had taken the wrong man. They must have already discovered their mistake and would try again, and this time they would make sure they got the right man – alive or dead.

That afternoon he asked to see Major Kemble, but was told that the Major was on leave in England. Instead he was seen by an American officer, Captain Gray, a young man with a crew-cut and the bland look of a Mormon missionary. Speaking atrocious German with a strong American accent, Gray assured him that the business of the names was "mere coincidence" and that Siebler would turn up again safe and sound. Kemble, he said, had exaggerated the danger of Stasi infiltration in the camp. In any case, as Hinnerk had already been in the camp for ten days, his papers were sure to arrive soon and he would then be able to leave.

The following day came news that Siebler's body had been found, stabbed to death, in a wood near Fulda, close to the GDR border. In vain, Hinnerk tried to seek out Captain Gray but he was too busy to see him in the morning and was out for much of the afternoon. So Hinnerk could not get any advice. According to the local press, the kidnappers on their way to the border with Siebler, had realised their mistake and not considered it worth taking him back to the GDR. So they had just killed him and dumped his body in the wood. When Hinnerk finally saw Captain Gray, the officer told him he was not in danger. Outside the camp, such kidnappings did happen occasionally, but there was really no reason to think that the similarity of the man's name to his own was more than a coincidence. Hinnerk should continue to exercise caution when away from the camp, as all inmates were warned to do.

Hinnerk decided to stay inside. At night he slept badly, wondering how long it would take the agents in the camp to realise that he was their true target. After three days he began to wonder whether the American officer had been right and he was being paranoid, but one evening, entering the dormitory for the night, he noticed that the door of his bedside locker was ajar. The locker was a metal cupboard of the kind used in hospitals. Scratch marks around the lock suggested that someone had picked it. Then the intruder had evidently been interrupted by someone coming into the room and had not had time to close the lock. Hinnerk looked through his few belongings in the cupboard. There was nothing missing and nothing to indicate his identity, but the very fact that the locker had been searched indicated that the Stasi agents had pinpointed him.

That night he lay awake wondering when they would choose to strike. Towards dawn he dozed off briefly, only to be woken by the sound of a church clock tolling five o'clock.

His mind was now made up. While the other occupants of the dormitory still slept, he dressed and stuffed a few possessions into a plastic carrier bag – toothbrush, shaving kit, a change of shirt, underwear and socks. When the canteen opened he ate an early breakfast and took some rolls, cheese and an apple away with him and added them to the bag. Then he left the camp and, taking the longest and most circuitous route, walked to the nearby station, where he bought a ticket to Flensburg, the town that he knew was closest to the Danish border. The ticket cost him 16 marks out of the 50 that were left from his two weeks' allowance.

He changed trains in Hanover and again at Hamburg, ate the frugal snack he had brought with him, and by mid afternoon he was in Flensburg, the northernmost city of Germany. A map that he bought in a souvenir shop on the harbour showed him that the town lay on a fjord, which ran north and then east into the Baltic. The border with Denmark joined the western side of the fjord just beyond the city boundary. He knew that crossing by one of the checkpoints would be impossible, since he had no passport, but if he could cross over by water he might stand a chance.

He settled on a hired rowing boat, which cost him half his remaining money, including the hire fee and a deposit. Now he had only 15 marks in his pocket, but he didn't care. His spirits rose as he plunged the oars into the gentle swell, smelt the breeze coming over the water and saw the Danish coast hoving into view. He passed a village which he knew from the map to be Kollund, the first village on the Danish side, but he kept on rowing up the coast. Ten minutes later he found what he was looking for – a house with grounds adjoining the water, a small jetty and no one in sight. He tied the boat to a post on the jetty, stepped ashore with tears in his eyes and kissed the ground.

44

They lay cocooned in the cabin, the movement of their lovemaking echoed by the gentle rocking and tossing of the boat. Henrik had lost count of the number of times they had come here, each time more intense than the last. The dim interior of the cabin, with the sound of the water lapping against the hull and the smell of coffee from the little galley – this had become their own separate world, their private Shangri-La. Here, for a few blessed hours, Henrik could forget the problems that besieged him in the world outside.

After they had made love he was startled to see that Kirsten was sobbing gently.

"Kirsten ..." He reached out and stroked her damp cheek. "Kirsten ... is there something ...?"

She put her arms around him and drew him close to her. "It's just ... No, we mustn't talk about it. Not now."

He was sure she must be referring to the need to deceive her own mother and felt an overpowering surge of tenderness. "I hate lying too," he murmured. "I never got used to it." For answer, she pulled him down so that he could kiss her – first lips, then her neck and breasts. Moments later they were making love once more.

Later, when they emerged on deck, the sky had darkened and the wind was dank with oncoming rain. Kirsten shivered slightly, struggling into a navy blue pullover. He smiled at her, but his smile froze as he looked over her shoulder and saw again the white motor launch in the distance, bumping along through the white-topped breakers.

"Anything wrong?" Kirsten asked, seeing his changed expression.

He shook his head. "A storm seems to be brewing. That's all. We should be getting back to harbour."

He didn't want Kirsten to notice the white boat. Several times he had seen it on their trips together, and each time he had dismissed it as coincidence. Now a tormenting suspicion hardened to near certainty. Although the light was poor and the view obscured by spray, he could see on the rear deck, someone who looked uncommonly like Kurt.

As they were walking away from the quay, having tied up at the mooring rings, Henrik glanced back and saw the white launch easing its way through the harbour mouth. This seemed to be Kurt's way of telling him that he wanted a meeting.

As soon as he had seen Kirsten back to the house, Henrik told her he had forgotten to close the boat's fuel valve and hurried back to the harbour. The white launch was moored at the end of the quay.

"You took your time," Kurt growled, as Henrik entered the cabin. Dressed in a smart, navy blue blazer and white, turtle-neck shirt, he gave a convincing impression of a playboy mariner. The décor of the cabin was commensurately plush. Soft spotlights lit up red leather upholstery, polished mahogany veneer surfaces and a drinks cabinet lined with mirror glass. "Who was the woman? Your pretend half-sister I suppose."

"Leave her out of it," Henrik snapped. "So what's up? Why are you here?"

Kurt drew at a cigarette, and now Henrik saw that he looked tired, and for the first time visibly worried.

"I'm here because the other man has fled the GDR."

"The other man …?" Henrik was gripped by a nauseating fear as it dawned on him whom Kurt meant.

"Yes, Hinnerk Siebert – or Henrik Karlssen, to use his real name – the man you are supposed to be. He left Berlin on a Saturday morning having told his wife he was going cycling in the Harz. In fact he headed for the Elbe. A motorist reported seeing someone of his description cycling late at night near the restricted zone. The border guards nearly caught him, but he managed to reach the river and a West German patrol boat picked him up."

"Shit!" Henrik took a long, deep breath. "So what do we do now?"

"We wait."

"Wait! Are you serious?"

"Calm down. You're not the only one who's going to be in deep trouble if this operation fails. Listen. Siebert was taken to a reception camp at Giessen. Our collaborators in the camp set a trap for him so that he could be kidnapped and brought back home, but the idiots got the wrong man. Then, when they found the right one, they were about to try again when he jumped camp. We can assume he's heading for his mother's house. We've got to take care of him before he reaches her."

"You mean kill him?" said Henrik, thinking: How can I be saying this?

"That's Plan B. Plan A is we render him unconscious, get him on board the boat and head for the East German coast. Of course if we can't take him alive then we'll have to do the other thing. We've got a Dormobile parked near the bridge to the mainland. Karla and I are taking it in turns to watch the road. If we miss him you'll have to deal with him."

"Karla?"

"The agent they've sent me as a reinforcement."

Henrik objected: "I can't watch round the clock till he comes. What would the family think?"

Kurt took Henrik's arm in an unusual gesture of reassurance. "We're probably talking about twenty-four hours, so buck up, man. Since he didn't show today, it's likely he'll come tomorrow."

"So what's your advice?"

"Find a suitable spot in the wood across from the house and tell the family this-evening that you're going to be up at dawn to spend a whole day drawing birds. I've got a couple of things to give you."

He handed Henrik a photograph of a big man with dark hair and eyebrows, and a large, pale face. Henrik was startled at how different this face was from his own.

"Ugly looking bastard," said Kurt, inviting Henrik to laugh at the double meaning. "Keep his picture with you."

The photograph looked as if taken covertly; the location was Berlin by the river Spree with the Museum Island in the background. Why had Kurt not simply produced an official mug shot from the files? Even as he posed the question, Henrik feared he knew the answer. The fact that the Stasi had taken a covert picture of Siebert meant that they had been keeping him under observation. They had wanted to make sure he did not escape to Denmark and expose the man they had put in his place. And now that was precisely what was going to happen unless Siebert was intercepted.

Kurt now rummaged in a canvas rucksack from which he took a metal box about the size of a car battery. Henrik recognised a portable radio transmitter with a telephone receiver attached by a cable. He had been trained to use the equipment several years ago.

"Keep this with you," Kurt said. Stay in regular contact, and if you spot him alert me immediately. Keep your binoculars and your gun about you."

"My gun?"

"What's wrong with you? To scare Siebert into keeping his trap shut till I can get to you. Of course we want to get him home alive, but if he won't play ball, you'll have to shoot him."

Henrik had the photograph in his hand. The face had an innocent, open expression which, despite himself, he found disarming.

"How long have you had this picture?" Henrik asked sharply.

Kurt hesitated for a moment before saying: "I had it sent to me when you discovered the mistaken identity ... I thought we should know what he looked like just in case."

"You're lying," muttered Henrik. "You've had this man under observation for a long time."

Kurt's startled expression told him his suspicion was correct.

"What the hell are you talking about?"

"You *know*," sneered Henrik. "There was never any mix-up in the records. You and the bosses knew all along that I wasn't Birthe Karlssen's son. You needed someone to impersonate him, and I happened to have a past that fitted."

Kurt stared at him with narrowed eyes. "Careful how you talk. It doesn't alter the present situation. We have a job to do, and we're going to do it."

"What if I refuse?"

Kurt threw back his head and laughed mockingly. "That pretty non-half-sister of yours won't have a face worth kissing if you start playing for the other side or screw up. Don't think I haven't been watching you with her, you unprofessional streak of shit."

"You bastard!"

Henrik lunged towards Kurt, and his fist flew out, but Kurt parried the blow and held Henrik's wrist in an iron grip.

"Steady now! I meant what I said. If you disobey orders, we'll both be arrested, but don't you worry, someone else will sort out your girlfriend." Kurt released his grip then pushed Henrik away. "You've got no choice, buddy boy. We sink or swim together. Now, take the two-way-radio and scram. And stay in contact throughout tomorrow." In silence Henrik slid the photograph into his breast pocket and picked up the rucksack. Ahead of him, unless he was very lucky, lay an act of murder.

45

As he sat down to the evening meal with the family he could not escape the thought that this was a "Last Supper" with himself cast in the role of Judas.

Seeing Kirsten's glowing face across the table, he could remember the feel of her body under his in the most tantalising detail, and, as he did so, an excruciating sense of loss overwhelmed him. Longing to be alone with her, he knew that the time for such happiness might already be at an end. Within a matter of hours, he was going to do something that she would never forgive him for if she ever found out about it. And then there was the rest of the family – Birthe more effervescent than he had ever seen her, Gertrud smiling in her calm, gentle way, and even Sven and Niels looking relaxed.

How ironic that this new harmony should have come about only on the eve of his most terrible betrayal. Birthe had put candles on the table, and the small dining room, with its old oak sideboard and lace curtains had taken on a warm, homely atmosphere which cruelly mocked his mood. At last, close to midnight, the meal was over and the three women stood up to clear away the dishes.

He waited in his room until he heard Kirsten coming up the stairs, then went out on the landing. In a second they were in each other's arms, kissing, their bodies clinging together as though drowning, neither of them saying anything. Henrik tried to memorise this moment in meticulous detail: the smell of her hair, the taste of her kiss, the soft pressure of her breasts against his chest. Finally Kirsten broke the silence.

"Henrik, dearest ..." Her voice trembled with regret. "We can't be together tonight."

"But ...," he pleaded, "if I came to your room for a while ..."

She shook her head. "No, it's too dangerous, and anyway it wouldn't feel right in this house with mother so close. The boat is different. That's our special place, away from the everyday world. We'll go there again soon."

"Yes," he said sadly "soon." The picture came to him of her real half-brother walking along a road towards the island – walking with the same determination that had made him climb on to the roof as a child. And this thought reminded him to tell her that he would be going out early in the morning to spend the day bird watching and drawing.

"How wonderful!" she cried, her eyes lighting up. "Draw something for me, won't you?" She kissed him once more, lightly, and then she was gone to her room.

Closing the door of his own room behind him, he reached for a bottle of aquavit which he had bought for the long vigil ahead, and poured himself the first of many glasses. Beyond tonight and the pain of knowing how soon he might lose her, lay the appalling certainty that Siebert would either be abducted or killed. Either way, how could he bear going on with Kirsten? Their love would be poisoned forever by his knowledge of what he had done to Henrik Siebert.

When he finally slid under the quilt, he was soon twisting back and forth. Even now, he could not stop seeking a solution to his dilemma. Yet over and over again he returned to the inescapable fact that even if he did not kill Siebert, but instead saved him, he would still lose Kirsten. He would not be able to live with himself if he remained here pretending to be the man he had murdered. As if caught in the coils of a snake whose grip became tighter the more he struggled, he abandoned all thought of sleep. He wanted to pray, but realised that the creed he had been brought up in had left him nothing to pray to, and nothing to defend him against the despair that seemed to seep out of the dark corners of the room, and swirl around him like a fog. He had to renounce Kirsten and yet doubted he could do it.

He wondered when his life had taken the turning that had led to this cruel choice between evils. Perhaps very early, when as a schoolboy he had signed the paper committing himself to the Stasi. In a flash of terrible clarity, he now saw how he had been set up for that decision. The headmistress had never intended to expel him, only to intimidate him into signing Petzold's paper. The two of them must have planned it in advance. The avuncular Petzold, the mentor whom he had so liked and trusted, was after all just a cold manipulator. He could not even console himself with the thought that he had served a good cause with unpleasant means, for the system he had worked for was corrupt and evil.

By the early hours of the morning he had convinced himself that there was really only one option open to him. As a thin grey light glowed in the gap between the closed curtains, a chill calm crept over him. He got out of bed and dressed, then tiptoed from the room and down the stairs to the front door, hoping that the creaking of the boards would not wake any of the family. Outside in the yard his car was parked. He opened the boot and fumbled in the space under the spare tyre where he had hidden the gun. After checking the ammunition he thrust it into his jacket pocket and stood for a moment wondering where he should do it. The environs of the house were out of the question. But the boat ... yes, he would take the boat out to sea, stand on the deck ... a shot, a plunge into the water, and oblivion. In the cabin he would leave a note for Kirsten and another for Birthe, explaining everything and asking for forgiveness.

Setting off down the road, he turned for a moment to look back at the house, wondering how long it would take before the family learned what had happened. When he peered ahead into the imperceptibly brightening road he saw a man, ghostly in the half-light, walking towards him. Eager to be seen by no-one on this last walk of his life, he thought of hiding in the shadows of the trees by the roadside. But, as the approaching figure grew more distinct, he felt a cold shiver of recognition. Only for a moment did he deceive himself about what he was seeing. Within seconds denial was impossible. Here, yards from the house, hours sooner than he had thought likely, was *the other man*. The hesitance of his gait, and the way he looked from side to side as if feeling his way, proclaimed him a stranger, just as surely as his heavy build and his large, pale face declared his identity. Henrik didn't need the photograph in his breast pocket. He knew in every fibre of his being that this was Hinnerk Siebert, the real Henrik Karlssen.

As if a self he had long disowned had suddenly taken possession of him, Henrik braced himself to act. All thoughts of suicide were gone. He could scare him away - yes - suddenly Henrik believed he could. When he was within a stone's throw of Hinnerk, he warned him in a loud whisper: "Your life's in danger, Siebert. I can help you, if you do as I say."

It was only as he spoke that Hinnerk seemed to see him, stopped, frowned and peered into the gloom.

"Who are you?" he said.

"I work for West German intelligence. There's a marksman who'll shoot you if you go any closer to that house." He jerked his thumb over his shoulder to indicate the Karlssens' home.

"Wh-why would they shoot me?"

"We can't talk till we find some cover." Henrik pointed to some bushes at the edge of the wood, just behind Siebert. Very reluctantly, the big man backed towards the bushes after a rapid glance behind him.

"Wh-who wants to shoot me?"

"The Stasi. The moment they knew you'd escaped they staked out the house." Suddenly the big man stopped backing away. Henrik whispered urgently: "You can only save yourself by leaving the island. I'll take you by boat and drop you on the mainland. We must go straight to the harbour." He pointed to a track leading through the trees. "That path cuts off a bend in the road and gets us there unobserved."

But Siebert stopped dead, his face registering deep mistrust.

"Do you think I'd fall for a trick like that? Once you get me on board, the next thing I know I'll be landing in East Germany, unless you shoot me and dump me over the side first."

"Please," murmured Henrik, "I'm trying to help you."

"I don't believe you."

Henrik moved closer and hissed: "The Stasi planted an agent in the Karlssen family. He's using your identity. They'll kill you to protect him."

Siebert still did not move. "Take me to the phone box in the village and we'll find out what's true."

"You'd never make it there alive."

"Because *you* will kill me?"

"No, because *they* will kill you." He looked Siebert in the eye, willing him to yield. But his persuasive powers were useless. Siebert merely looked back at him stolidly. "Fine," rasped Henrik, "I don't care whether you believe me or not." Then he released his gun from its shoulder holster and made sure Hinnerk saw it. "Do as I say, or you're dead. Now start walking."

Siebert stood firm for what seemed an age then took several faltering steps. "My m-m-mother would know an imp-p-poster any day. You must be lying about the agent."

"Know you by your birth mark, would she?" Henrik laughed and was gratified by the look of shock on Hinnerk's broad face. He jabbed the gun into Hinnerk's ribs. "Now move."

To Henrik's relief Hinnerk allowed himself to be prodded slowly along the track. "Birth marks can be faked like everything else," said Henrik, softly.

Siebert stopped about twenty metres down the path. Henrik was dimly aware of a cloud of white blossom to his left – wild cherry, he guessed. Around him millions of tender new leaves would soon be reaching towards the light. From deep within the wood, came the opening notes of the dawn chorus. It struck him that mentioning the birthmark had been madness. No western counter-intelligence officer could possibly have known about it. Even Kurt had not known until told by him. In the grey light, as the birds sang louder, the real bird watcher's son was regarding him closely.

"You're *him*, aren't you?" demanded Hinnerk. "You were sent to pretend to be me."

"Keep walking." Henrik gestured with the gun, but Hinnerk shook his head. This movement was not emphatic, but Henrik knew he meant it. For the first time since he had seen Siebert, Henrik felt the adrenalin that had sustained him until now, drop away, making everything seem infinitely hard. For a few brief minutes he had really believed he might scare Hinnerk so badly that he would abandon his plan to be re-united with his mother. But that hope was all but dead now. He wondered how Hinnerk had reached the island without being seen by Kurt or the woman. Perhaps he had hitched a lift from a lorry during the night, in which case he would have been hard to spot. Kurt and Karla would probably still be looking out for him, so Henrik calculated that he had perhaps a couple of hours before they became suspicious. Henrik knew the big man would only escape them if he could be landed in some remote place on the mainland. And if that could be achieved Henrik felt he might one day persuade Kirsten that he had done his best to make amends by saving her half-brother's life. After taking Hinnerk to a safe place, Henrik would alert the Danish police to Kurt's presence and intentions, so that he could be arrested before Hinnerk could walk back again and blunder into his nemesis on the bridge. After that, Henrik meant to give himself up to the West German police and offer to co-operate. Kirsten would expect no less.

Hinnerk was staring at him with angry incredulity. "You fooled my whole family and then thought you'd shoot me like a dog?"

Since Kurt and Karla might arrive at any moment, the time for explanations was over. To save him, all Henrik could do was threaten. He raised the gun. "We go to the harbour or I shoot you here."

"Shoot if you like. I've faced death often enough on the way here." As Siebert moved towards him, Henrik could not help feeling admiration. "I've come here in spite of everything you could do. If I'm going to die, then I'll die on Danish soil."

Henrik had played his last card. A dull rage rose within him. What recompense would he ever have for what the Stasi had done to him? Not a thing. This lumbering man would take away everything that he had briefly enjoyed, just because he was lucky enough to be who he was. I, he thought, was tricked into thinking *I* was Birthe's son. Tricked into feeling love for a mother not my own, made to feel the worst guilt in the world for nothing that was my fault. And now this oaf will destroy my last hope of salvaging something from the wreckage. Why couldn't he do what he was told? Everyone else from the GDR could manage that. But not him. The blood in Henrik's head seemed to boil as his whole body trembled with rage. Despite himself, he began to squeeze the trigger, though his hand shook uncontrollably. Stupid, bloody fool. Through the head -

yes. *Yes.* The barrel of the gun was circling and dipping. Shoot him, he heard Kurt whisper in his ear. Do it, man! Siebert's face was ashen, his lips trembling. *Do it!* roared Kurt's voice in every corner of his mind. Just then Henrik felt an explosion of pain in his wrist and the gun went off. Siebert was lying on the ground. A moment earlier he had tried to kick the gun out of Henrik's hand. As Henrik's arm had been jerked aside by the kick, his finger had tightened and the gun had fired. Henrik pocketed the gun and knelt next to Hinnerk. He reached down and touched his leg close to where he was holding it. At once Henrik felt warm blood welling.

Henrik saw a light come on in one of the upper windows of the house. Then Niels leaned out and called: "What's happening?" in a scared voice

"There's been an accident," Henrik cried back in German. "In the wood." He was pressing down hard on Siebert's wound in an effort to stem the flow of blood. His victim was moaning aloud, all assertiveness gone. It flashed through Henrik's mind that he still might manage to bluff it out by claiming that Hinnerk had been sent by the Stasi to kill him. Yet this thought withered at once. The truth would be sure to emerge. One look at Hinnerk's solemn, honest face would be enough for anyone to see that he was genuine.

Henrik was still crouched over the wounded man, when Niels stumbled towards them, thrusting aside saplings, and breathing hard. "I heard a shot," Niels gasped, in English, the language they usually spoke together. "What's happened?"

"This man has been shot in the leg," Henrik told him slowly, as if explaining to a child. He prayed he would have an opportunity later to explain things to Birthe and Kirsten. But perhaps he would not.

"Who shot him?" Niels' mouth hung open as he stared at Henrik.

"He did," groaned Hinnerk, directing accusing eyes at Henrik, and surprising him with his heavily accented English.

"Because you flung yourself at me and knocked my arm." Henrik turned to Niels. "He's losing a lot of blood. We must get him to the house and call an ambulance."

After a great effort they got Siebert to his feet, one on either side.

"Try to put your weight on your good leg," Niels said, speaking in German, "and use us as crutches. Can you manage that?"

Siebert nodded, his face tight with pain, and slowly he hobbled forwards with the two men holding him and trying to stamp down the undergrowth ahead of him until they reached the road. Then they half carried him across the tarmac. By the time they reached the house, more lights were on, and Birthe, Sven, Kirsten and Gertrud, all in their night clothes, came down the stairs as the injured man was carried through the hall and into the living room.

"What the devil's going on?" Sven muttered, rubbing his eyes.

"Put him on the sofa," Gertrud ordered. "And call an ambulance right away."

"I'll do it," Niels volunteered and went to the telephone in the hallway.

"You're in safe hands," Gertrud told Siebert in her capable, reassuring voice, though it was clear he understood very little Danish. "I used to be a nurse. We need to expose that wound with the minimum of movement and then stop the bleeding. Kirsten, could you bring the first-aid kit and a pair of scissors from the kitchen so that we can cut away the trouser leg? And Birthe, could you fetch a bowl of warm water and cloth for a tourniquet?"

"I've called the ambulance," Niels said, coming back into the room. "They have to come from the mainland, so they'll be here in about half an hour."

"What about the police?" demanded Sven. "That man's been shot."

"I'll call them," insisted Henrik.

"But you shot him," objected an outraged Niels.

"It was an accident."

A moment later Kirsten came in with the scissors and first-aid kit. To Henrik's relief she had not heard Niels' accusation. But he could see how confused she was, and wished he could think of what to say. Gertrud took the scissors and other things from Kirsten, and said sternly, "Please be quiet everyone. I don't want him to become agitated." Then she carefully cut away the trouser leg above the thigh. "Fortunately the bullet's gone through without hitting the bone. Help me tighten the tourniquet, someone."

Birthe and Kirsten came forward to help. When the tourniquet was tied Birthe saw something that made her draw breath sharply. Kirsten followed the direction of her mother's gaze in stunned silence. Then Gertrude, who had not noticed the diamond-shaped birthmark, covered it with a dressing. Birthe turned to Henrik. "I don't understand, I don't...." Kirsten was standing beside her with an anguished look on her face. Henrik assumed that Kirsten now suspected that he had just tried to murder her real half-brother to save his own skin. What else could she suppose?

"Will *someone please* tell me, what's going on?" roared Sven.

Birthe began to tell him about Hinnerk's birthmark.

"I always knew your precious Henrik was a no good, lousy fraud," roared Sven.

By then Henrik had rushed from the room and made for the telephone. When Kurt and the woman realised that something was wrong they would either escape in Kurt's yacht or come to the house to kill or kidnap Siebert. *To hell with that.* Henrik gripped the phone and dialled rapidly. First he would tell the police where Kurt and Karla could be picked up, and then where he could be found. Perhaps, before the police took him away, he might be lucky enough to have a few minutes with Kirsten to explain to her what had really happened in the wood. Yet as he heard the operator's voice asking which emergency service he wanted, Niels and Sven fell on him and ripped the phone from his hand.

"You've got some explaining to do! Filthy imposter."

He felt Sven's fist connect with his cheekbone, and then Niels hit him on the head with a walking stick.

"You owe mother more than an apology, you bastard."

As they dragged him into the sitting room, Birthe's white face was shining with tears. Standing motionless by her mother, Kirsten was dry-eyed but trembling uncontrollably. Unable to look at her, Henrik closed his eyes and bowed his head.

46

Across the road, concealed in the wood, among some stunted yew trees and a clump of unpleasantly prickly holly bushes, Kurt was training a pair of powerful Zeiss binoculars on the house. Beside him on the ground lay a small canvas rucksack holding a walkie-talkie, and a long, narrow leather bag containing a rifle. Despite the early hour he could have done with a swig of Schnapps to clear his head and ease the furious mood he was in. For one thing he hated woods. They worsened the hay fever that seemed to get worse every year, making his nose run and his head feel like a ball of lead. He had only come to this spot because of an instinct that something had gone wrong with the ambush. And he had been right. Erdmann should have been here watching for his Doppelgaenger, reporting at regular intervals using his walkie-talkie. And instead, where was he? Inside the house, where something odd seemed to be going on. The whole family, apart from the children, were awake and gathered in the living room.

Kurt shifted his position, trying to see more. One of the women was bending over a sofa where a man was lying stretched out. Kurt could not see the man's head because the master of the house was standing with his back to the window, partly blocking the view. But a disquieting suspicion was growing in Kurt's mind.

He blew his nose and swore. Right from the start he had felt uneasy about this whole Danish operation and Kobitz's crazy scheme with the "unwitting Doppelgaenger". Somehow you knew in your bones when a plan had "a worm in it". Now it was turning into a whole can of worms, with him right in the middle of it.

Kurt hated many things, but most of all he hated being seen as a loser. Life had taught him early on that to be *that* was the worst fate in the world. Born in Göttingen in the year of the Nazi take-over, as a child he had loved the parades, the uniforms, the martial music, the endless rows of swastika flags, the sound of Hitler's voice over the radio. After the war began he had been thrilled at the news of victory after victory for the glorious Wehrmacht, in which his own father was an officer, on the Russian front. Then, out of the blue, had come the unthinkable – defeat at Stalingrad, his father "missing, presumed dead", the food shortages, and the realisation that Germany was fighting for its life. His nightmare had begun – he and his mother cowering in the cellar all night waiting to be entombed by bombs. Afterwards, the devastation, the mangled corpses lying in the streets. And then the invasion – American soldiers looting the house and raping his mother. He had vowed to get his own back when he grew up, and had never stopped trying.

While a stream of refugees flowed continuously west, he and his mother had headed east, to her parents in Weimar, inside the Russian zone, and there they had stayed while the maelstrom around them gradually subsided. Life under the Russians had been hard, but he had got used to it. And having known every taste, touch, texture and smell of humiliation, he had vowed never again to be on the losing side.

Eventually he had found the perfect winning side in the Stasi. Their football club, Dynamo Berlin, for which he had played in the reserve team, had been given the nation's best players, best trainers, best doctors, all to ensure victory. As a Stasi agent he had started doing the same. If there was a tough assignment to be carried out – say a dangerous renegade from the GDR to be kidnapped or eliminated – he could always be relied upon to deliver. His winning streak had gone on long enough for him to have hoped to reach the highest echelons of the organisation - until this miserable Danish affair.

Any fool could be wise after the event, but he still wished he had acted differently when Erdmann had told him about the birthmark. At that point he should have put the interests of the mission before his own. He should have advised them to pull Erdmann off the job, but he hadn't done that because Kobitz wouldn't have liked it, and a bad mark from Kobitz would have damaged his chances for promotion. Then Siebert had escaped to the west. That was Kobitz's cock-up, but his agents were the ones who'd have to carry the can. Everyone had thought Siebert was a docile nobody with no intention of leaving the GDR. How had his interrogators been *that* wrong?

But there was no point in looking back. He had to deal with Erdmann, and he was glad that the Stasi had sent an experienced agent to help him – Karla, with her hatchet face and bleached blond hair, ice-cold but tough, resourceful and incredibly fit. He was going to need all the help she could give him if they were going to salvage anything from the catastrophe.

From inside the house he heard raised voices. The big man had moved away from the window, giving Kurt a clear view into the living room. As his gaze fell on the sofa he realised that his suspicion had been right. The man lying there was Hinnerk Siebert. A moment later he saw Erdmann being manhandled into the room by the big one (Sven?) and another man (presumably his son, Niels), who pushed him violently to the floor. As it dawned on Kurt what had happened, his fingers tightened painfully on his binoculars. Erdmann had lost his nerve and botched the job with Siebert, merely injuring him. Siebert had been brought into the house, and in no time the family had discovered the truth. So the whole mission was a write-off, and threatened to become a disaster.

Erdmann was now sitting in a chair with one of the men pointing a gun at him. They would hand him over to the police for sure, and Erdmann wasn't going to lie for the sake of his country. Not him. Kurt lowered his binoculars. No, the treacherous little shit would blow the whole Doppelgaenger programme wide open. Kurt put down the binoculars, opened the leather bag and took out the rifle, a Russian SVD gas-operated semi-automatic, a state-of-the-art sniper's weapon. He weighed it in his hands for a moment, admiring its sleek lines and the powerful telescopic site mounted above the barrel. Then, with a practised movement, he raised the stock to his shoulder and drew a bead on Erdmann's head. He could almost see his skull breaking open. Just one squeeze. Kurt lowered his arm with an angry expiration of breath. A young woman had suddenly blocked his view and remained in that position. Kurt grimaced and returned the rifle to its bag. Maybe it would be best to get him back home alive so that he could take the blame for the whole fiasco.

Kurt lifted the rucksack from the ground beside him, took out the walkie-talkie and spoke into the receiver. When he heard Karla's answering voice he said: "Erdmann's botched the job. He and Siebert are both inside the house. We need to act fast."

47

He lay sprawled on the floor like a fallen angel. Strangely, in that terrible moment what was uppermost in his consciousness was not the horror of his situation but the threadbare carpet with its faded rose pattern and Birthe's sensible brown shoes a few inches from his head. In his humiliation his mind clutched at these mundane things as though they might offer a momentary comfort.

Sven gave him a vicious kick in the ribs then snatched the gun that had been protruding from his pocket. "You won't be needing this any more," he heard Sven growl. Then he felt the cold muzzle pressed against his temple.

"Worm!" Sven shouted. "I've a good mind to shoot you right now, but first I want to see you grovel. Now lick Birthe's boots and beg for forgiveness."

He lay doubled up, his ribs aching from the pain of the kick and his head throbbing from the blow that Niels had given him. He did not try to move, hoping that Sven might after all fire the gun and end his pain for ever.

"Why don't you do it!" he shouted.

As Niels hit him again with his stick, Kirsten screamed: "No more. Stop!"

"What's it got to do with you, Kirsten?" demanded Sven.

"Nothing," shouted Henrik. "Leave her alone."

Sven lunged at Henrik as he tried to get to his feet and knocked him down again. Kirsten grabbed a small table and jabbed at her father with its legs.

Too dazed to help her, Henrik clung to the hope that she did not think him guilty of trying to kill Hinnerk. Sven caught hold of the little side-table and shoved it back at Kirsten so hard that she fell against the large country sideboard by the door and slipped slowly to the ground, clutching her back.

"Why are you taking his side?" he yelled at his daughter.

Henrik staggered between Kirsten and her father but was stopped by another blow from Niels's stick, this time in the face. Blood was filling his mouth by the time he managed to reach out and touch Kirsten's arm. "Don't fight them," he begged.

She shook her head violently and cried: "I'm taking his

side because he's not a monster."

"But that's exactly what he is, little sister," jeered Niels. "He betrayed you and all of us."

Sven was about to administer another kick to stop Henrik standing up, when Birthe screamed: "Stop it, Sven! Stop it! There's been enough violence for one day." She gave Kirsten her hand and helped her to reach an armchair. "How dare you hurt your own daughter, Sven. Shame on you. Now Henrik, sit down and tell us who you are if you're not my son."

He rose to his feet and lowered himself gingerly into a chair, glancing at Kirsten who was clearly in pain. Mercifully the children were asleep in their rooms at the back of the house and had missed the mayhem.

"I ... I don't expect you to believe me," Henrik began "but when I came here I really thought I was your son."

"Just answer the question!" Niels snapped, in English. "Who the hell are you?"

"All right," he began in a subdued voice.

Kirsten smiled at him encouragingly. Overwhelmed, he looked away, fearing he might break down. "You needn't call me Henrik any longer. As most of you now know ..." – he pointed to the man on the sofa, now lying still with his eyes closed – "this is the real Henrik ... or Hinnerk, as he calls himself. My name is Lutz Erdmann."

"Lutz?" Birthe repeated in a puzzled tone, as though she found it impossible to associate the clipped sound with the man she had known as Henrik.

"Yes. I am an agent of the Ministry of State Security of the German Democratic Republic."

Sven gave a snort. "Ha! A filthy spy, all along."

Gertrud now spoke for the first time. "Please, let him

speak. Go on Henrik … Lutz."

Now that his true identity was revealed, he felt as though he had shed the dead weight of an iron mask. Relief, shame and a great weariness remained. Haltingly he told them his story: the unknown circumstances of his birth in Denmark, the unrecorded sojourn in a Lebensborn home, the brief period in Königsberg, the loss of his adoptive mother in Dresden, then the second set of adoptive parents, the way he had been tricked as a schoolboy into pledging himself to the Stasi, the fake discovery of the Lebensborn documents, the mission to Denmark.

"How do we know *any* of this is true?" jeered Sven. "You could have come here knowing perfectly well you weren't a member of our family."

"You're right. I can't prove I didn't know my identity was false. But I swear I didn't. I was fooled too. I never meant to harm to any of you."

"Just use us as your trusting stooges," muttered Sven.

The moth-eaten stag's head on the wall seemed to stare down at Lutz with a mocking expression. "Yes," it seemed to say, "the Stasi deceived you, but you deceived yourself as well. You naively thought you could keep your work for the Stasi separate from the people whose lives you touched. You say you didn't intend to harm them, but that's exactly what you did. Poor Claudia is dead, Kirsten will never be forgiven by her family when they find out that she knew the truth about you, and now the whole family is in danger. Your training never prepared you for that, did it?"

"Don't expect us to feel sorry for you," chipped in Niels.

"I don't," replied Lutz, grateful for Niels' anger. It was their pain he couldn't stand. "Why not, kick me again."

"It's what you deserve," grunted Sven.

"Keep quiet," snapped Kirsten, unexpectedly getting up. "How did this shooting happen?" She pointed in the direction of Siebert's bandaged leg.

"Early this morning," Lutz replied, speaking in English to Kirsten, "I decided to end my life." A cry left Kirsten's lips, and her hand flew to her mouth. "I took the gun," continued Lutz, "and started to walk down to the harbour, intending to go to the boat, put out to sea and shoot myself. But on the road I met him approaching the house" – he glanced at Hinnerk with lowered eyes. "I warned him that my colleagues had a plan to ambush him, and said I would take him by boat to the mainland to avoid them. He didn't believe me, so I tried to force him to come with me at gunpoint. When he tried to kick the gun from my hand it went off accidentally and he was shot in the leg. The rest you know."

There was a long silence, before Birthe said: "How could you live here thinking you were really one of us and yet all the time be spying on our country? And then, when you saw the photograph with the birthmark and knew you were someone else ... how could you go on pretending? What kind of person must you be?"

"I was a man out of my depth." He looked directly at her kindly, tear-streaked face. "I was happy with you all. I swear it. I felt I'd found my real family at last. Okay, I was working for the Stasi. At first I really believed in the cause, then I came to realise that I'd always been used by them. I was told I couldn't quit without risking a bullet in the head. Even after I discovered the birthmark, I had to go on pretending. You have no idea how ruthless these people are. If they'd ever suspected that one of you knew my secret, that person would have had an accident in no time."

Lutz turned and met Kirsten's unhappy gaze, trying, by simple force of will, to remind her of the other reason why he had gone on pretending. I loved you, his eyes told her, and I still do. I was desperate not to lose you.

Suddenly Hinnerk spoke up. He had pulled himself up into a sitting position and was pointing at his Doppelgaenger. Somehow he had grasped the sense of what had been said. "He's telling the truth," he said in German, and everybody turned in surprise to look at him. "He did try to help me escape, but I didn't trust him. The shooting accident was my fault."

"What's he saying?" asked Sven impatiently.

"That I told the truth," said Lutz in Danish, jumping to his feet. "You may not care what happens to me, but for Siebert's sake you need to call the police immediately. There are two Stasi agents on the island looking for him and me."

Now Sven and Niels were confused. They were no longer in control. While they stood uncertainly, Gertrud said: "Well someone's got to call the police, so I will." She stood up. "What shall I tell them?" she asked Lutz.

"There's a man and a woman near this house, and they're armed. They'll be driving a dormobile and they have a white motor launch moored in the harbour which they'll use for their escape."

She nodded and went to telephone from the hallway, where they heard her explaining the situation in her calm, sensible voice.

"I spoke to Officer Andersen," she told them when she came back. "He's only got himself and one other man, so he's calling for reinforcements from Nykobing. He'll be here as soon as he can."

While Gertrud had still been speaking, Lutz had been relieved to see an ambulance with a blue light on its roof drawing up in front of the house. With ambulance men about, and one or two policeman expected at any moment, Kurt and the woman would be unlikely to make their move.

He jumped as he heard Kirsten's familiar voice right beside him. "I need to talk to you, urgently ... it can't wait ... Come to the kitchen."

He started to follow, but as they reached the doorway something heavy smashed through the window from outside and lay on the floor – a metal object that Lutz for a second took for a beer can thrown by the louts who had attacked him. But they were in jail, and the object was making a hissing noise and giving off smoke from a hole in each end.

"A smoke grenade!" he shouted. "Get out of the room! Someone help Hinnerk!"

He felt his way towards the spot where the grenade lay. Half closing his eyes against the stinging smoke and trying not to breathe it in, he reached down to pick up the canister, but already the metal was hot, and he immediately dropped it. Pulling his sleeve down over his hand, he tried again, and this time held the thing long enough to fling it out through the smashed window. Through the veil of smoke he saw Hinnerk hobbling out through the door, leaning on Niels's shoulder. The others were already out of the room. Coughing helplessly, he went towards the door, and now a figure loomed in front of him. Lutz made out a blue uniform, a peaked cap and goggles, and this person's nose and mouth were covered by a white gauze surgical mask. It was only when he saw a woman - similarly masked and uniformed - just behind this man, that he realised who they were.

"You're coming with us," he heard Kurt say through his mask, as he felt a gun pressed to his head.

Simultaneously the woman, Karla, twisted his right arm behind his back and held his little finger in a skilled grip that sent pain flashing up his arm.

"Now move!" she ordered in a steely voice. "Try anything and I'll make it ten times worse."

Kurt led the way through the door and out into the hallway, now also half-filled with smoke. From the floor above he heard Niels shouting to the children to leave by the back stairs. The rest of the family appeared to have left the house already by the back door.

Outside in the road the ambulance was waiting. Kurt opened the rear doors and climbed in. Karla ordered Lutz to follow, giving his little finger one last agonising twist as she pushed him onto a bunk at the side of the compartment. On the floor, between the bunks were the ambulance driver and his assistant, bound and gagged.

"I'd like to show you something," Kurt murmured to Lutz in a pleasant, confiding voice. He had what looked like a small leather travelling bag. "Take a look at this." He opened the bag and held it up to Lutz's face. Too late, Lutz saw the white gauze pad and smelt the pungent aroma of chloroform. Kurt pulled the bag over his head, so that the pad pressed against his mouth and nose, while Karla held him down. His last thought before he lost consciousness was that now he would never know what Kirsten had wanted to tell him.

48

When Police Officer Andersen and his deputy stepped out of their car and approached the house they found the Karlssen family assembled in the courtyard, ashen-faced and clearly shaken, including the two children who were still in their night clothes. The dog was running about in circles, barking and whining by turns. A pungent, burnt-out smell hung in the air, and the house was still wreathed in wisps of smoke from the now extinguished grenade. Someone had fetched a chair for the wounded Hinnerk, who sat wrapped in a blanket. Two more police cars drew up.

"We'd better get him off to hospital," Andersen said after he had been given a rough account of the drama by Gertrud, the only one who seemed able to speak coherently. "There isn't time to order another ambulance, so one of the cars can take him." He signalled to two of his colleagues, who helped Hinnerk to the car and eased him into the back seat. Birthe, appearing to wake up out of a daze, picked up the blanket, dashed with it to the car and gently tucked it around Hinnerk. Her hand rested for a moment on his shoulder before one of the policemen closed the door. Hinnerk managed a wave as the car drove off.

"The kidnappers," Andersen said. "You say there were two of them …"

Kirsten spoke up: "Yes, a man and a woman. Henrik said they had a dormobile near by and also a white motor yacht at the harbour. Please do something to stop them. God knows what they'll do to Henrik …"

"Serve him right!" Niels snorted. "The bastard."

Kirsten turned to him with a venomous look. "Would you

have refused to obey the Stasi in his position?"

Andersen held up a placating hand. "I'll send out an alert for them right away." They watched him walk to his car and speak into a walkie-talkie attached to the dashboard. When he returned he said as reassuringly as he could: "I've sent out a description and instructions to look both for the Dormobile and the yacht. Don't worry, they can't get very far. We'll catch them."

"What do you think will happen to Henrik ... Lutz?" Kirsten asked.

"I don't want to hear that man's name again!" Sven shouted. "As far as I'm concerned I hope his East German friends throw him into the sea."

Birthe began to weep. "I know what he did was wicked, but I feel so sorry for him."

"Save your pity for your real son, Mother," Niels said sharply. "He's the one who has suffered most in all of this."

"Yes," Birthe sobbed "I know I'll have to get used to the idea that he is my real son. It will just take me a while. All this has been such a terrible shock."

Andersen had walked over to his car to take a call on the walkie-talkie, and now he came back with a worried look on his face.

"Not such good news, I'm afraid. They located the dormobile standing empty outside the village, and the ambulance was found abandoned near the harbour with the two ambulance men tied up inside it. They also found the white yacht, still in the harbour with no one on board."

49

In his dream he heard the lapping of waves and felt Kirsten's body beneath him moving in rhythm with the swell, and he kept whispering to her that she was his "Little Mermaid" and that they were safe here, cocooned in the cabin of the *Jasmin*. Then, as the dream faded, he realised he was indeed in the *Jasmin*, but he was not making love to Kirsten. He was alone on the bunk where they had lain together, and when he tried to sit up he couldn't because he was tightly bound, the ropes digging painfully into his wrists and ankles. For a moment he could not work out why he was here, then he remembered Kurt, the ambulance, the chloroform. So the bastards had taken his boat instead of their own, well aware that the police and the coast guard would be looking for a modern white launch, not an old converted fishing craft.

He could hear them talking on the deck beyond the main cabin, evidently unaware that he had returned to consciousness.

"I tell you, we'll need him as a witness," Kurt was saying urgently. "If he confesses to having screwed up then it'll take the heat off us."

"Get real," Karla snapped back, "his testimony won't do you any good. You should have called the thing off as soon as he found out who he was. That's going to count against you."

"It was headquarters' decision to keep him on. Everything would have been fine if those idiots hadn't let Siebert escape."

"And fine if Erdmann had shot him when he had the chance. He disobeyed orders so he'll be shot the moment he gets back home, so we might as well shoot him now. HQ will be grateful to us for saving them the trouble."

Terrified, Lutz twisted his hands slightly to see if he could loosen the knot, but it was hopeless.

"They might not see it that way," Kurt said. "Killing one of our own agents is a serious matter …"

"We have the authority to kill traitors - that's what he is. We'll reach the ship pretty soon. So we need to do it while we're still out of sight. If you won't, I will."

Kurt was silent for about a minute – the longest, most agonising silence Lutz had ever known.

"Maybe you're right," Kurt said at last. "All right, take care of it while I keep watch here."

Certain he was about to die, Lutz heard her footsteps as she crossed the main cabin. Out of the corner of his eye, he saw her framed in the doorway, raising a gun. He closed his eyes.

"Wait!" Kurt called from the deck.

"What is it now?" demanded Karla fiercely, but she lowered the gun and left the cabin.

"Listen," urged Kurt, once he thought both he and Karla were out of Lutz's hearing, "it's Kobitz who's to blame for thinking up this crazy scheme. I can use Erdmann's testimony against him and then step into his job. Imagine what that would do for your career as well as mine – I'll see to that. But it means we have to bring Erdmann back alive."

"You'd better be right." Karla said, then glanced into the cabin. "Oh, I do believe the traitor's awake."

"All right," Kurt ordered "get him up on deck. I can see the ship."

After Karla had untied him she propelled him on to the deck using her vicious finger grip. His wrists and ankles were numb, and he felt sick from the swell and the after-effects of the chloroform. Looming ahead to starboard was a frigate of the People's Navy of the GDR with a group of seamen lowering a ladder over her side.

As they came up to the side of the vessel, Lutz saw the name *Stadt Wismar* painted in white against the drab grey of the hull. As he began to climb the ladder his nausea grew worse. At the top, he was grasped by sailors' hands and pulled roughly onto the deck. Before they took him below he caught a last glimpse of the *Jasmin*, floating away like a lost dream, with the Danish coast already far in the distance.

50

"I tell you, I forbid you to go!" Sven, red-faced and fuming, blocked the front door of the house, while Birthe and Kirsten faced him defiantly. "I've had just about enough of all these Germans barging in and playing havoc with our lives." His breath smelt of beer and his voice was slurred.

Birthe stared at him, her face pale and tight with anger.

"And I tell you we're going, whether you like it or not. He's my son, and he's lying there injured in hospital. I'm going to visit him."

She made to push past him, but he shoved her back, so that she staggered and almost fell. "You're not! And that's final!"

"Father!" Kirsten yelled at him. "You're drunk. He's my brother and we're going."

"Your brother!" Sven guffawed. "How do you know he's not a spy as well, like that other little shit?"

At that moment Niels came up to the door from outside. His car stood in the drive with the engine running.

"OK," he said briskly "let's go."

Sven turned and looked at him in astonishment. "What? You're going as well? What's come over you Niels?"

Niels said quietly: "Hinnerk nearly died trying to get here. It's the least we can do."

The women had slipped past Sven and climbed into the car. While Sven lumbered after them Niels was already in the driver's seat. The car moved off with Sven hammering his fists on the windows and shouting incoherently.

* * *

"You're all very kind," Hinnerk said, looking at the flowers and the fruit that they had brought, "especially when I've caused you so much trouble." He lay in a casualty ward in a hospital in Vordingborg, with six other occupants. Behind a curtain they could hear the occupant of the next bed, a half-demented elderly man on a drip, moaning continuously.

"Caused us trouble! …" Niels repeated. "Are you serious? You deserve a medal after what you've been through."

Kirsten added: "You're a hero, Hinnerk. You don't mind if we call you Hinnerk, do you? After all, you are our half-brother …our true half-brother." She said the words a little hesitantly, as though it hadn't quite sunk in that this large, pale man lying in the bed was really the person that Lutz had claimed to be.

She and Niels spoke German with Hinnerk, while Birthe silently arranged the flowers in a vase that one of the nurses had brought. When she had finished Hinnerk thanked her and smiled, touching her arm. Birthe said something in Danish and Kirsten translated:

"Mother says there is a lot that she wants to talk to you about, but she doesn't feel up to it now. The past couple of days have been very confusing for her. But she wants you to know that she's glad you're here."

"Tell my mother I understand," Hinnerk said. "There is so much I want to talk to her about, but everything can wait. When I'm discharged from here, I'll have to go back to Germany to complete the asylum process and apply for Danish residence. By the way, what happened to the other man and the ones who dragged him off?"

"Not a trace," Niels said. "They got clean away. They are probably back in East Germany by now."

"And what do you think will happen to him." Kirsten's voice shook with anxiety.

From behind the curtain came a series of loud moans from the old man in the next bed. When they had subsided Hinnerk said: "I'm afraid at best he'll get a long prison term, at worst a death sentence."

Kirsten's hand flew to her mouth.

"It's no more than he deserves," Niels said.

"He saved my life by not handing me over to his colleagues," Hinnerk reminded them. "We mustn't forget that."

By the time visiting hours were over it was raining. While Niels dashed off to fetch the car, Kirsten and Birthe waited in the entrance porch, looking gloomily out at the rain-swept car park, the row of rubbish containers at one side, the signs pointing to "X-Ray Unit", "Casualty", "Physiotherapy".

"I'm thinking about Henrik ... I can't seem to call him Lutz," Kirsten said. "Do you think they'll really execute him?"

Birthe sighed. "I don't know, dear, but there's nothing we

can do to help him now."

"But Mother..." Kirsten's voice was cracking: "I... I loved him ... I still do. I found out his secret some time ago, but I couldn't betray him. I know I should have told you, but I was desperate not to lose him."

"I guessed as much the moment you stood up for him. Luckily for you, Sven and Niels didn't draw the same conclusion. I'll say nothing to them, but you must forget him, Kirsten." Her tone was resigned but emotional.

"I hated not telling you," Kirsten insisted.

Her mother turned away. "I loved him too...and wish I never had."

An ambulance drew up and a heavily bandaged patient was lowered from the rear compartment on to a trolley.

"There's something else, Mum ..." Kirsten began, but she couldn't go on. Niels had drawn up in the car and was signalling to them through the glass to run out to him and brave the curtain of rain.

PART IV

51

Berlin, summer 1990

From the Friedrichstrasse station he boarded a suburban train going west. He had a sense of unreality as the train crossed the remains of the Wall. He could still scarcely believe that this journey was now so simple. No checkpoints, no guards, no barbed wire along the sides of the track. He alighted at the Tiergarten station and entered the park, breathing in the smell of flowers and the warm summer air. After twice asking directions, he found himself walking along a path that led through a thickly wooded area and across a waterway, which was spanned by a pedestrian bridge with a pair of bronze lions at either end. As he reached this bridge, he saw a young woman sitting on the parapet, one leg half slung over the railing, face turned towards the water where some ducks were feeding. She was wearing jeans and a white summer jacket. Propped up against the parapet beside her was a red umbrella. There was something strangely familiar about her posture, the line of her slim figure, and the way her dark hair hung down over the side of her face. And when she turned and looked at him, he blanched as if he had seen a ghost, but still kept on walking towards her.

As she saw him she smiled, slid down from the railing and came towards him.

"Miss Warrington?" he ventured hesitantly as he came up to her.

She held out a slim hand and he took it. "Call me Sonia."

Her manner was open and friendly, and he relaxed a little. "All right, Sonia. I am Lutz."

"I know you are... but my mother always called you

Henrik."

He looked at her, speechless for a moment. "Your mother ...You are Kirsten's daughter?"

"Yes."

He shook his head as if in disbelief. "You look so much like her. When I saw you just now ..." He broke off, simply staring at her face.

She took his arm and steered him to a bench in the shade of a chestnut tree. A woman walked past pushing a pram. Two children and a dog played with a ball on the grass by the waterside, while an elderly man fed the ducks. She put a hand on his and said: "Do I look like anyone else?"

"Anyone else ..." he repeated, puzzled. Then it began to dawn on him what she might be saying. "Your mother married...your name is Warrington...?"

"She married an Englishman when I was eight years old. They divorced years ago."

"So I am...?"

She nodded, unable to speak.

For a minute they sat in silence, he gently squeezing her hand.

"Sonia ...," he said, "Sonia ...," There was so much he wanted to say to her if he could only think where to begin.

She smiled through her tears. "You like my name?"

"It's beautiful."

Watching the children playing with the dog, he wondered what she had been like at that age – and later, as she had grown into a young woman. His heart swelled with joy but also with immense sadness at the thought of all the years when he might have watched her grow up, had he not been shut away behind the Wall. He turned towards her and they hugged tearfully, holding each other for several minutes, saying nothing.

Sonia broke the silence, wiping away her tears with a handkerchief and saying brightly: "Let's walk a little. We have so much to talk about."

She took his arm and they walked over the bridge and on through the park.

"Your mother… ," he said, "Does she know you are here?"

Sonia gave a light laugh. "Of course she does."

He wondered how much Sonia knew about what had happened. What had Kirsten told her?

As though guessing his thoughts, she said: "Mum has told me everything."

"Everything?"

"Yes, and she forgave you long ago for what happened. In fact, she feels the family were hard on you. They should have been grateful to you for saving Uncle Hinnerk's life. When she realised she was pregnant with me, she was desperate to contact you. She made enquiries everywhere and always drew a blank. Finally she went to some East German office in Copenhagen, but they denied that you were working for the Stasi and said the story of the kidnapping was absurd. She was so depressed that she almost killed herself. She boarded a ferry to Oslo and nearly threw herself overboard, but at the last moment she couldn't bear the thought of killing me." Lutz shook his head, shocked.

"After that she vowed not to give up searching for you. She tried again and again, even though the East German authorities kept stonewalling her. After she'd pestered them for about two years they finally admitted that you were in prison, but claimed you couldn't be contacted. Years went by and she married Michael Warrington. We moved to England, but the marriage failed and we were back in Denmark within six years. When the Wall came down, we felt we had a real chance of finding you at last. In fact it turned out to be easier than we'd thought. We made enquiries through the German Consulate, and a few days later they gave us your address but no phone number – apparently you are ex-directory! We wrote you a letter, but you never replied …"

"I never received it."

"We kept hearing how chaotic it was in Berlin, and we thought the letter might have got lost, so I decided to come in person. I have friends here and I speak German. Mum was happy for me to come alone. She wasn't quite ready to meet you yet. She knew what an ordeal you'd been through and was terrified you might have come to hate her. She couldn't have endured that. Do you feel very bitter, Papa?"

Hearing her call him that, as if she were still a little girl, brought tears to his eyes. He shook his head. "No, I'm not bitter with her – only with the system that used me and with myself for choosing to serve it."

"Don't be hard on yourself. If it hadn't been for you, Uncle Hinnerk might have been killed."

"Uncle Hinnerk …," he repeated, realising that he and his Doppelgaenger were now linked by family ties. "What became of him? And the rest of the family?"

They walked on slowly, arm in arm, and she told him the main things that had happened to them in the intervening years. Birthe had spent several days in shock, but had gradually adjusted to Hinnerk being her real son. He had moved into the house, and in time had won over the rest of the family, except for Sven – having grudgingly accepted one bastard son he refused to go through the process again. Hinnerk made friends with Pastor Arup and helped him set up the Grundtvig school on the island, which had always been Arup's dream. When Arup moved away the Grundtvig people put Hinnerk in charge of the school, which he was still running. Sven went to pieces on learning about Kirsten's pregnancy. Coming after Henrik's exposure and Hinnerk's arrival, it had been the final straw. He had started drinking heavily again and died of liver failure two years later. Then Niels and Gertrud took over the farm."

Lutz asked: "Did the family find out that Kirsten had known who I really was?"

"Yes. Her mother guessed it on the day you were kidnapped. The others found out later. Her father never forgave her until the day he died. Niels didn't speak to her for years. It was Gertrud who finally brought him round – she was always the sensible one."

"And after your mother got divorced, were there other men in her life?"

"There was someone for about a year. But he let her down. I was a teenager at the time and hadn't wanted to come back from England. I was really difficult. Maybe it was my fault."

He squeezed her hand again. "What happened to you both after the divorce from Warrington?"

"Mum and I went to live in Copenhagen. I was fourteen, and always in trouble with my teachers. But somehow I finished school and studied photography in Hamburg. It was the one thing I enjoyed. I'm a fashion photographer now, and make a good living."

"That's wonderful." An old man in a wheelchair was pushed past them. "I don't suppose Birthe is still alive?" Lutz murmured. "I wish I could have told her how ashamed I felt."

"I'm sorry, Papa. She died five years ago."

"What happened to the farm?"

"Niels sold it. Poor Hinnerk wanted to stay on. He said he'd only ever felt happy there. Now he's living in a small house in the village. He has a woman friend in Copenhagen who comes to stay with him at weekends."

Lutz smiled. "I'm glad for him. He deserves some happiness after all he went through."

She nodded. "Years later he heard that there had been a great uproar in the Stasi after his escape. His adoptive parents were questioned, but they convinced the Stasi that they'd known nothing of his plans. It was harder for the people who had helped him – his old nurse Astrid from the Lebensborn home and her husband and brother-in-law. The Stasi burst into their home and threatened to execute them unless they told them where Hinnerk was. The nurse's brother-in-law was caught by the police on his way to help Hinnerk escape. They were all given prison sentences. Hinnerk was terribly shocked when he learned what had happened. It took him months to get over it. Eventually they were released from prison, but they both died before the Wall came down, so Hinnerk never saw his nurse and her husband again. He still grieves over it."

Lutz shook his head sadly. "To think that I was part of that awful system."

Sonia squeezed his arm. "Don't blame yourself, Papa. You paid your debt long ago. Let's talk of happier things."

They came to a festive looking café with an open-air terrace, and sat at a table in the shade of a big red umbrella. Looking at the menu, Sonia said, with a mischievous look: "I know what I'm going to order for you – Black Forest gâteau!

In fact I'll have some too. And let's have a pot of coffee to go with it."

For a moment he looked startled then laughed. "So Kirsten even told you that!"

While they waited for their coffee and cakes, she looked serious suddenly. "Will you come to Copenhagen, to talk to Mum? I hope you will. It still makes her cry to describe how you were dragged away before she could speak to you." She squeezed his arm tightly. "Please come."

Lutz was silent while the waitress put out their order. Over the past twenty-four years he had often thought about Kirsten and re-lived their brief, intense affair. But faced with the prospect of actually seeing her again, he drew back inwardly. Memories could so easily be spoiled, and the pain of the past obliterate its pleasures

She seemed to read his thoughts. "Oh, I know you can't recapture those times, but maybe something different is possible ...?"

"A fresh start?" He couldn't help sounding wearily ironical.

"Stranger things have happened. I don't think she really knows what she wants. Are you always so certain, Papa? You could meet ... then take it from there." Seeing him still looking doubtful, she added: "At least you could call her on the phone. There are things she's anxious to tell you."

"Things?"

"Things about the past she would rather tell you in person."

Seeing her wide, eager eyes, he looked down and stirred his cup. "I don't know ... You're very young, Sonia. For you the future is full of infinite possibility. For me it's quite different. Life has scarred me terribly. Your mother and I...we're no longer the people we were then."

"I see... " she said in a small, listless voice. "Well, if that's how you feel ..." She pushed away her plate, leaving her cake half-eaten, then placed a twenty-mark note on the table. "Have the coffee and cake on me. I have to go."

As she walked away between the tables, he cursed himself. Must he avoid every conceivable risk in order to protect himself from the pain of regret? The flaw was that, even at his age, no risks meant no rewards. Wasn't it time he tried to make something from what was left of his life? He saw her reach the end of the terrace and walk down some steps to where a gravel path led off into the park. He leapt up, overturning his chair and dashed after her. "Your change!" he heard the waitress call after him. Where the hell had she gone? He saw her walking past some rhododendron bushes.

"Sonia!" he called at the top of his voice, "Sonia! Wait!" Only when he was a stone's throw from her did she relent and stop. "I'll call her!"

52

It took him two days to pluck up the courage to call the number that Sonia had given him. Fortified by a large glass of Schnapps, he picked up the phone in his cramped little flat and dialled the number. As he heard the ringing tone, a worrying thought struck him. What language should he use? By now his Danish had mostly vanished, and he knew that she spoke little German.

"Ja, Warrington" he heard a woman's voice say. So she had kept her married name.

He decided to opt for English, their first medium of communication. "Is that you, Kirsten?"

There was a long silence before she said: "Hello, Henrik."

"It's been ages since I was called that."

"Was I the very last person?"

"I think so."

"I'd like to think I was. You know you'll always be Henrik to me?"

He felt an unexpected tightness in his throat. Her voice was older now, inevitably, but otherwise eerily unchanged. She sounded slightly out of breath, as if she was as nervous as he. The noises coming from the flat above were worse than usual – raised voices, stamping feet - so he knew he was going to have to listen hard to catch each nuance. She remained silent.

Awkwardly he said: "Sonia's a wonderful person. Meeting her meant such a lot to me. You must be very proud of her."

"You should be proud too, Henrik."

"But I did nothing."

"Not quite nothing," she murmured, and he sensed that she was smiling – and remembered how her eyes creased when she did.

"I wish I could have been a real father..."

"The day they dragged you away, this is what I'd wanted to tell you, that I was pregnant and you were the father." They were both close to tears.

"I had no idea ..."

"If you had known, it could have made it even worse for you in prison. All those years. Poor Henrik – did they treat you very badly?"

"They broke stronger wills than mine. The worst thing was living with the knowledge of what I had done to you and

Birthe. Can you ever forgive me?"

Her voice choked a little as she said: "Oh Henrik, of course I forgive you. I realised years and years ago that you were being punished out of proportion to what you had done. I wanted you to meet your daughter, but you were locked away somewhere and I couldn't contact you."

The Alsatian dog in one of the flats below was howling as he often did in the daytime. Lutz hardly heard him.

"What are you thinking, Henrik?"

He blurted out: "Sonia wants me to come to Copenhagen. Is that what you want?"

"Yes, I do want to see you."

"Then I'll come. Tell me where."

"What about the Langelinie, by the Little Mermaid, where we first met?"

"And how shall we recognise each other?"

"What a silly question, Henrik."

*   *   *

"You're very chirpy today," the manager of the Jupiter said to him a few days later. "Full of the joys of summer, eh?" And it was true – he felt more alive than he had done for years, even exchanging light-hearted banter with the waitresses, who gave him puzzled looks. It was Monday and he was to go to Copenhagen the following weekend. He was both excited and nervous. How would they react to each other? Would any of the old spark still be there after all these years?

That evening he did a late shift at the restaurant. The customers had gone, he had locked the front door and was clearing up before going home. It was dark and raining outside.

He was in no hurry to leave until the rain had stopped, so he took his time going round the tables, emptying the ashtrays, brushing away the crumbs and snuffing out the candles. As he passed the window on to the street he caught a glimpse of a figure in a hooded raincoat, peering in, blurred by the condensation on the glass. A moment later he heard a knock at the front door. Perhaps it was a customer, who had left something behind, or a beggar looking for scraps. He opened the door and said: "We're closed." But the figure pushed past him into the restaurant, lifting back the hood to reveal the almost bald head and fleshy face of Kurt.

"You and I need to talk," Kurt told him, sitting down in the nearest chair and stretching his legs out.

"I've nothing to say to you," Lutz replied, continuing with his work. "You must leave now or I'll call the police."

"I don't think so." Kurt leaned back and looked at Lutz through narrowed eyes. "We both have an interest in seeing that certain things from the past remain buried. That's why those old files are a problem for some of us. I happen to know that my own file has been destroyed, but sadly yours has not. In case you haven't seen it, I took the precaution of making photocopies of everything in it, including the report of the Borup operation and the forged confession." He took a sheaf of papers from his briefcase and waved it mockingly at Henrik. "If the report becomes public the Danes will want to prosecute you for blackmail. You could face a long prison sentence." Kurt replaced the papers.

Lutz felt suddenly cold and sick. Kurt might be lying, but that seemed unlikely. Kurt had always been thorough. It was just like him to have copied the file. Something more comforting struck Lutz. It was true he didn't have a copy of

Kurt's file, but he knew things that Kurt would be desperate to keep from coming to light.

As if reading his thoughts, Kurt sneered: "Don't think you can blackmail me. You've no proof of anything, whereas I have." He patted his briefcase. "But it would be annoying to have you going around spreading rumours about me. So it's in both our best interests – especially yours – to keep quiet."

Lutz breathed deeply trying to calm his anger. "You're forgetting something."

Kurt smiled blandly. "You'd better enlighten me."

"Unlike you, I no longer have anything to lose – so a prison sentence doesn't frighten me – but you have everything to lose, Major."

Kurt lunged forward and seized him by throat, pinning him down on the nearest table. As Lutz began to choke, he could smell Kurt's boozy breath and his rancid body odour. Remembering a trick he had learnt in his Stasi martial arts training, he brought his hands together between Kurt's arms, locking the wrists together, and then twisted hard. Kurt's grip loosened enough for Lutz to break free and grab a chair. He swung it at Kurt, who ducked and came at him with a knife. Still holding the chair, Lutz moved to the other side of the table, where a burning candle had toppled over in the struggle, setting fire to some paper napkins. Lutz dropped the chair and tried to reach out to extinguish the flames, but Kurt lunged at him with the knife, gashing Lutz's wrist as he checked the blow.

All of Lutz's accumulated rage at Kurt suddenly erupted. He seized the hand holding the knife and wrestled with Kurt. Although Kurt was bigger, he had run to fat and moved clumsily. Lutz tried to trip him up, but before he could do so, the whole table went over, and flames began to lick at the curtains. As the fire spread, they wrestled their way around the room like some frenzied dancing couple, smashing crockery and upsetting more tables.

The room was filling with smoke. Lutz broke free and ran to a short stairway that led to an extra dining area on a mezzanine level. Half way up he felt Kurt's hand clawing at his right leg. Lutz kicked out with his left and heard Kurt roar with pain as his foot struck the side of the ex-Stasi man's closely cropped head. Lutz scrambled up to the mezzanine. On one side there was a door marked "Toilets", on the other a small window looking on to the street. He glanced back and saw through the haze of smoke, that Kurt was crouching on the stair, nursing his head. Lutz unfastened the window catch and pushed the wooden frame outwards, but it was warped and wouldn't budge. He tried again with his shoulder, and it moved a fraction. Then he thrust himself at the frame again and again, until it finally gave way and the window swung open.

Leaning out, he gulped in lungfuls of the moist night air, hearing the sirens of approaching fire engines. He looked down, wondering if he should attempt the twenty-foot drop to the street. There was no way back down the stairs – a wall of dense acrid smoke now filled the mezzanine. He clambered out on to a narrow stone window ledge. Still unwilling to risk the drop, he wondered whether he could climb down the façade as though down a rock face. His feet searched desperately for a toehold, but found nothing. Then he lost his balance and dropped, feeling an intense shooting pain in his right ankle as he hit the pavement. He keeled over and passed out moments after the rest of his body struck the ground.

When he came to again, he was lying on the pavement

wrapped in a blanket. A fireman was crouching beside him. Lutz had no idea how much time had passed since he had jumped.

"Don't move," the fireman told him. "There's an ambulance on its way. The lads are in there now putting out the last remnants of the fire."

Lutz remembered how he had seen Kurt crouched on the stairs, the smoke swirling around him. If his old enemy had died in the fire, Lutz realised his troubles would be over.

"Was there anyone else in the building?" he asked, his lungs hurting as he spoke.

"We don't know yet. They're searching it room by room now. Here's the ambulance now."

* * *

In the ambulance, with an oxygen mask over his face, Lutz was driven to an emergency ward of the sprawling Charité hospital complex across the river Spree. Over the next two days, they examined his lungs and made him breathe and blow into a variety of tubes and bags; finally declaring his lungs to be sound. They shone lights in his eyes, and asked him if his head still ached and whether he was seeing double - he wasn't. Then they strapped up his ankle, which he was amazed to discover had been sprained but not broken. On the morning after his arrival he asked to see the newspapers and eagerly scanned them for reports of the fire. All the dailies mentioned it and a couple of them reported his own rescue, but none of the reports said anything about a second person having been found in the building, dead or alive. He began to worry that

Kurt might somehow have escaped from the building at the last minute.

On the third morning, just before he was due to be released from hospital, an eager young policeman came to see him. He appeared new to the job, to judge by the almost pedantically correct way in which he described his task as being "to take a preliminary report of the events connected with the fire". Lutz wondered whether to tell him about Kurt and the fight, knowing how improbable it sounded. In the end he told the whole story.

The policeman looked up from his notebook and said: "You say you saw this man ... Barschke ... on the stairs just before you left the building."

"Yes."

"That's very curious. No firemen mentioned seeing anyone else leave the building, nor have any human remains been found in the debris."

The young officer seemed to expect Lutz to express an opinion, but he merely gazed down the ward between the beds with an expression of utter dejection.

53

Before boarding the train to Copenhagen Lutz looked up and down the platform, half expecting to see Kurt in the crowd. over his shoulder and taking evasive action if anyone resembled his former colleague. One day – unless Lutz murdered him first – Kurt would either kill him or expose him for his part in the Borup affair. The police wanted to interview Kurt to check his version of how the fire had started against Lutz's account, but they had been unable to find him. Kurt would be well in with the new elites in Russia and eastern Europe, and could be in hiding anywhere from Berlin to Moscow, planning his revenge.

Looking around at the other passengers settling into their seats and getting out their newspapers, it struck Lutz that – despite money worries, illnesses, cheating wives or husbands, problem children – hardly any would be living their daily lives in fear that each new day might be the one to bring them face to face with their deadly enemy. He would just have to live with that knowledge as best he could. But should he tell Kirsten and Sonia about Kurt? Probably not straight away. Although in the long run they would have to know for their own safety. But since there might not be a "long run", why spoil what might only be a short time together? Kurt wasn't his only problem either. There was the enquiry into the fire coming up soon, and there was the problem of earning a living while the restaurant was being renovated. Forget all that, he told himself. If there was still a little happiness to be grasped from this journey back into the past, then he felt he owed it to himself to take advantage of it.

By mid afternoon he was walking along the Langelinie. He was still using a stick since the accident. There were no British sailors or Japanese tourists this time, and the graffiti on the statue had gone. Otherwise everything felt much the same as on that afternoon twenty-four years ago when he had come here to meet Kirsten and Birthe. And something of the apprehension he had felt then came back to him now. He could have done with a cigarette although he had given up smoking years ago.

He was twenty paces away when he spotted her, seated on a bench, her figure a little fuller and her dark hair streaked with grey, but immediately it struck him that, like Birthe, she had kept her beauty over the years. She wore a yellow blouse that picked up the colouring of her flared floral skirt. Clothes for a celebration, he couldn't help thinking, though his nerves still tormented him.

She looked in his direction, holding up a hand to shade her eyes against the sunlight. The moment she saw him she stood up, waved and hurried towards him. In another second or two he would be able to see that she was smiling.

AFTERWORD AND ACKNOWLEDGEMENTS

The Lebensborn Boy is loosely based on real events no less extraordinary than those described here. The idea for the novel was sparked off by an article in a German magazine describing how one of the East German intelligence agencies had used former Lebensborn inmates for its own sinister purposes in the Cold War, with often tragic consequences. For much of the background information on the Stasi, on the dissidents bought free by West Germany and on life in the German Democratic Republic generally, we are indebted to Peter Unkart. Thanks are also due to Dorothee Schmitz-Köster, a leading expert on the Lebensborn programme and author of several authoritative works on the subject, which were of immense value in writing the parts dealing with the Lebensborn homes. Donate Pahnke McIntosh and Joyce Jeal read the book carefully at various stages and provided crucial advice and feedback. We are indebted to Matthew Hamilton, Karl French and Maria White for their helpful input, and to Jane Conway-Gordon for her fine-tuning..

Made in the USA
Charleston, SC
06 February 2015